Elvis Puffs Out

OTHER BOOKS IN THE SERIES:

Breaking Cat News

Lupin Leaps In

Take It Away, Tommy!

Elvis Puffs Out

GEORGIA DUNN

 A **BREAKING CAT NEWS** ADVENTURE

Andrews McMeel
PUBLISHING®

FOR MY NANA, DOROTHY "DEE DEE" QUINN

"TAKE GOOD CARE OF YOURSELF, YOU BELONG TO ME."

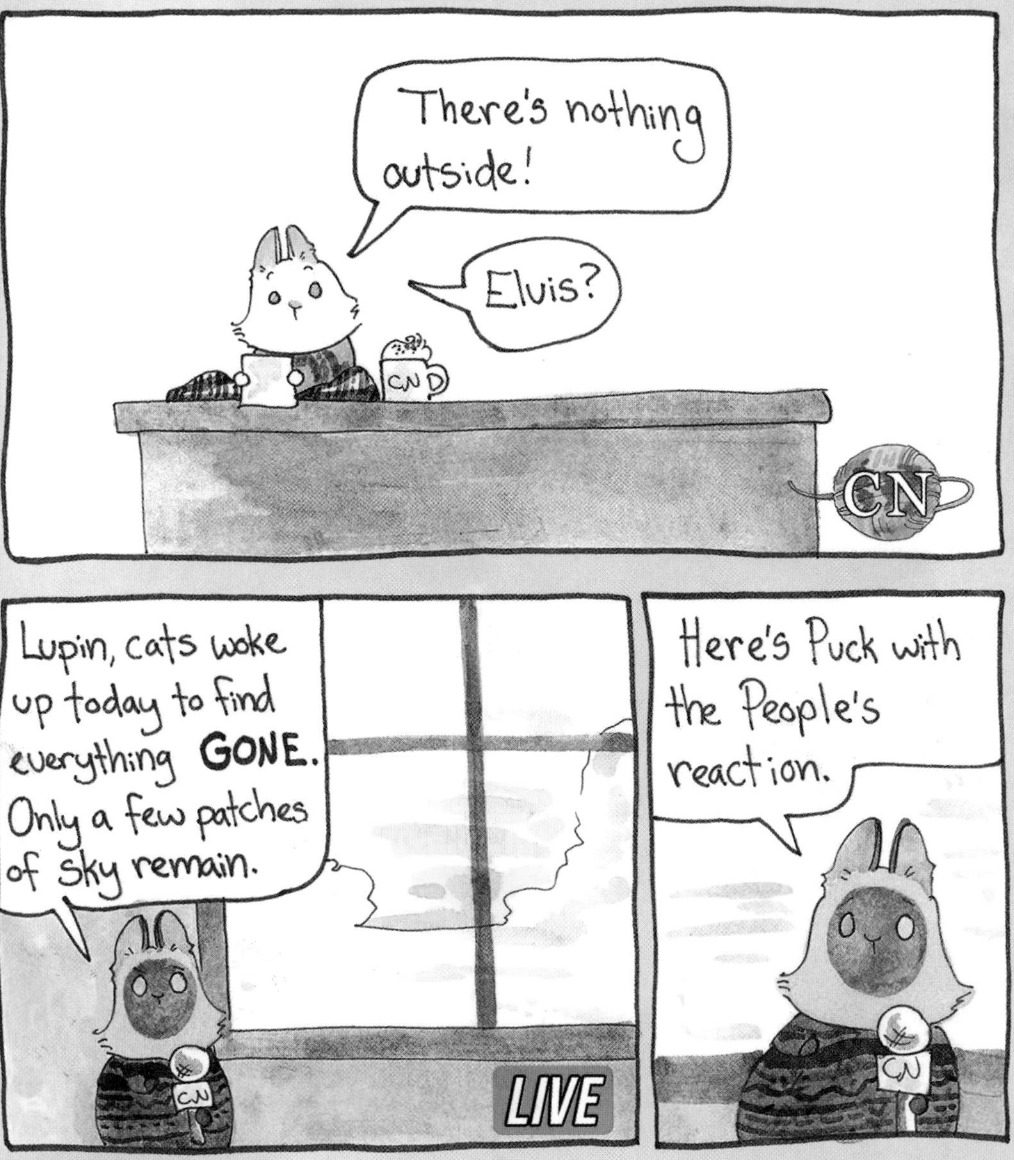
There's nothing outside!
Elvis?
CND
CN
Lupin, cats woke up today to find everything GONE. Only a few patches of sky remain.
CN
LIVE
Here's Puck with the People's reaction.
CN

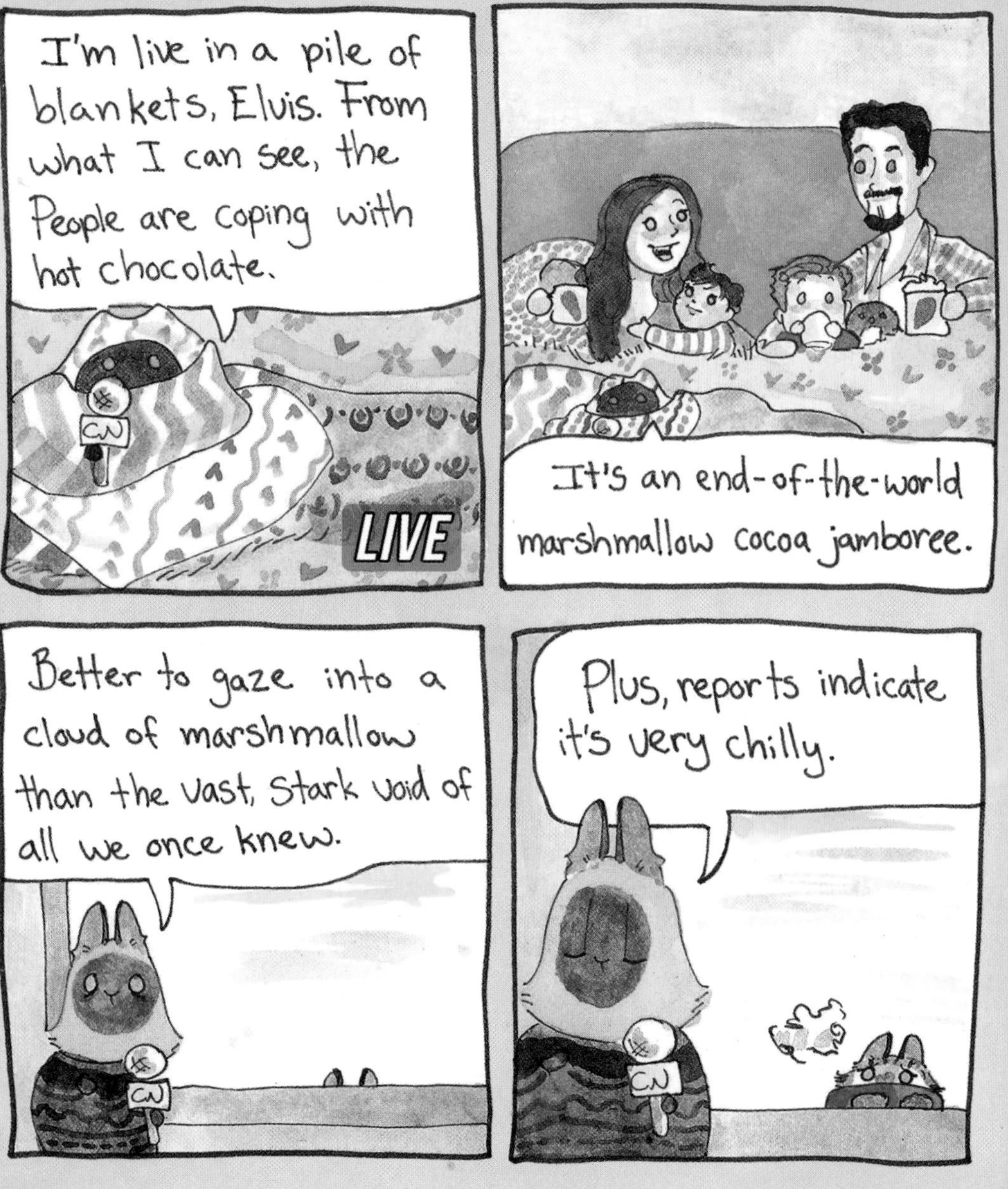

I'm live in a pile of blankets, Elvis. From what I can see, the People are coping with hot chocolate.
CN
LIVE
It's an end-of-the-world marshmallow cocoa jamboree.
Better to gaze into a cloud of marshmallow than the vast, stark void of all we once knew.
CN
Plus, reports indicate it's very chilly.
CN

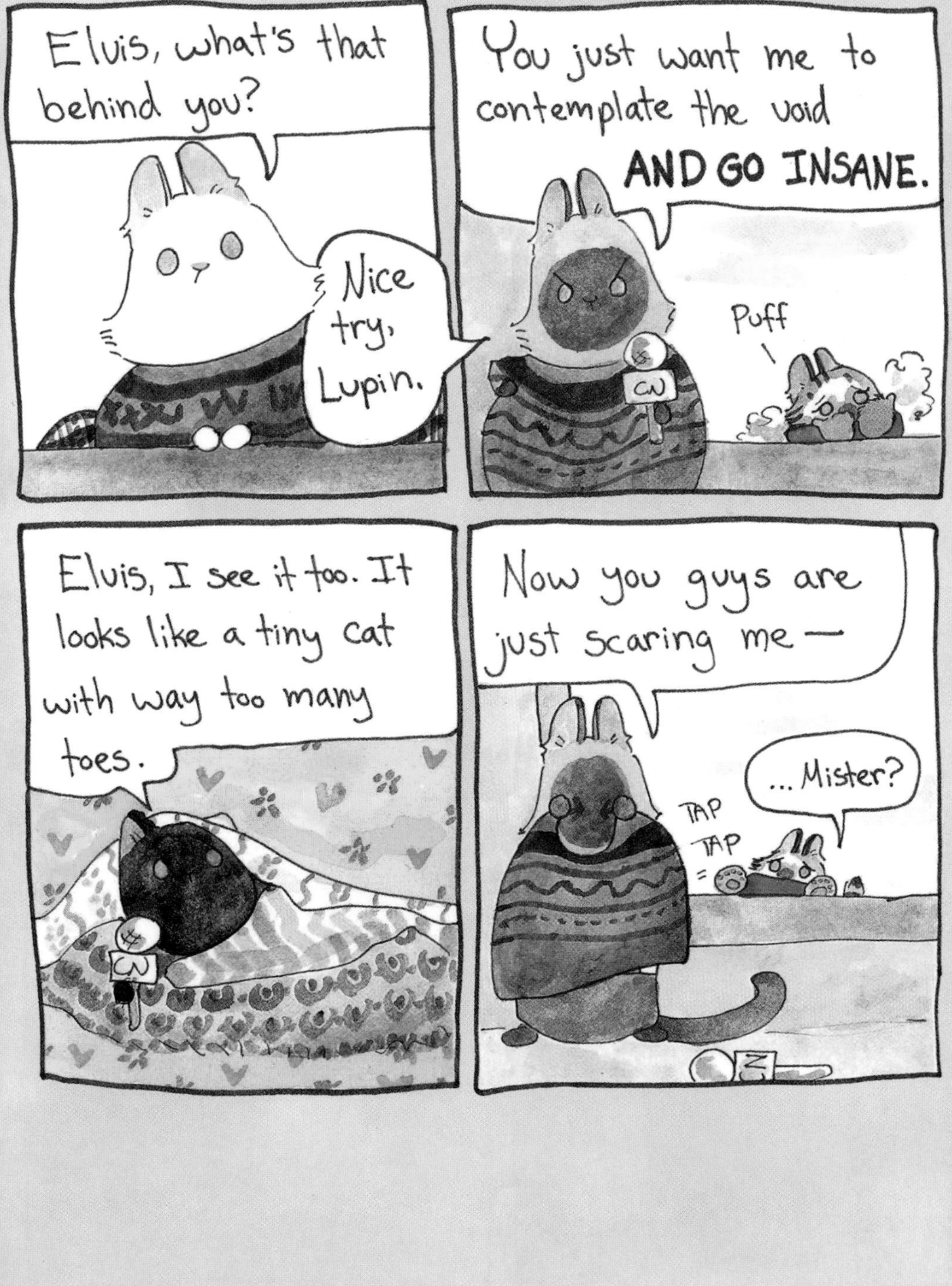
Elvis, what's that behind you?
Nice try, Lupin.
You just want me to contemplate the void AND GO INSANE.
Puff
CW
Elvis, I see it too. It looks like a tiny cat with way too many toes.
CW
Now you guys are just scaring me—
... Mister?
TAP
TAP

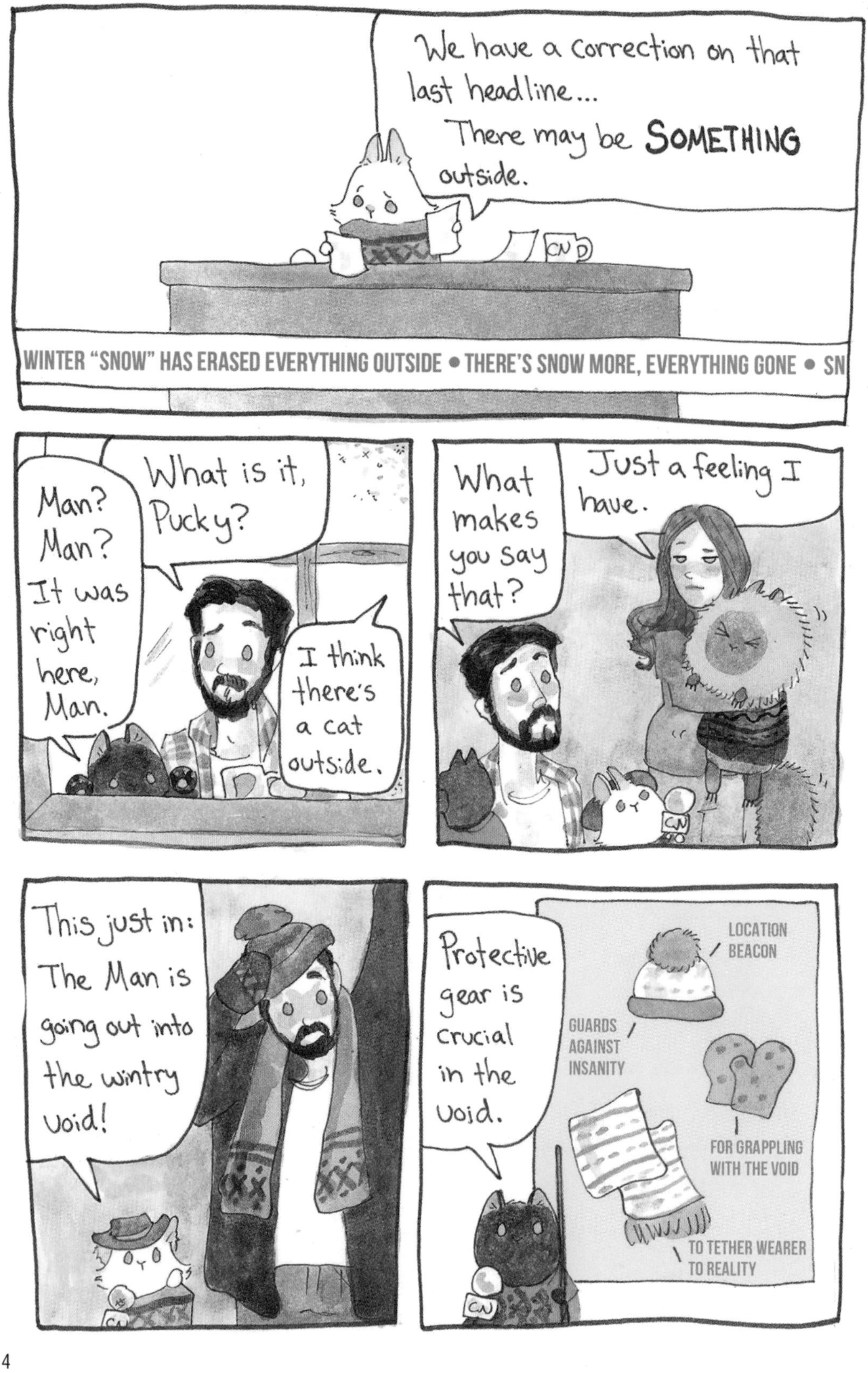

We have a correction on that last headline... There may be SOMETHING outside.
WINTER "SNOW" HAS ERASED EVERYTHING OUTSIDE • THERE'S SNOW MORE, EVERYTHING GONE • SN
What is it, Pucky?
Man? Man? It was right here, Man.
I think there's a cat outside.
What makes you say that?
Just a feeling I have.
This just in: The Man is going out into the wintry void!
Protective gear is crucial in the void.
LOCATION BEACON
GUARDS AGAINST INSANITY
FOR GRAPPLING WITH THE VOID
TO TETHER WEARER TO REALITY

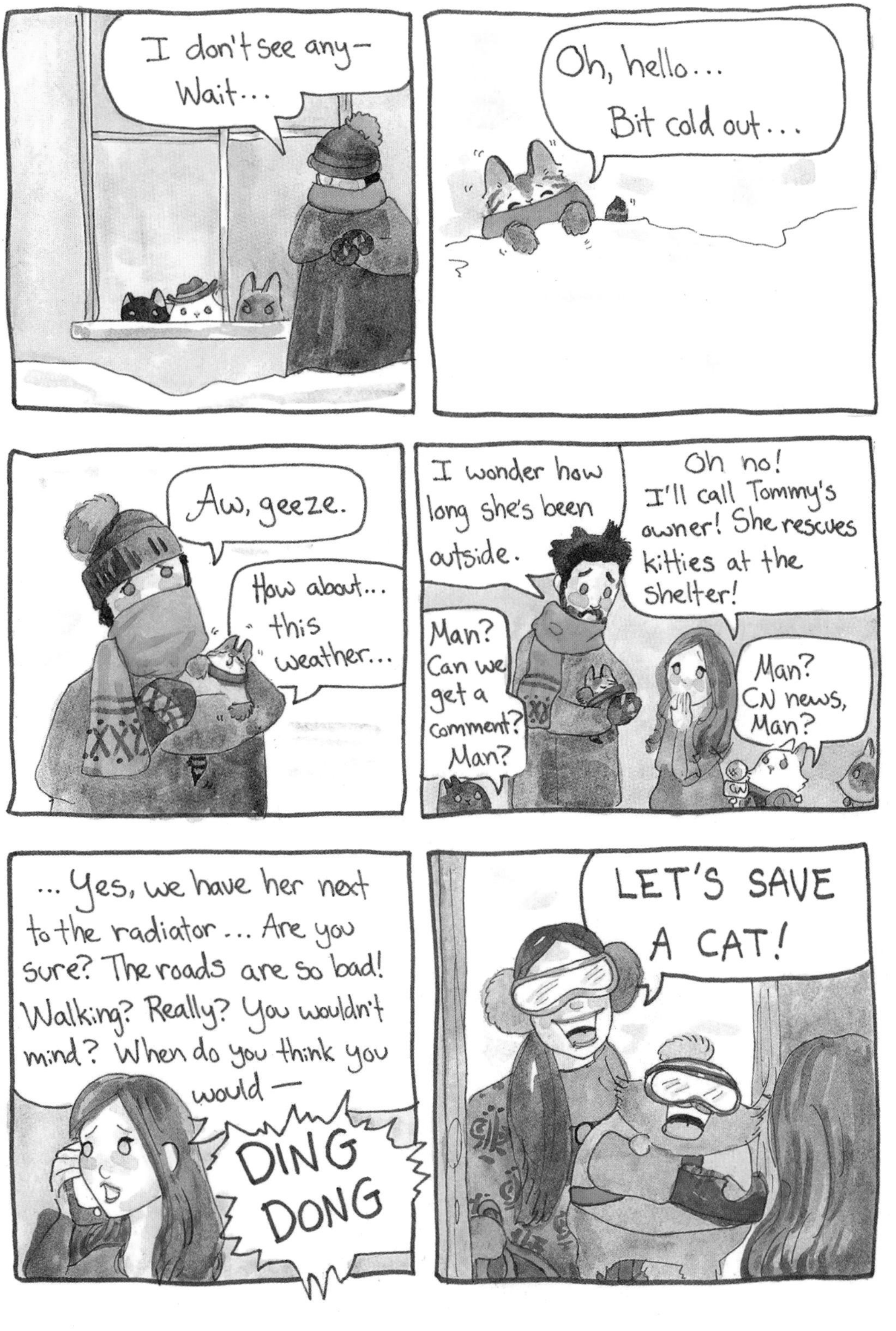
I don't see any-
Wait...
Oh, hello...
Bit cold out...
Aw, geeze.
How about... this weather...
I wonder how long she's been outside.
Oh no! I'll call Tommy's owner! She rescues kitties at the shelter!
Man? Can we get a comment? Man?
Man? CN news, Man?
... Yes, we have her next to the radiator ... Are you sure? The roads are so bad! Walking? Really? You wouldn't mind? When do you think you would —
DING DONG
LET'S SAVE A CAT!

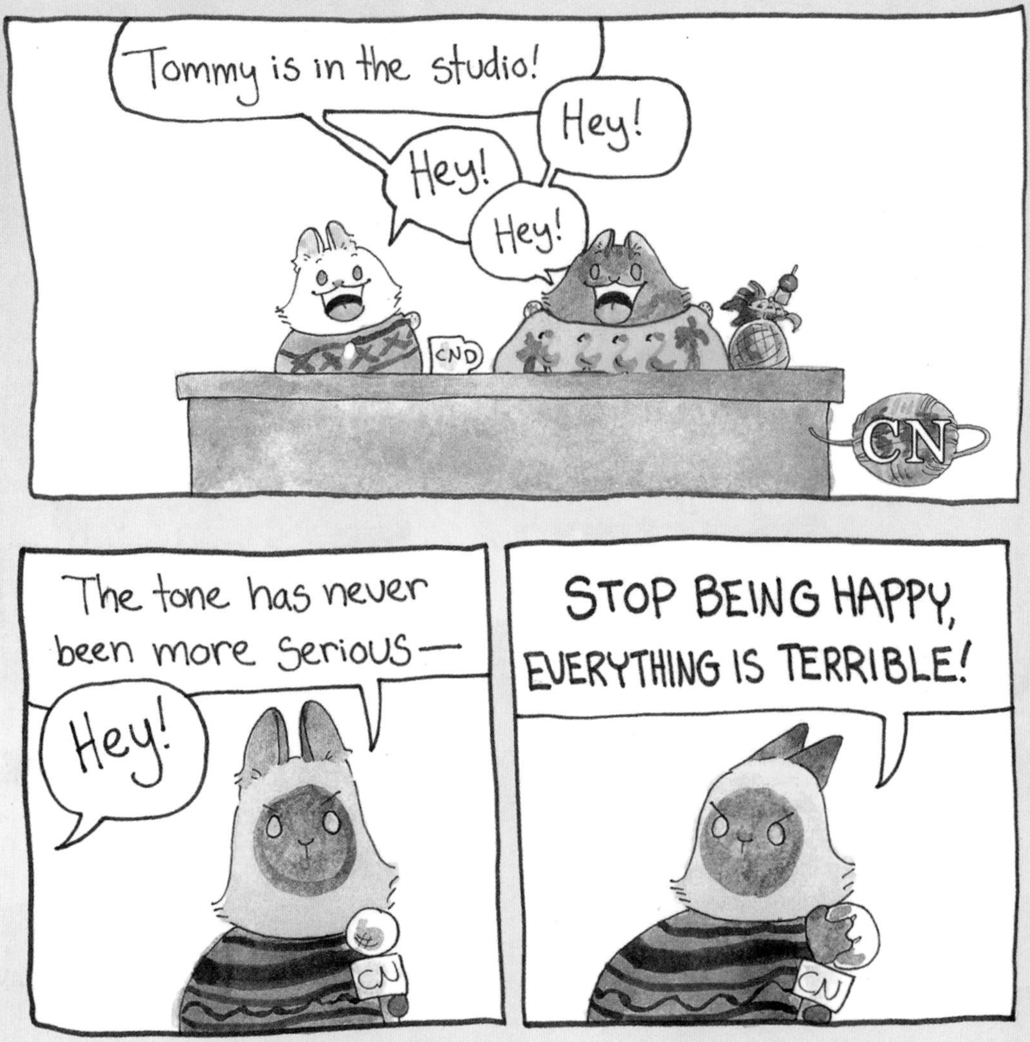
Tommy is in the studio!
Hey!
Hey!
Hey!
CND
CN
The tone has never been more serious—
Hey!
CN
STOP BEING HAPPY, EVERYTHING IS TERRIBLE!
CN

Here's the towel from the dryer you asked for!
Excellent! Let's get you toasty!
PURRRRR
PURRRRRRRRR
Do you think she'll be ok?
Tough to say... She wolfed down that kitten food, though.
That's a good sign.
I don't want to bring her outside again any time soon, though. Do you happen to know a friendly, cat-loving family that could foster her for a few weeks?
Well, do we?
CN

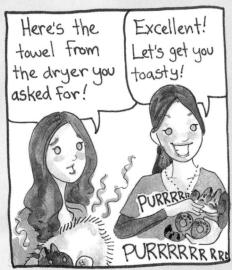

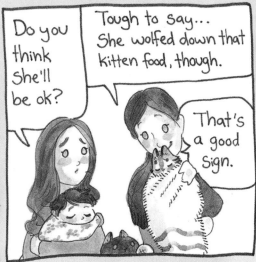

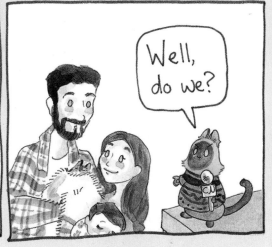

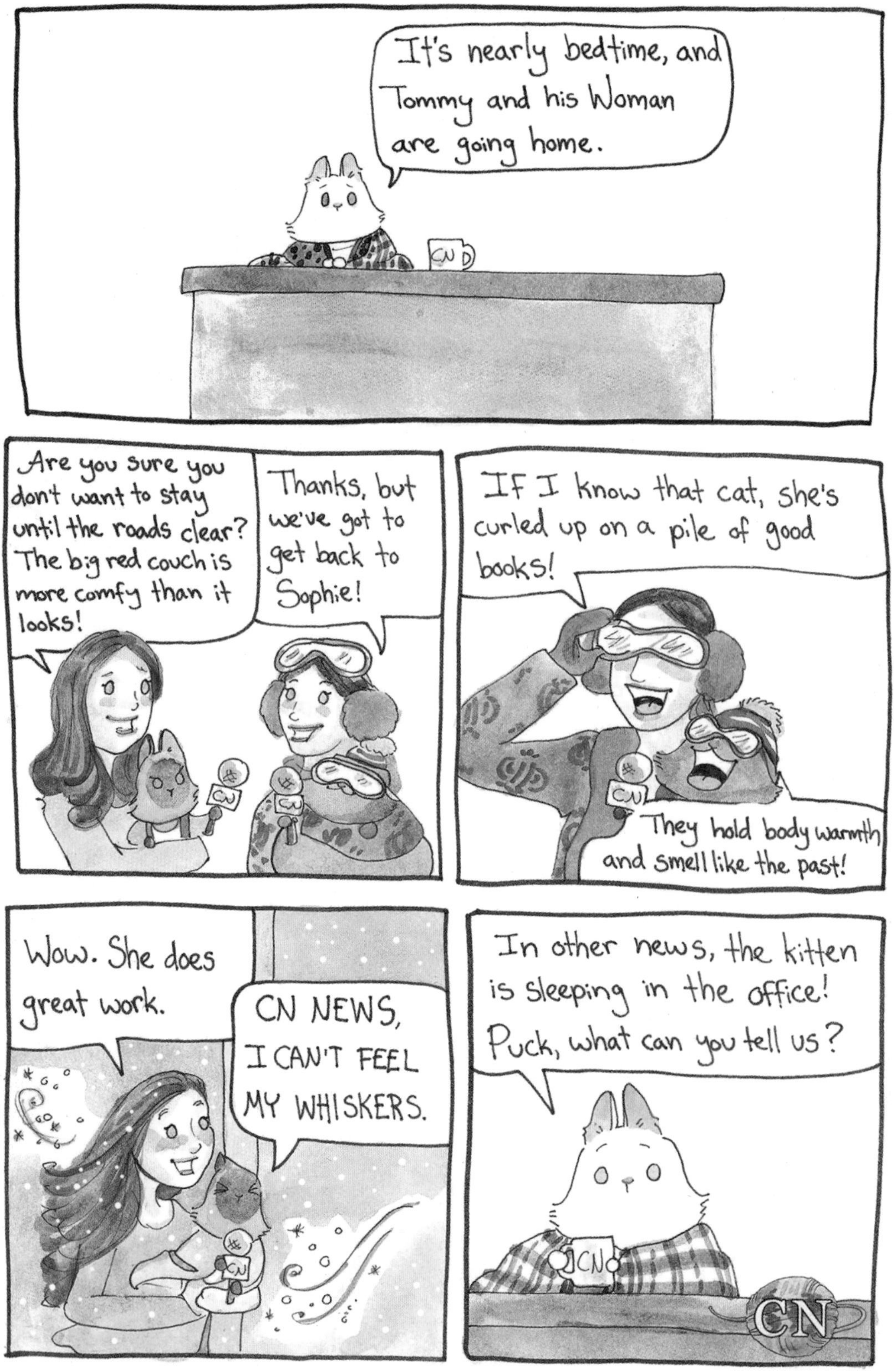

It's nearly bedtime, and Tommy and his Woman are going home.
CN
Are you sure you don't want to stay until the roads clear? The big red couch is more comfy than it looks!
Thanks, but we've got to get back to Sophie!
CN
IF I know that cat, she's curled up on a pile of good books!
CN
They hold body warmth and smell like the past!
Wow. She does great work.
CN NEWS, I CAN'T FEEL MY WHISKERS.
CN
In other news, the kitten is sleeping in the office! Puck, what can you tell us?
CN
CN

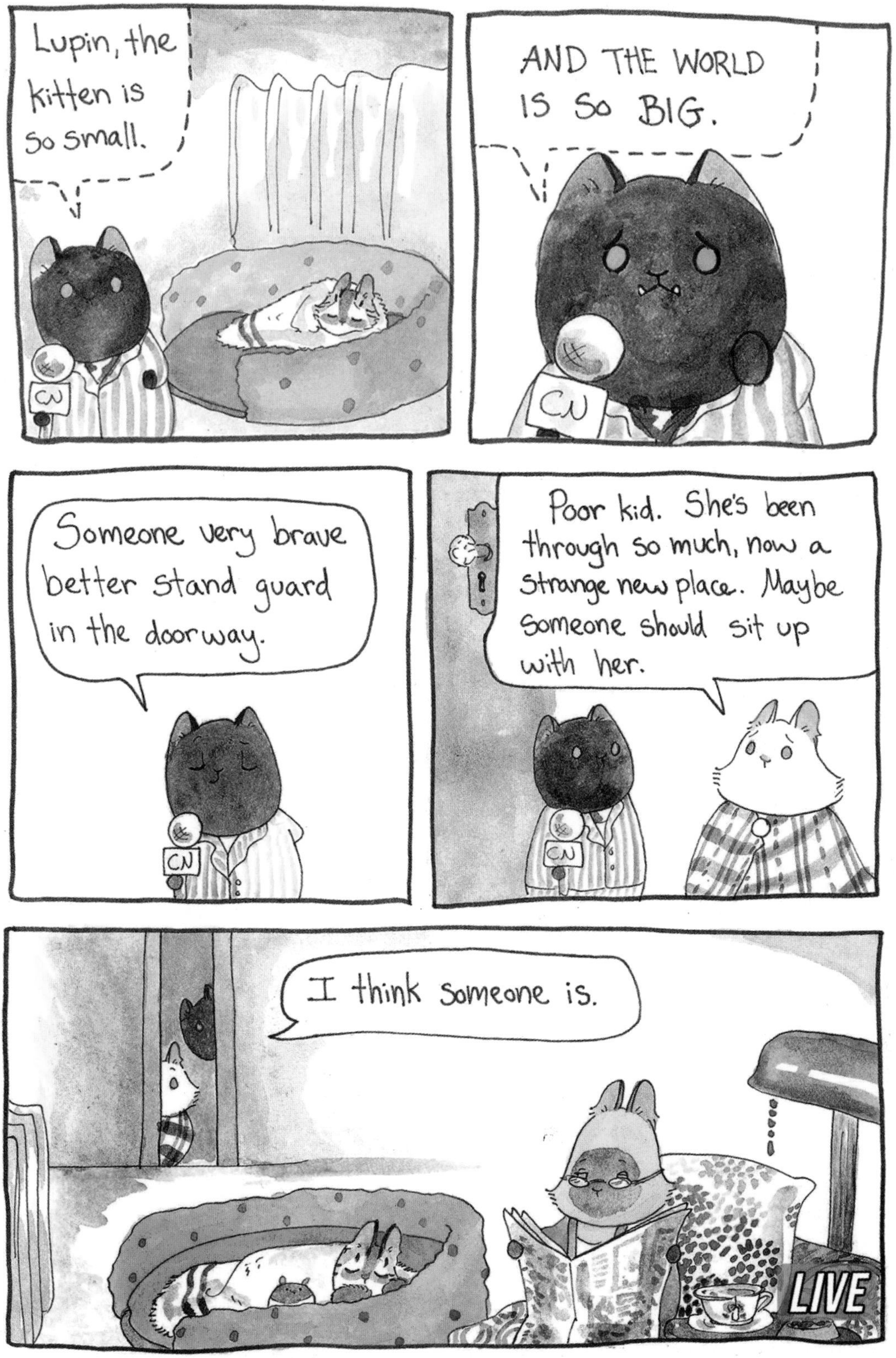
Lupin, the kitten is so small.
AND THE WORLD IS SO BIG.
Someone very brave better stand guard in the doorway.
Poor kid. She's been through so much, now a strange new place. Maybe someone should sit up with her.
I think someone is.
LIVE

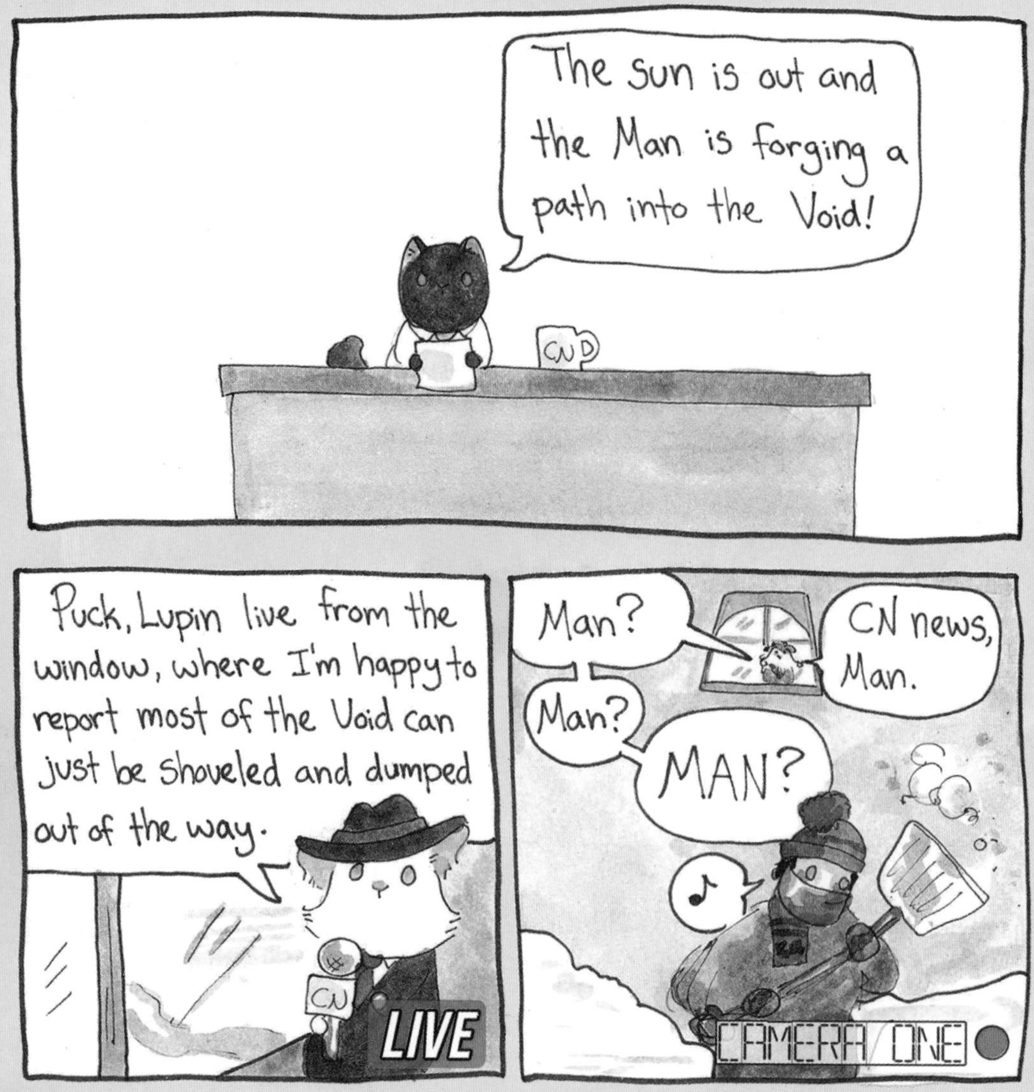
The sun is out and the Man is forging a path into the Void!
CN
Puck, Lupin live from the window, where I'm happy to report most of the Void can just be shoveled and dumped out of the way.
CN
LIVE
Man?
Man?
MAN?
CN news, Man.
CAMERA ONE

Always dodging the press...
Reality perseveres! Moving on, we have an update on the kitten!
Elvis?
Thanks, Puck. The kitten is awake and alert! She ate well this morning, and now she is resting.
With some company.

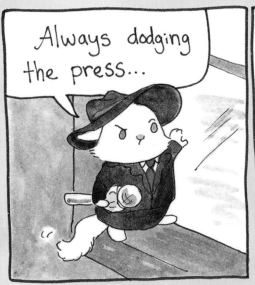

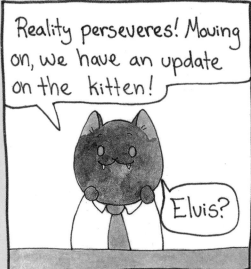

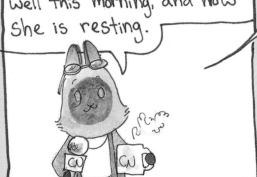

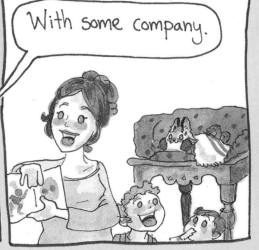

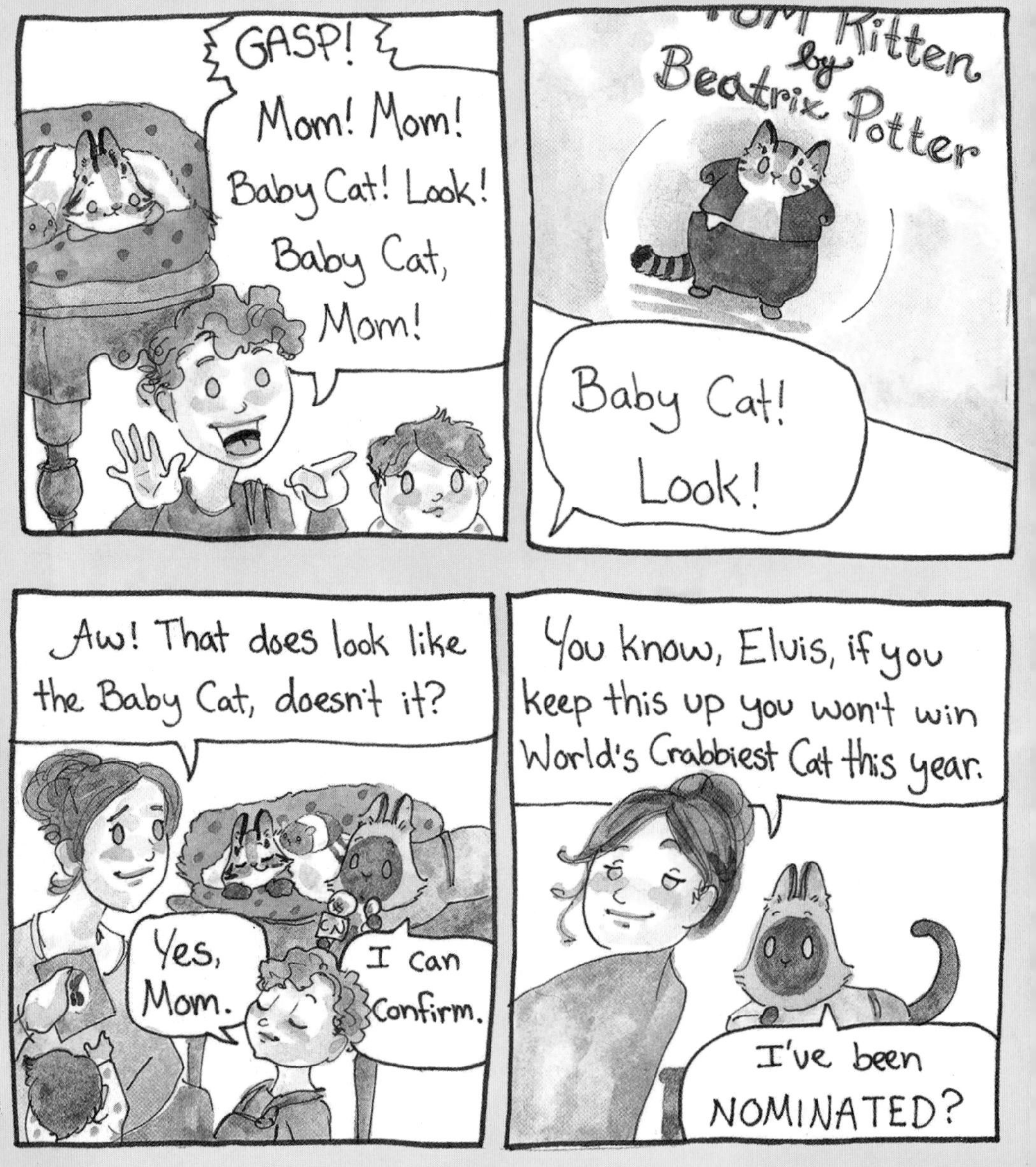
GASP!
Mom! Mom! Baby Cat! Look! Baby Cat, Mom!
Kitten
by
Beatrix Potter
Baby Cat! Look!
Aw! That does look like the Baby Cat, doesn't it?
Yes, Mom.
I can confirm.
You know, Elvis, if you keep this up you won't win World's Crabbiest Cat this year.
I've been NOMINATED?

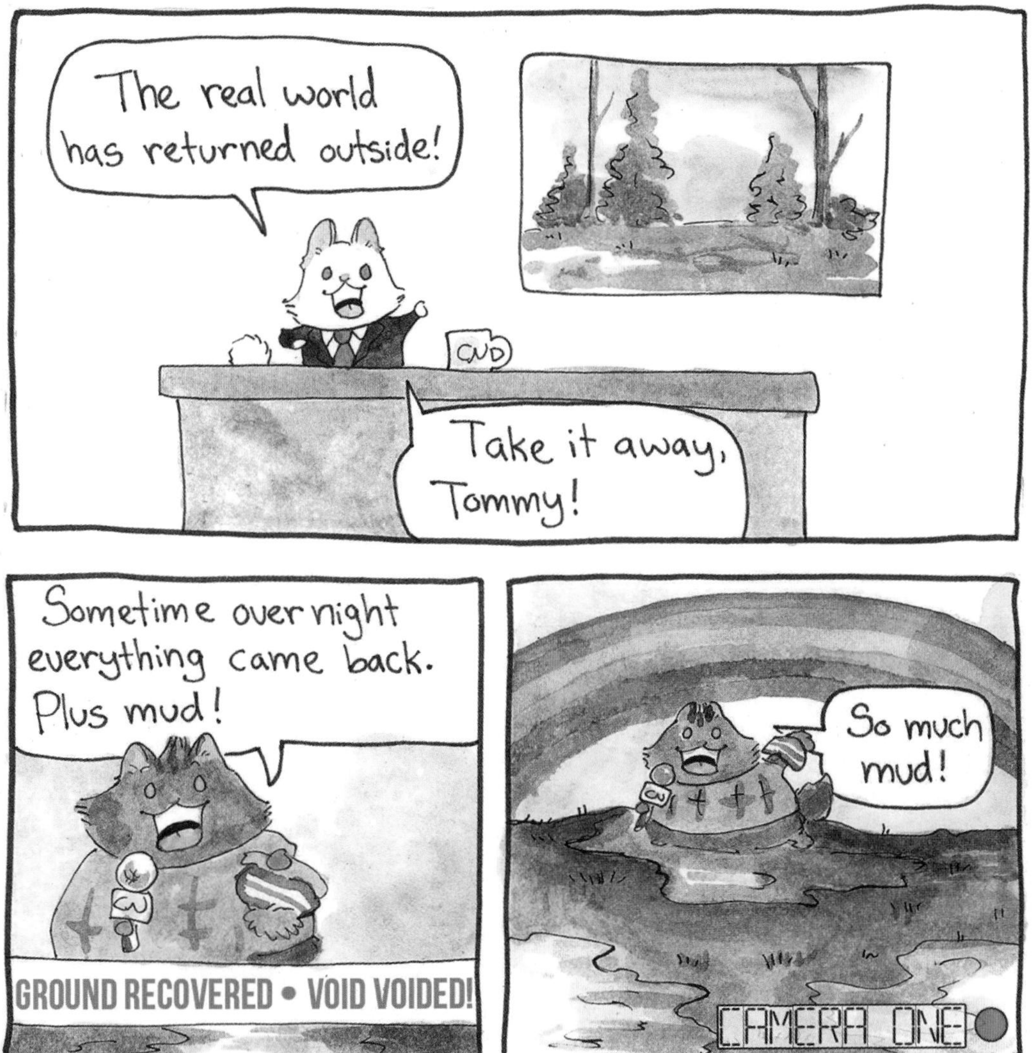
The real world has returned outside!
Take it away, Tommy!
Sometime over night everything came back. Plus mud!
GROUND RECOVERED • VOID VOIDED!
So much mud!
CAMERA ONE

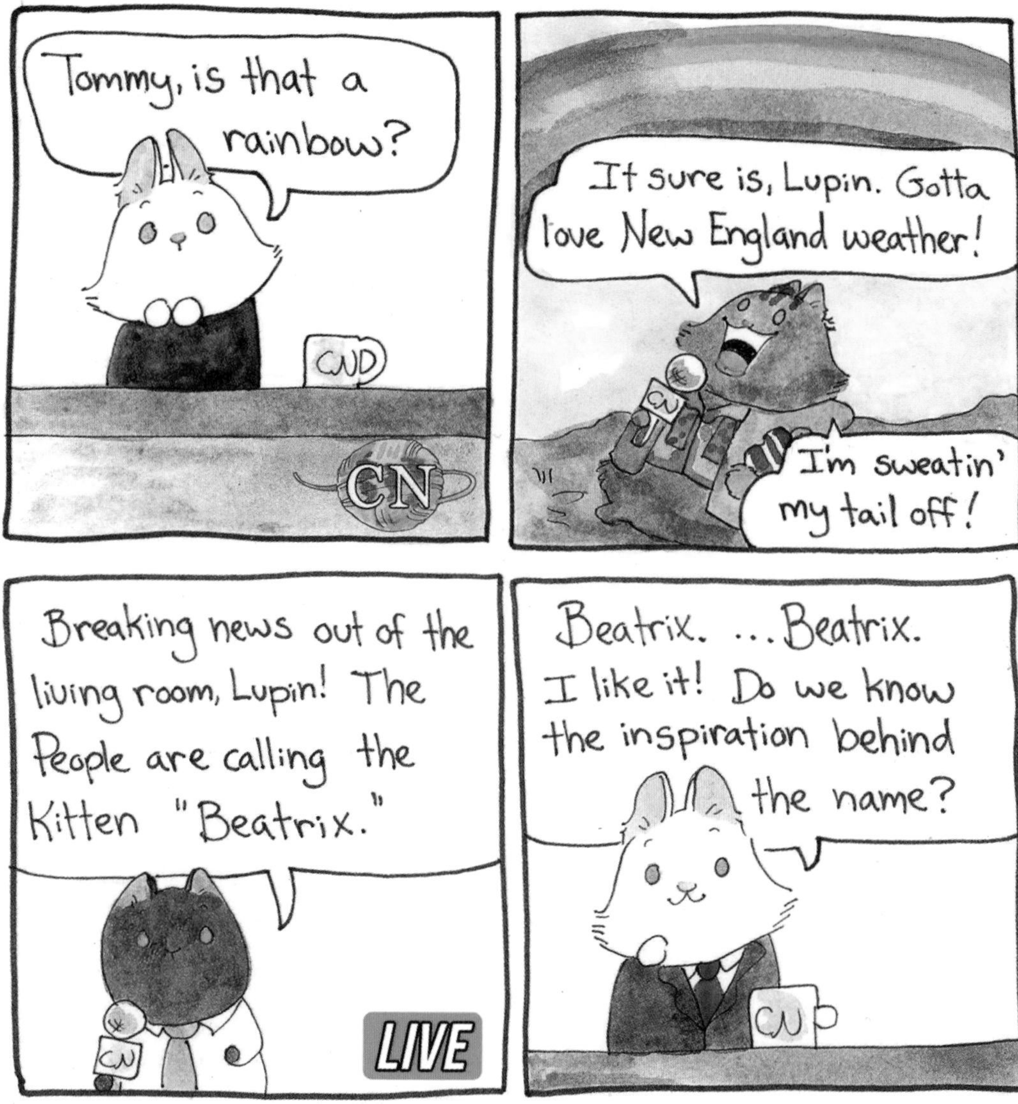
Tommy, is that a rainbow?
CND
CN
It sure is, Lupin. Gotta love New England weather!
CN
I'm sweatin' my tail off!
Breaking news out of the living room, Lupin! The People are calling the Kitten "Beatrix."
CN
LIVE
Beatrix. ...Beatrix. I like it! Do we know the inspiration behind the name?
CN

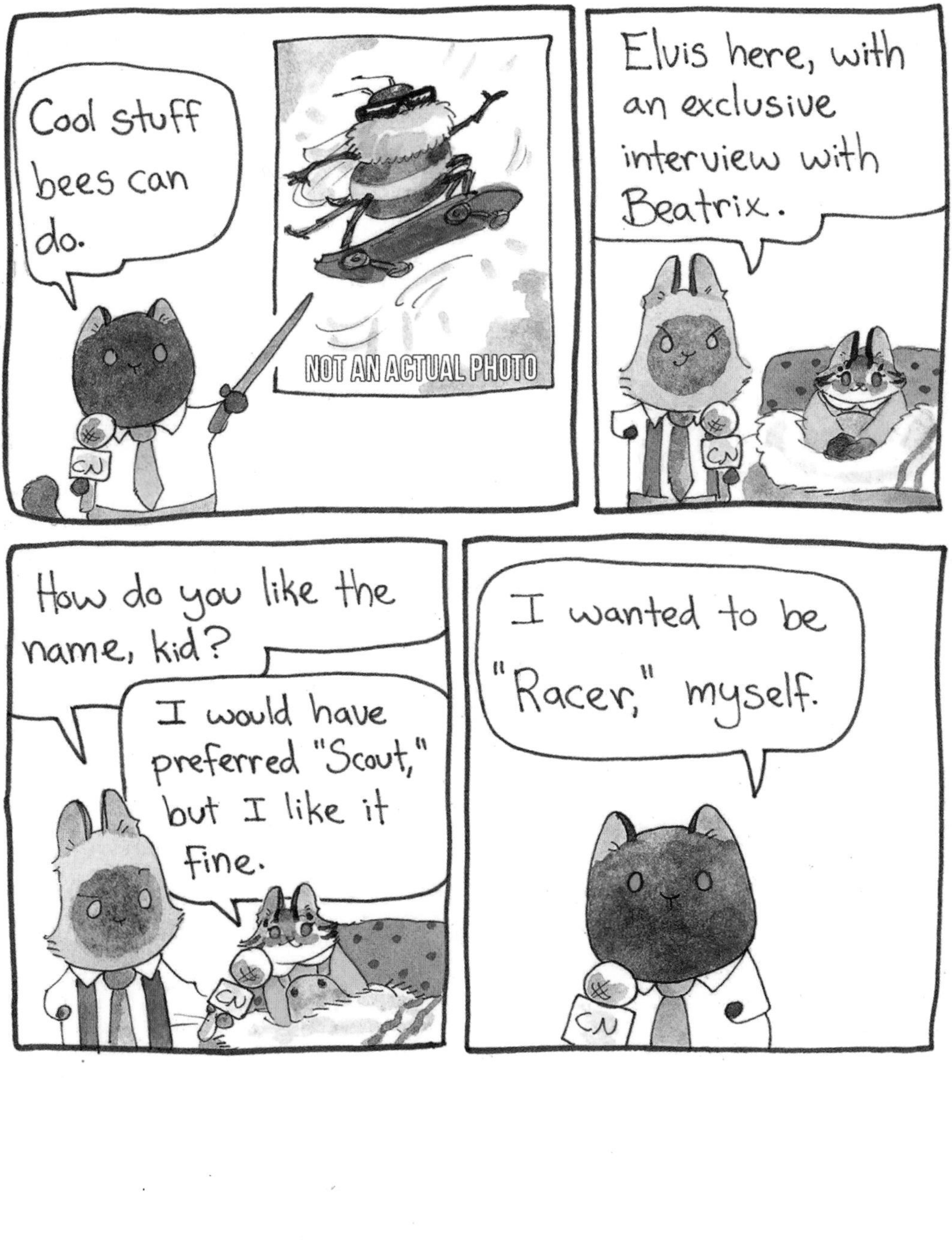
Cool stuff bees can do.
NOT AN ACTUAL PHOTO
CN
Elvis here, with an exclusive interview with Beatrix.
CN
How do you like the name, kid?
I would have preferred "Scout," but I like it fine.
CN
I wanted to be "Racer," myself.
CN

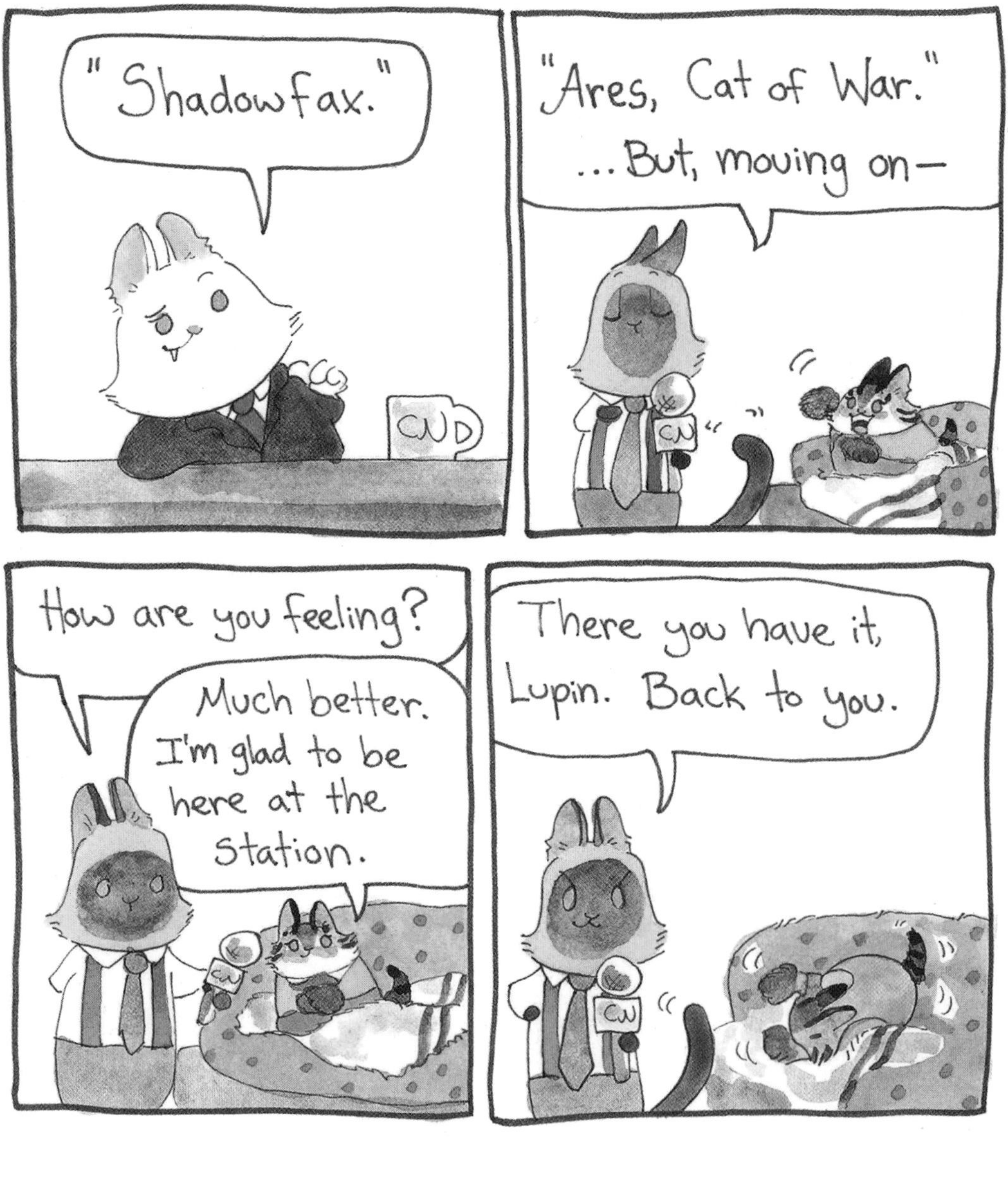
"Shadowfax."
"Ares, Cat of War." ...But, moving on—
CWD
CW
How are you feeling?
Much better. I'm glad to be here at the station.
CW
There you have it, Lupin. Back to you.
CW

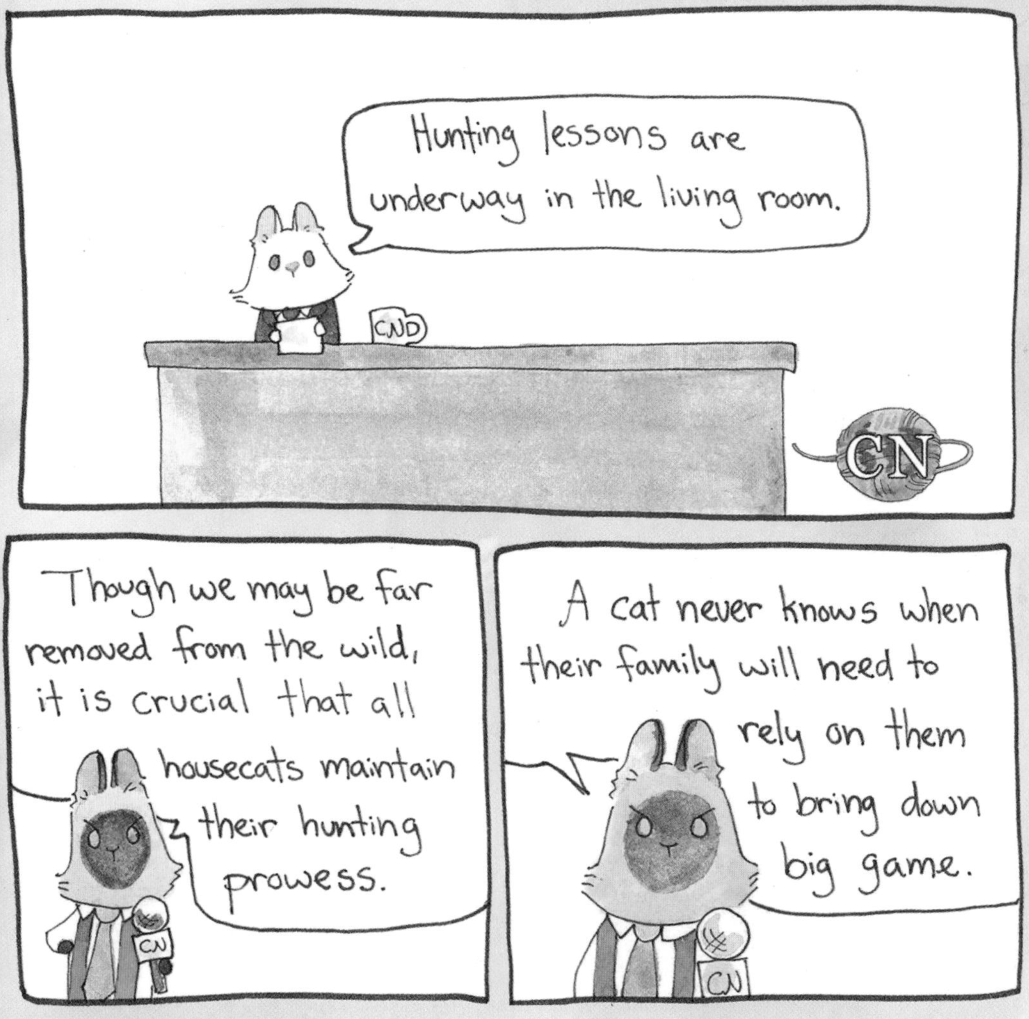
Hunting lessons are underway in the living room.
CND
CN
Though we may be far removed from the wild, it is crucial that all housecats maintain their hunting prowess.
CN
A cat never knows when their family will need to rely on them to bring down big game.
CN

Like an ice cream cone or a can of tuna.
MAYBE A HAM SANDWICH
Steady now... Don't want to spook it...
LIVE
Steady...
Oh, buttons.

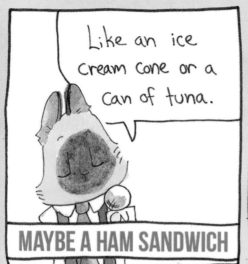

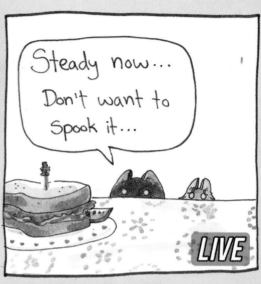

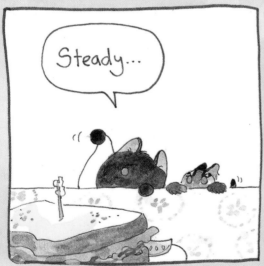

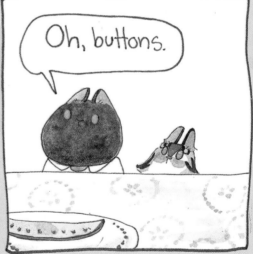

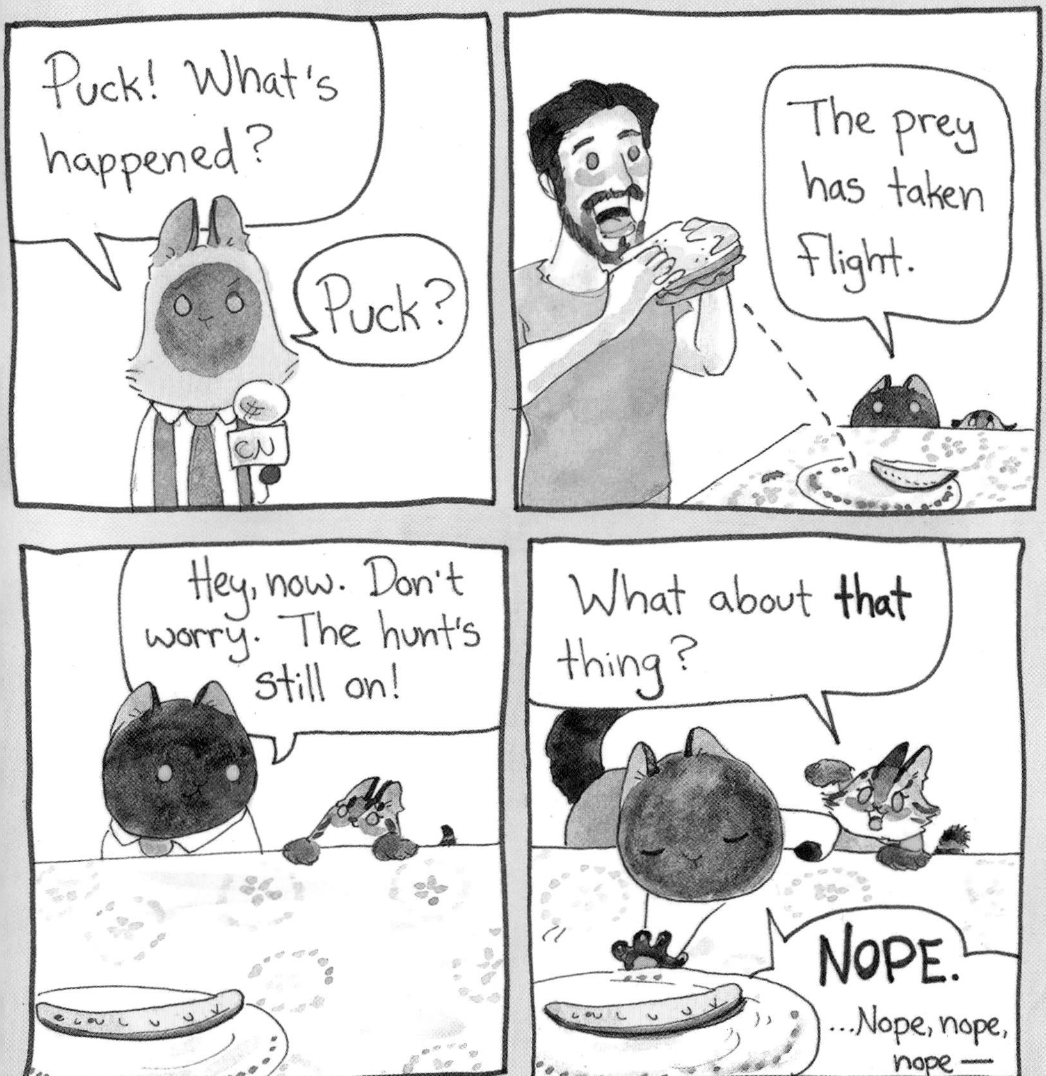
Puck! What's happened?
Puck?
CN
The prey has taken flight.
Hey, now. Don't worry. The hunt's still on!
What about **that** thing?
NOPE.
...Nope, nope, nope —

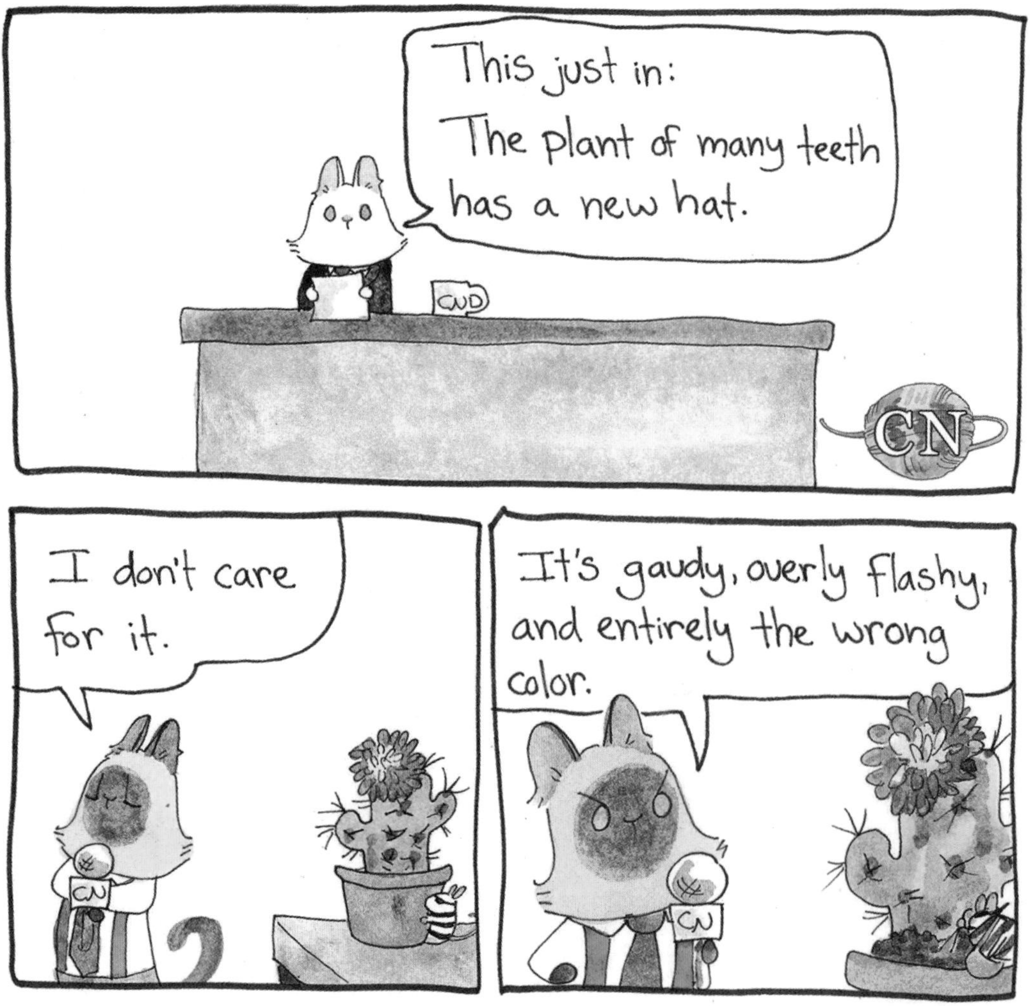
This just in:
The plant of many teeth has a new hat.
CN
I don't care for it.
It's gaudy, overly flashy, and entirely the wrong color.

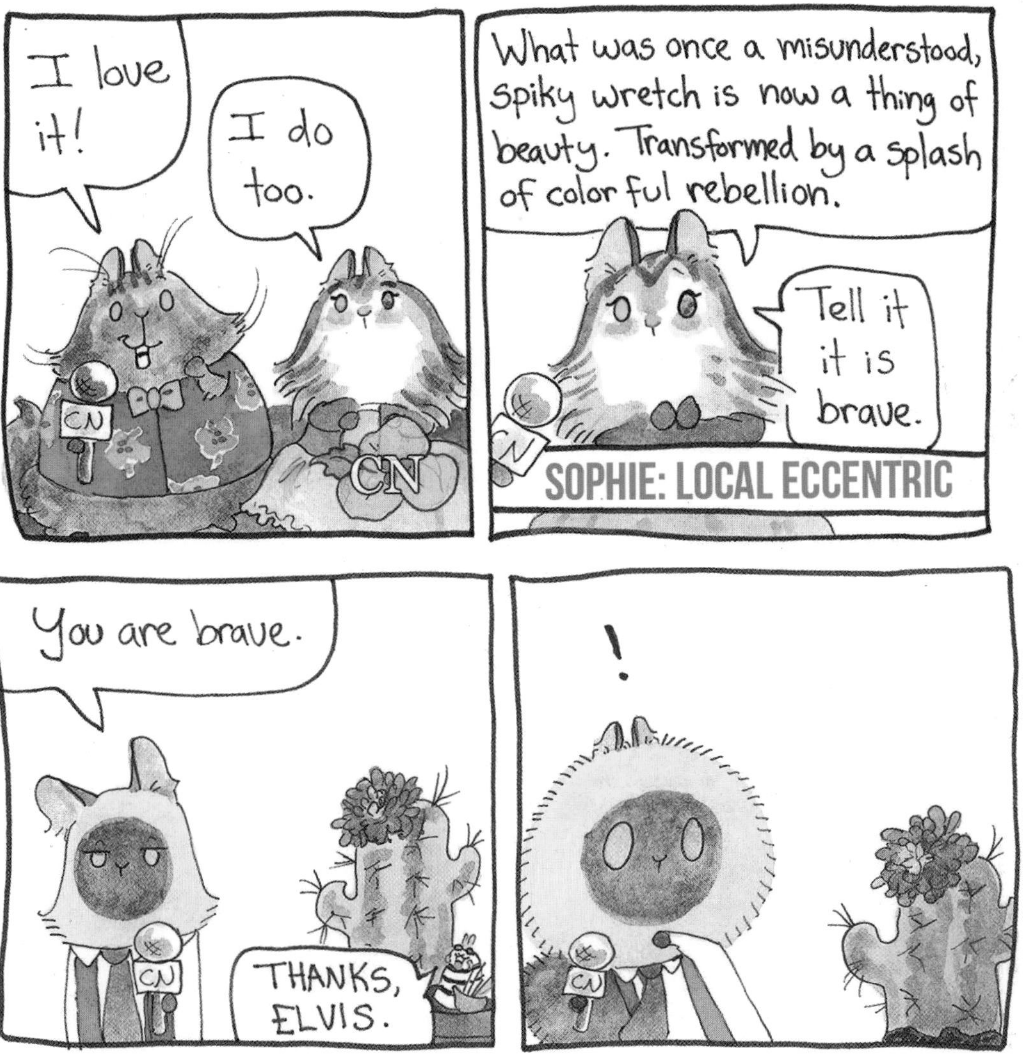
I love it!
I do too.
What was once a misunderstood, spiky wretch is now a thing of beauty. Transformed by a splash of color ful rebellion.
Tell it it is brave.
SOPHIE: LOCAL ECCENTRIC
CN
CN
CN
You are brave.
THANKS, ELVIS.
CN
!
CN

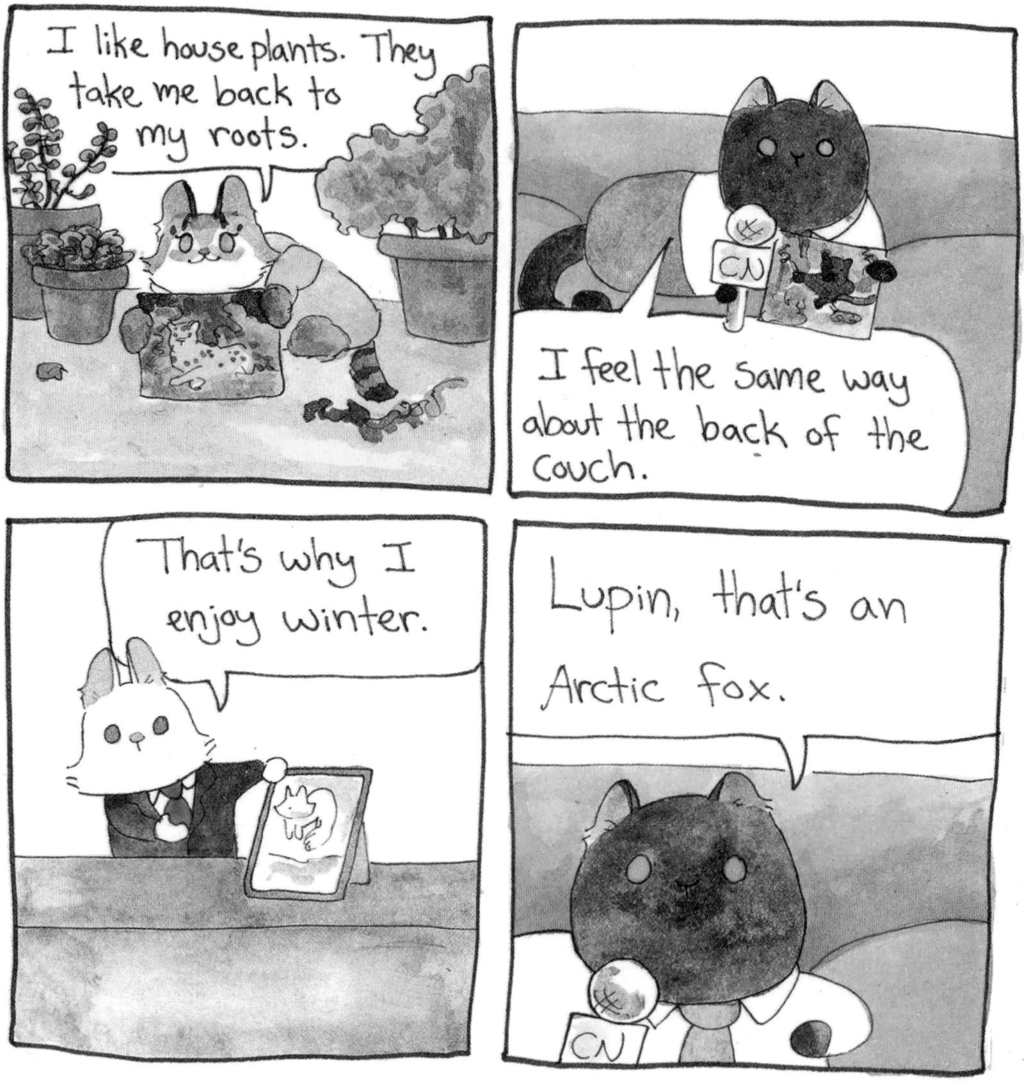
I like house plants. They take me back to my roots.
CN
I feel the same way about the back of the couch.
That's why I enjoy winter.
Lupin, that's an Arctic fox.
CN

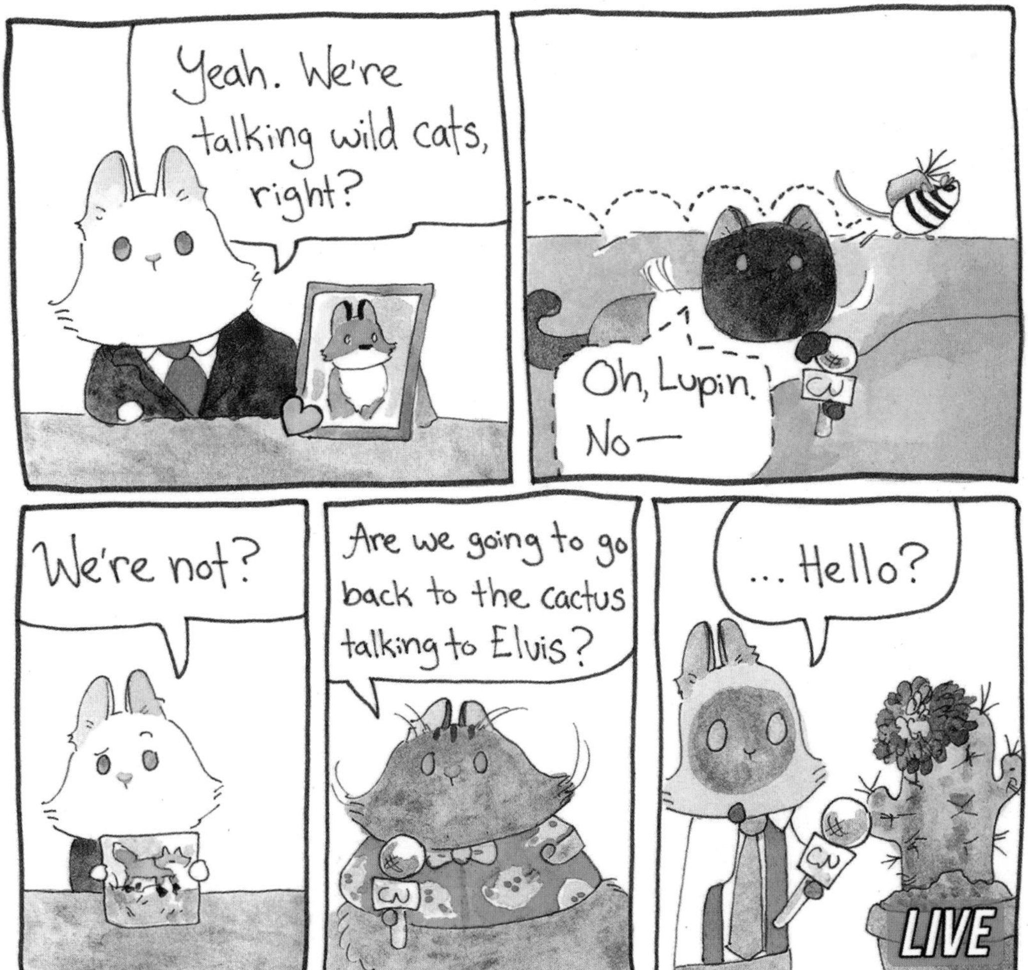
Yeah. We're talking wild cats, right?
Oh, Lupin. No—
CW
We're not?
Are we going to go back to the cactus talking to Elvis?
CW
... Hello?
CW
LIVE

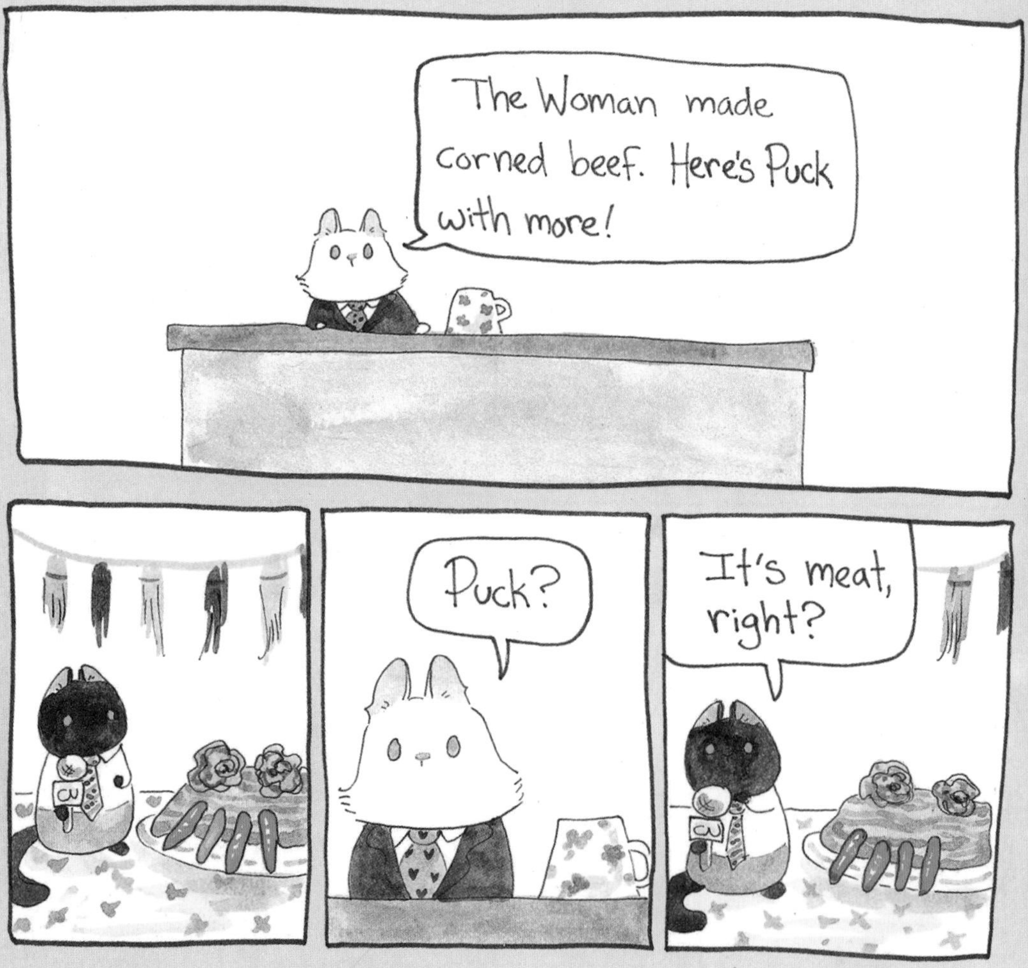
The Woman made corned beef. Here's Puck with more!
Puck?
It's meat, right?

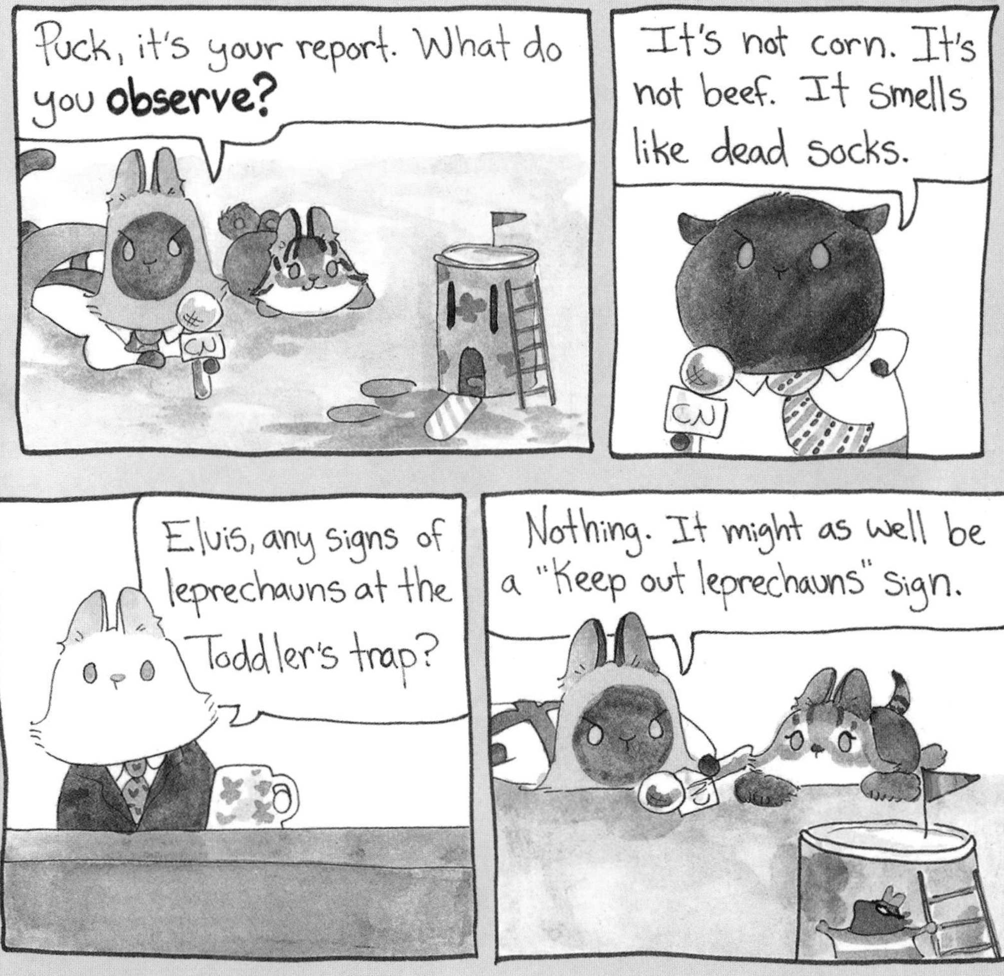
Puck, it's your report. What do you observe?
It's not corn. It's not beef. It smells like dead socks.
Elvis, any signs of leprechauns at the Toddler's trap?
Nothing. It might as well be a "Keep out leprechauns" sign.

Are leprechauns a problem in this house?
They seem to be seasonal.
LIVE
This isn't gold, it's chocolate.
CAMERA ONE

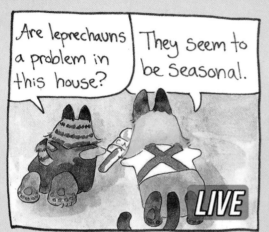

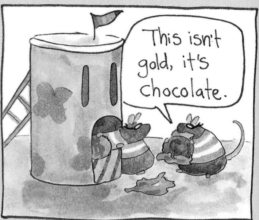

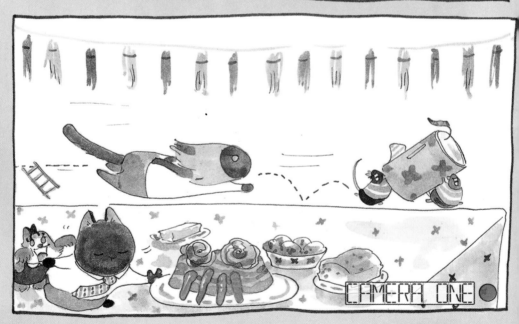

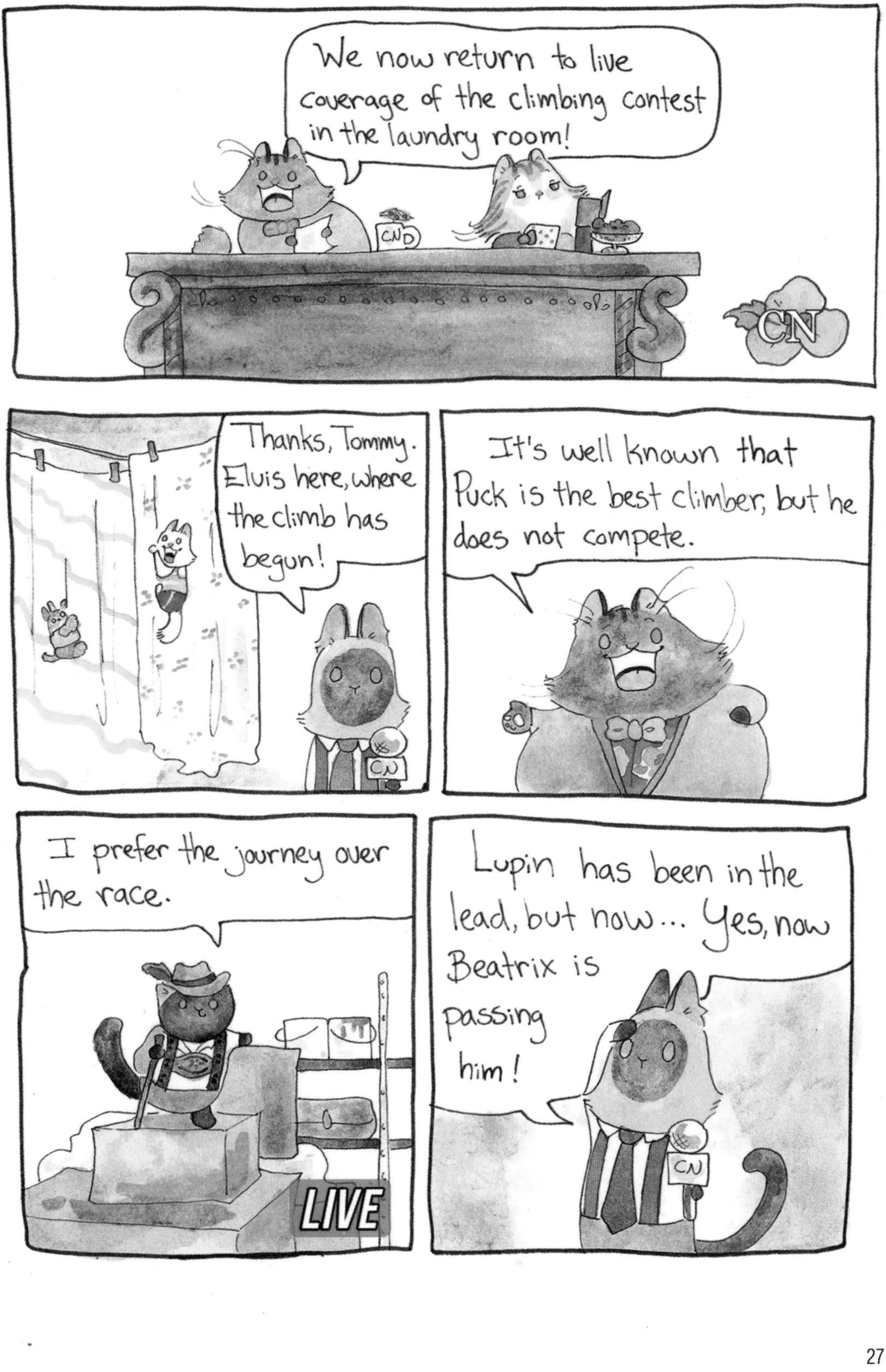

We now return to live coverage of the climbing contest in the laundry room!
CND
CN
Thanks, Tommy. Elvis here, where the climb has begun!
CN
It's well known that Puck is the best climber, but he does not compete.
I prefer the journey over the race.
LIVE
Lupin has been in the lead, but now... Yes, now Beatrix is passing him!
CN

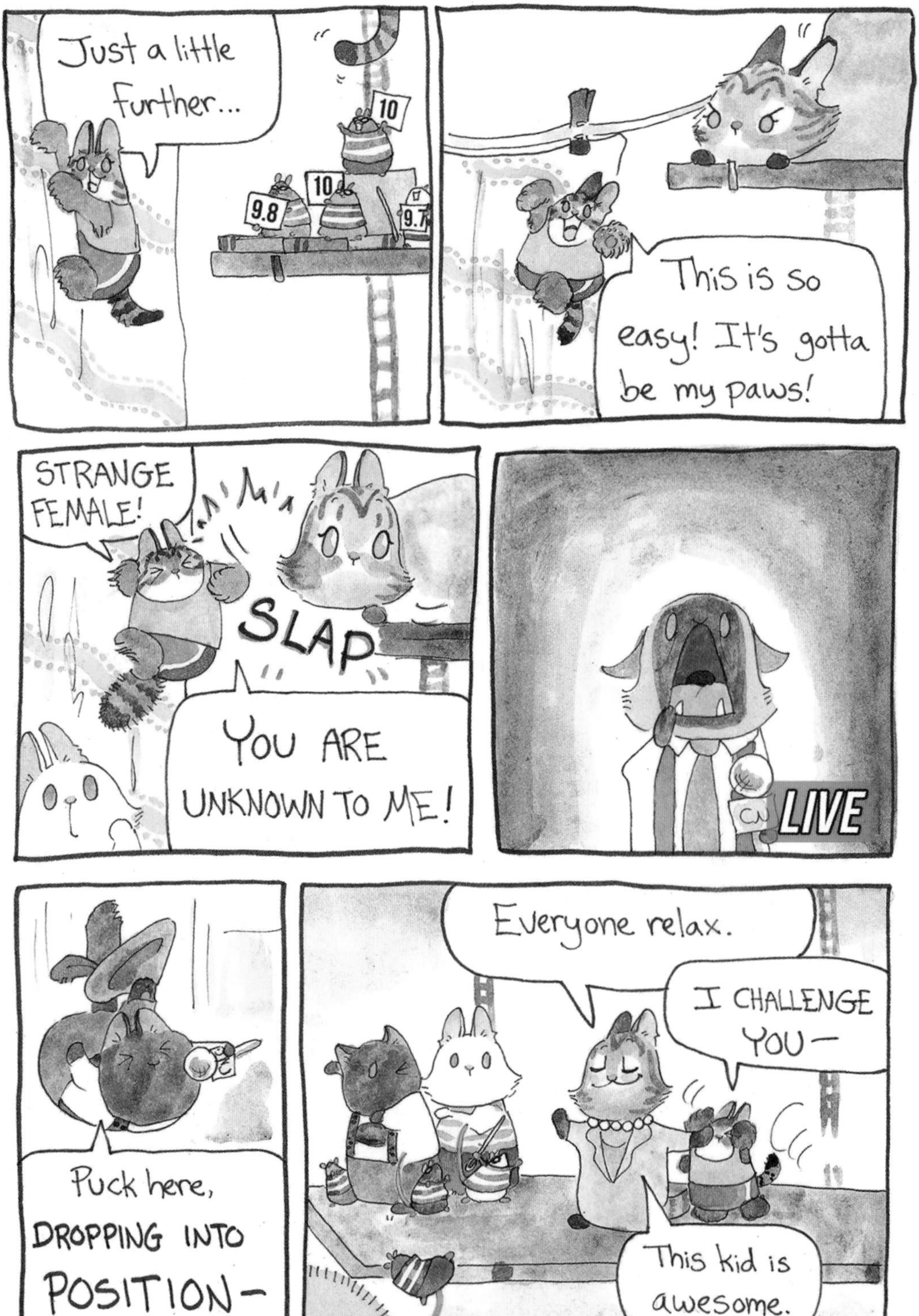
Just a little further...
10
9.8
10
9.7
This is so easy! It's gotta be my paws!
STRANGE FEMALE!
SLAP
YOU ARE UNKNOWN TO ME!
LIVE
Puck here, DROPPING INTO POSITION–
Everyone relax.
I CHALLENGE YOU–
This kid is awesome.

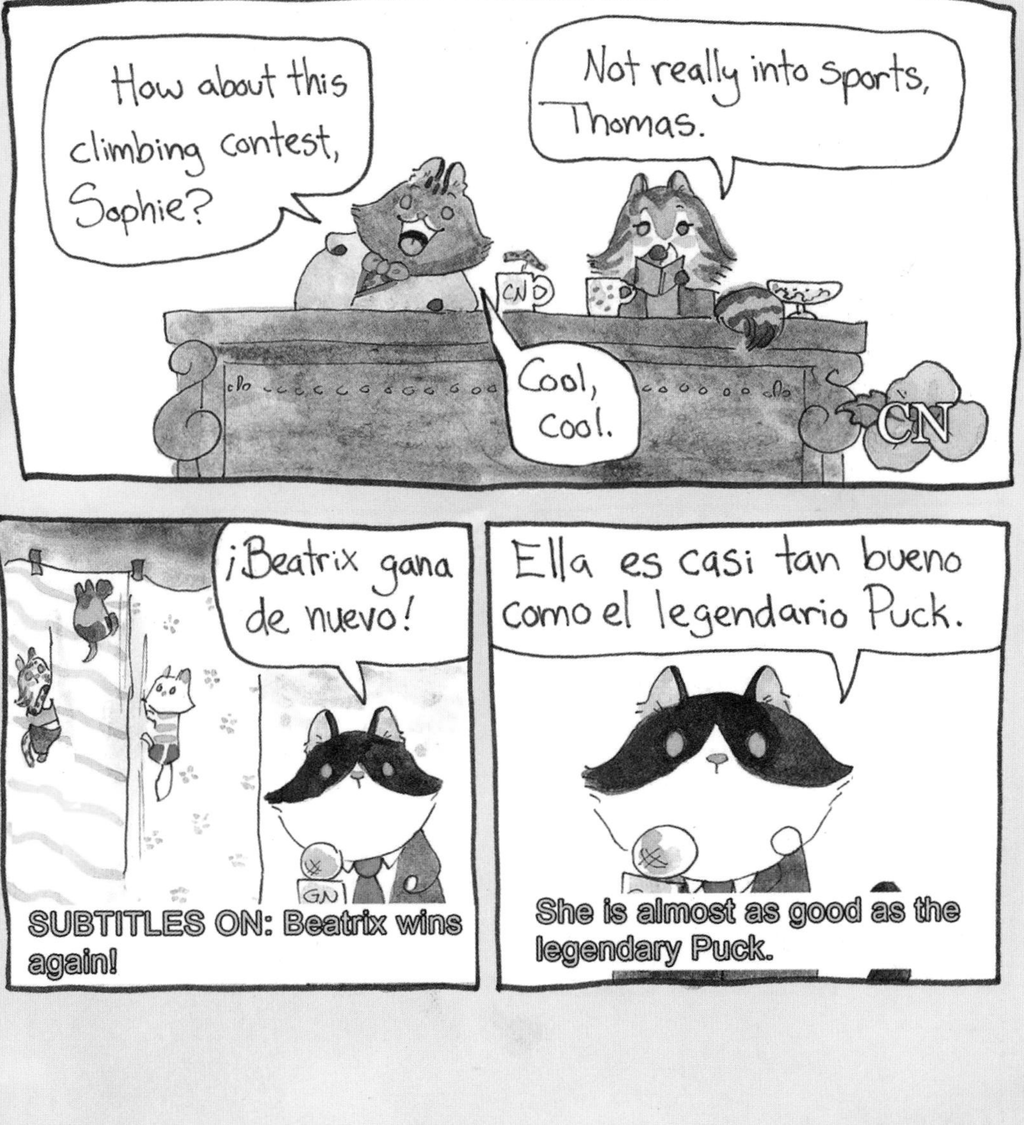
How about this climbing contest, Sophie?
Not really into sports, Thomas.
Cool, cool.
CN
¡Beatrix gana de nuevo!
SUBTITLES ON: Beatrix wins again!
Ella es casi tan bueno como el legendario Puck.
She is almost as good as the legendary Puck.

Who does not compete.

Beatrix, how does it feel to take the race?

Great!

You did good, kid.

Thanks! I'm going to go tell Puck!

Whew! What a little go-getter!

She'll make a great reporter some day.

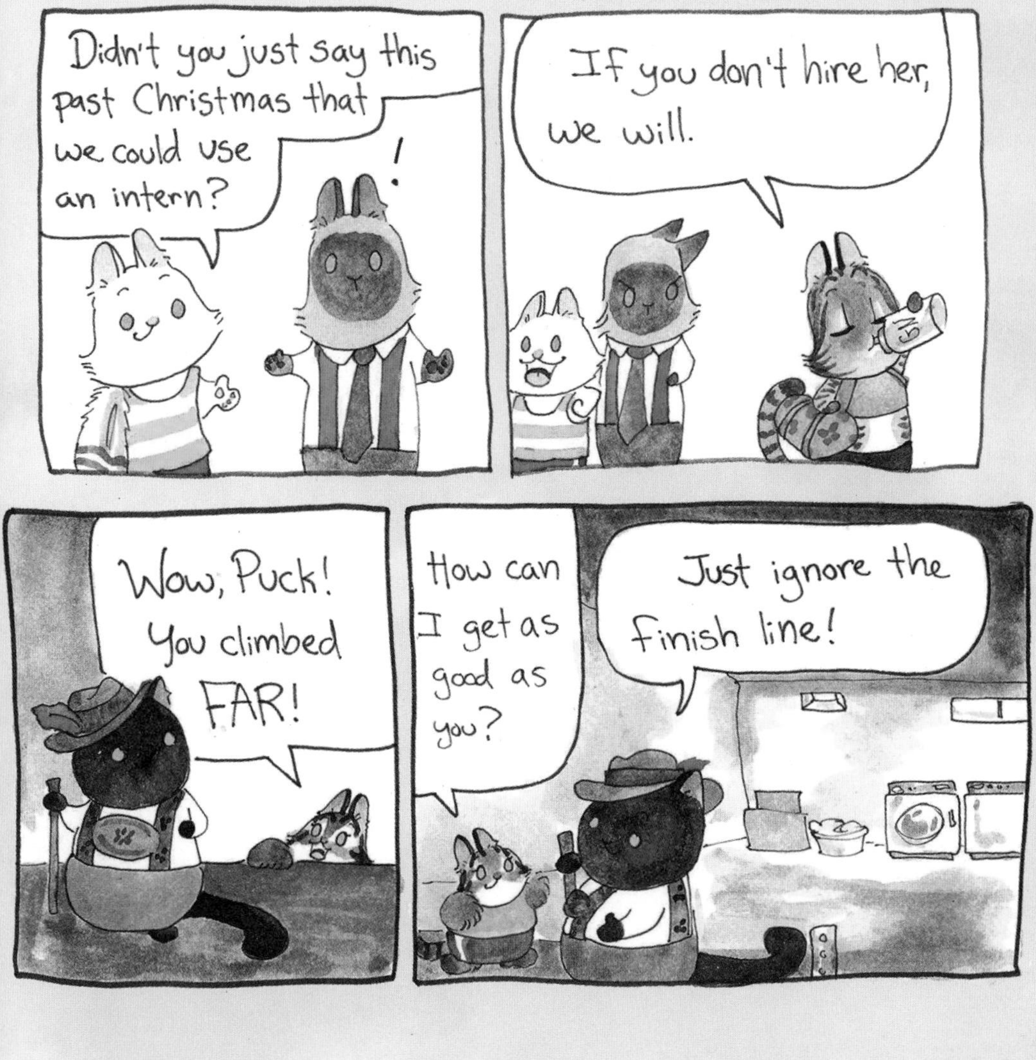
Didn't you just say this past Christmas that we could use an intern?
!
If you don't hire her, we will.
Wow, Puck! You climbed FAR!
How can I get as good as you?
Just ignore the finish line!

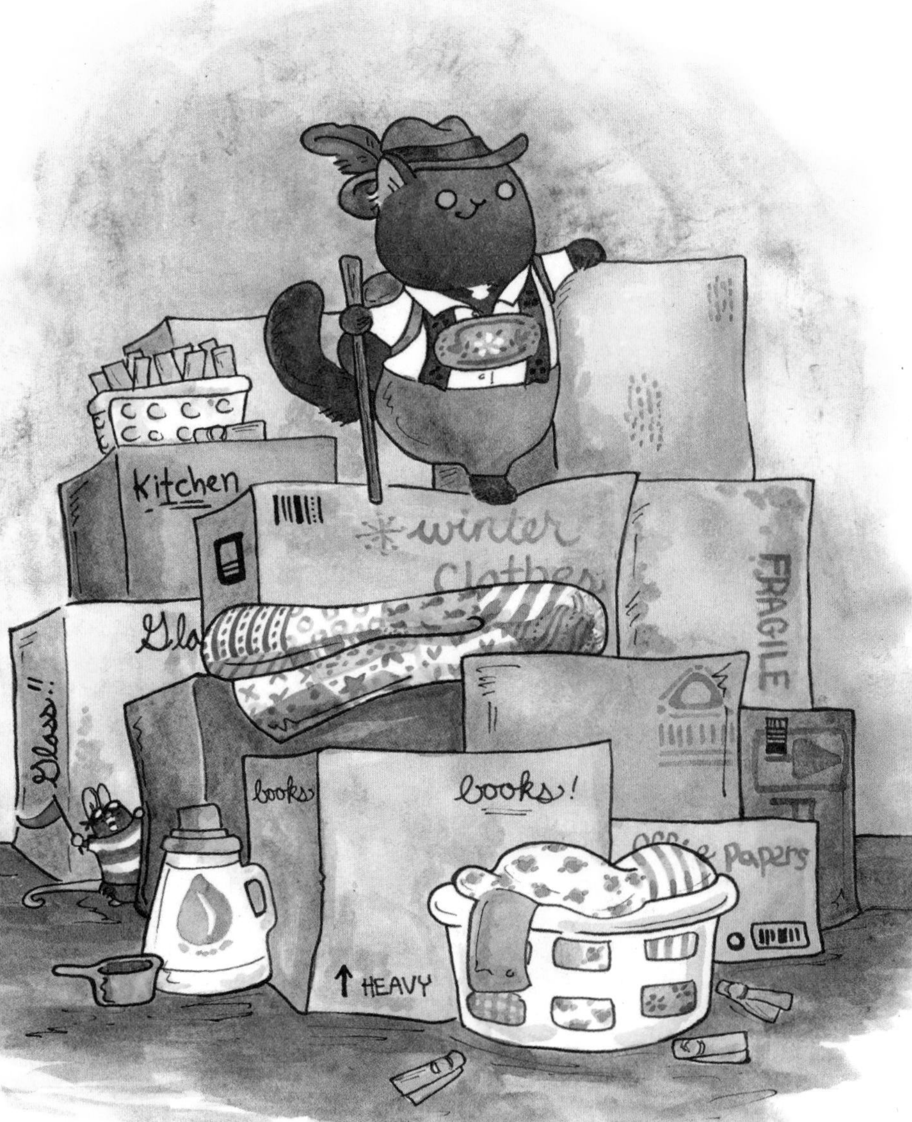
Kitchen
winter
FRAGILE
Glass!!
books
books!
↑ HEAVY
Papers

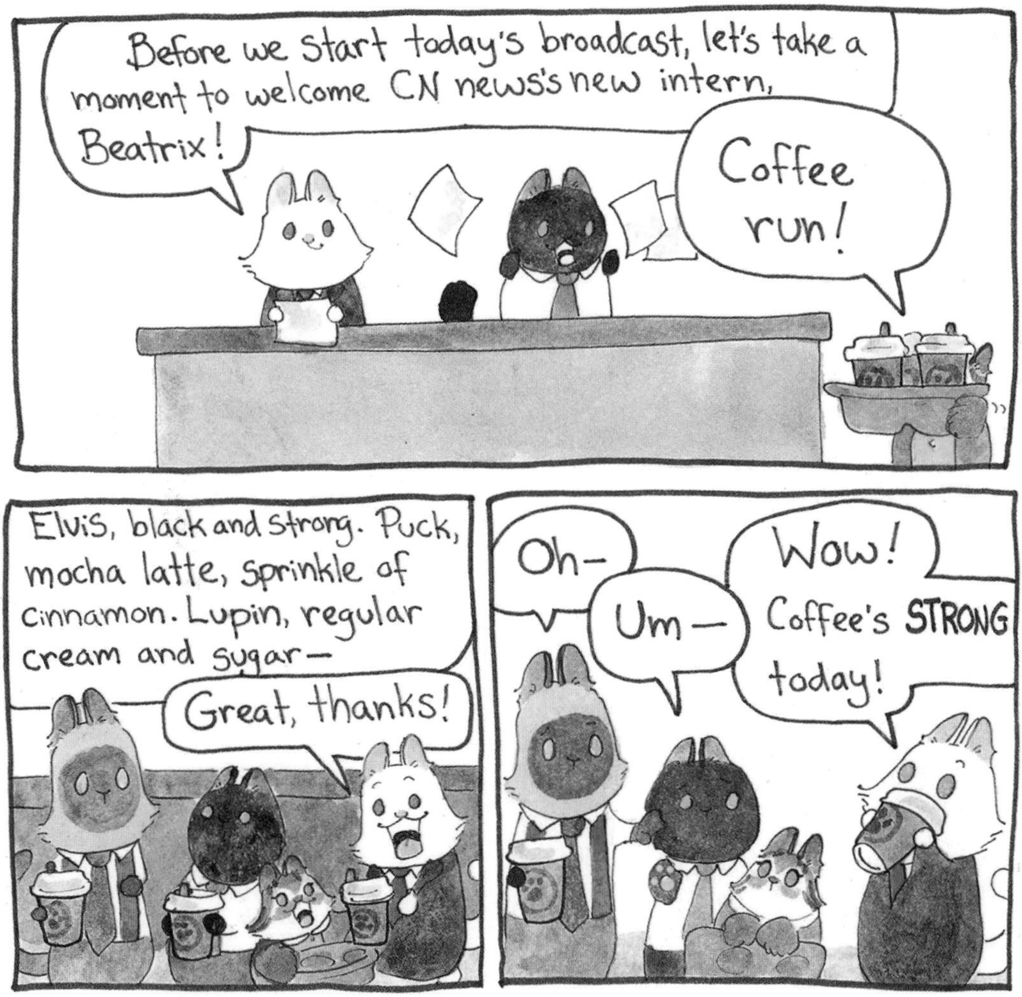
Before we start today's broadcast, let's take a moment to welcome CN news's new intern, Beatrix!
Coffee run!
Elvis, black and strong. Puck, mocha latte, sprinkle of cinnamon. Lupin, regular cream and sugar—
Great, thanks!
Oh—
Um—
Wow! Coffee's STRONG today!

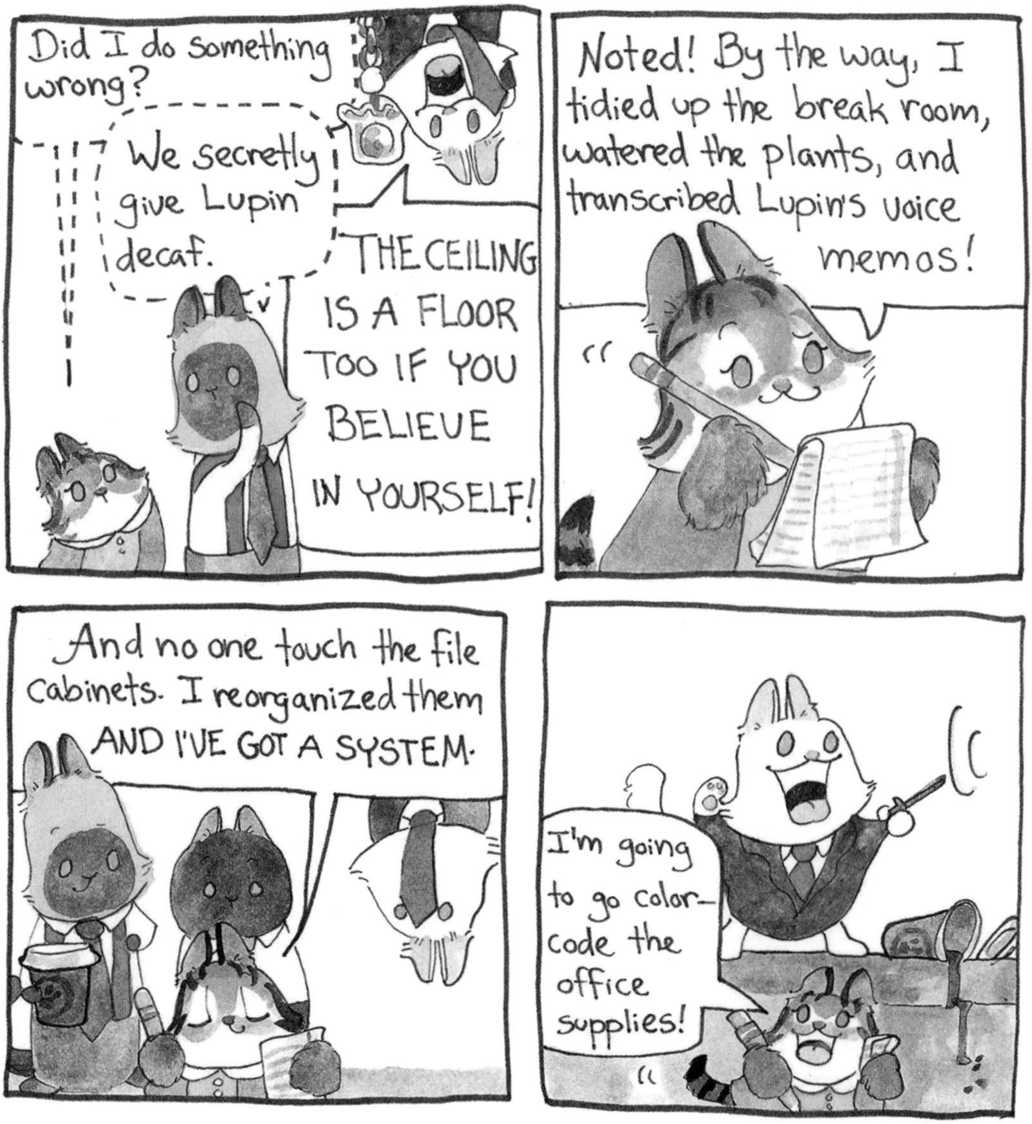
Did I do something wrong?
We secretly give Lupin decaf.
THE CEILING IS A FLOOR TOO IF YOU BELIEVE IN YOURSELF!
Noted! By the way, I tidied up the break room, watered the plants, and transcribed Lupin's voice memos!
And no one touch the file cabinets. I reorganized them AND I'VE GOT A SYSTEM.
I'm going to go color-code the office supplies!

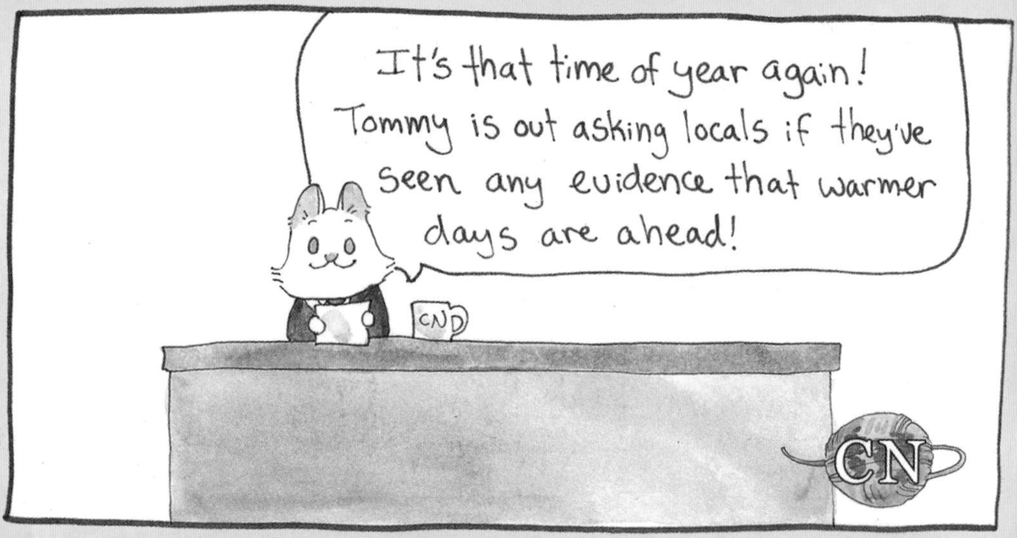
It's that time of year again! Tommy is out asking locals if they've seen any evidence that warmer days are ahead!
CND
CN

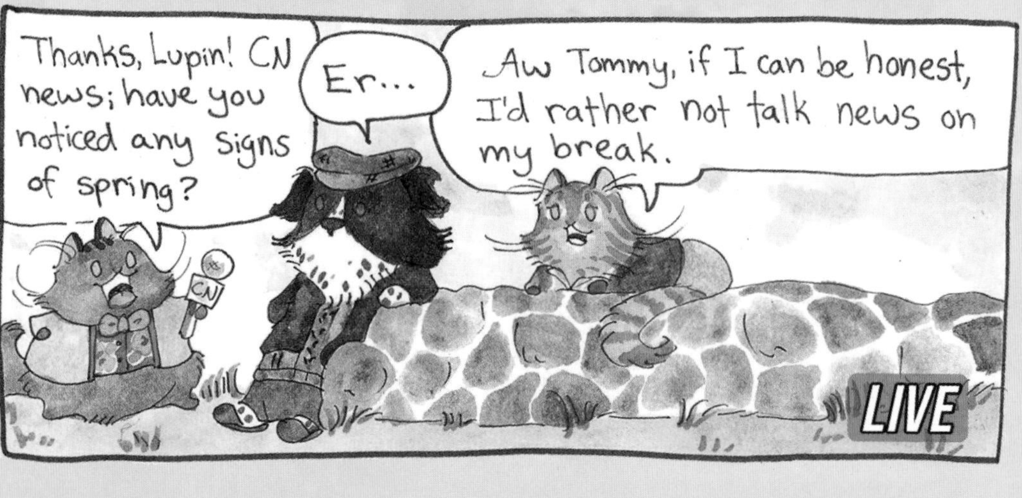
Thanks, Lupin! CN news; have you noticed any signs of spring?
Er...
Aw Tommy, if I can be honest, I'd rather not talk news on my break.
CN
LIVE

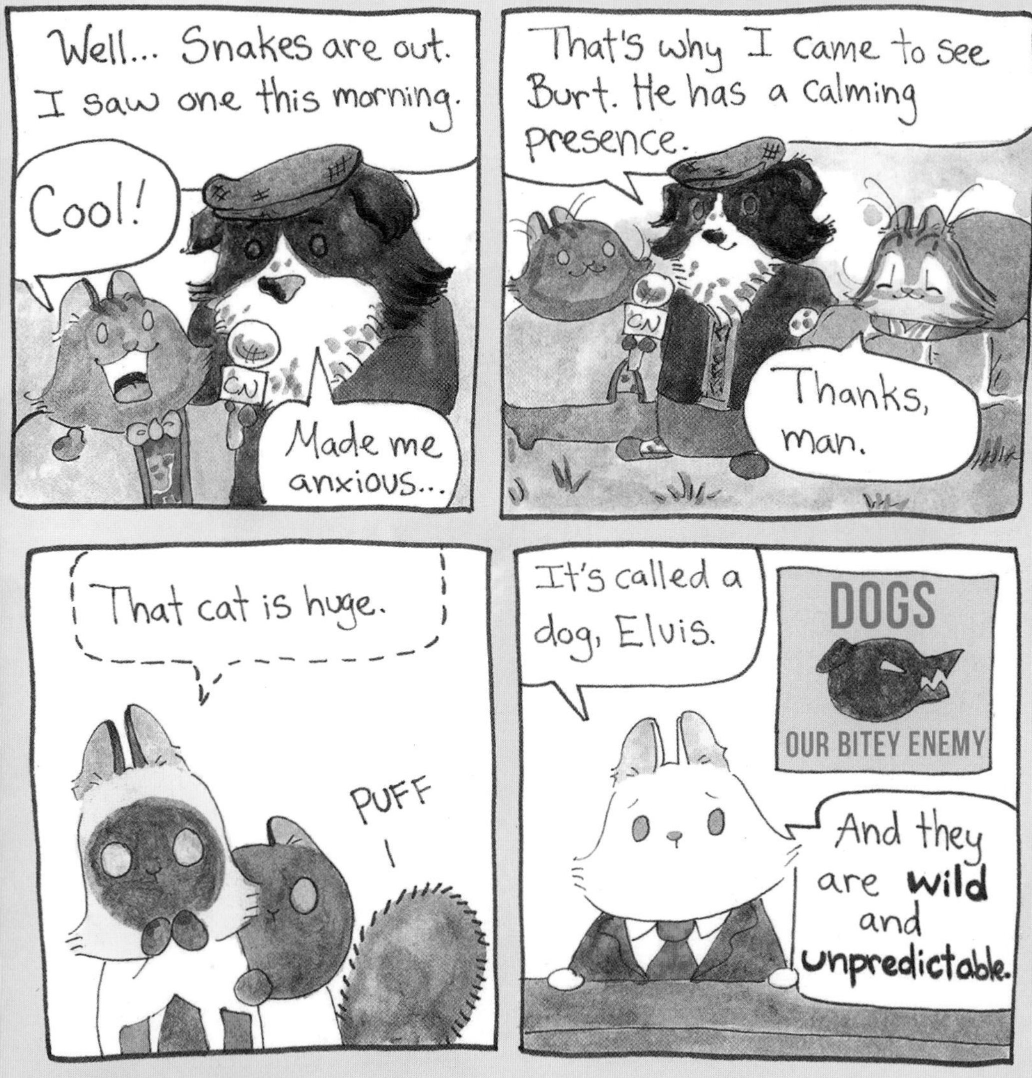
Well... Snakes are out. I saw one this morning.
Cool!
Made me anxious...
That's why I came to see Burt. He has a calming presence.
Thanks, man.
That cat is huge.
PUFF
It's called a dog, Elvis.
DOGS
OUR BITEY ENEMY
And they are **wild** and **unpredictable.**

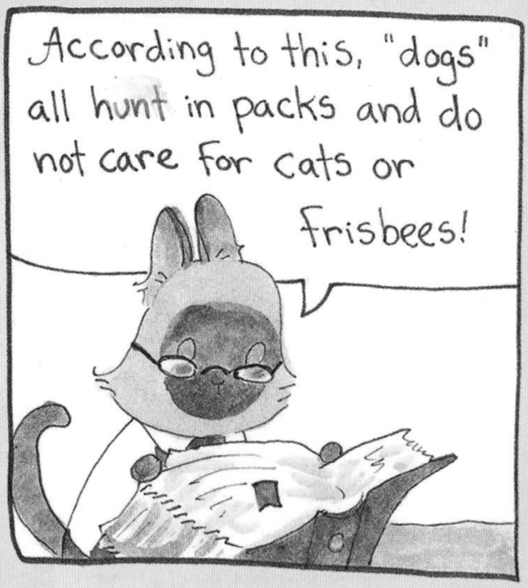
According to this, "dogs" all hunt in packs and do not care for cats or frisbees!

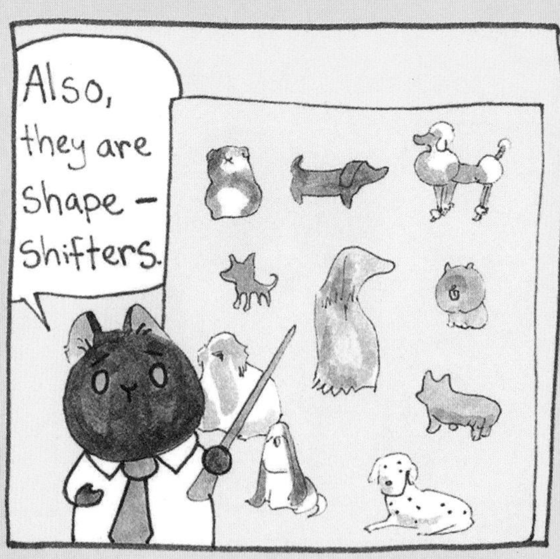
Also, they are Shape-Shifters.

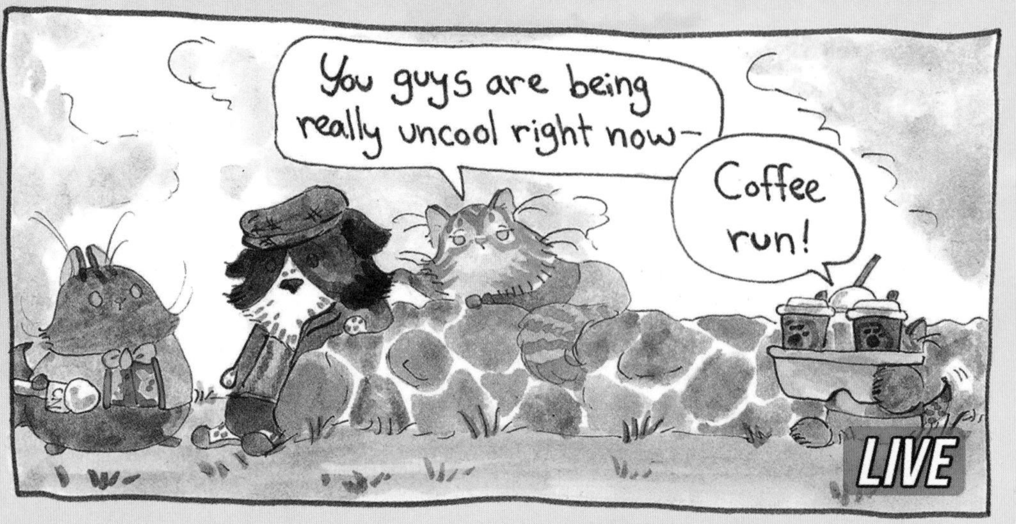
You guys are being really uncool right now—
Coffee run!
LIVE

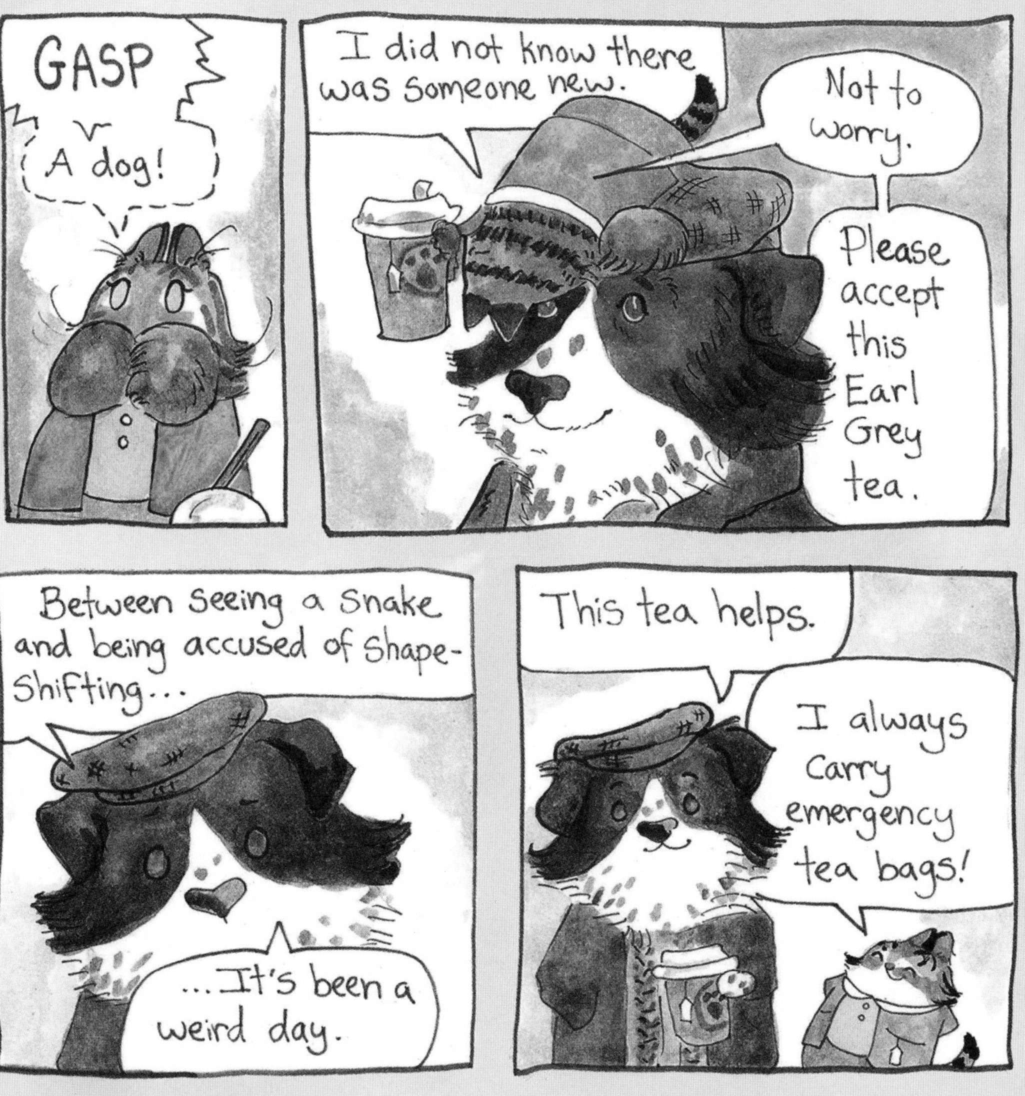
GASP
A dog!
I did not know there was someone new.
Not to worry.
Please accept this Earl Grey tea.
Between seeing a snake and being accused of shape-shifting...
...It's been a weird day.
This tea helps.
I always carry emergency tea bags!

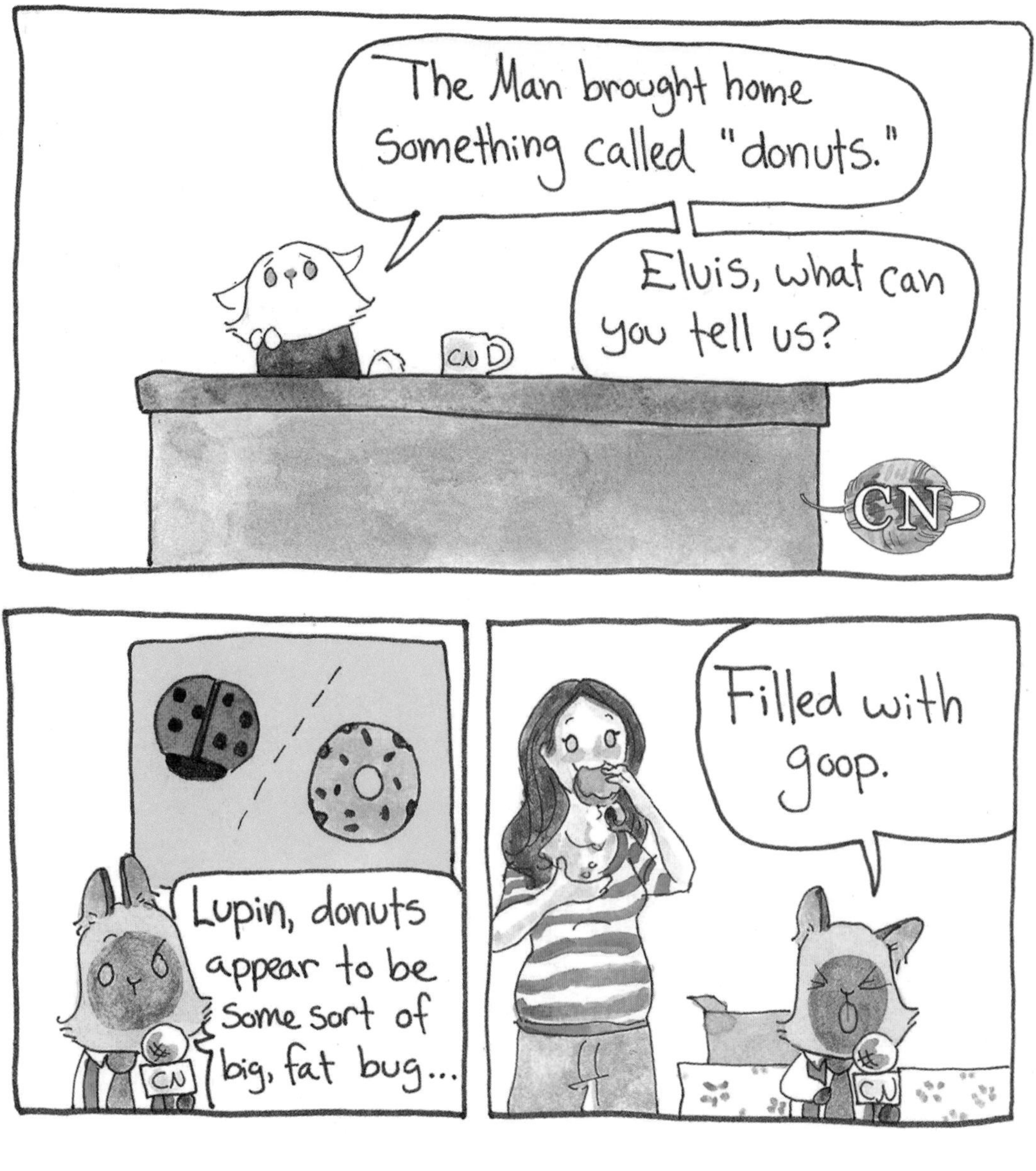

The Man brought home Something called "donuts."
Elvis, what can you tell us?
CN
Lupin, donuts appear to be Some sort of big, fat bug...
CN
Filled with goop.
CN

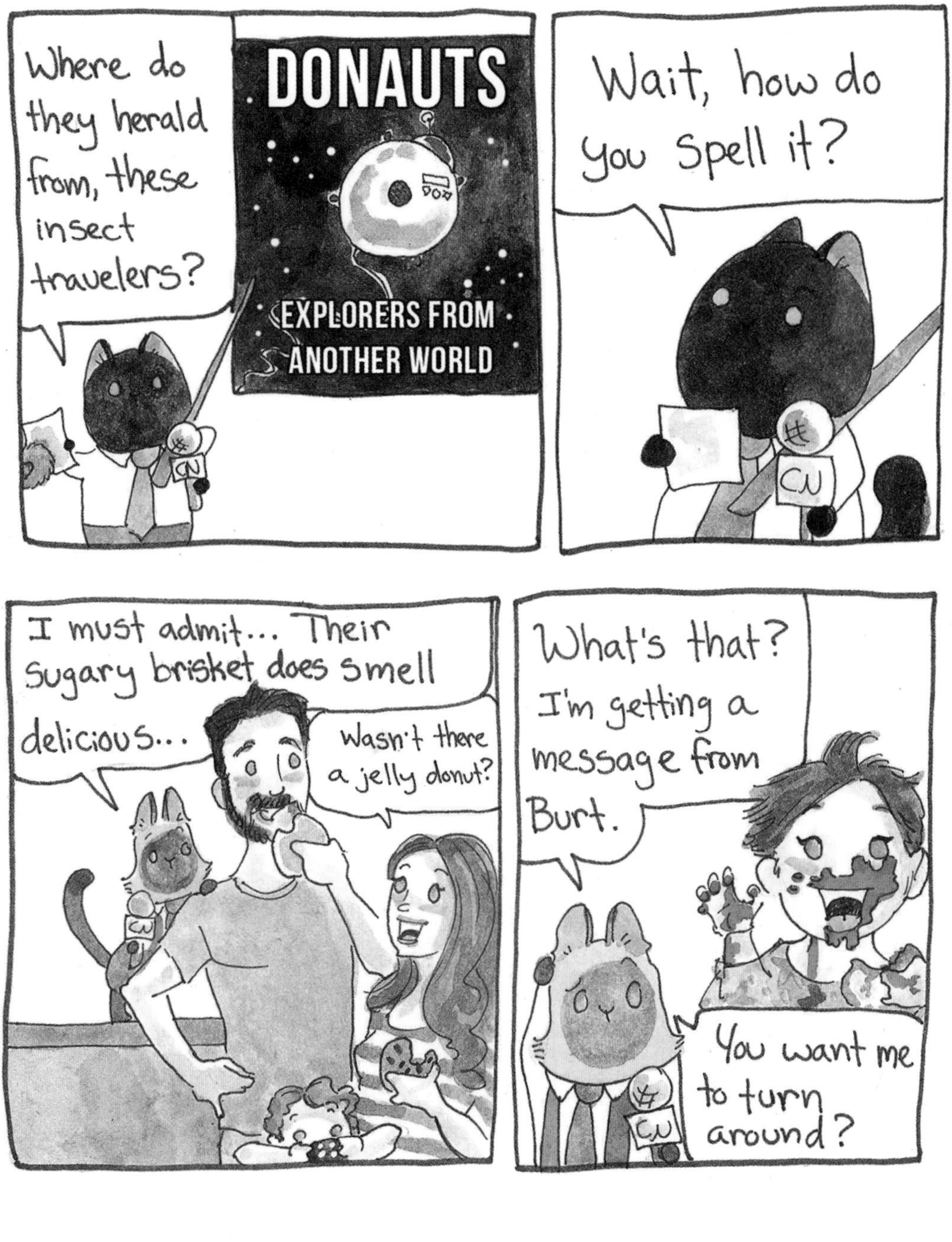
Where do they herald from, these insect travelers?
DONAUTS
EXPLORERS FROM ANOTHER WORLD
Wait, how do you Spell it?
I must admit... Their sugary brisket does smell delicious...
Wasn't there a jelly donut?
What's that? I'm getting a message from Burt.
You want me to turn around?

I've just been handed a bulletin – the doorbell rang!
Someone at the door, DROP TO THE FLOOR.
Hey!
Hey! Your books came in! And I've got a Christmas cactus cutting for you!

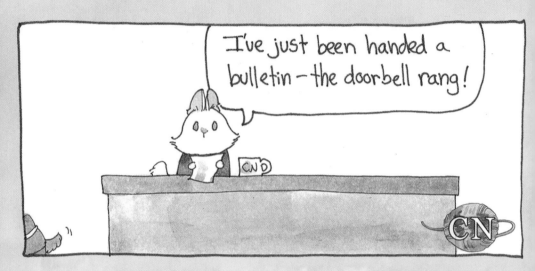

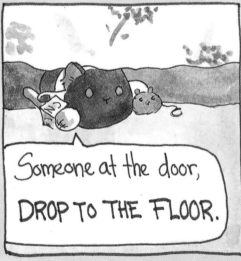

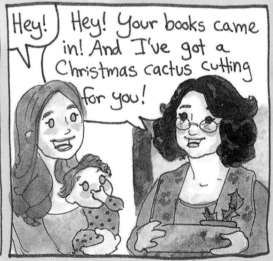

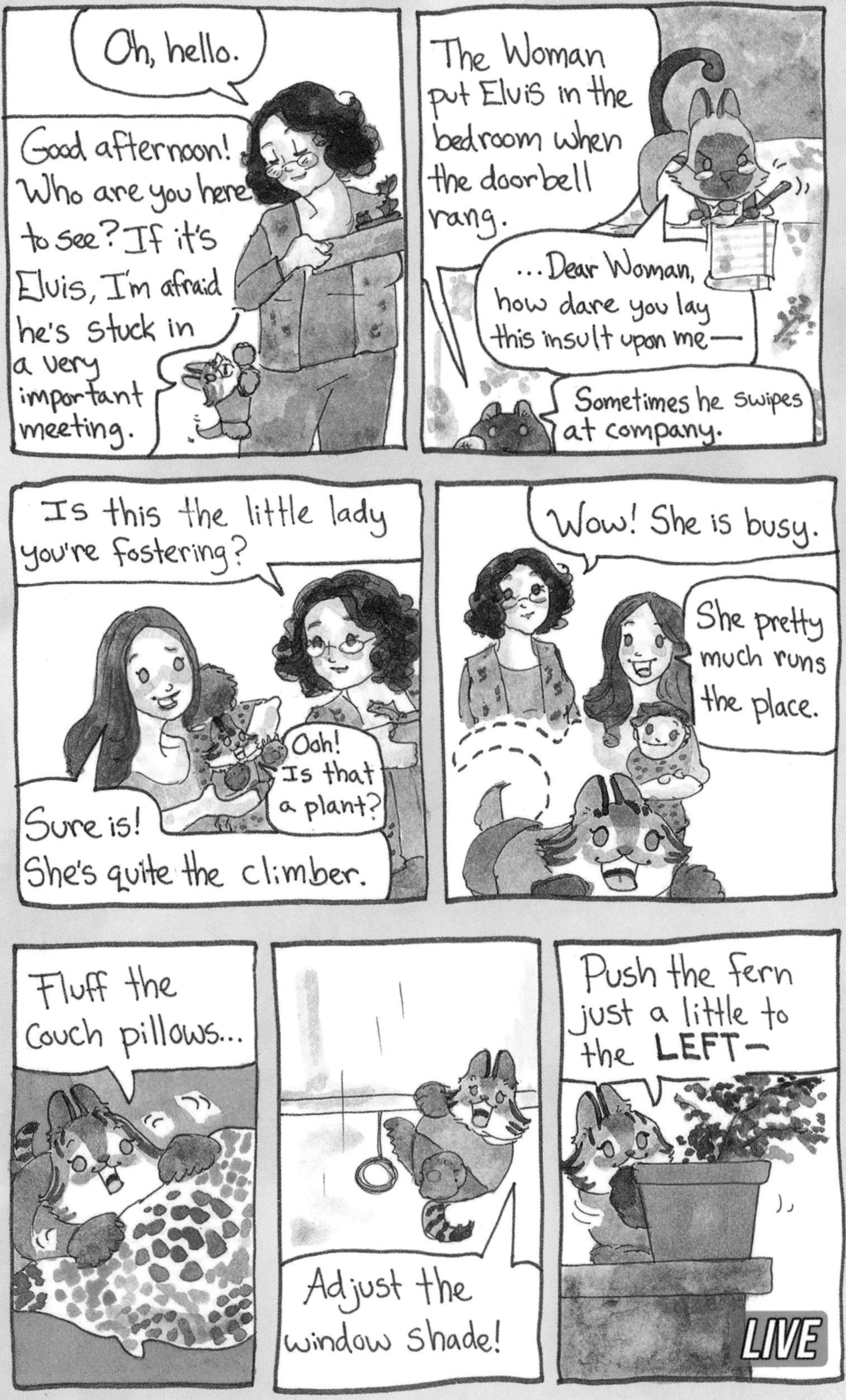
Oh, hello.
Good afternoon! Who are you here to see? If it's Elvis, I'm afraid he's stuck in a very important meeting.
The Woman put Elvis in the bedroom when the doorbell rang.
...Dear Woman, how dare you lay this insult upon me—
Sometimes he swipes at company.
Is this the little lady you're fostering?
Ooh! Is that a plant?
Sure is! She's quite the climber.
Wow! She is busy.
She pretty much runs the place.
Fluff the couch pillows...
Adjust the window shade!
Push the fern just a little to the LEFT—
LIVE

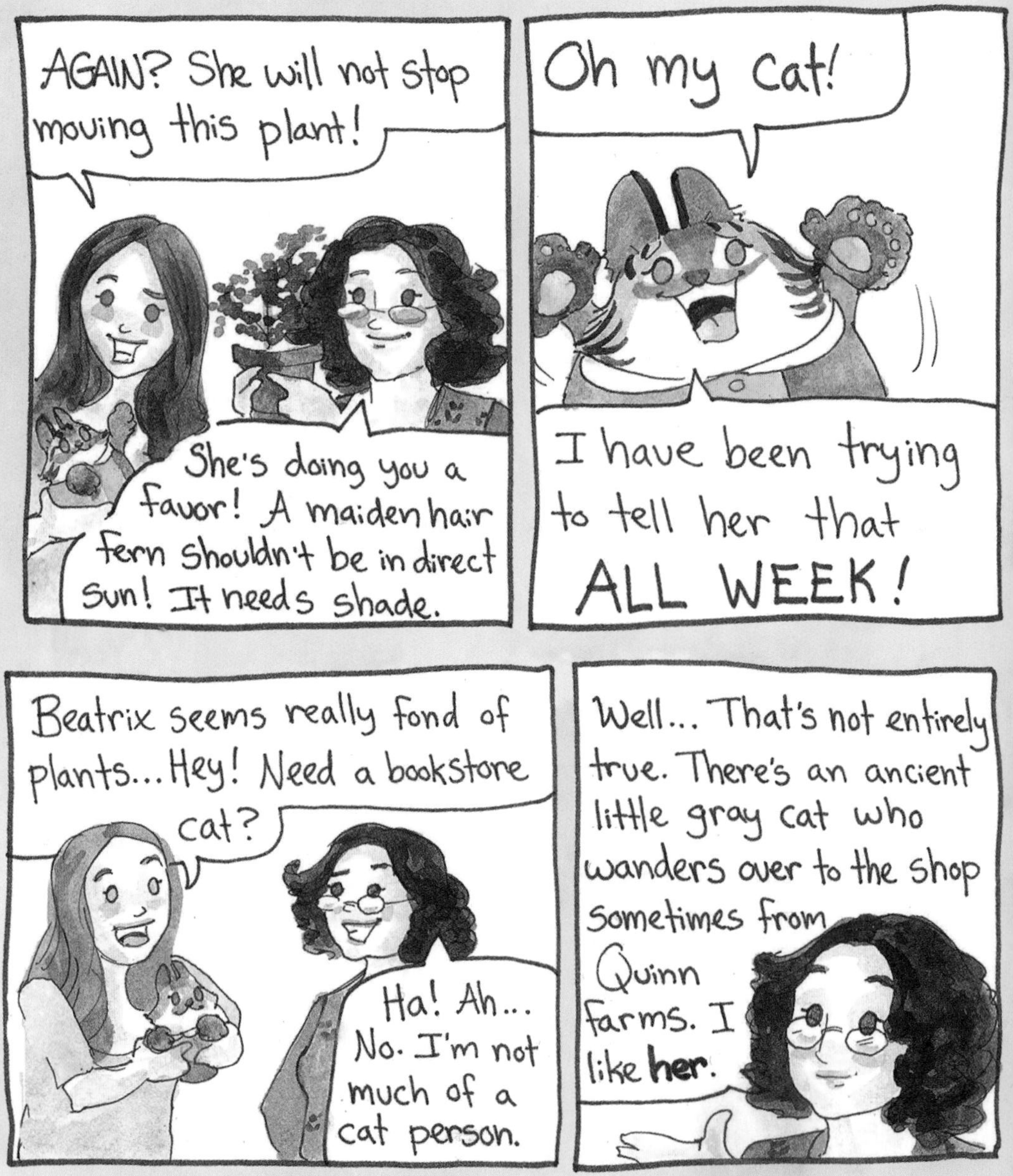
AGAIN? She will not stop moving this plant!
She's doing you a favor! A maiden hair fern shouldn't be in direct sun! It needs shade.
Oh my cat!
I have been trying to tell her that ALL WEEK!
Beatrix seems really fond of plants... Hey! Need a bookstore cat?
Ha! Ah... No. I'm not much of a cat person.
Well... That's not entirely true. There's an ancient little gray cat who wanders over to the shop sometimes from Quinn farms. I like **her**.

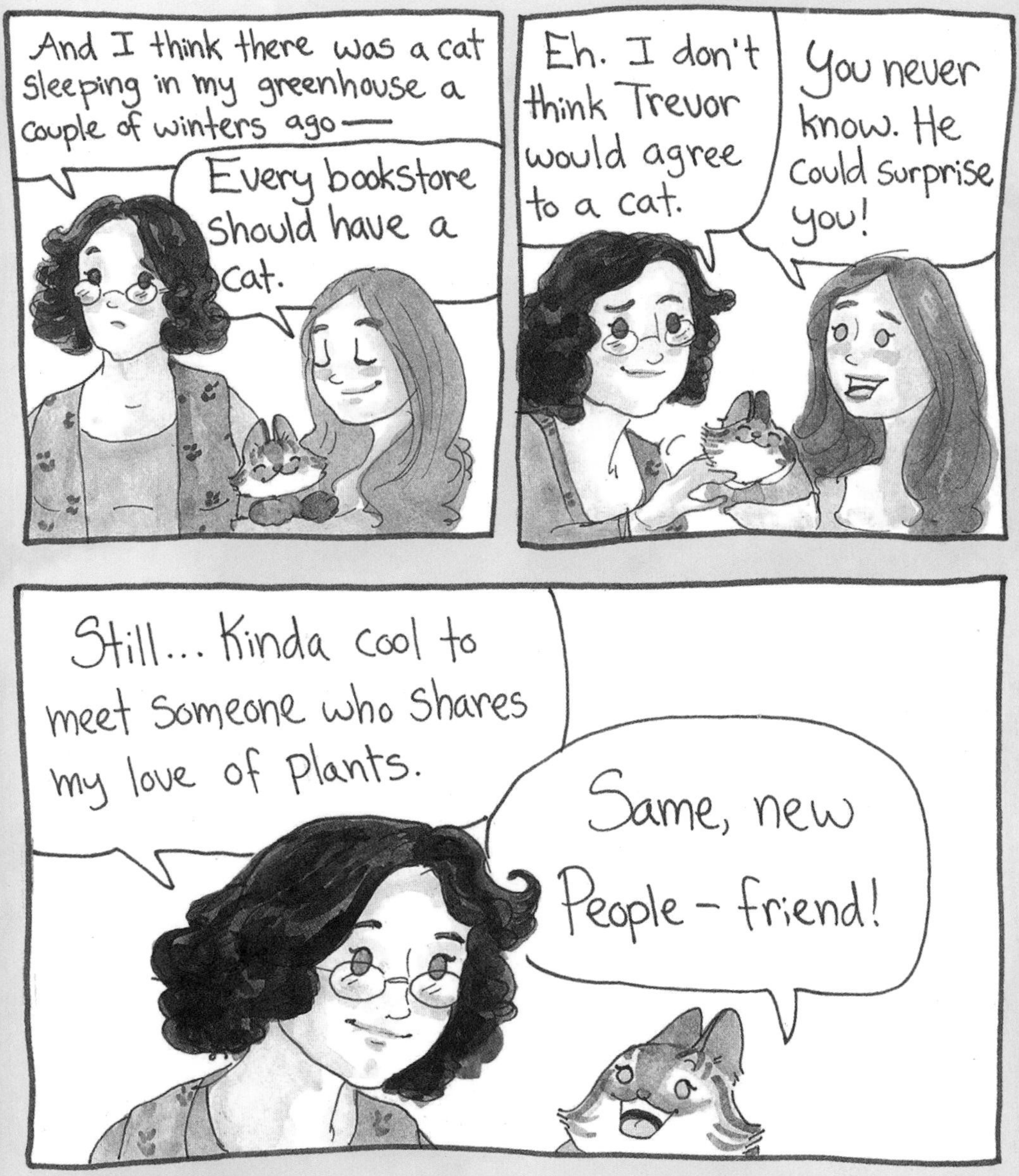
And I think there was a cat sleeping in my greenhouse a couple of winters ago—
Every bookstore should have a cat.
Eh. I don't think Trevor would agree to a cat.
You never know. He could surprise you!
Still... Kinda cool to meet someone who shares my love of plants.
Same, new people-friend!

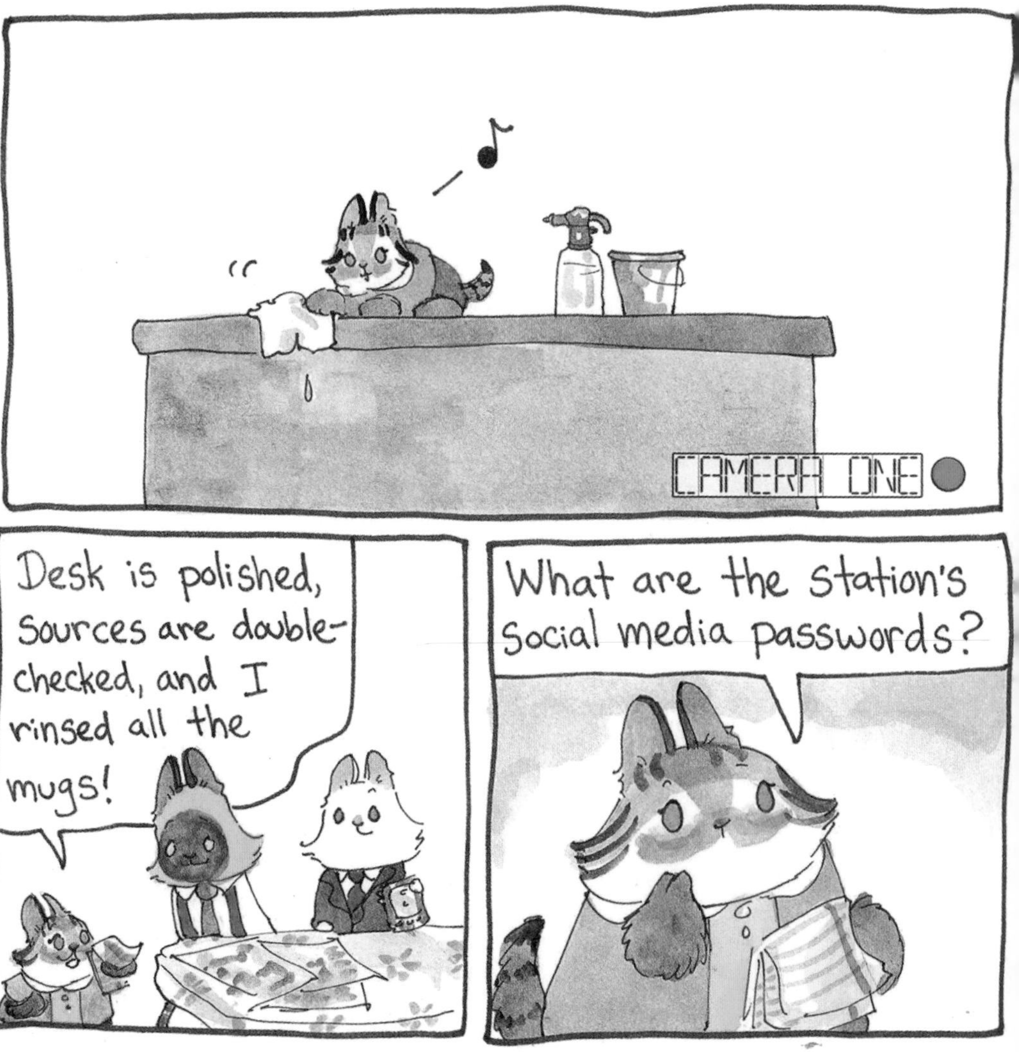
CAMERA ONE
Desk is polished, sources are double-checked, and I rinsed all the mugs!
What are the station's social media passwords?

Oh— We don't really—
No, we don't do that.
WHAT?
It's the 21st century! How does the station tweet?!
Beatrix.
Birds have their own news.
Whew! Ok. Not to worry. I am appointing myself "Social media intern."
Maybe we could ask Burt to set up—
All in favor, say aye.
Aye!
No need! Just set up a Twitter account for the station.
Is that a bank?
@breakingcatnews
I don't want my name on this—

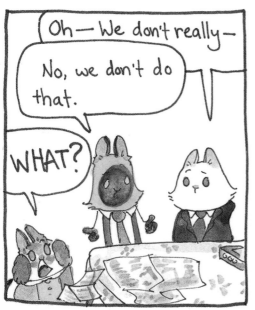

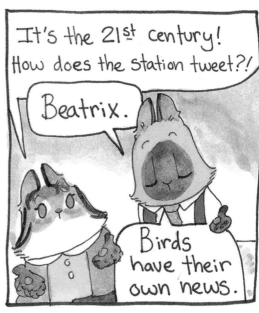

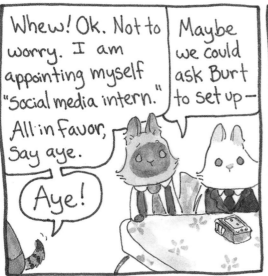

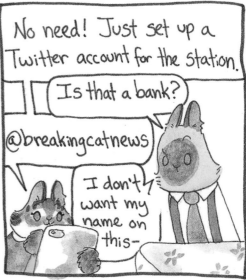

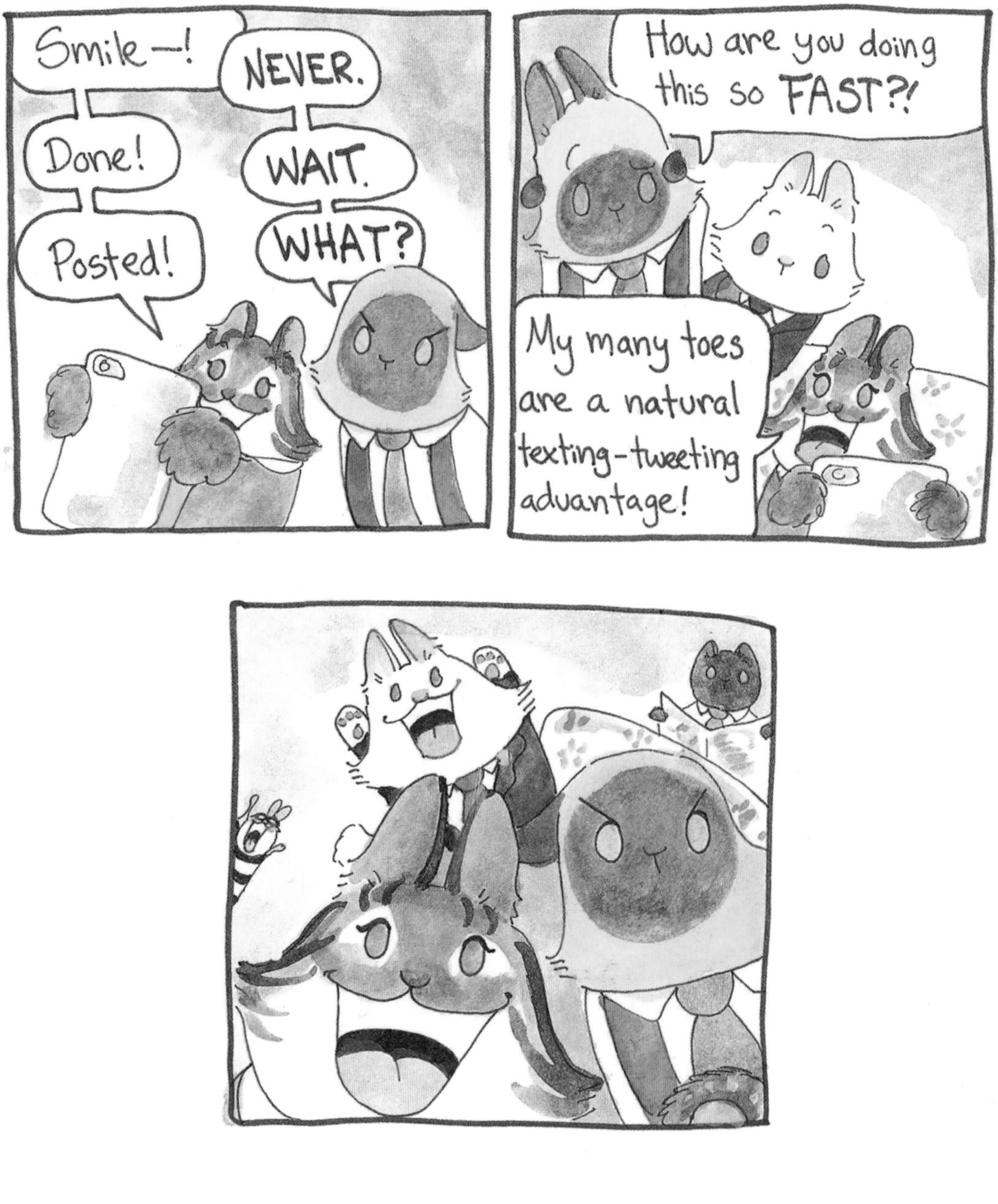
Smile—!
Done!
Posted!
NEVER.
WAIT.
WHAT?
How are you doing this so FAST?!
My many toes are a natural texting-tweeting advantage!

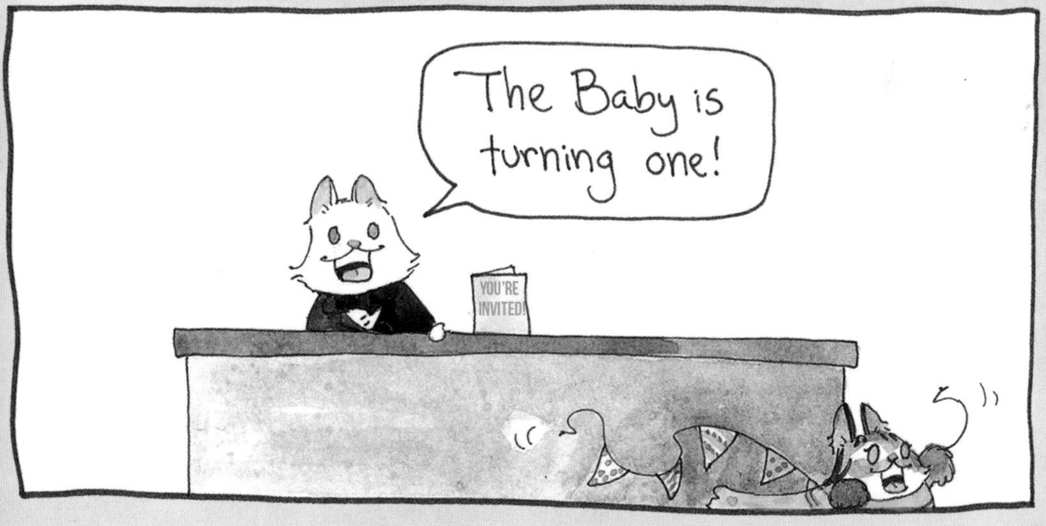
The Baby is turning one!
YOU'RE INVITED!

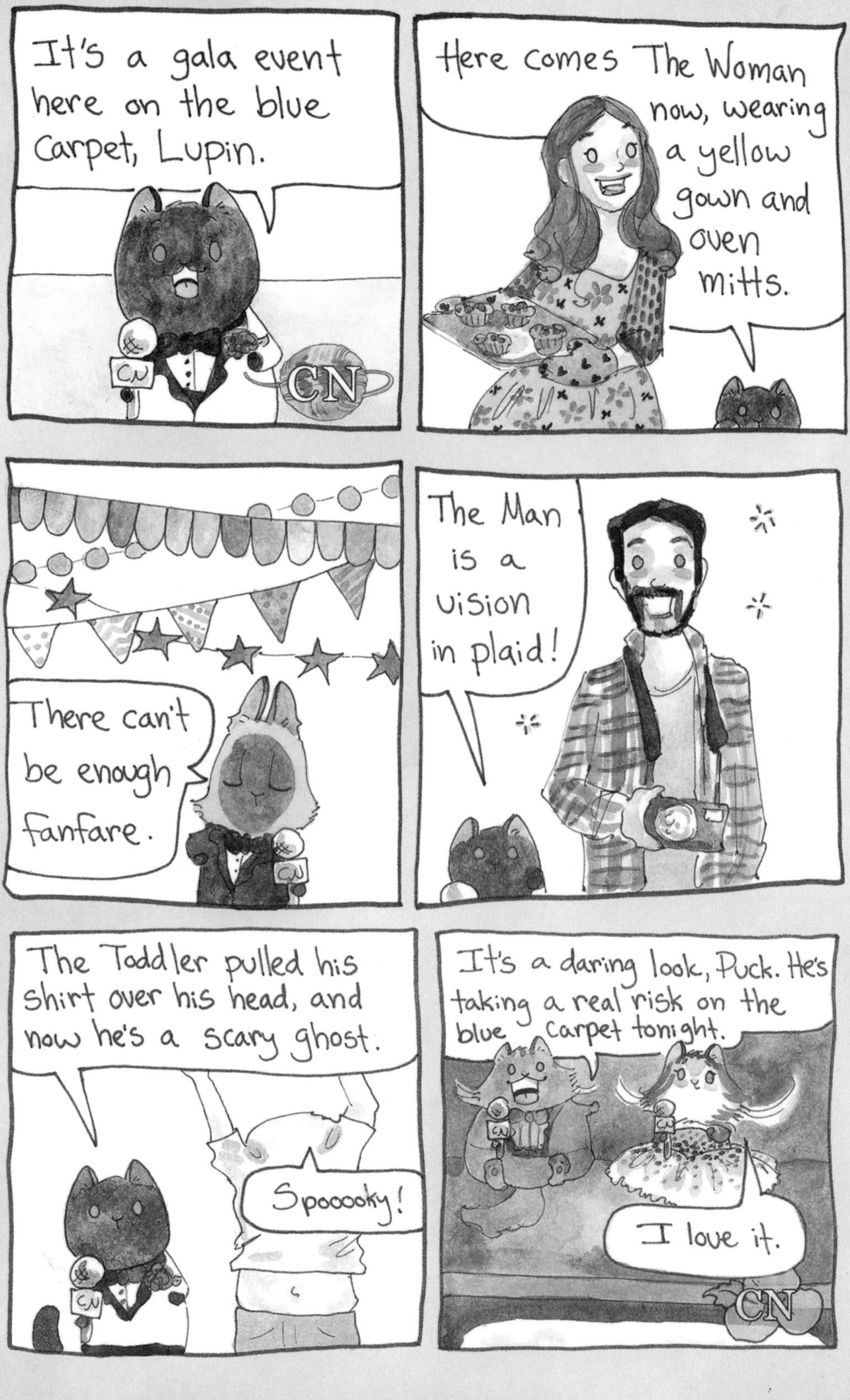

It's a gala event here on the blue carpet, Lupin.
CN
CN
Here comes The Woman now, wearing a yellow gown and oven mitts.
There can't be enough fanfare.
CN
The Man is a vision in plaid!
The Toddler pulled his shirt over his head, and now he's a scary ghost.
CN
Spooooky!
It's a daring look, Puck. He's taking a real risk on the blue carpet tonight.
CN
CN
I love it.
CN

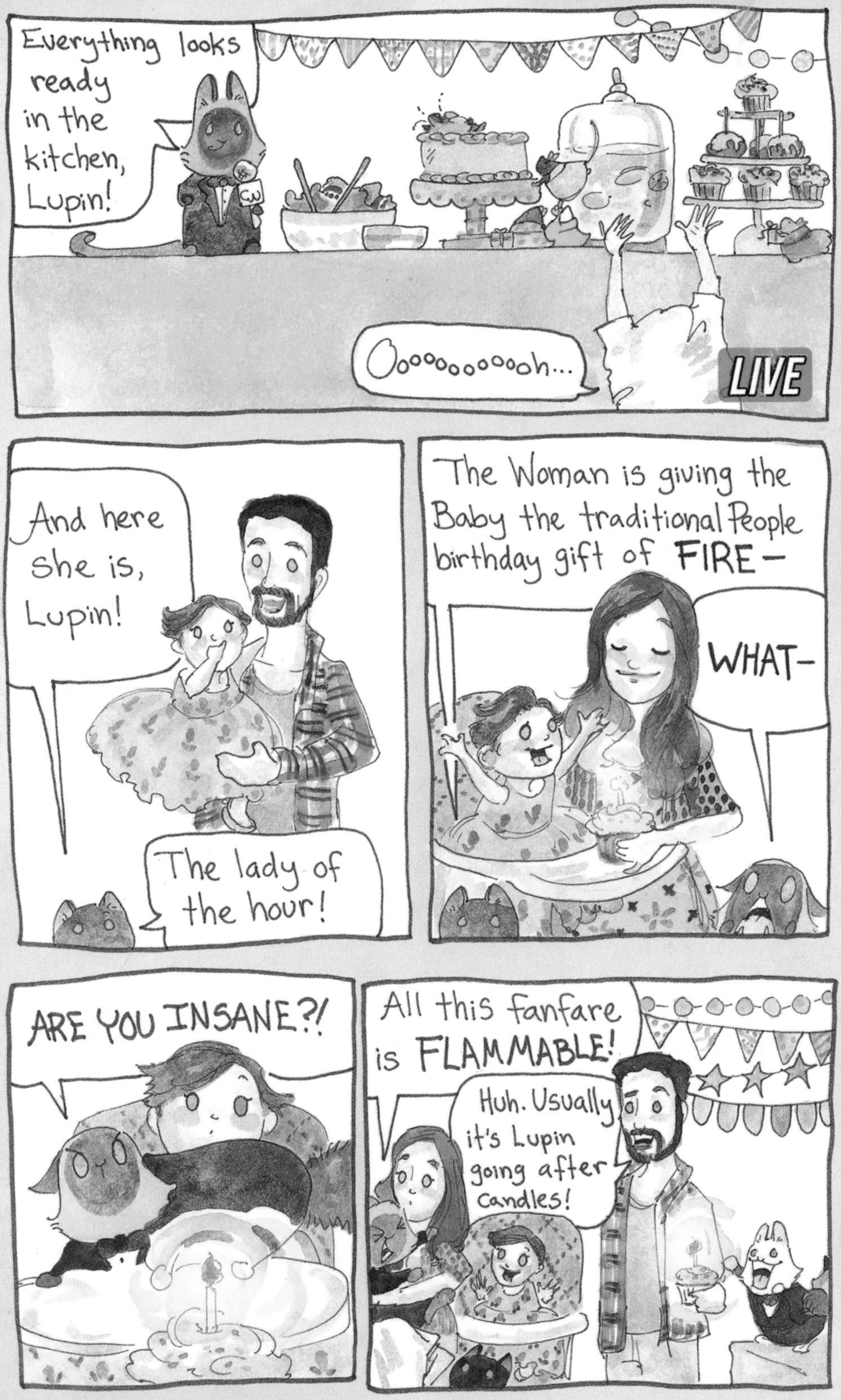
Everything looks ready in the kitchen, Lupin!
Oooooooooooh...
LIVE
And here she is, Lupin!
The lady of the hour!
The Woman is giving the Baby the traditional People birthday gift of FIRE–
WHAT–
ARE YOU INSANE?!
All this fanfare is FLAMMABLE!
Huh. Usually it's Lupin going after candles!

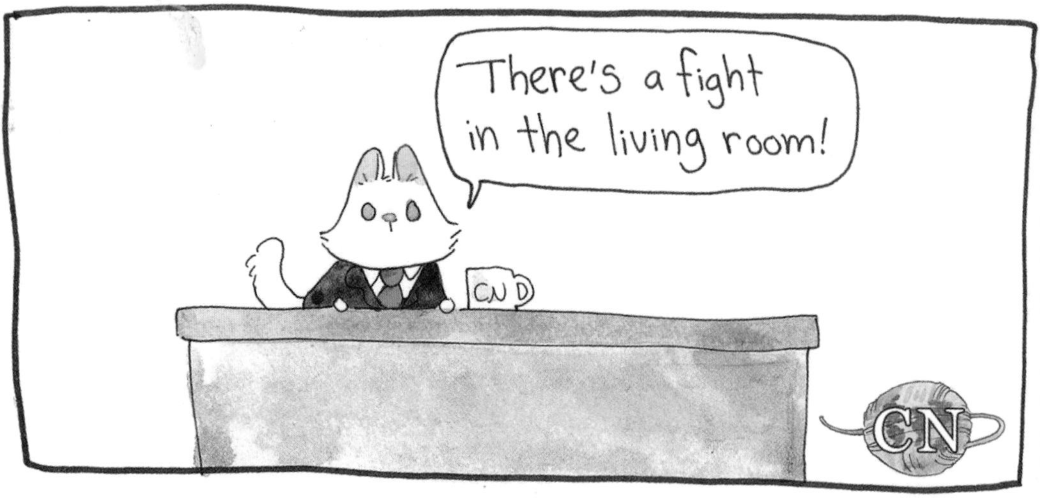
There's a fight in the living room!
CN
CN

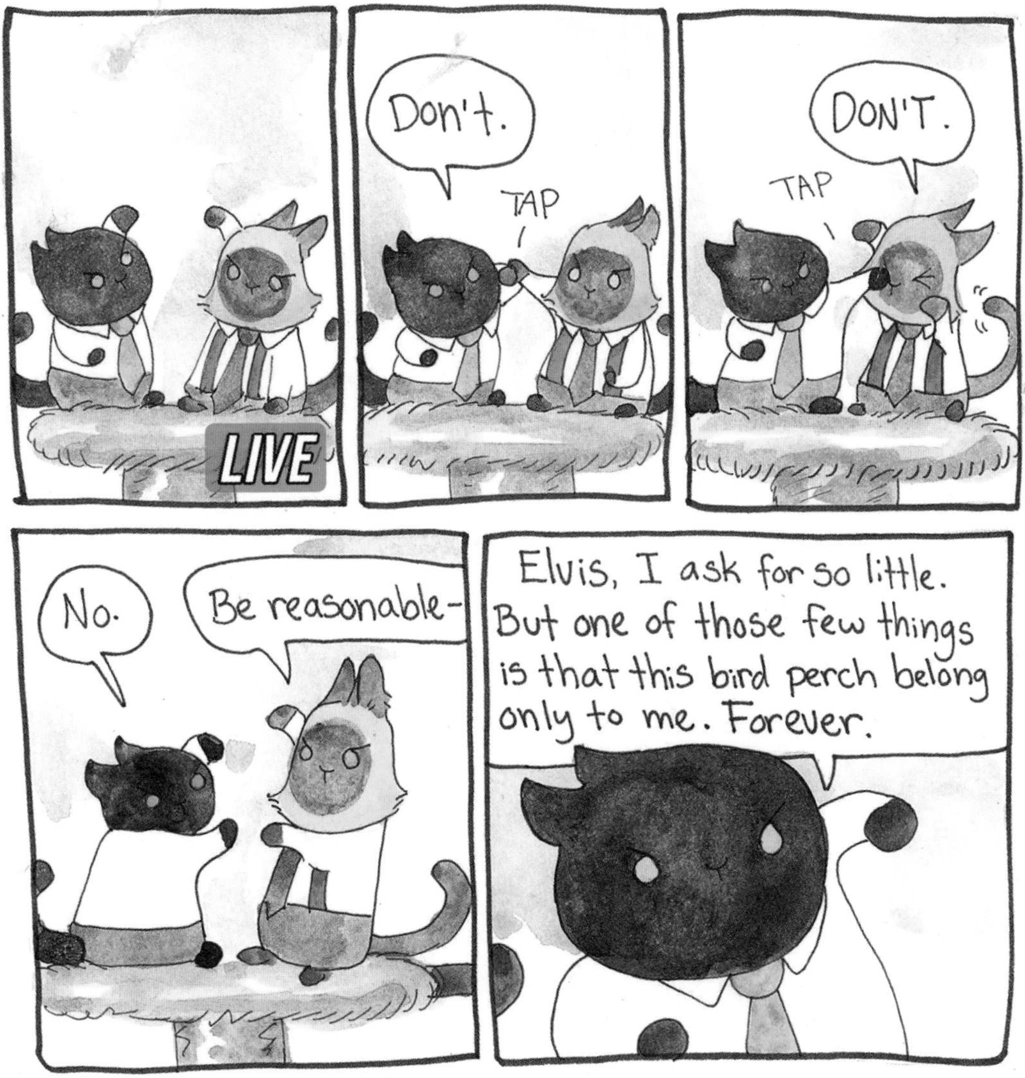
LIVE
Don't.
TAP
TAP
DON'T.
No.
Be reasonable-
Elvis, I ask for so little. But one of those few things is that this bird perch belong only to me. Forever.

I, too, have initiated FREEZE TAG COMBAT!

— Sigh.

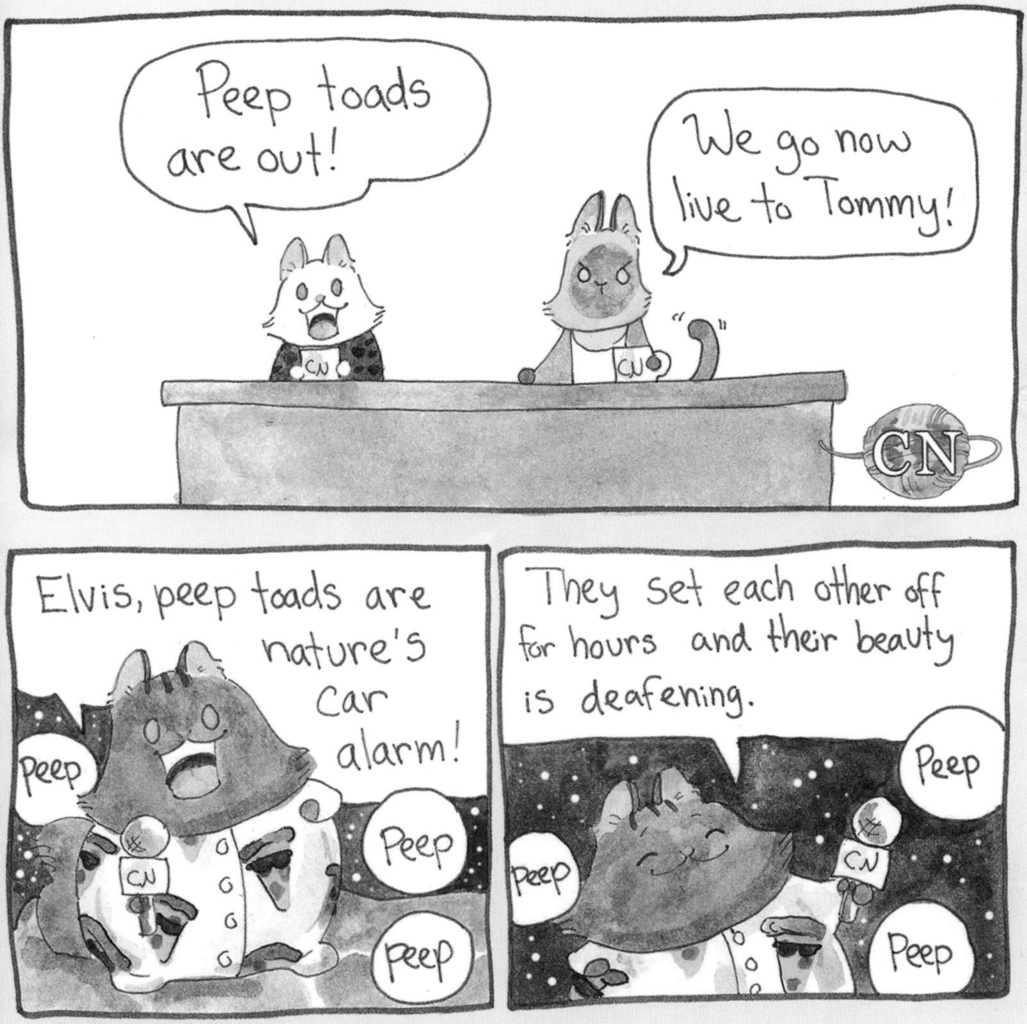
Peep toads are out!
We go now live to Tommy!
CN
Elvis, peep toads are nature's car alarm!
Peep
Peep
Peep
They set each other off for hours and their beauty is deafening.
Peep
Peep
Peep

On warm nights when the peep toads are out, I like to press my nose to the screen and contemplate the majesty of nature.

Sigh.

Peep

Peep

Peep

Peep

Peep

Peep

Cocoa run!

How do you keep getting outside?!

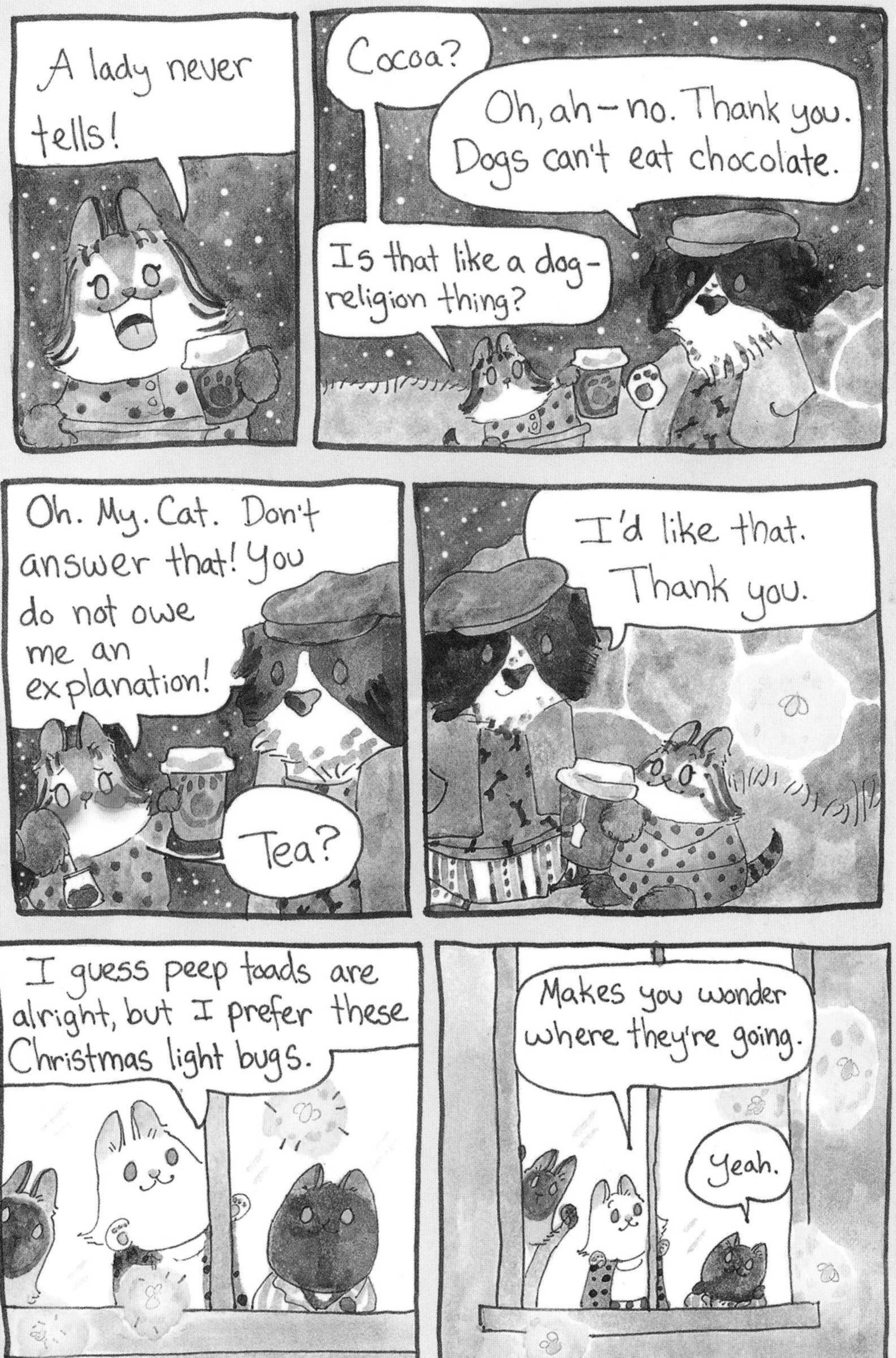
A lady never tells!
Cocoa?
Oh, ah—no. Thank you. Dogs can't eat chocolate.
Is that like a dog-religion thing?
Oh. My. Cat. Don't answer that! You do not owe me an explanation!
Tea?
I'd like that. Thank you.
I guess peep toads are alright, but I prefer these Christmas light bugs.
Makes you wonder where they're going.
Yeah.

Peep
Peep
Peep
Peep

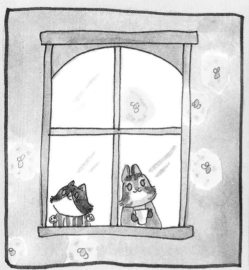

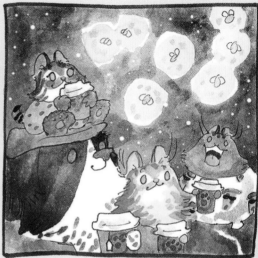

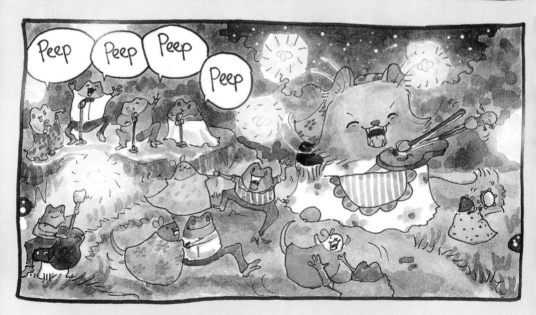

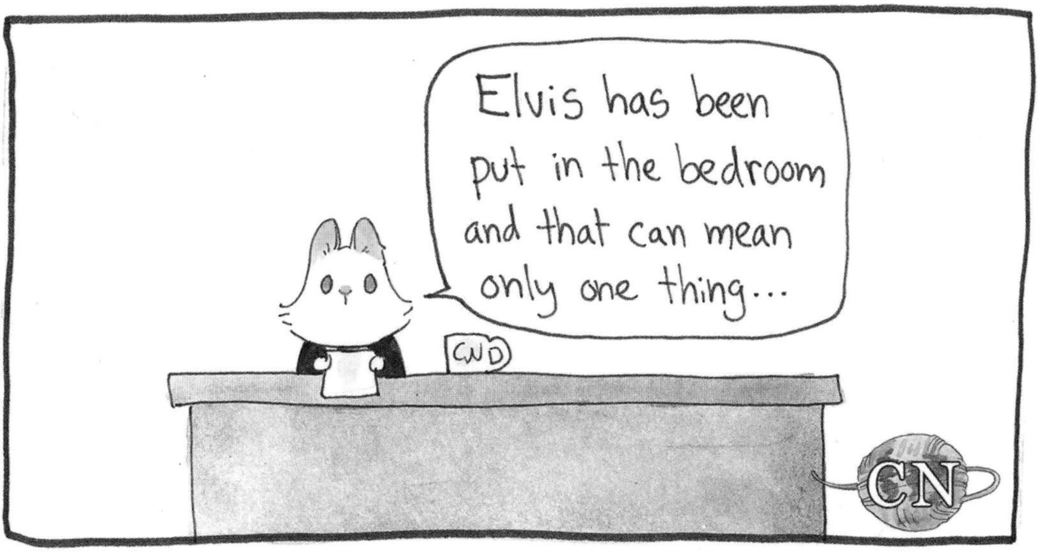
Elvis has been put in the bedroom and that can mean only one thing...
CN

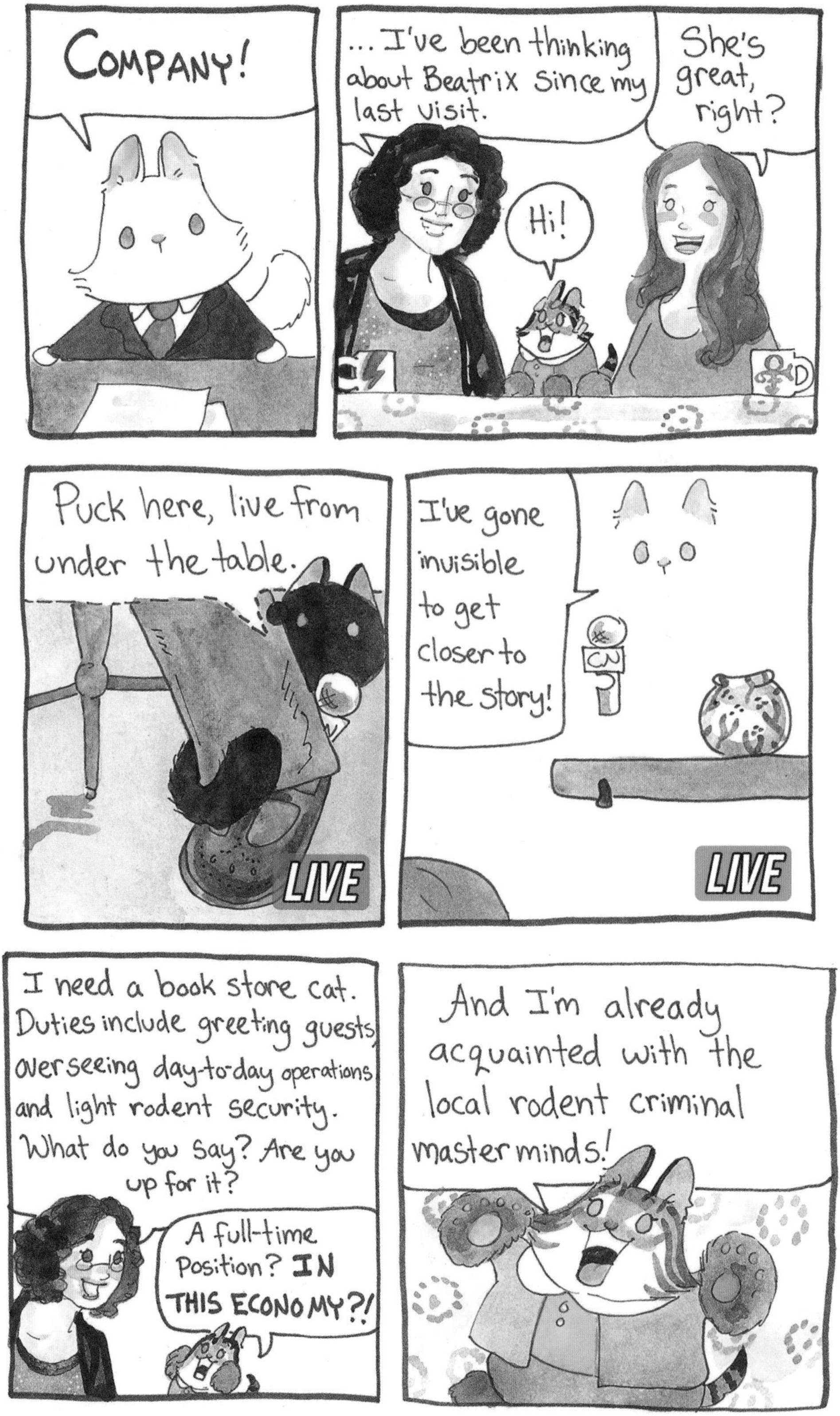

COMPANY!
...I've been thinking about Beatrix since my last visit.
She's great, right?
Hi!
Puck here, live from under the table.
LIVE
I've gone invisible to get closer to the story!
CN
LIVE
I need a book store cat. Duties include greeting guests, overseeing day-to-day operations and light rodent security. What do you say? Are you up for it?
A full-time Position? IN THIS ECONOMY?!
And I'm already acquainted with the local rodent criminal masterminds!

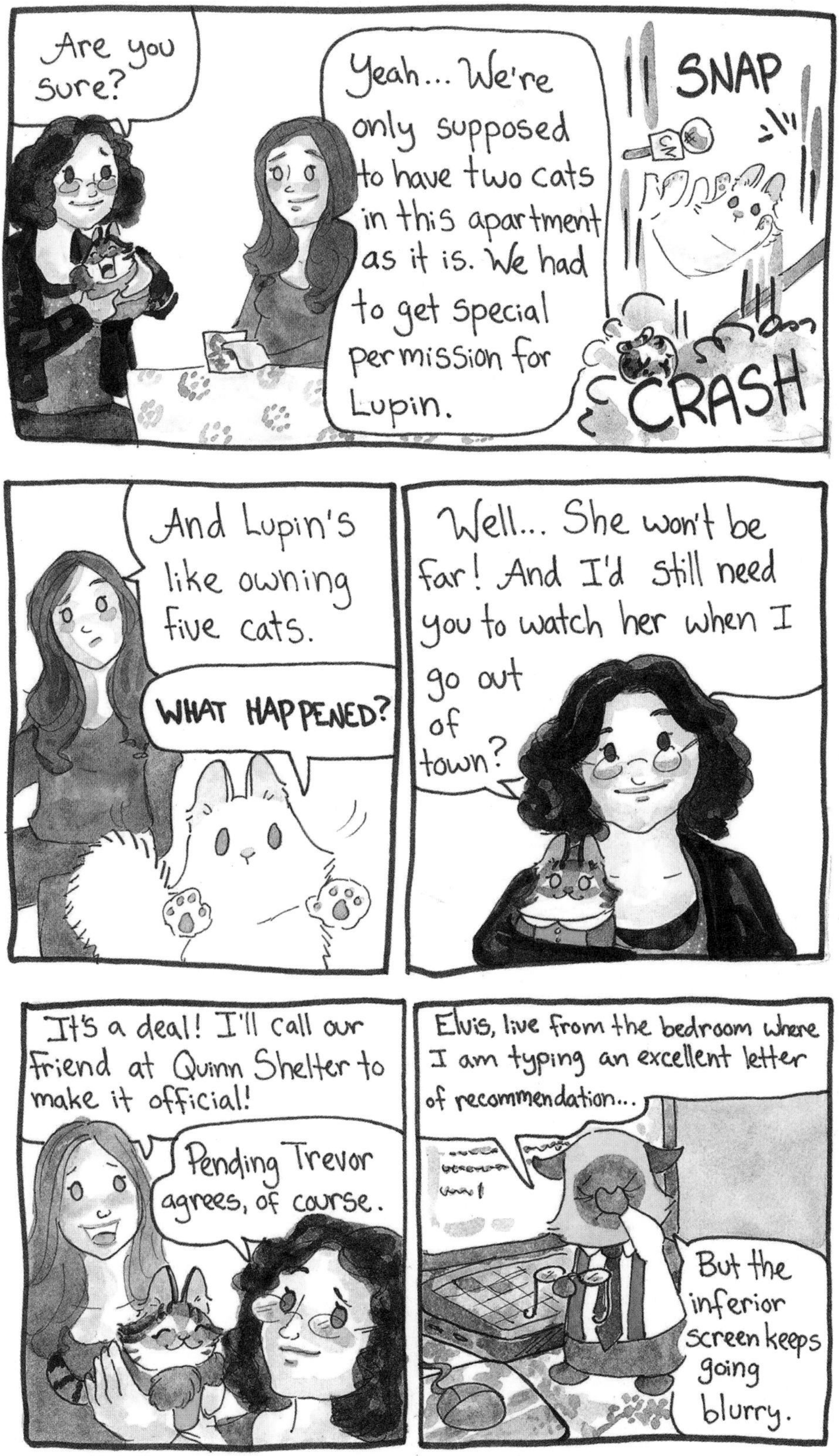

Are you sure?
Yeah... We're only supposed to have two cats in this apartment as it is. We had to get special permission for Lupin.
SNAP
CRASH
And Lupin's like owning five cats.
WHAT HAPPENED?
Well... She won't be far! And I'd still need you to watch her when I go out of town?
It's a deal! I'll call our friend at Quinn Shelter to make it official!
Pending Trevor agrees, of course.
Elvis, live from the bedroom where I am typing an excellent letter of recommendation...
But the inferior screen keeps going blurry.

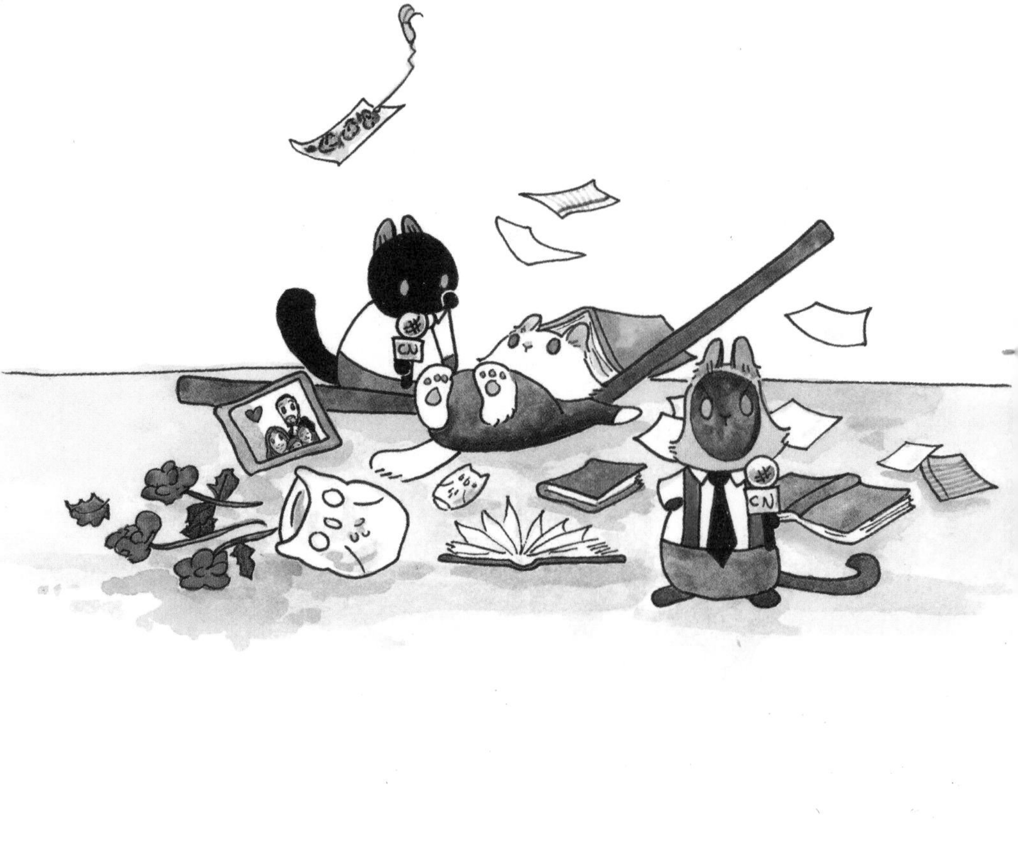
CN
CN

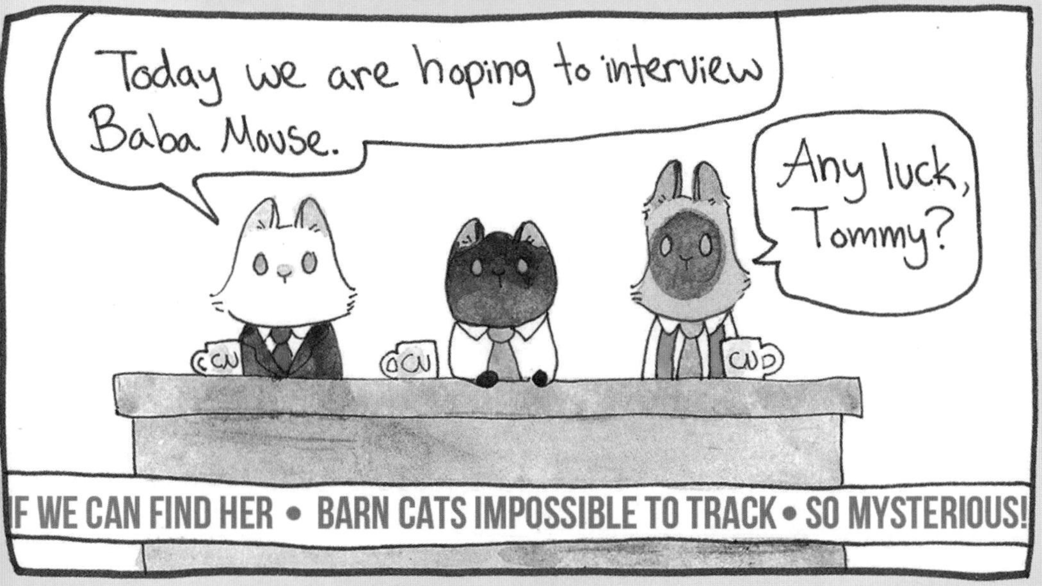
Today we are hoping to interview Baba Mouse.
Any luck, Tommy?
CN
CN
CN
IF WE CAN FIND HER • BARN CATS IMPOSSIBLE TO TRACK • SO MYSTERIOUS!

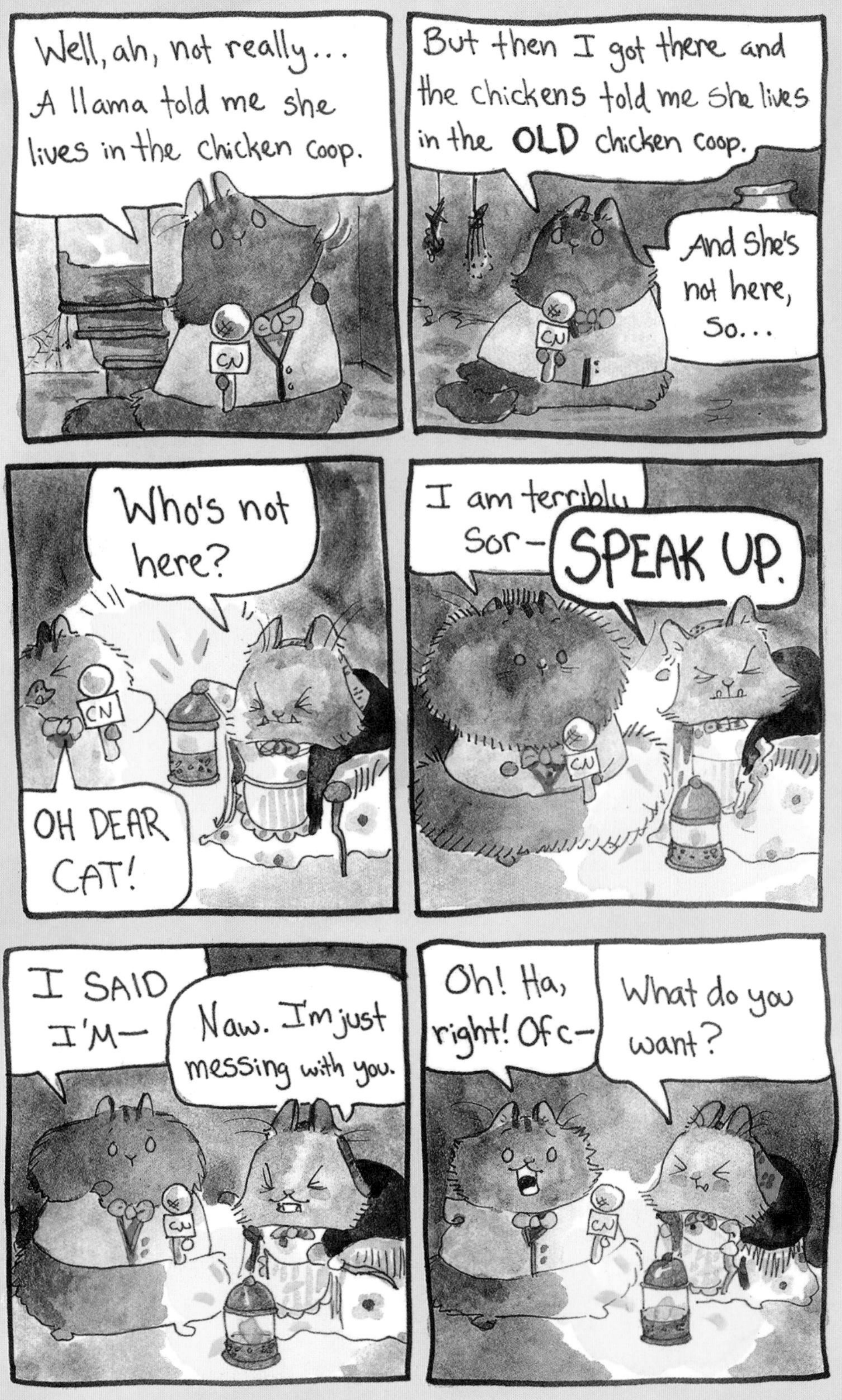
Well, ah, not really... A llama told me she lives in the chicken coop.
But then I got there and the chickens told me she lives in the OLD chicken coop.
And she's not here, so...
Who's not here?
OH DEAR CAT!
I am terribly sor—
SPEAK UP.
I SAID I'M—
Naw. I'm just messing with you.
Oh! Ha, right! Of c—
What do you want?

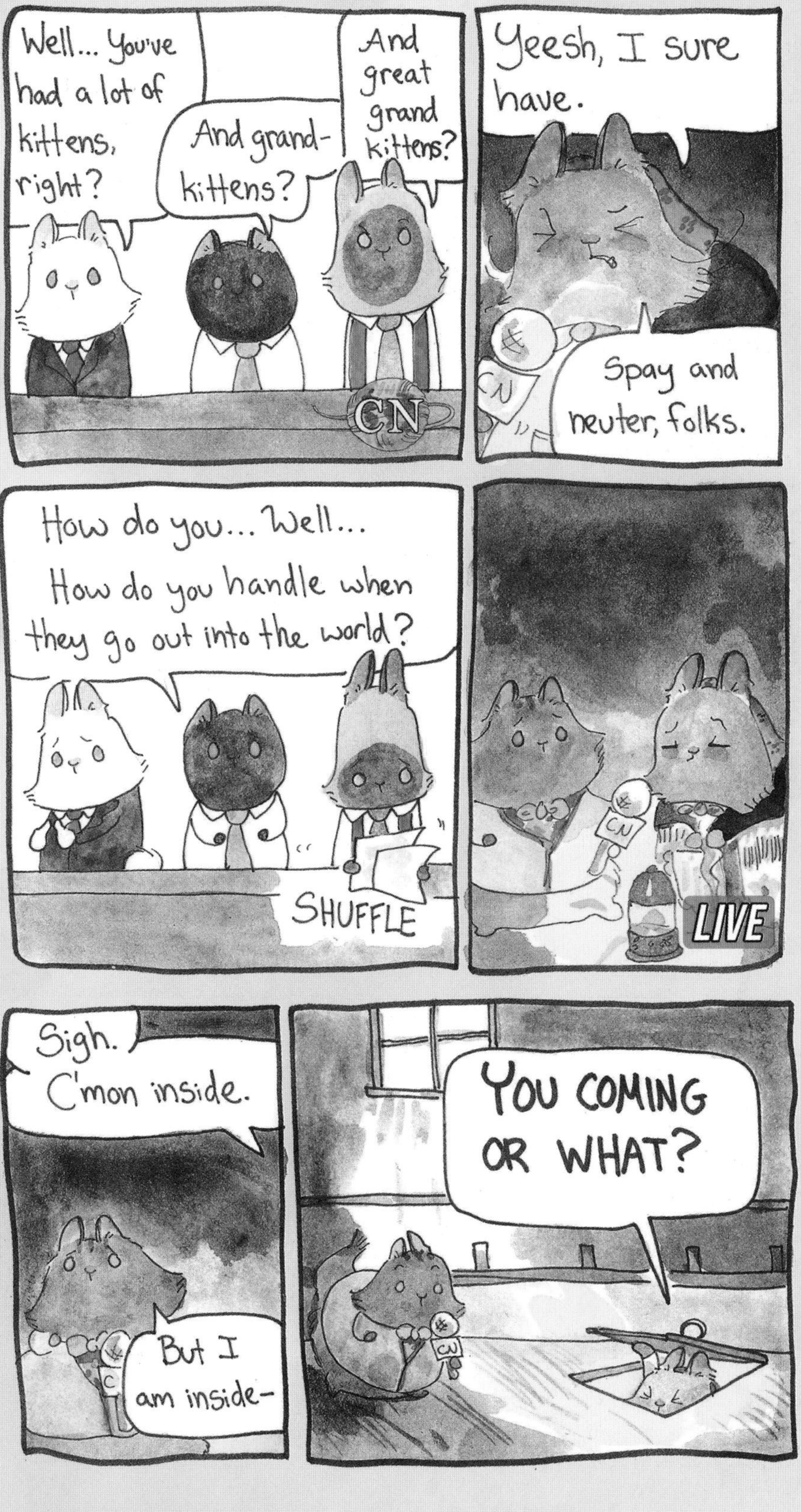

Well... You've had a lot of kittens, right?
And grand-kittens?
And great grand kittens?
Yeesh, I sure have.
Spay and neuter, folks.
CN
How do you... Well... How do you handle when they go out into the world?
SHUFFLE
LIVE
Sigh. C'mon inside.
But I am inside-
YOU COMING OR WHAT?

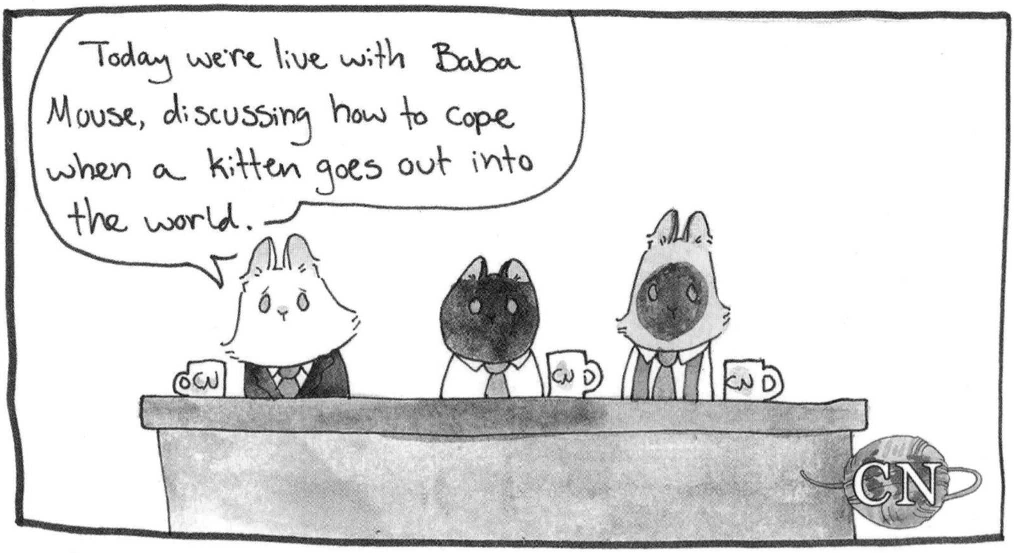
Today we're live with Baba Mouse, discussing how to cope when a kitten goes out into the world.
CN

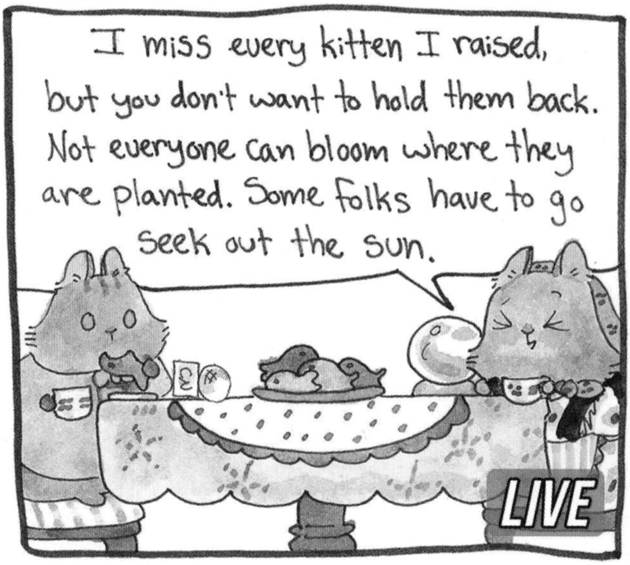
I miss every kitten I raised, but you don't want to hold them back. Not everyone can bloom where they are planted. Some folks have to go seek out the sun.
LIVE

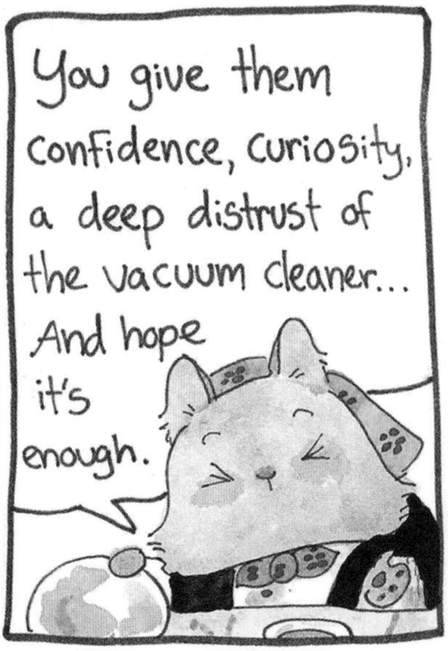
You give them confidence, curiosity, a deep distrust of the vacuum cleaner... And hope it's enough.

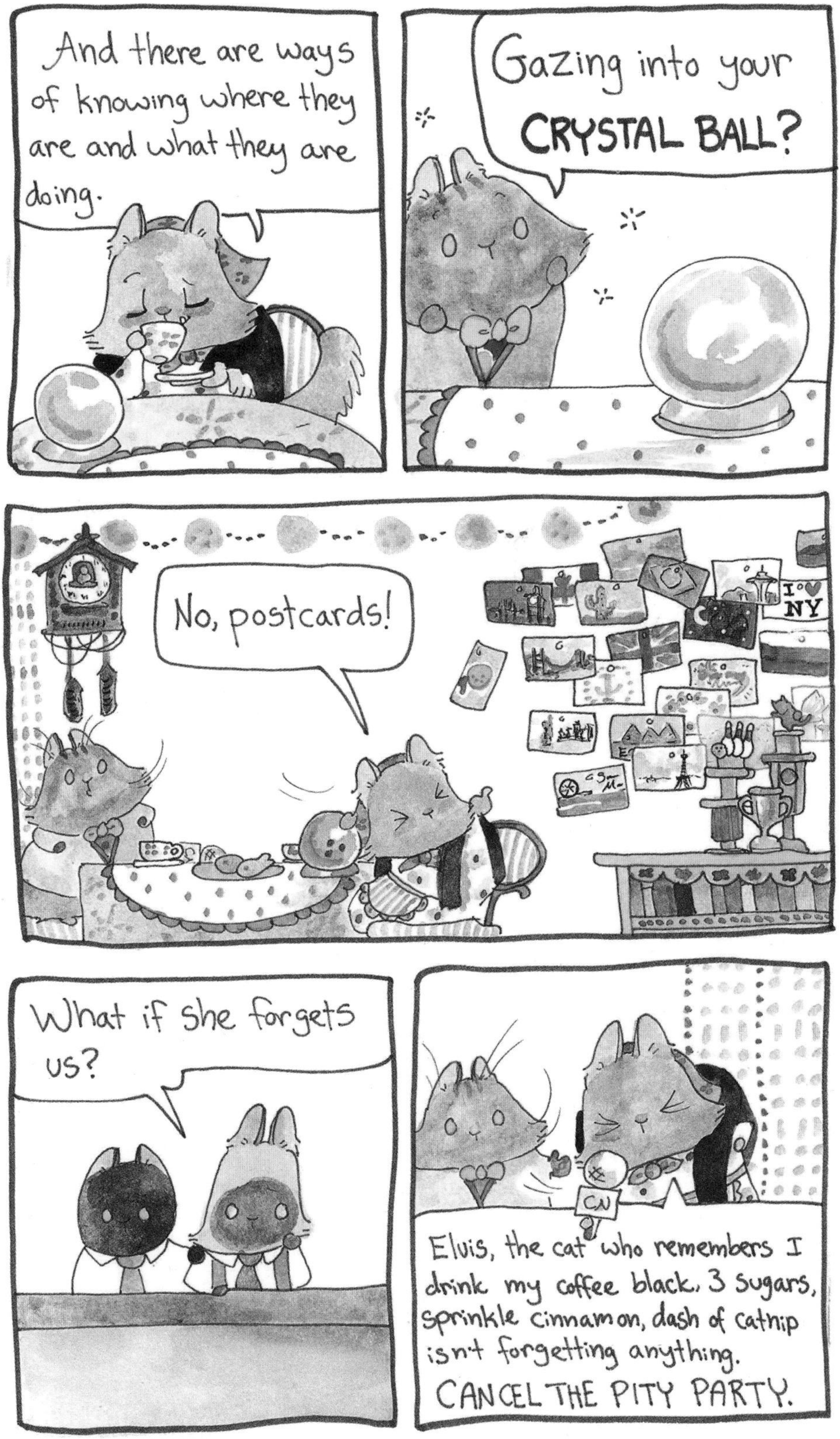
And there are ways of knowing where they are and what they are doing.
Gazing into your CRYSTAL BALL?
No, postcards!
I ♥ NY
What if she forgets us?
CN
Elvis, the cat who remembers I drink my coffee black, 3 sugars, sprinkle cinnamon, dash of catnip isn't forgetting anything.
CANCEL THE PITY PARTY.

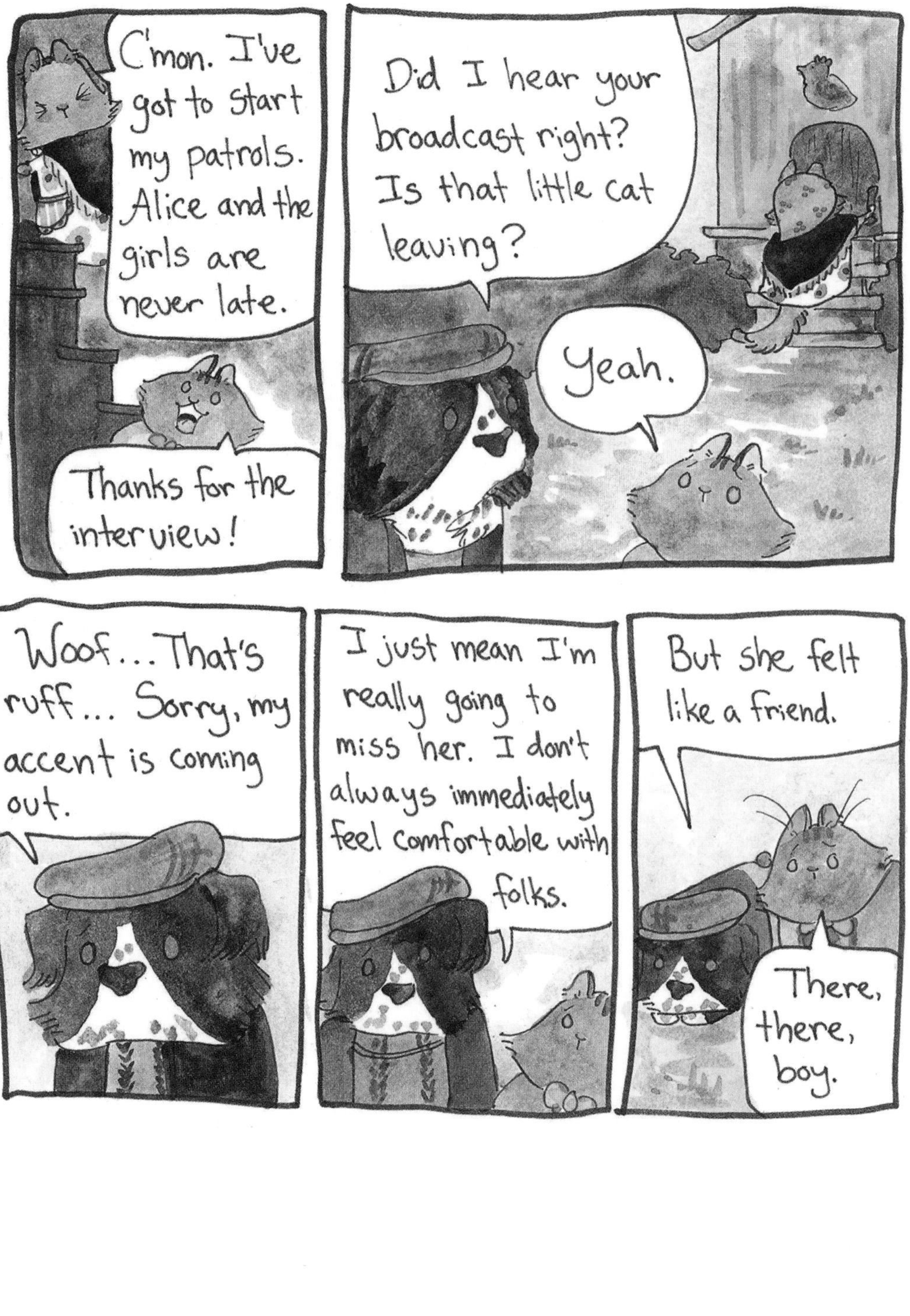
C'mon. I've got to start my patrols. Alice and the girls are never late.
Thanks for the interview!
Did I hear your broadcast right? Is that little cat leaving?
Yeah.
Woof... That's ruff... Sorry, my accent is coming out.
I just mean I'm really going to miss her. I don't always immediately feel comfortable with folks.
But she felt like a friend.
There, there, boy.

You gonna be ok?
Yeah, Tommy. Thanks, man.
Sigh.
'Morning, Baba.
'Morning, Trevor.

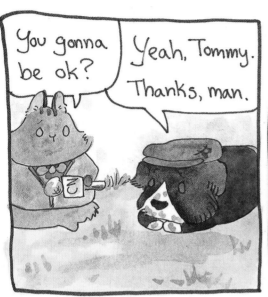

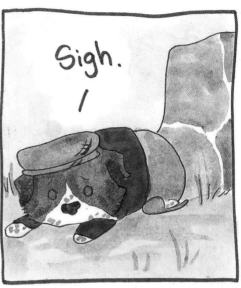

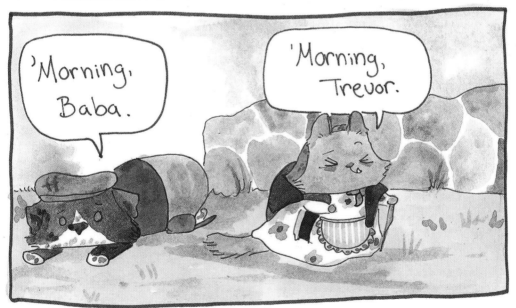

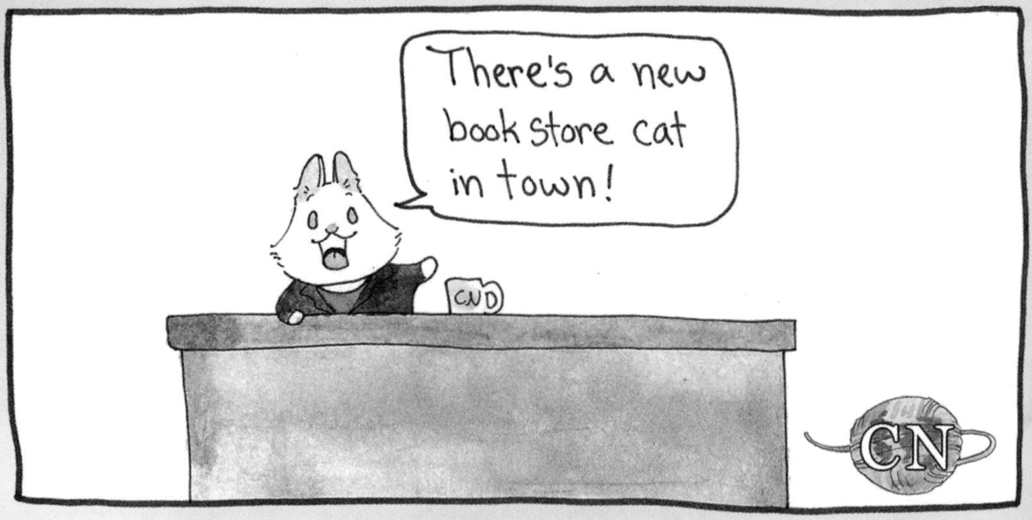
There's a new book store cat in town!
CND
CN

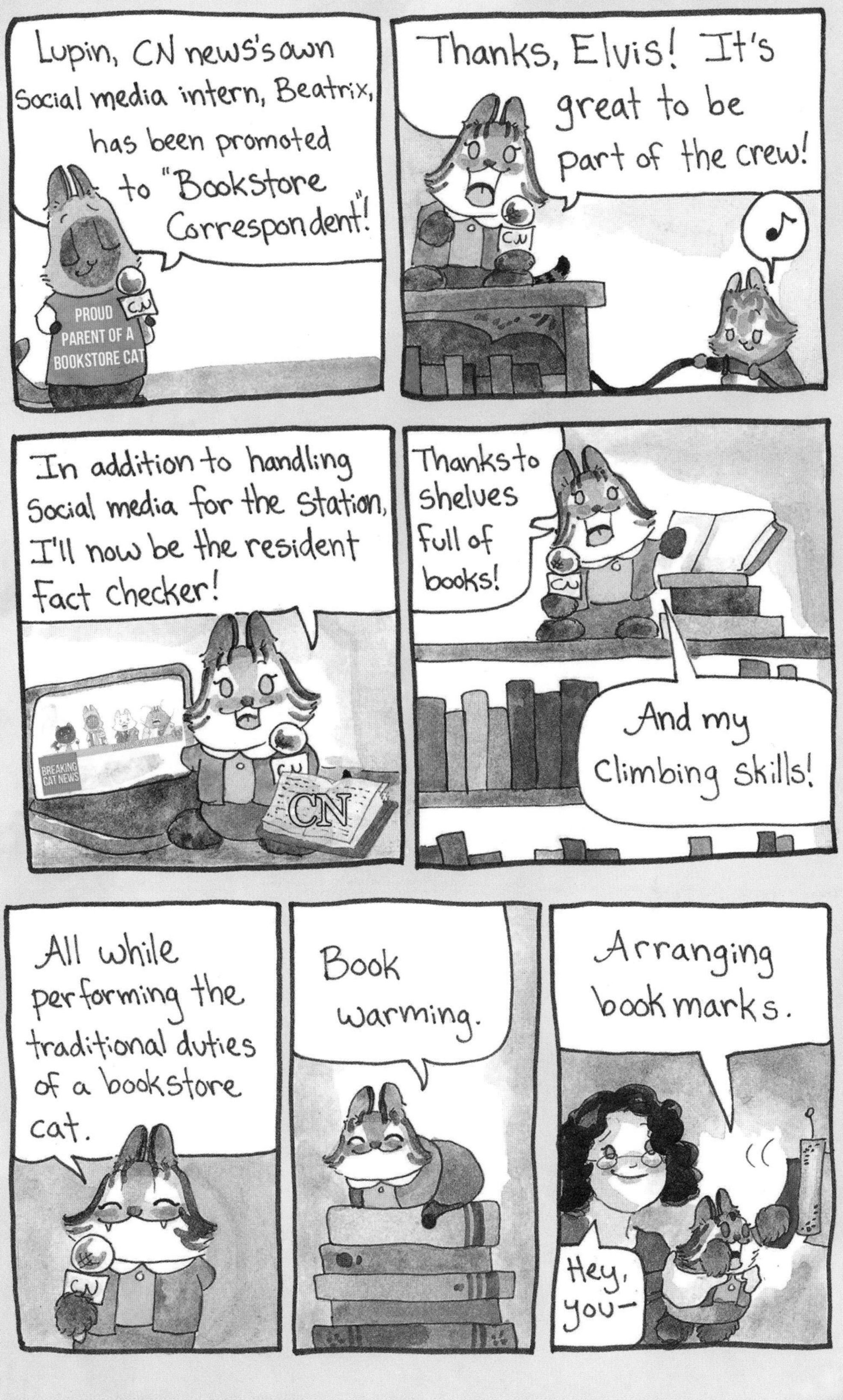
Lupin, CN news's own Social media intern, Beatrix, has been promoted to "Bookstore Correspondent"!
PROUD PARENT OF A BOOKSTORE CAT
CN
Thanks, Elvis! It's great to be part of the crew!
CN
♪
In addition to handling Social media for the station, I'll now be the resident Fact checker!
BREAKING CAT NEWS
CN
CN
Thanks to shelves full of books!
CN
And my Climbing skills!
All while performing the traditional duties of a bookstore cat.
CN
Book warming.
Arranging bookmarks.
Hey, you—

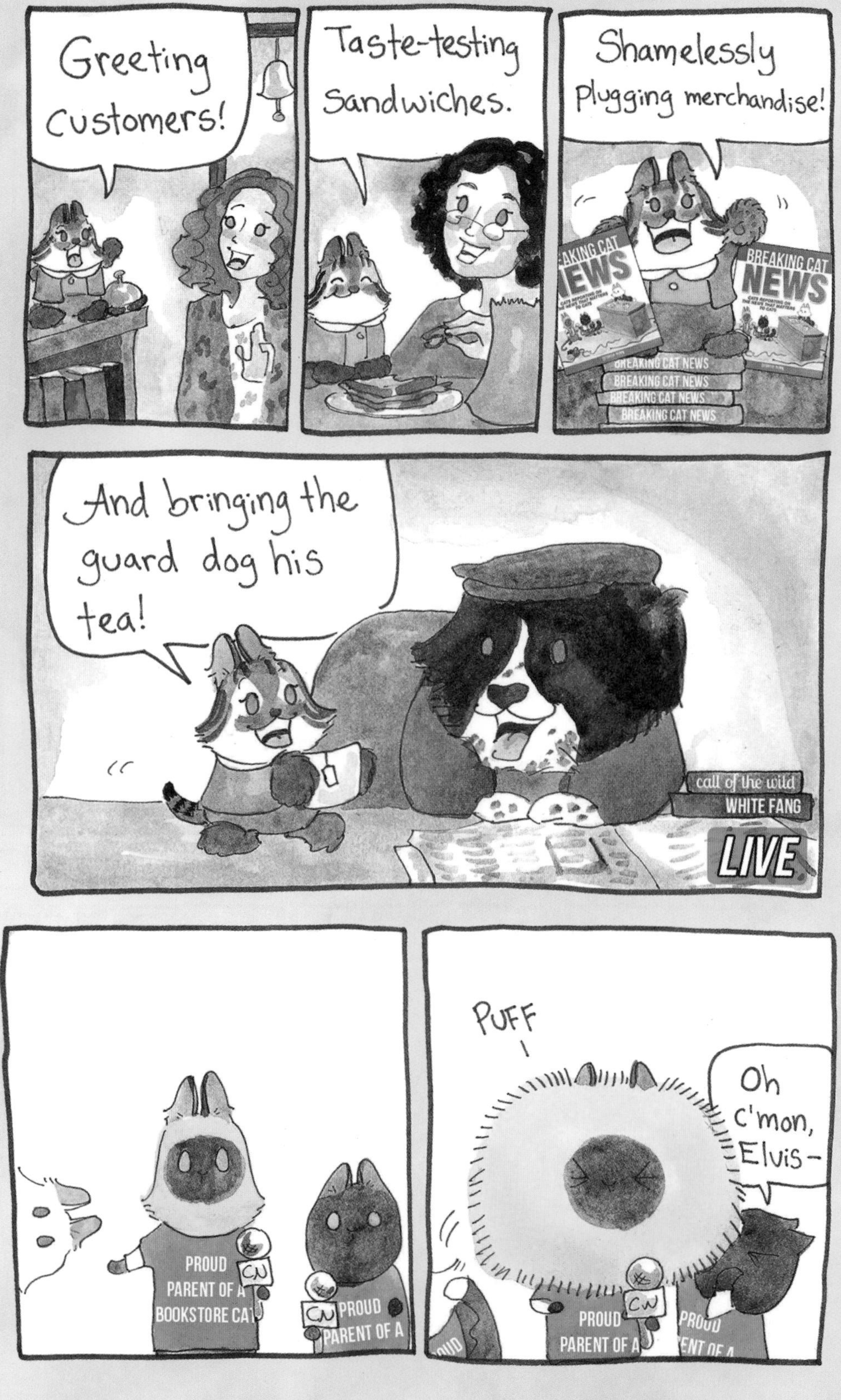
Greeting Customers!
Taste-testing Sandwiches.
Shamelessly Plugging merchandise!
BREAKING CAT NEWS
BREAKING CAT NEWS
BREAKING CAT NEWS
BREAKING CAT NEWS
BREAKING CAT NEWS
BREAKING CAT NEWS
And bringing the guard dog his tea!
call of the wild
WHITE FANG
LIVE
PROUD PARENT OF A BOOKSTORE CAT
CN
PROUD PARENT OF A
CN
PUFF
Oh c'mon, Elvis-
PROUD PARENT OF A
CN

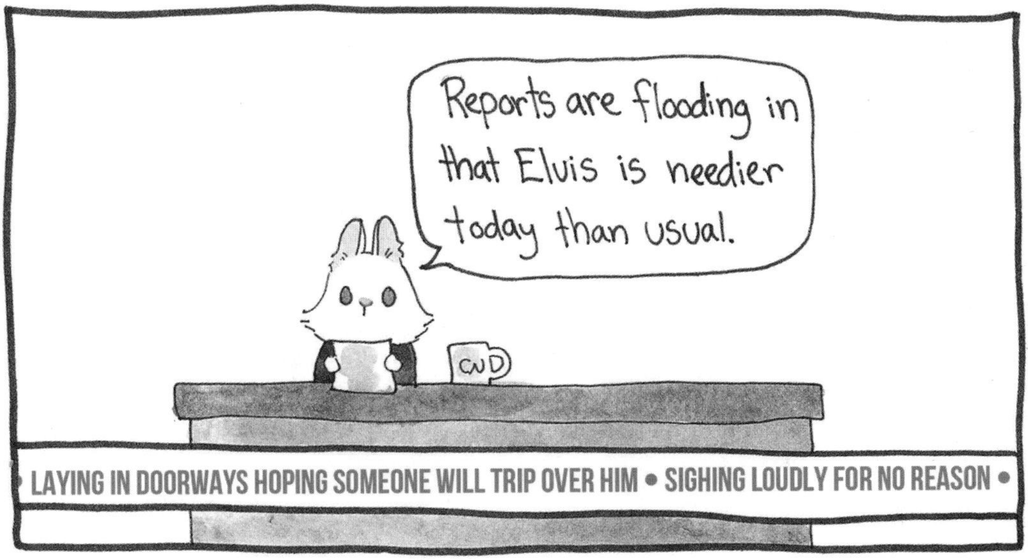
Reports are flooding in that Elvis is needier today than usual.
CWD
• LAYING IN DOORWAYS HOPING SOMEONE WILL TRIP OVER HIM • SIGHING LOUDLY FOR NO REASON •

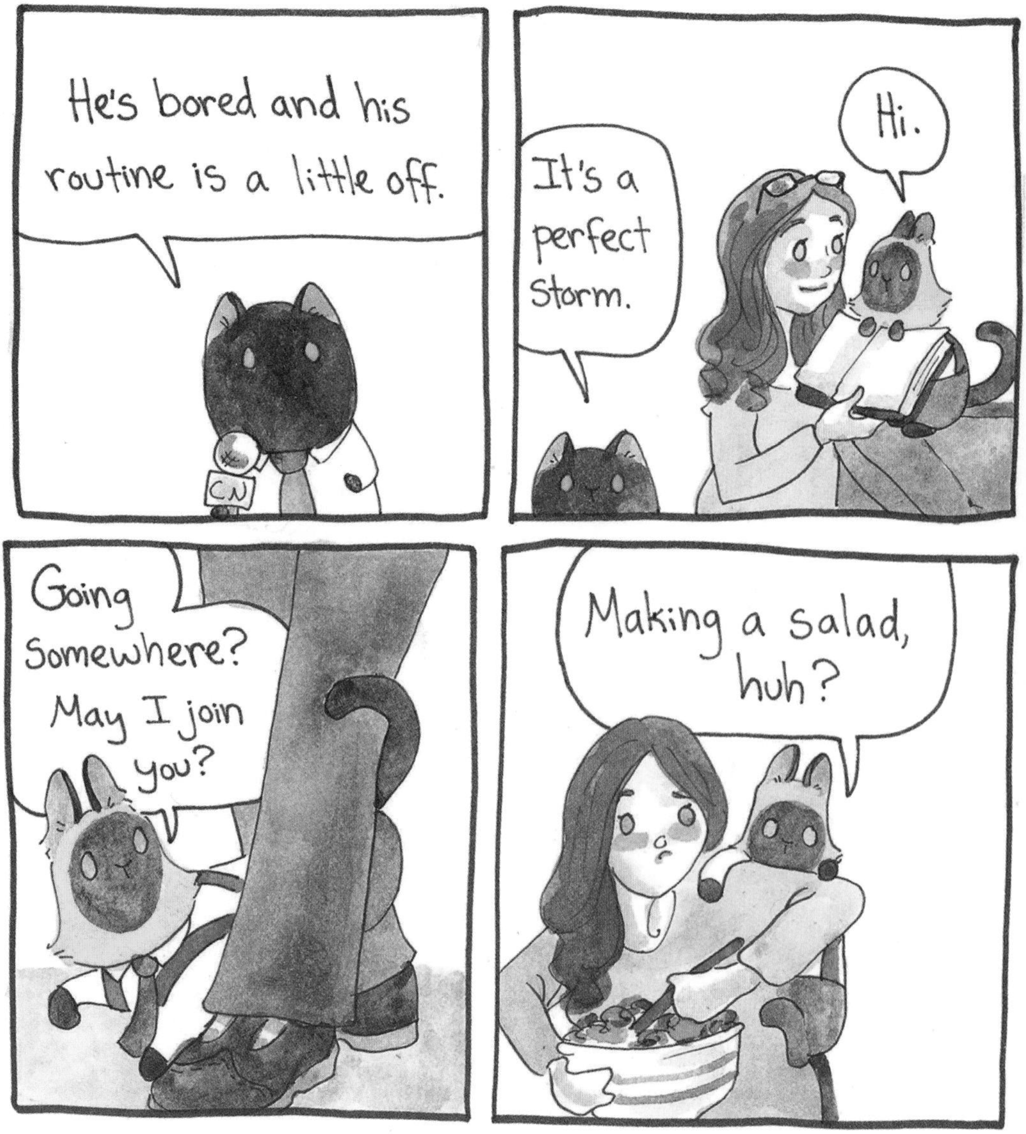
He's bored and his routine is a little off.
CN
It's a perfect storm.
Hi.
Going somewhere? May I join you?
Making a salad, huh?

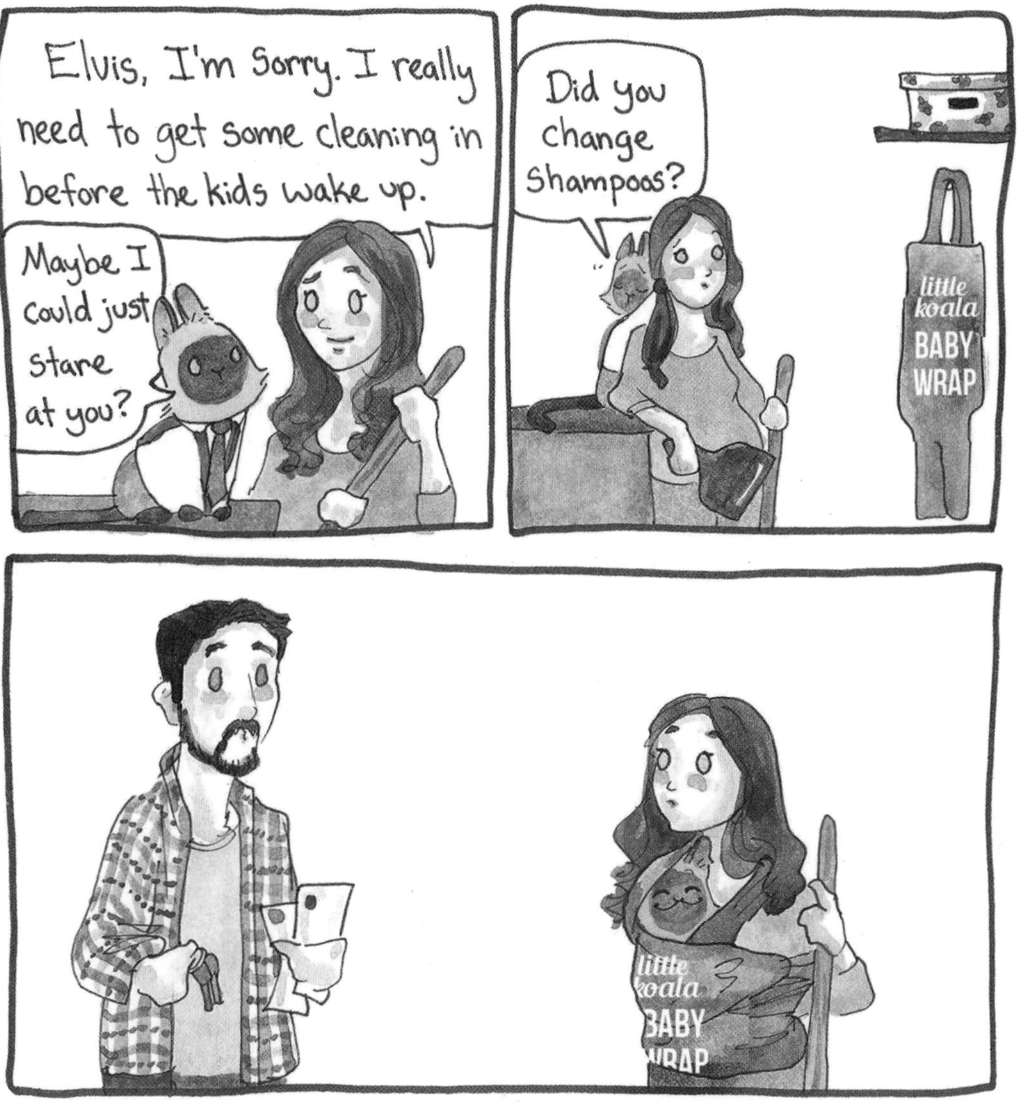
Elvis, I'm Sorry. I really need to get some cleaning in before the kids wake up.
Maybe I could just stare at you?
Did you change Shampoos?
little koala BABY WRAP
little koala BABY WRAP

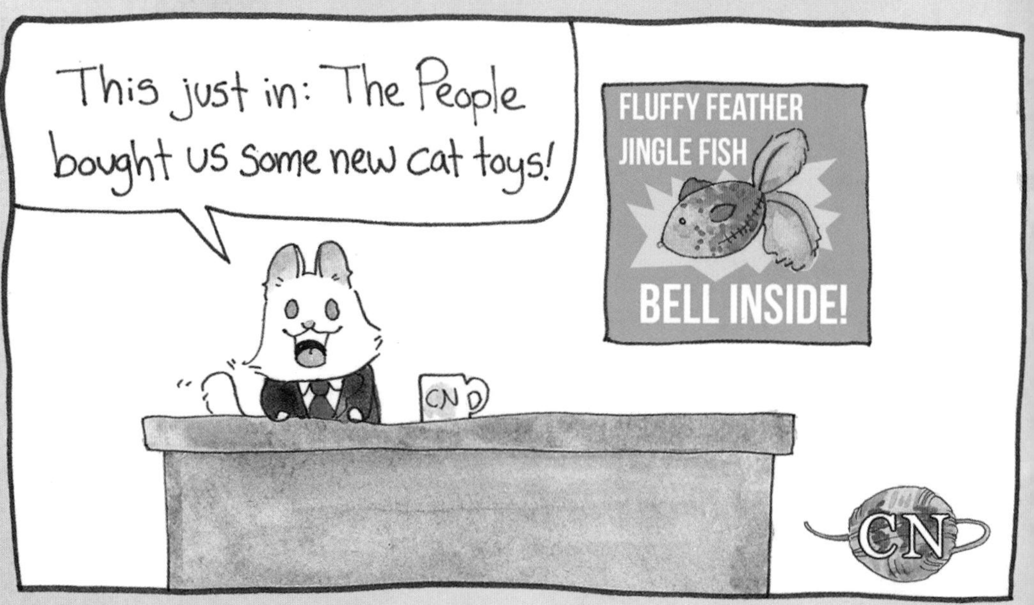
This just in: The People bought us some new cat toys!
FLUFFY FEATHER
JINGLE FISH
BELL INSIDE!
CN
CN

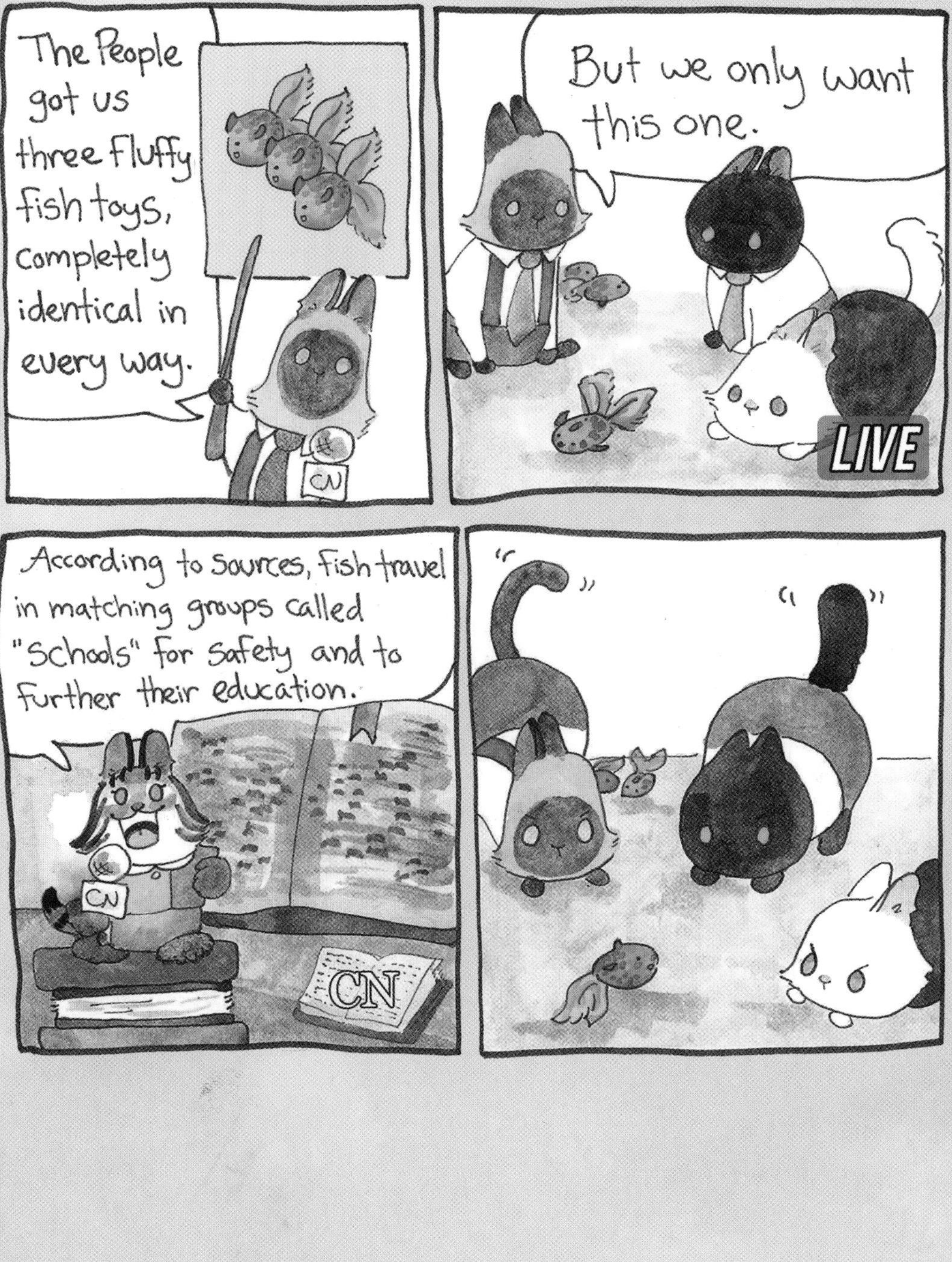
The People got us three fluffy fish toys, completely identical in every way.
CN
But we only want this one.
LIVE
According to sources, fish travel in matching groups called "Schools" for safety and to further their education.
CN
CN

Guys. We got one for each of you! They're exactly the same!
HISS
HISS
HISS
HISS
HISS
But **this** one's impossible perfection is matched only by its singular uniqueness.
NO, ONLY I CAN APPRECIATE ITS TIMELESS BEAUTY!
POUNCE
So rare....
JINGLE
JINGLE
JINGLE

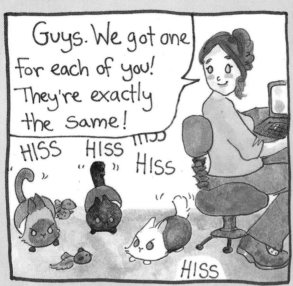

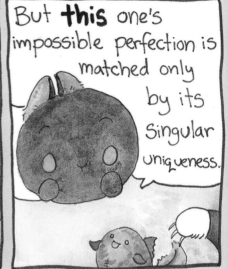

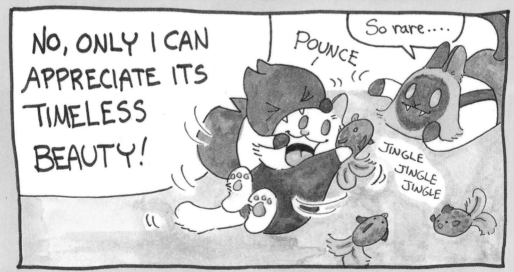

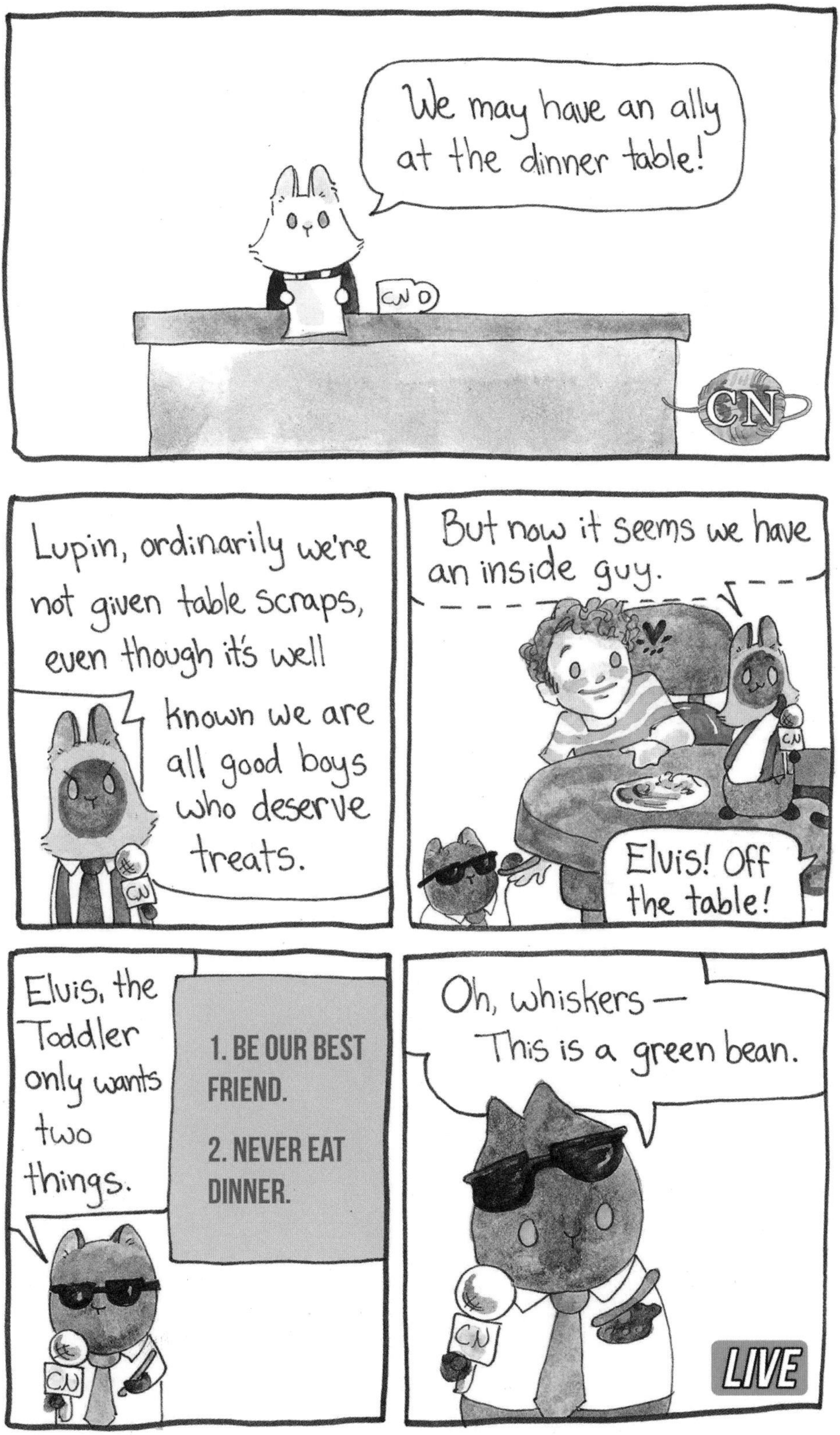
We may have an ally at the dinner table!
CN
Lupin, ordinarily we're not given table scraps, even though it's well
known we are all good boys who deserve treats.
CN
But now it seems we have an inside guy.
CN
Elvis! Off the table!
Elvis, the Toddler only wants two things.
1. BE OUR BEST FRIEND.
2. NEVER EAT DINNER.
CN
Oh, whiskers— This is a green bean.
CN
LIVE

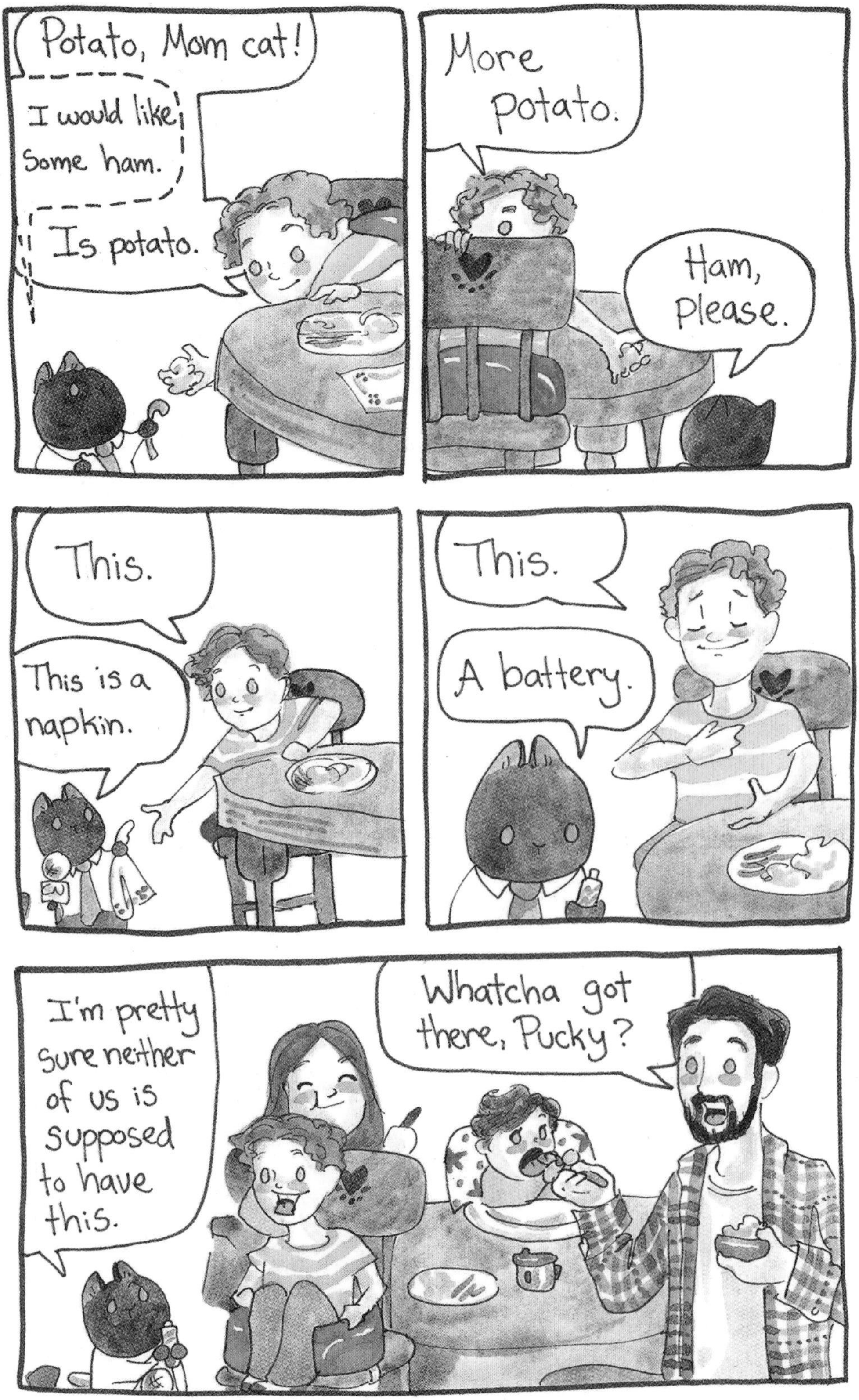
Potato, Mom cat!
I would like some ham.
Is potato.
More potato.
Ham, please.
This.
This is a napkin.
This.
A battery.
I'm pretty sure neither of us is supposed to have this.
Whatcha got there, Pucky?

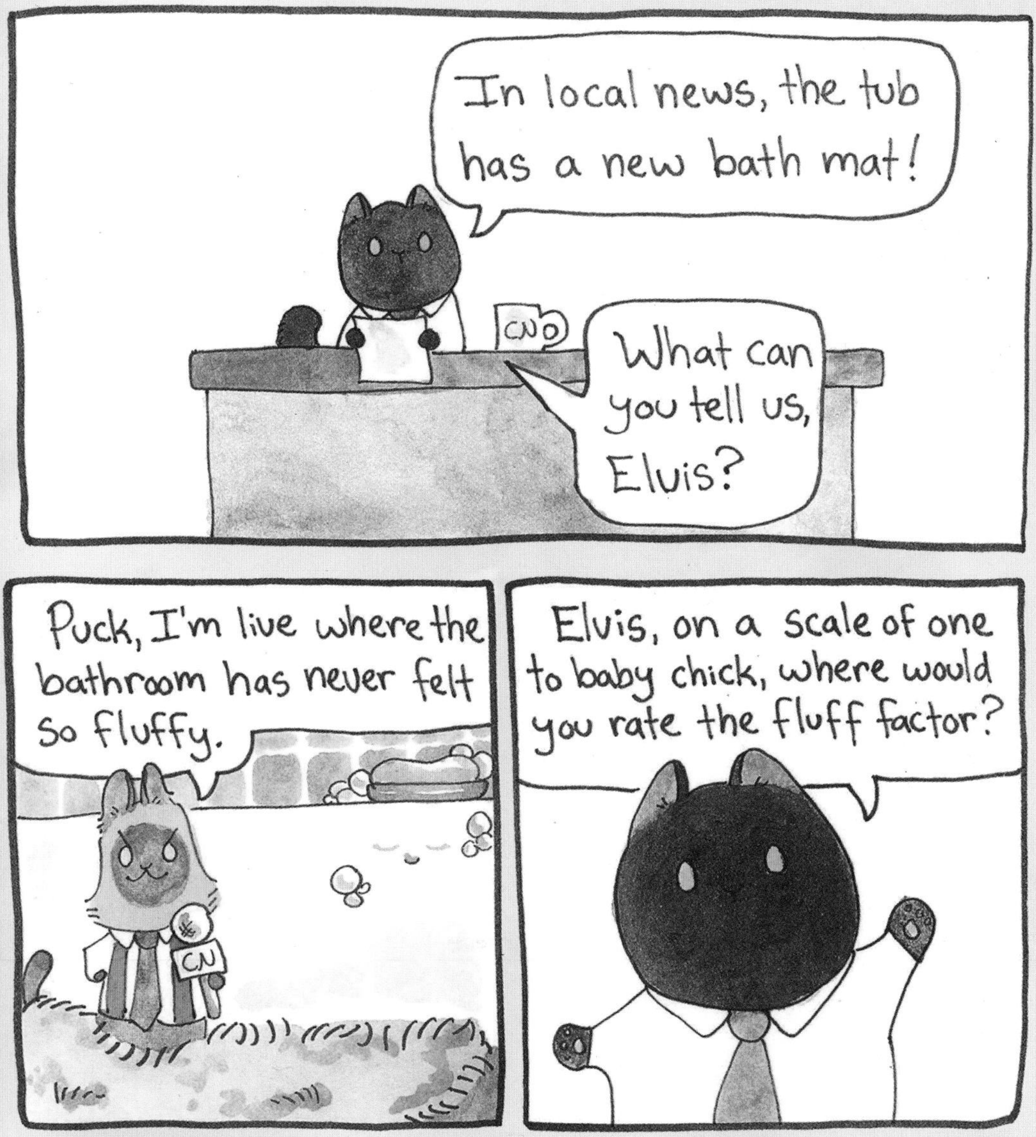
In local news, the tub has a new bath mat!
What can you tell us, Elvis?
CN
Puck, I'm live where the bathroom has never felt so fluffy.
CN
Elvis, on a scale of one to baby chick, where would you rate the fluff factor?

A solid "bunny rabbit."
CN
Gah!
1 FLUFF FACTOR
Yes, Puck. It **IS** shockingly fluffy.
I've never felt so RELAXED.

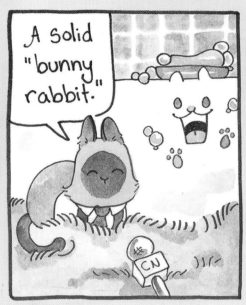

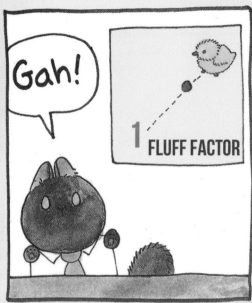

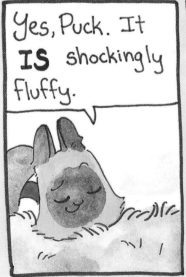

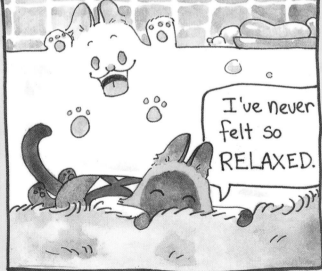

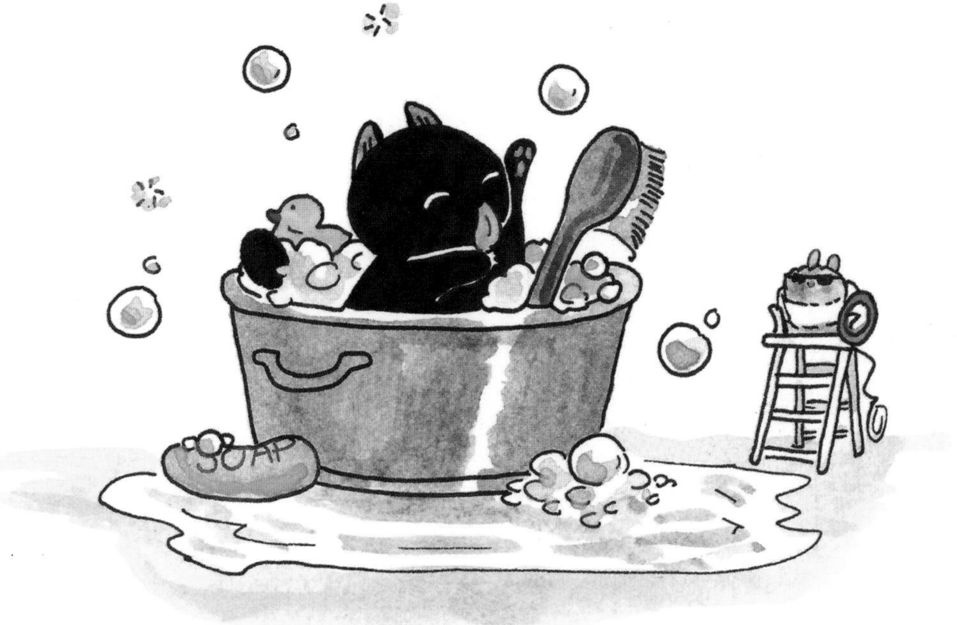
SOAP

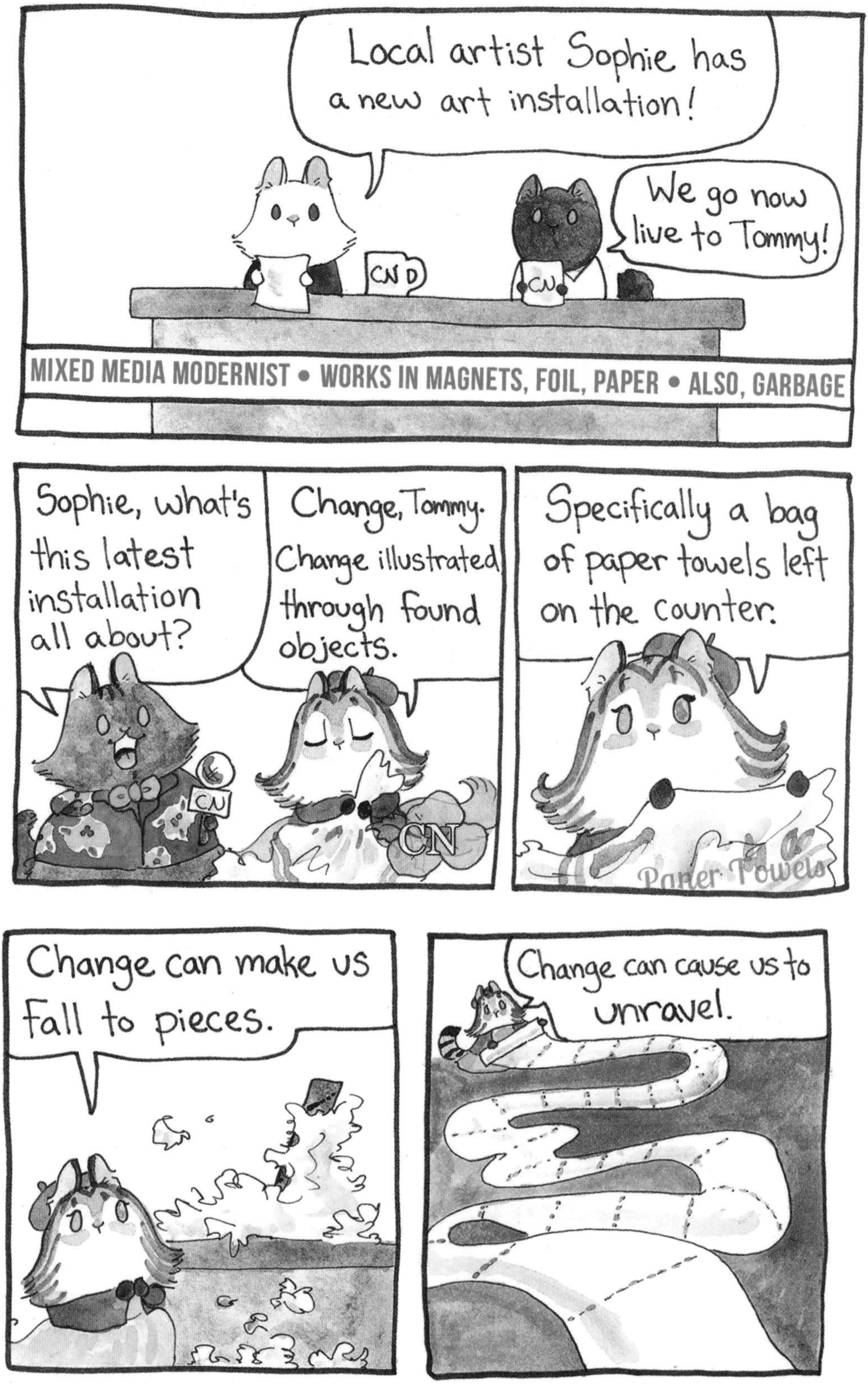
Local artist Sophie has a new art installation!
We go now live to Tommy!
CN D
CN
MIXED MEDIA MODERNIST • WORKS IN MAGNETS, FOIL, PAPER • ALSO, GARBAGE
Sophie, what's this latest installation all about?
Change, Tommy. Change illustrated through found objects.
CN
CN
Specifically a bag of paper towels left on the counter.
Paper Towels
Change can make us Fall to pieces.
Change can cause us to unravel.

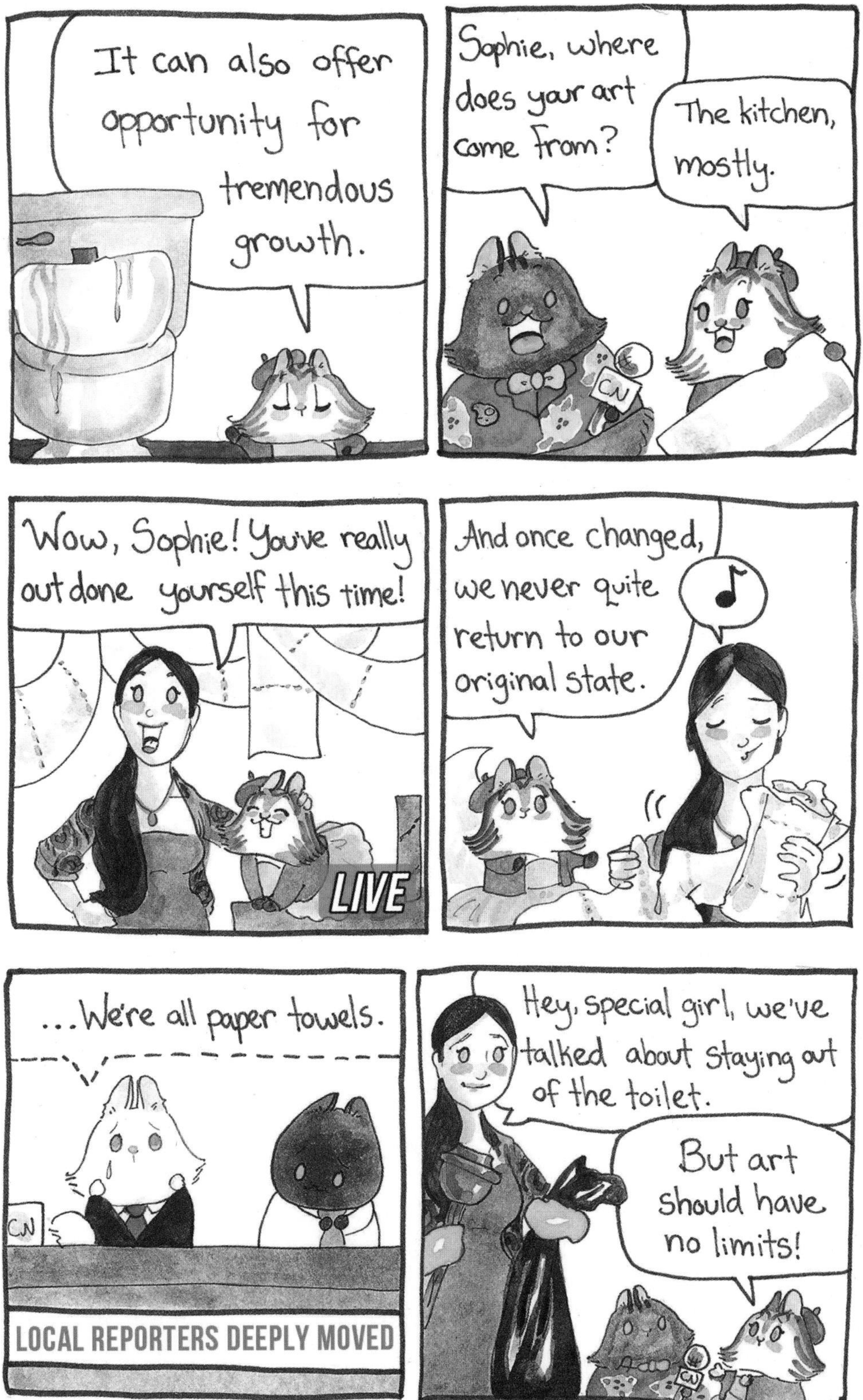
It can also offer opportunity for tremendous growth.
Sophie, where does your art come from?
The kitchen, mostly.
CN
Wow, Sophie! You've really outdone yourself this time!
LIVE
And once changed, we never quite return to our original state.
...We're all paper towels.
CN
LOCAL REPORTERS DEEPLY MOVED
Hey, special girl, we've talked about staying out of the toilet.
But art should have no limits!
CN

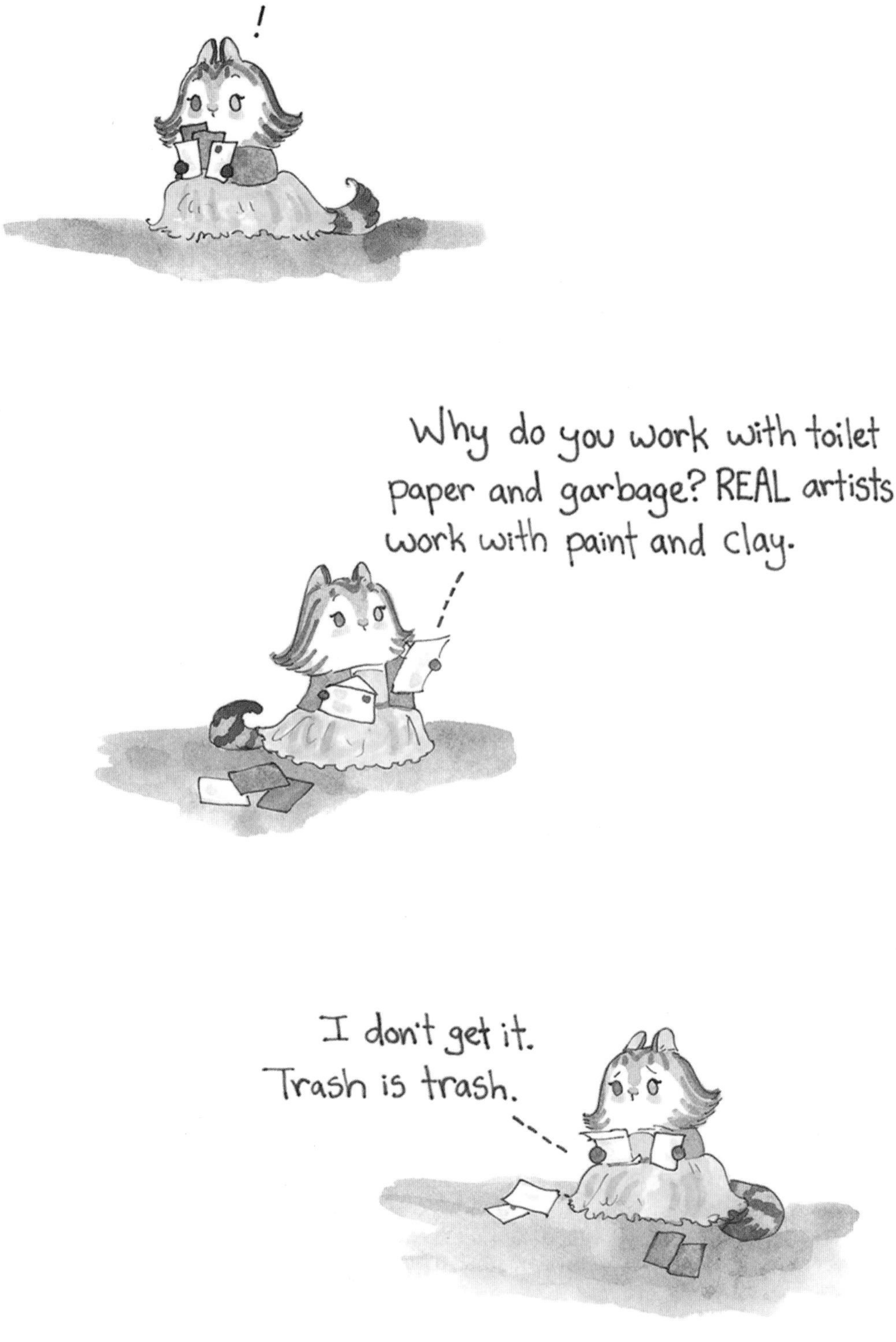
!
Why do you work with toilet paper and garbage? REAL artists work with paint and clay.
I don't get it. Trash is trash.

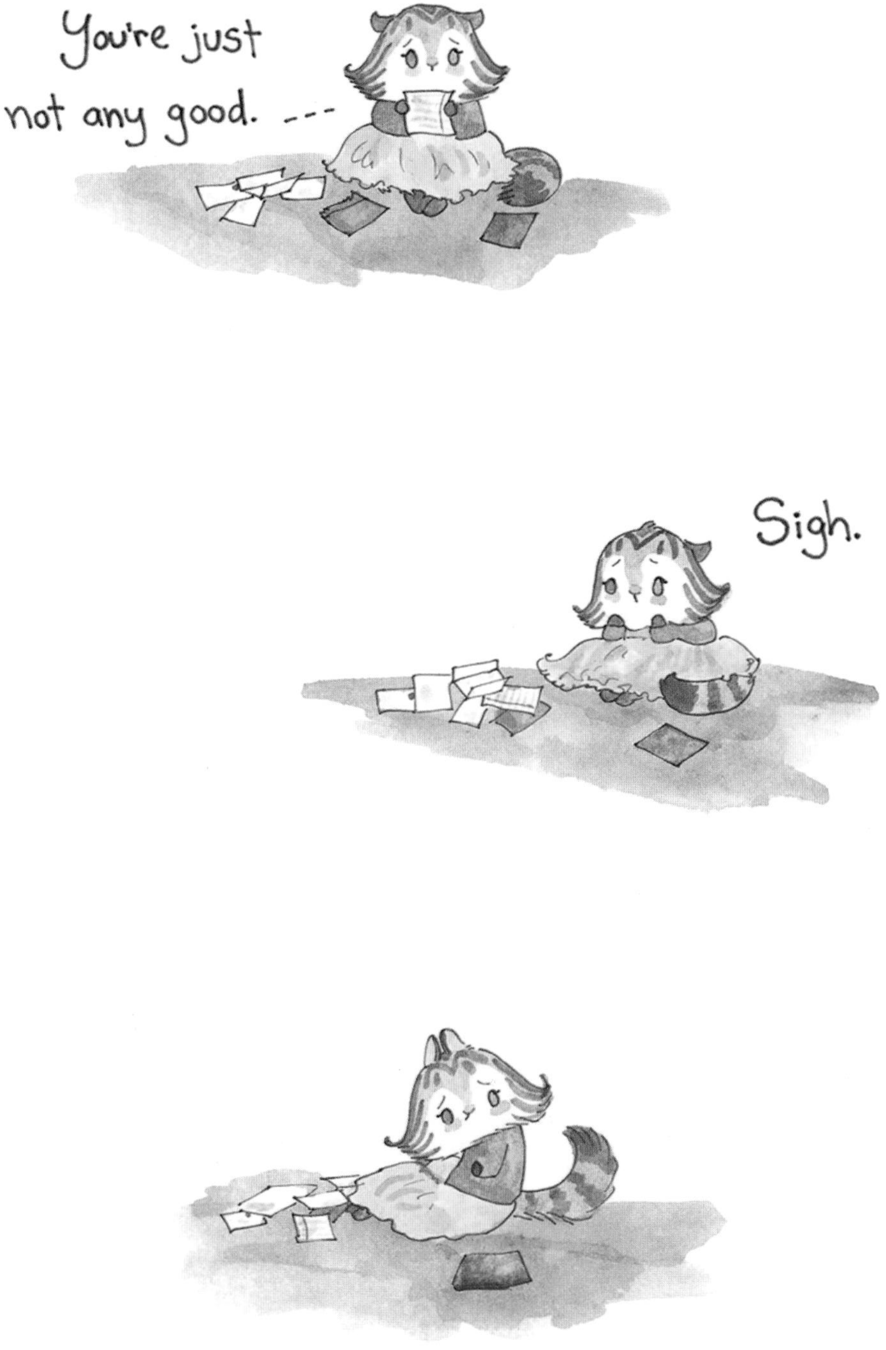
You're just not any good. ---
Sigh.

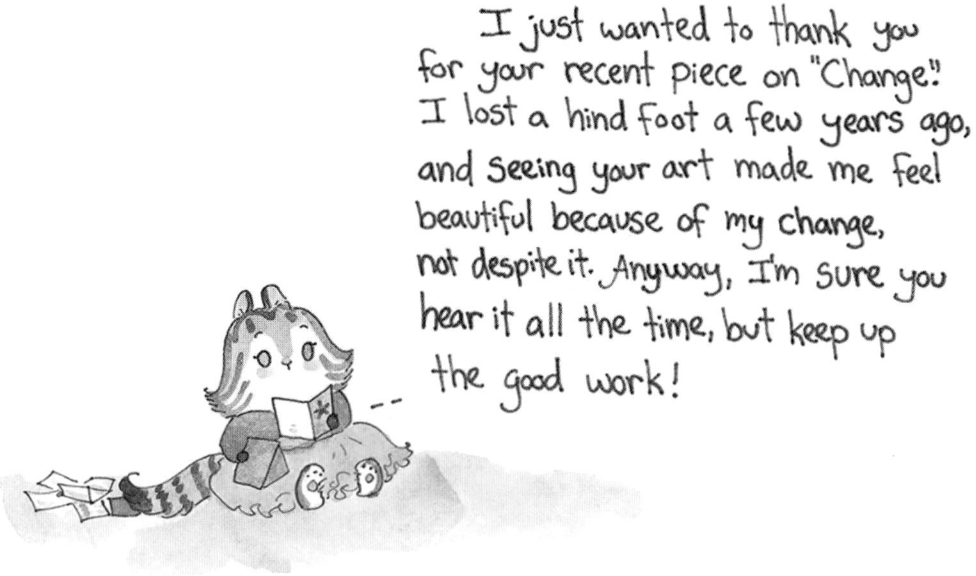
I just wanted to thank you for your recent piece on "Change." I lost a hind foot a few years ago, and seeing your art made me feel beautiful because of my change, not despite it. Anyway, I'm sure you hear it all the time, but keep up the good work!

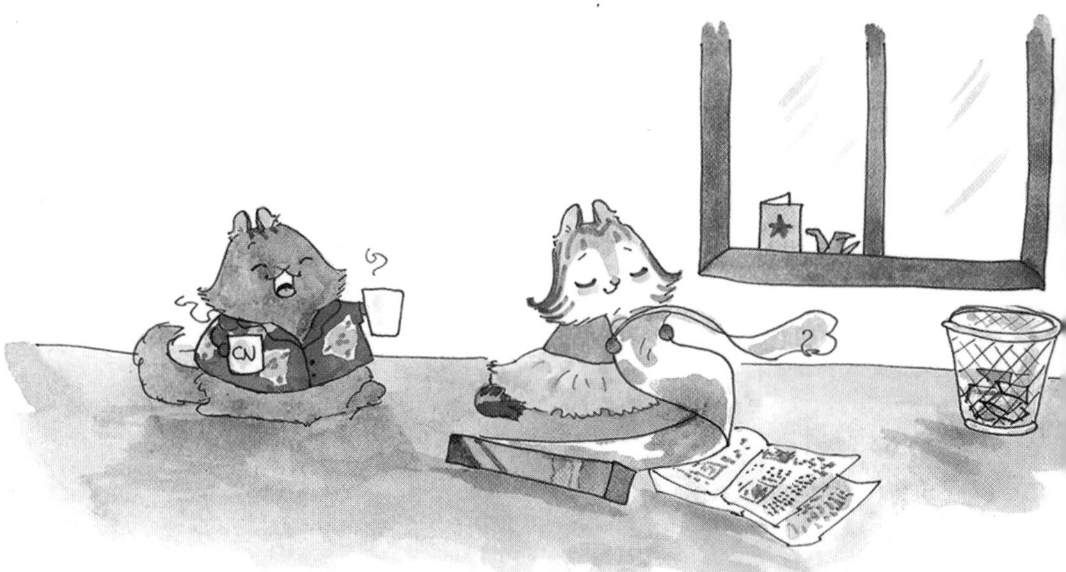
CN

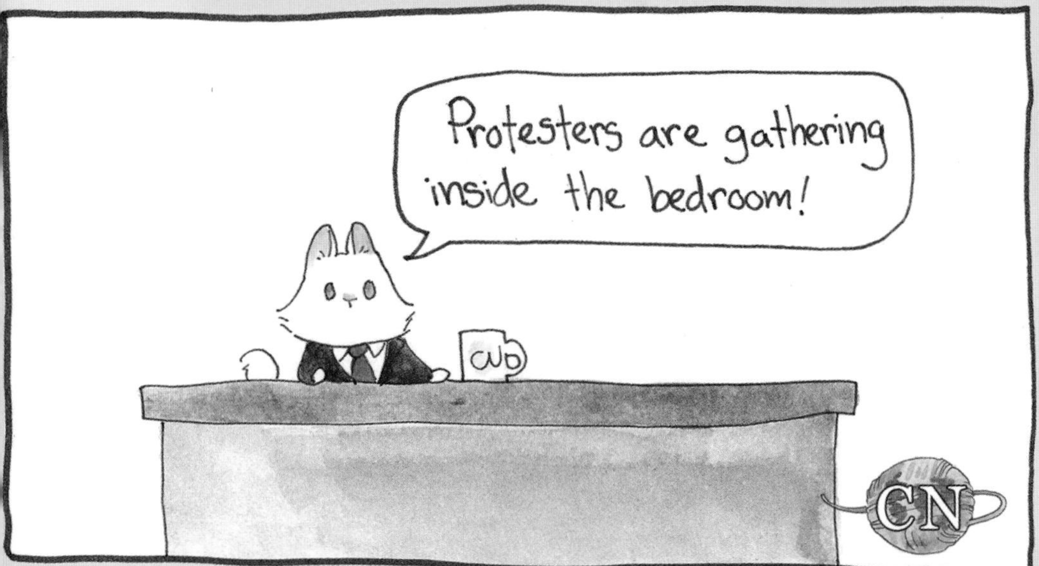
Protesters are gathering inside the bedroom!
CNN
CN

Lupin, Elvis here, live at the scene of the protest.
WAKE UP
Man?
CN
Elvis, what inspired this protest?
CN
The People decided to sleep past 8am.
WE HAVE RIGHTS!
I feel inspired to join.
DON'T BE RUDE GIVE US FOOD

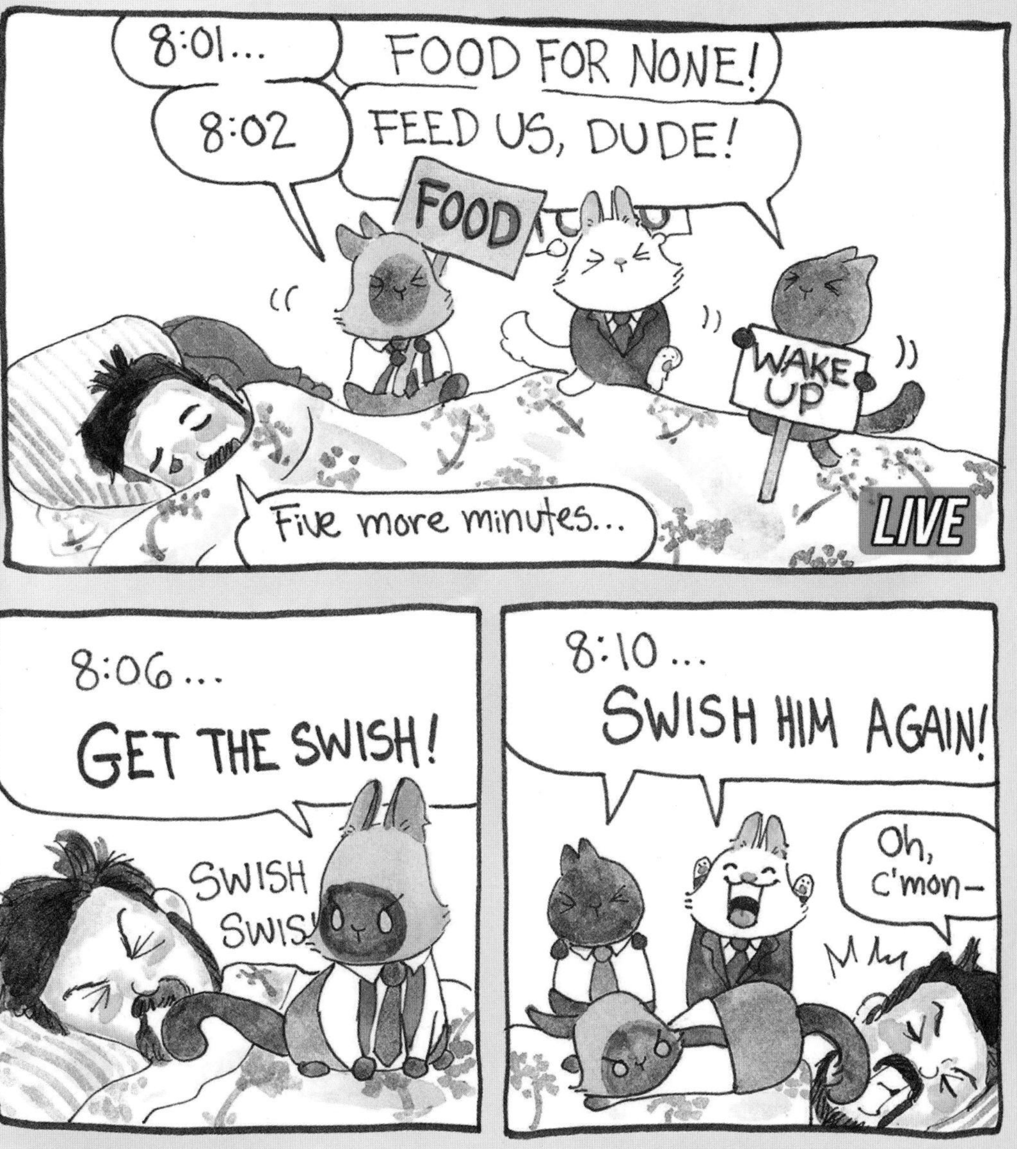
8:01...
FOOD FOR NONE!
8:02
FEED US, DUDE!
FOOD
WAKE UP
Five more minutes...
LIVE
8:06...
GET THE SWISH!
SWISH SWIS
8:10...
SWISH HIM AGAIN!
Oh, c'mon-

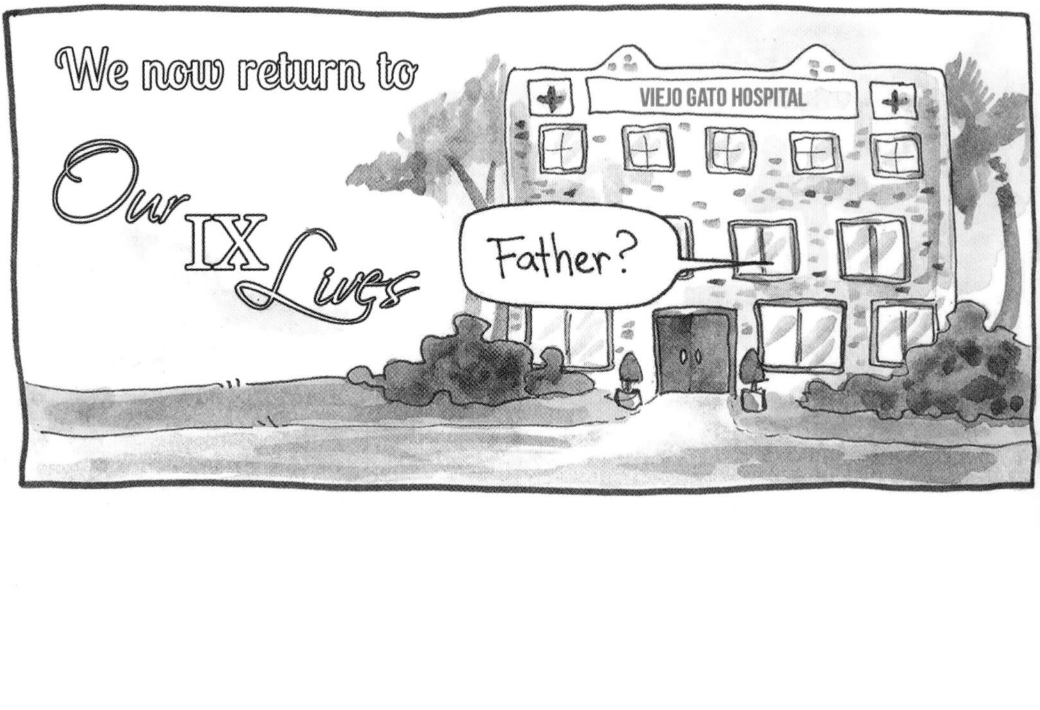
We now return to
Our IX Lives
VIEJO GATO HOSPITAL
Father?

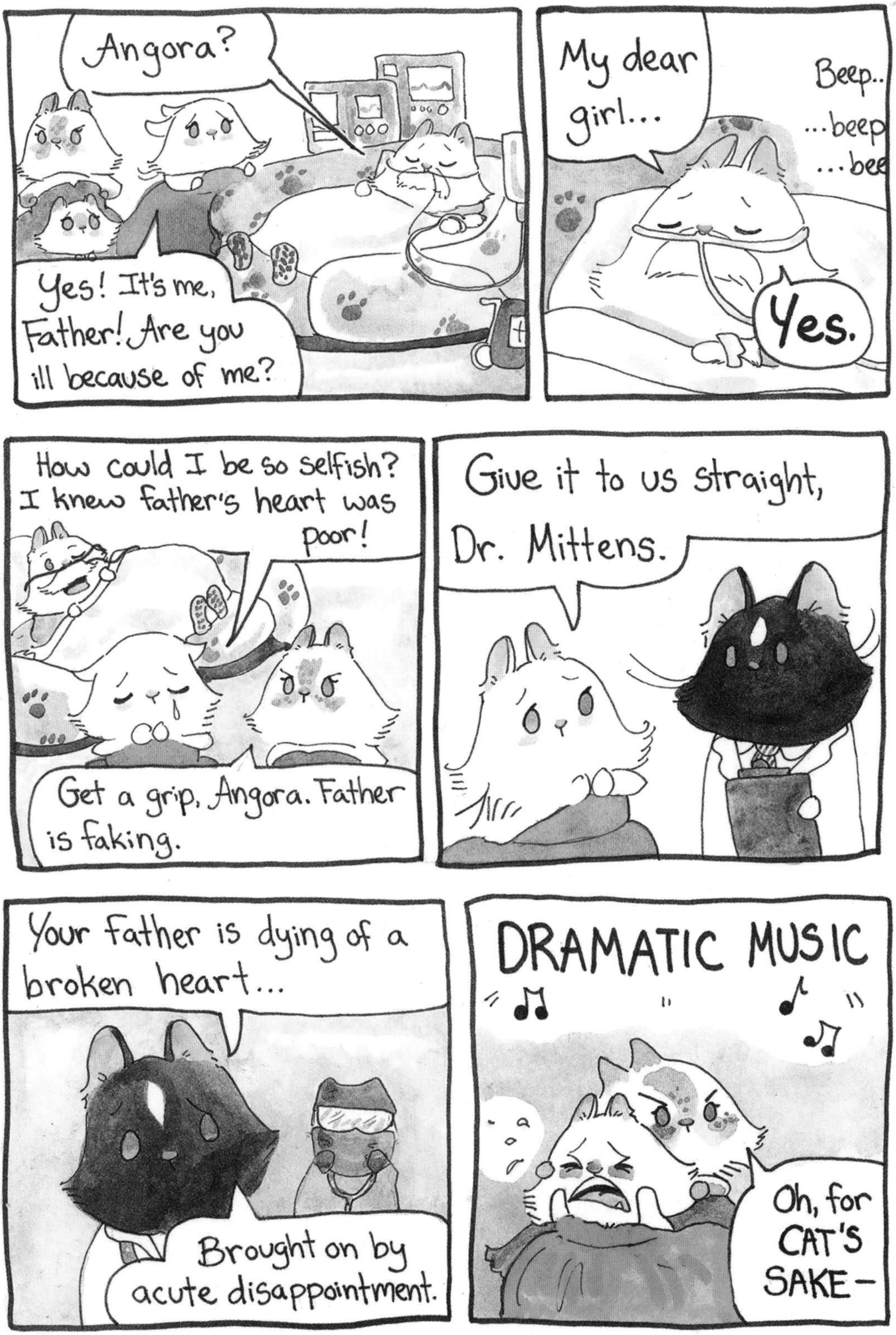
Angora?
Yes! It's me, Father! Are you ill because of me?
My dear girl...
Beep.. ...beep ...bee
Yes.
How could I be so selfish? I knew father's heart was poor!
Get a grip, Angora. Father is faking.
Give it to us straight, Dr. Mittens.
Your father is dying of a broken heart...
Brought on by acute disappointment.
DRAMATIC MUSIC
Oh, for CAT'S SAKE—

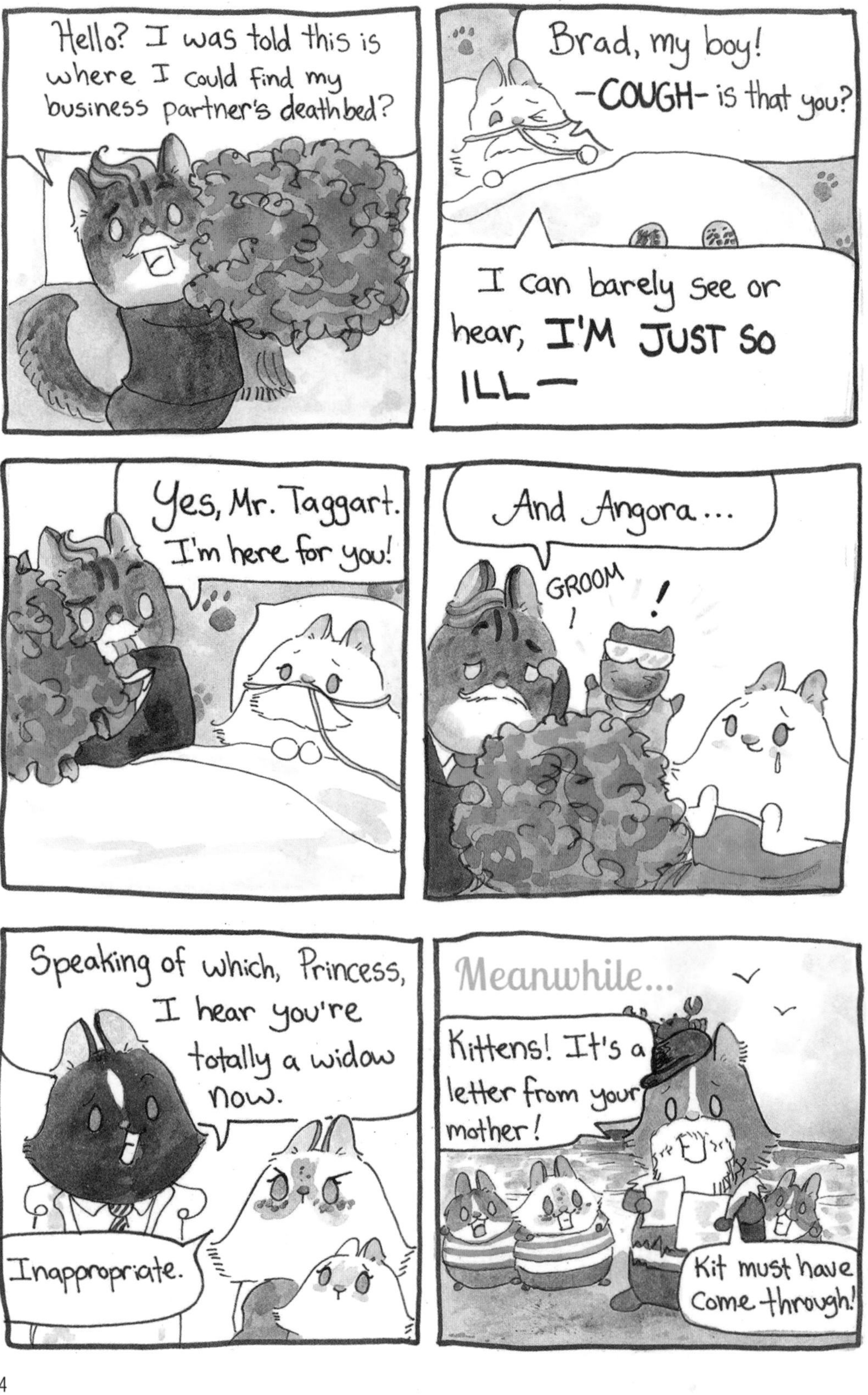
Hello? I was told this is where I could find my business partner's deathbed?
Brad, my boy! -COUGH- is that you?
I can barely see or hear, I'M JUST SO ILL—
Yes, Mr. Taggart. I'm here for you!
And Angora...
GROOM
!
Speaking of which, Princess, I hear you're totally a widow now.
Inappropriate.
Meanwhile...
Kittens! It's a letter from your mother!
Kit must have come through!

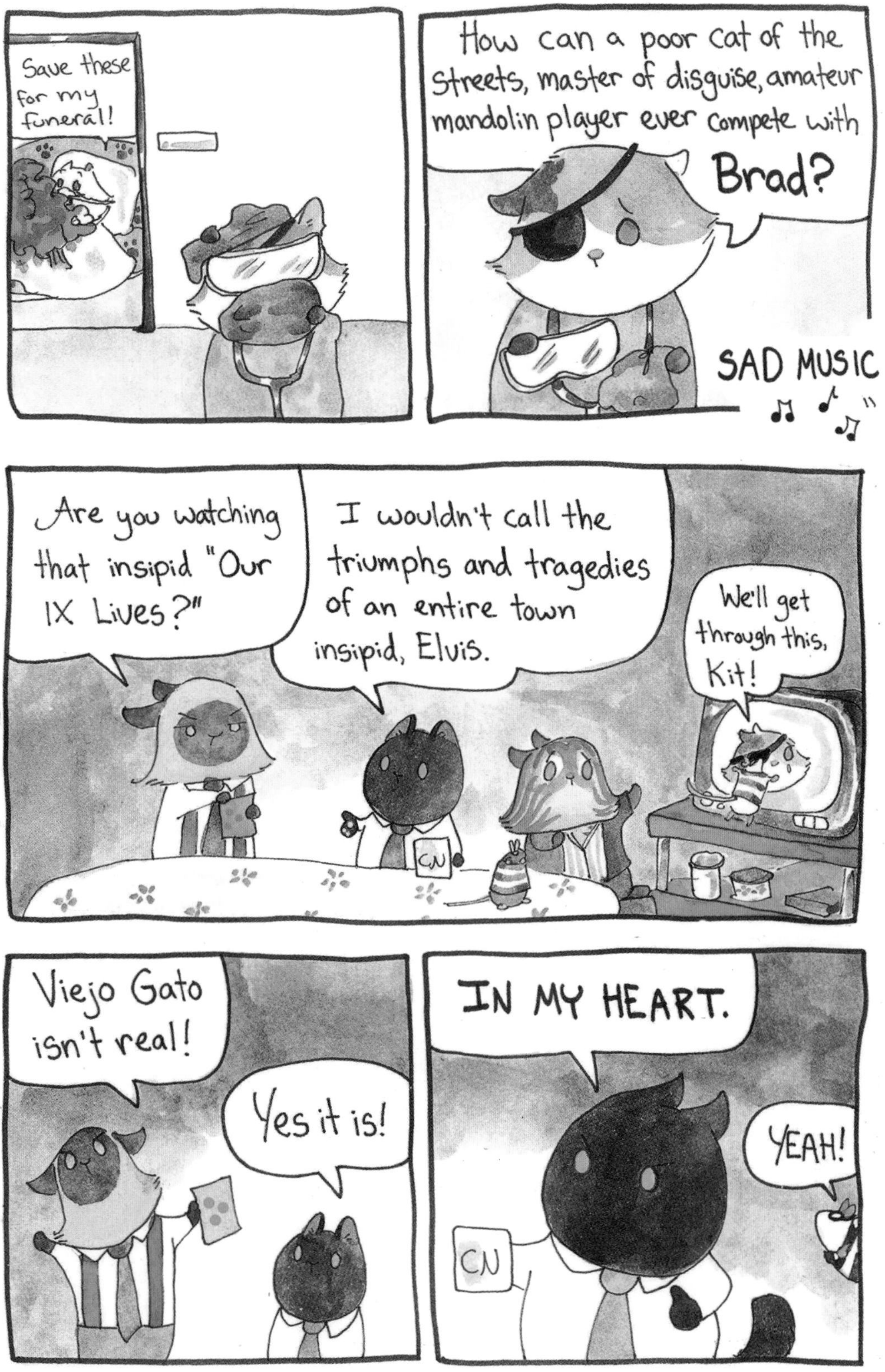
Save these for my funeral!
How can a poor cat of the streets, master of disguise, amateur mandolin player ever compete with Brad?
SAD MUSIC
Are you watching that insipid "Our IX Lives?"
I wouldn't call the triumphs and tragedies of an entire town insipid, Elvis.
We'll get through this, Kit!
CN
Viejo Gato isn't real!
Yes it is!
IN MY HEART.
YEAH!
CN

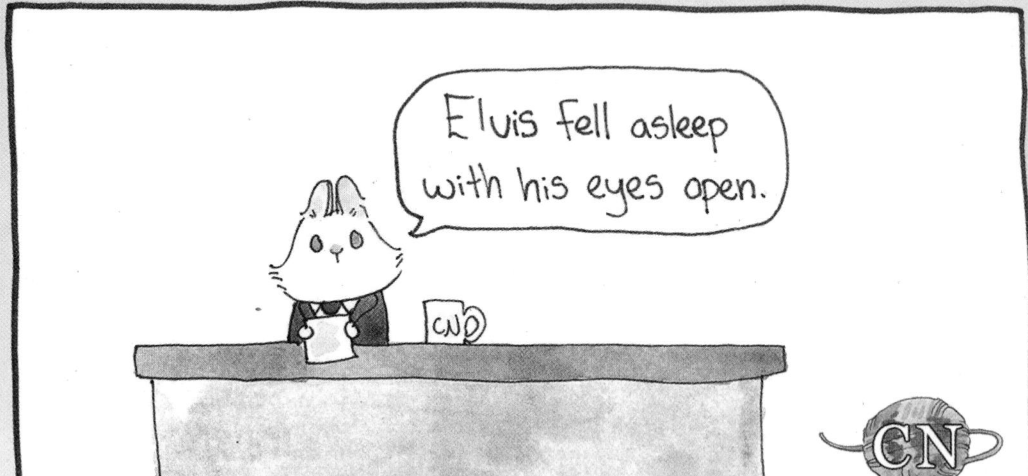
Elvis fell asleep with his eyes open.
CN
CN

Puck here, live on the scene and feeling uncomfortable.
LIVE
Are we sure he's asleep?
Oh, there's no doubt.
Poke.
!
LIVE
CN news... Should we wake him up?
CN news, dare me to boop his nose?

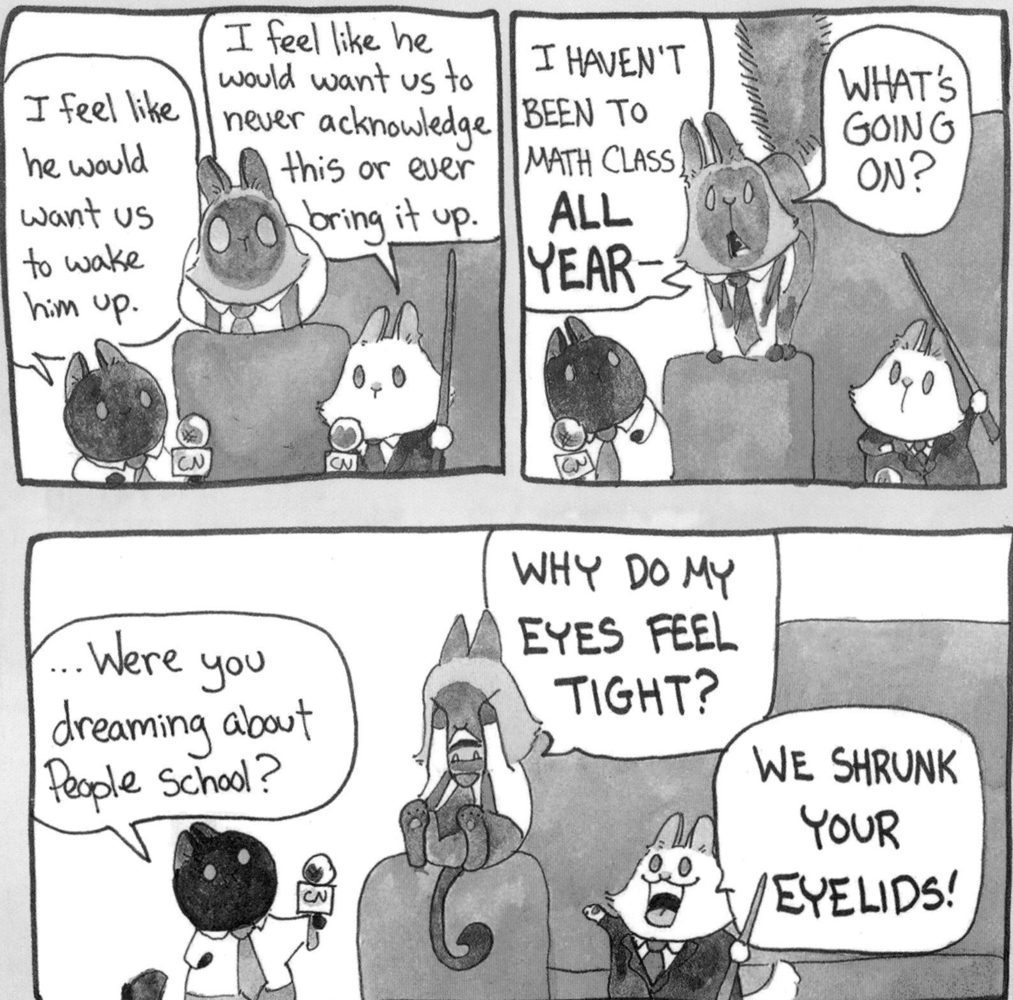
I feel like he would want us to wake him up.
I feel like he would want us to never acknowledge this or ever bring it up.
I HAVEN'T BEEN TO MATH CLASS ALL YEAR—
WHAT'S GOING ON?
CN
...Were you dreaming about People School?
WHY DO MY EYES FEEL TIGHT?
WE SHRUNK YOUR EYELIDS!

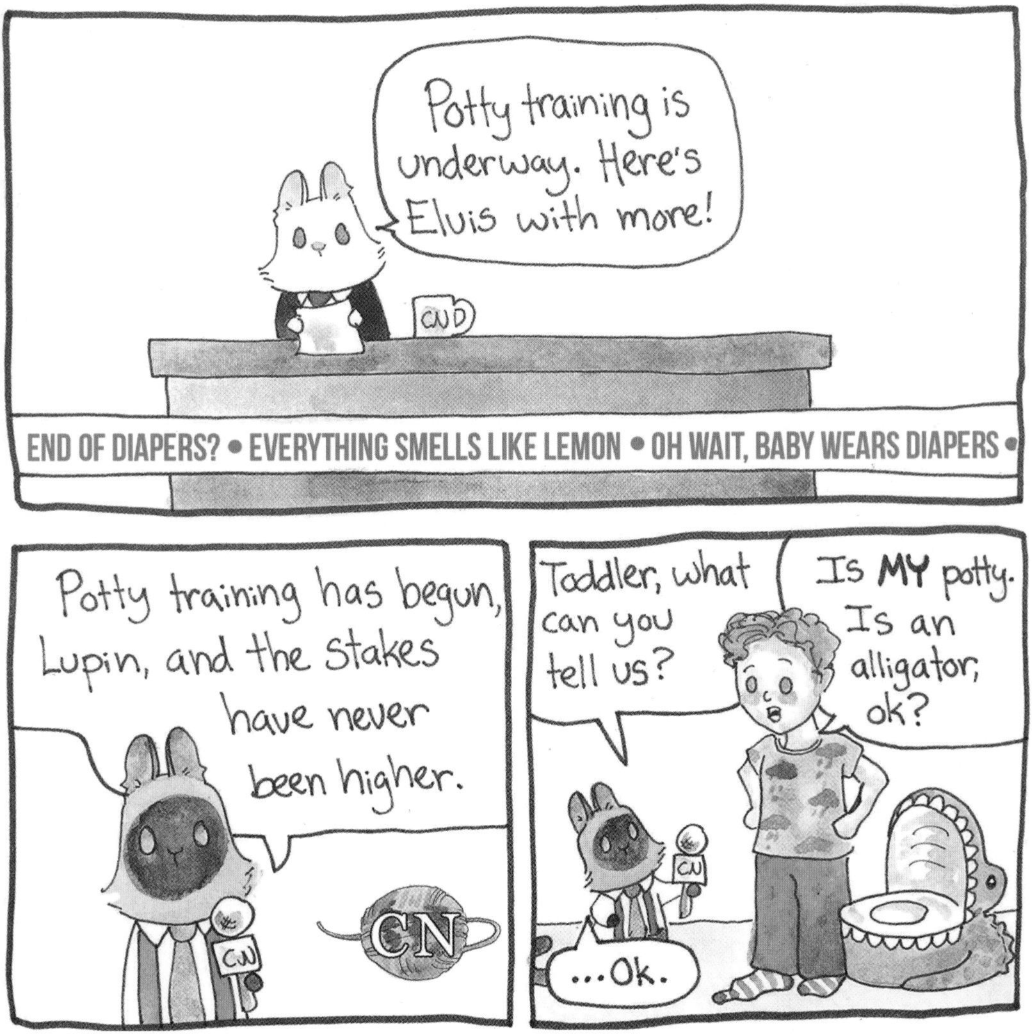
Potty training is underway. Here's Elvis with more!
CWD
END OF DIAPERS? • EVERYTHING SMELLS LIKE LEMON • OH WAIT, BABY WEARS DIAPERS •
Potty training has begun, Lupin, and the stakes have never been higher.
CN
CW
Toddler, what can you tell us?
Is MY potty. Is an alligator, ok?
CW
...Ok.

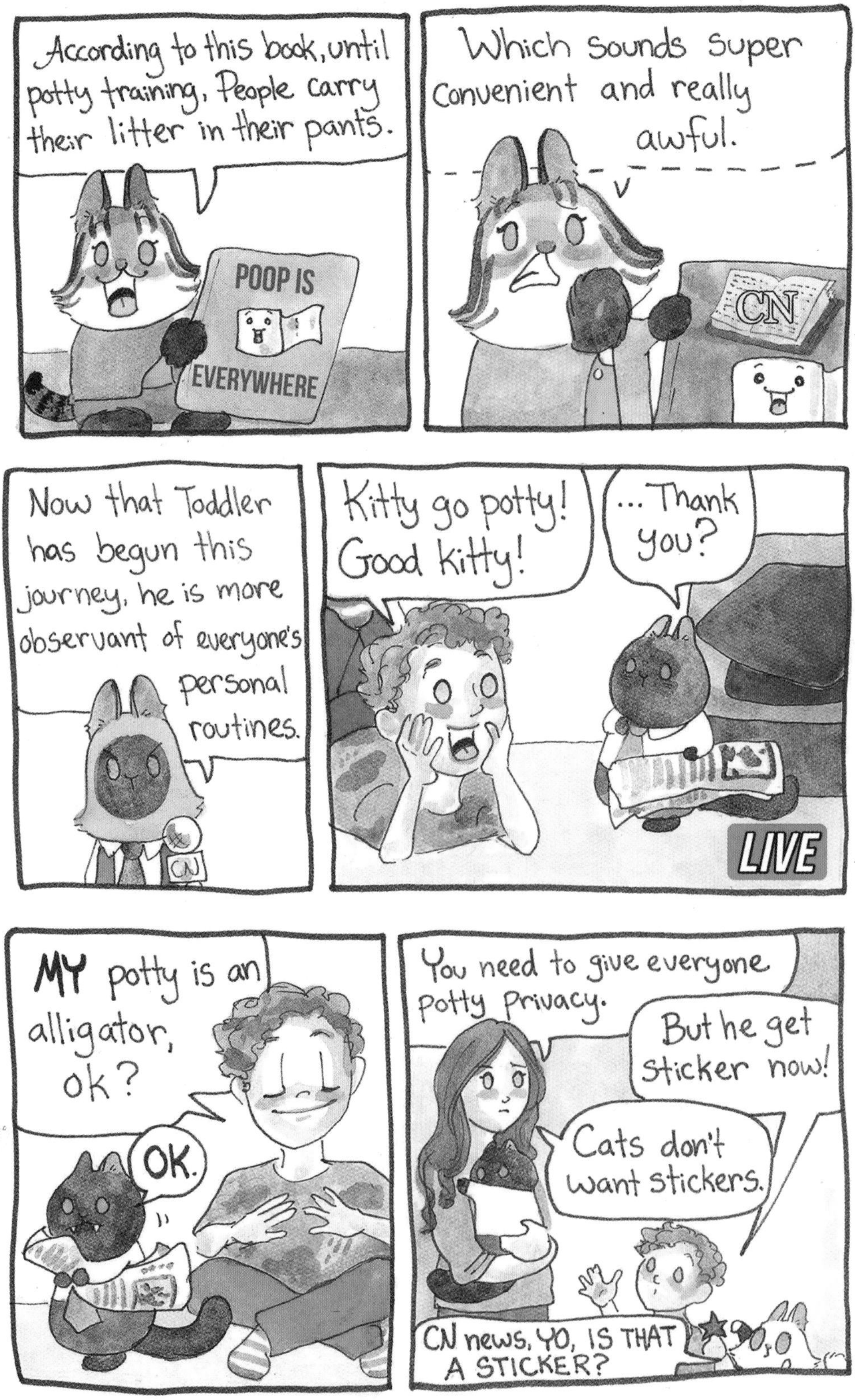
According to this book, until potty training, People carry their litter in their pants.
POOP IS EVERYWHERE
Which sounds super convenient and really awful.
CN
Now that Toddler has begun this journey, he is more observant of everyone's personal routines.
CN
Kitty go potty! Good kitty!
...Thank you?
LIVE
MY potty is an alligator, ok?
OK.
You need to give everyone potty privacy.
But he get sticker now!
Cats don't want stickers.
CN news. YO, IS THAT A STICKER?

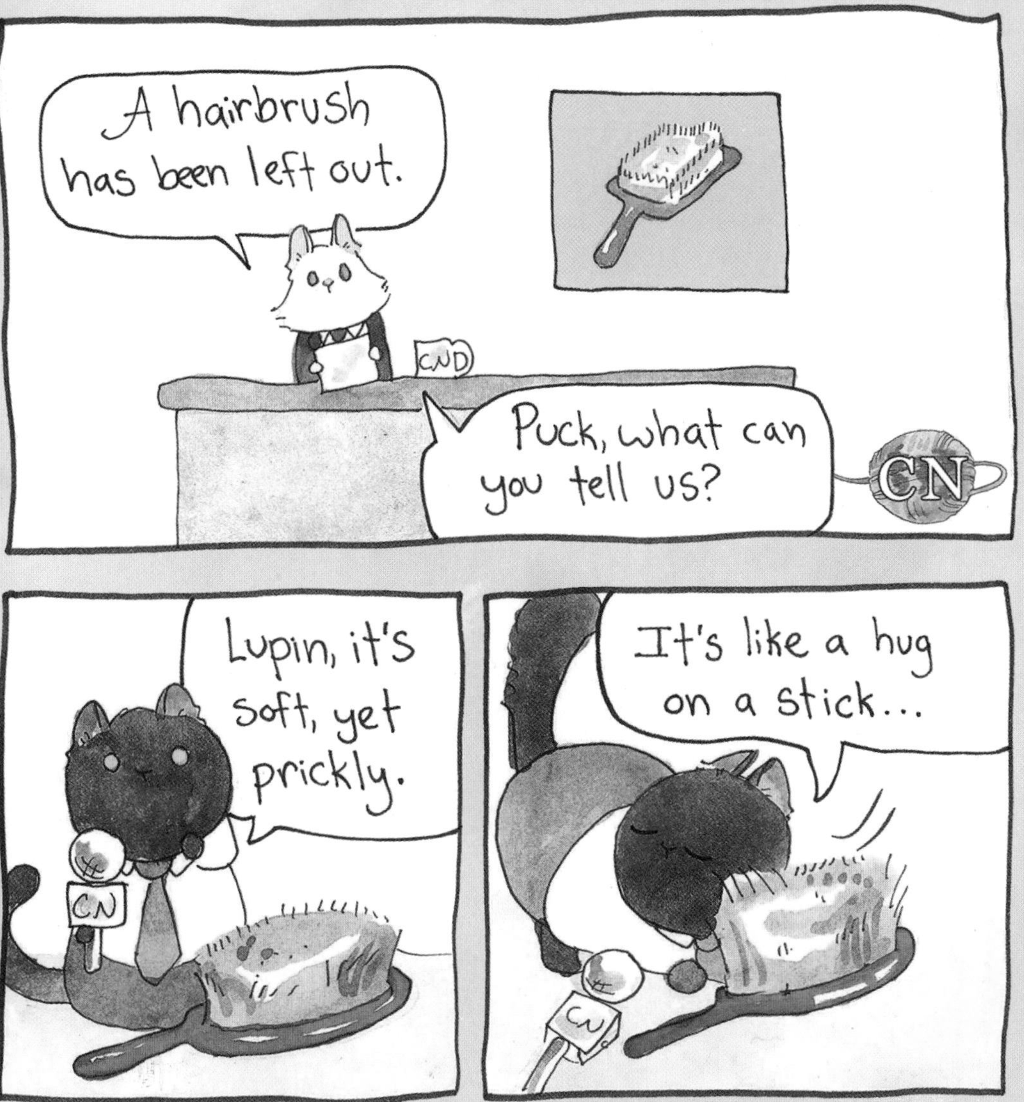
A hairbrush has been left out.
CND
Puck, what can you tell us?
CN
Lupin, it's soft, yet prickly.
CN
It's like a hug on a stick...
CN

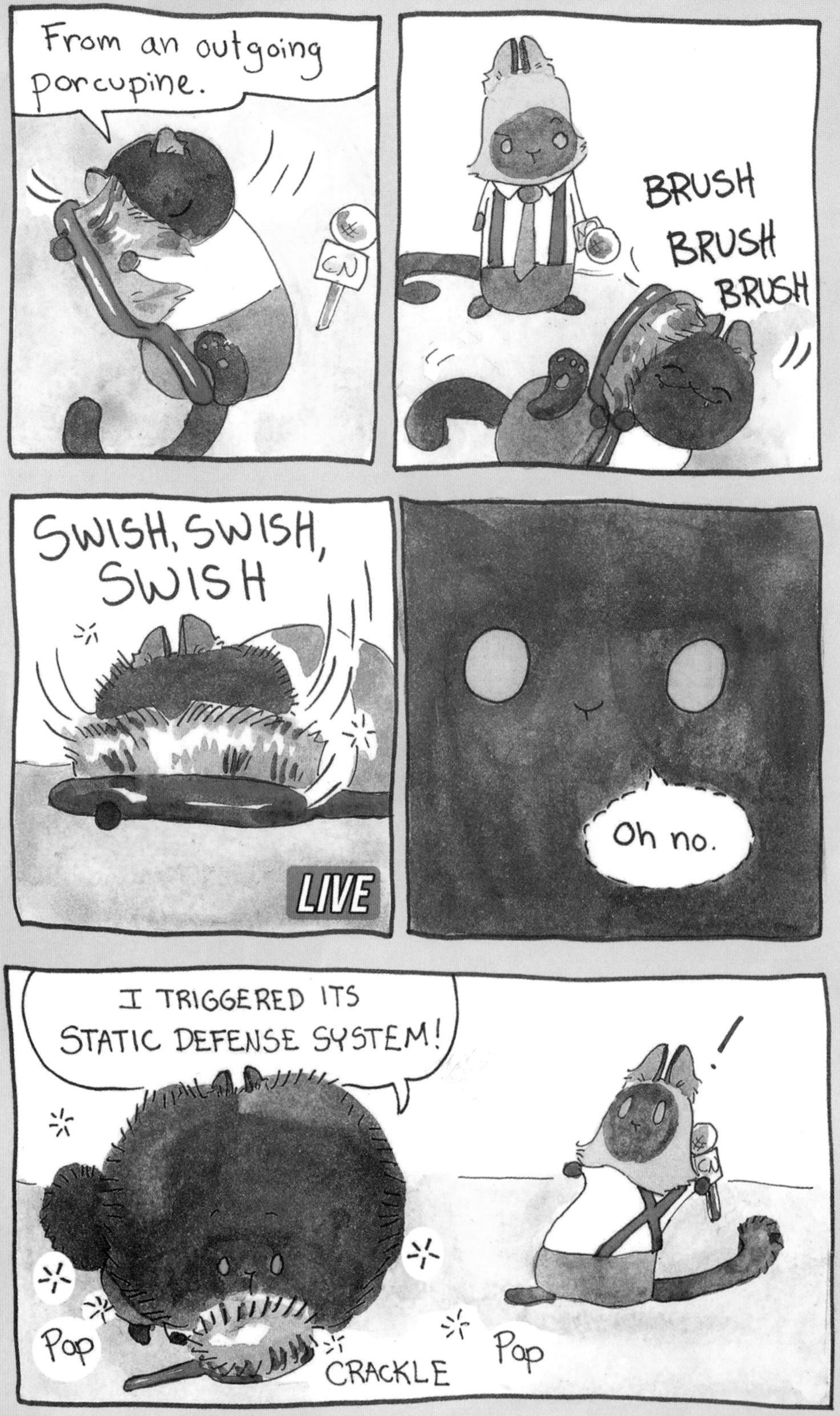
From an outgoing porcupine.
CN
BRUSH
BRUSH
BRUSH
SWISH, SWISH, SWISH
LIVE
Oh no.
I TRIGGERED ITS STATIC DEFENSE SYSTEM!
!
CN
Pop
CRACKLE
Pop

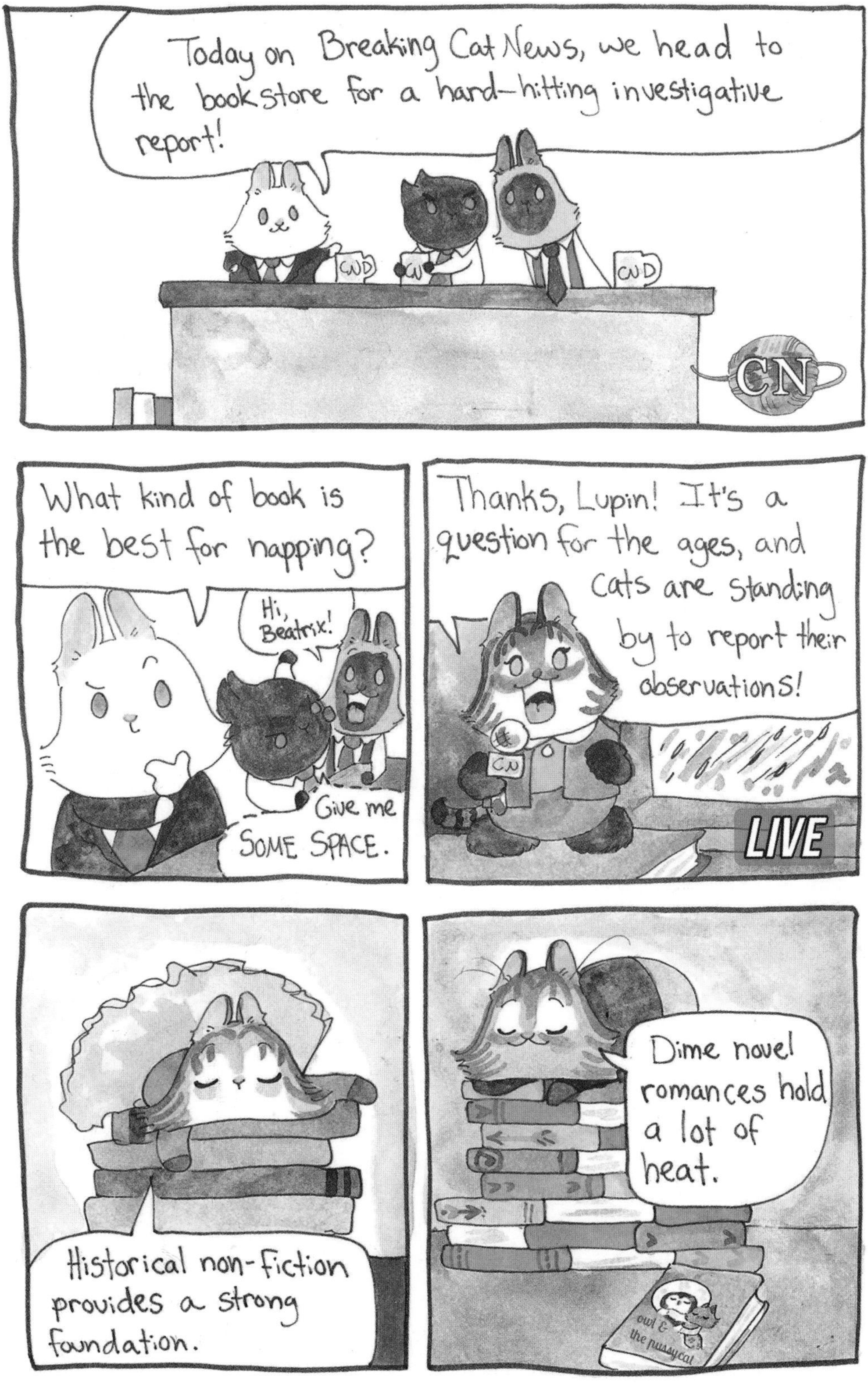
Today on Breaking Cat News, we head to the bookstore for a hard-hitting investigative report!
CWD
CN
What kind of book is the best for napping?
Hi, Beatrix!
Give me SOME SPACE.
Thanks, Lupin! It's a question for the ages, and cats are standing by to report their observations!
CN
LIVE
Historical non-fiction provides a strong foundation.
Dime novel romances hold a lot of heat.
owl & the pussycat

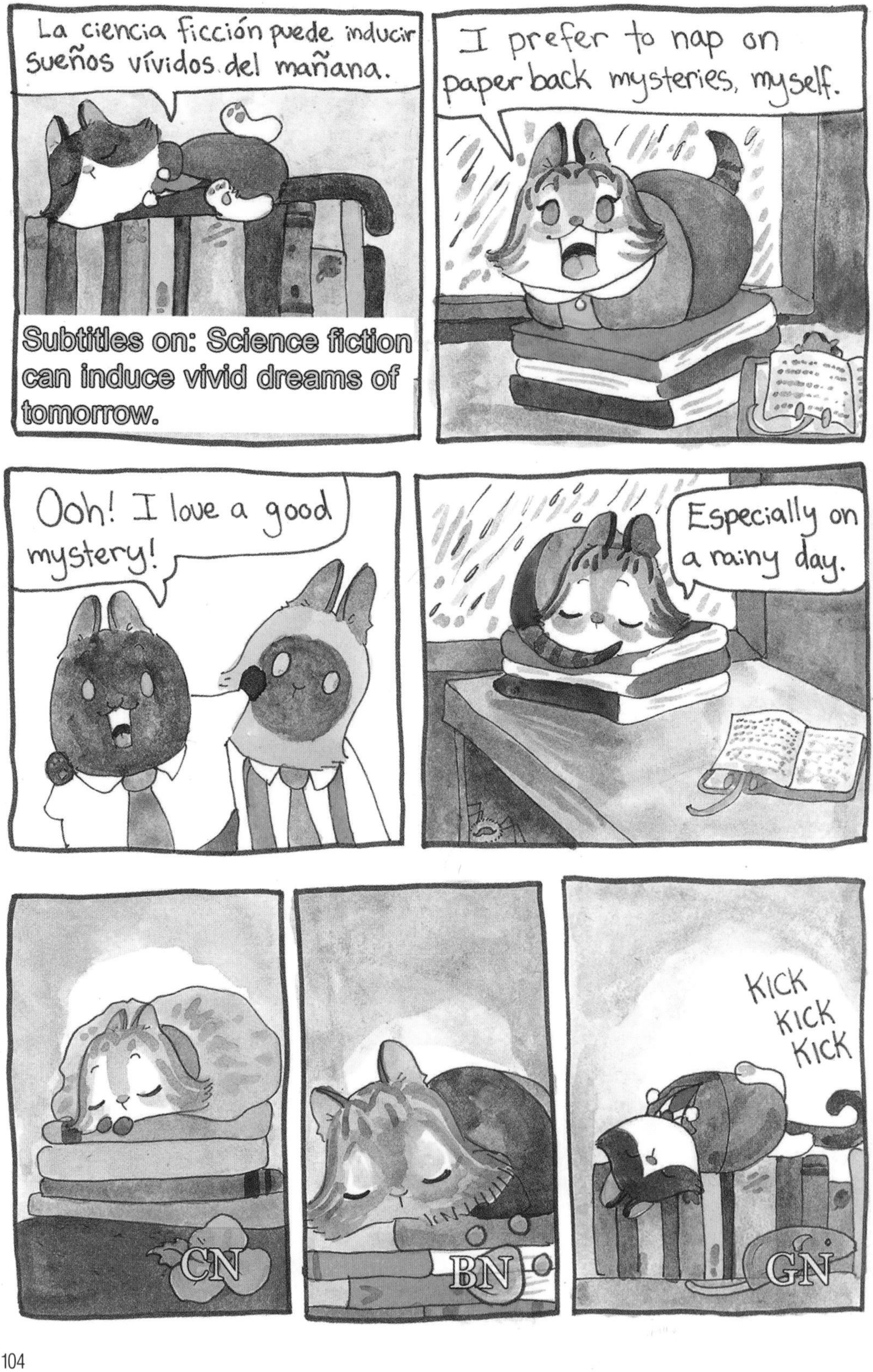
La ciencia ficción puede inducir sueños vívidos del mañana.
Subtitles on: Science fiction can induce vivid dreams of tomorrow.
I prefer to nap on paperback mysteries, myself.
Ooh! I love a good mystery!
Especially on a rainy day.
CN
BN
KICK KICK KICK
GN

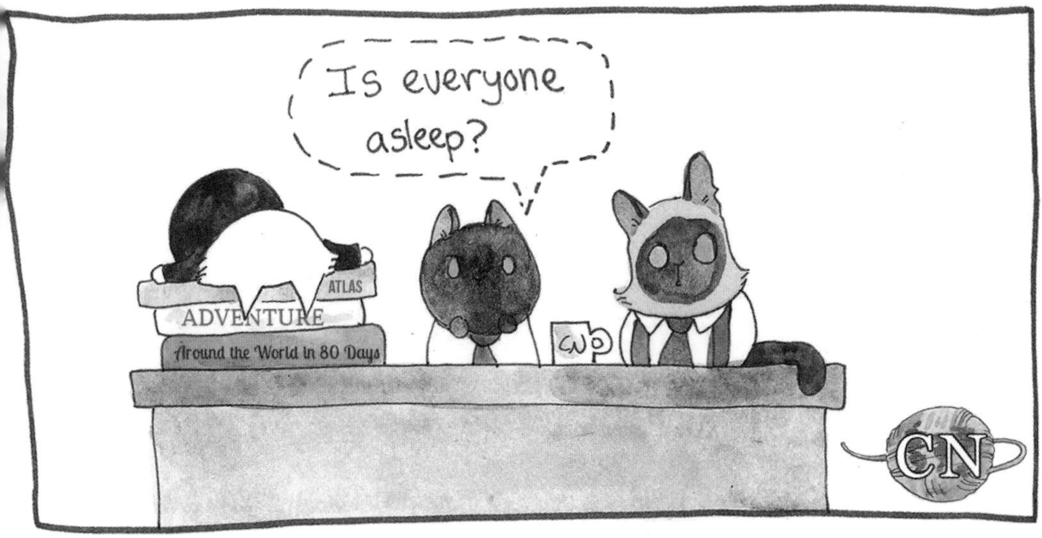
Is everyone asleep?
ATLAS
ADVENTURE
Around the World in 80 Days
CN
CN

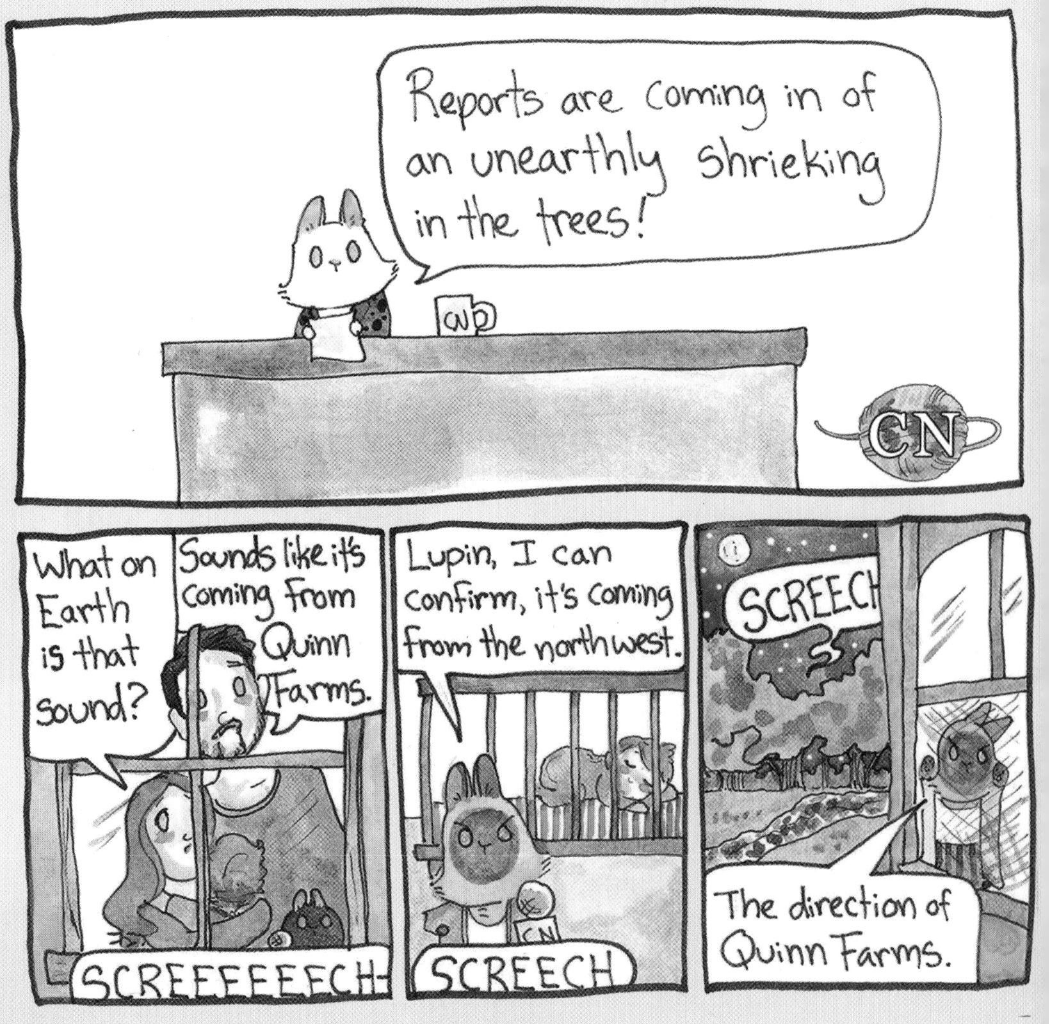
Reports are coming in of an unearthly shrieking in the trees!
CN
What on Earth is that sound?
Sounds like it's coming from Quinn Farms.
SCREEEEEEECH-
Lupin, I can confirm, it's coming from the northwest.
CN
SCREECH
SCREECH
The direction of Quinn Farms.

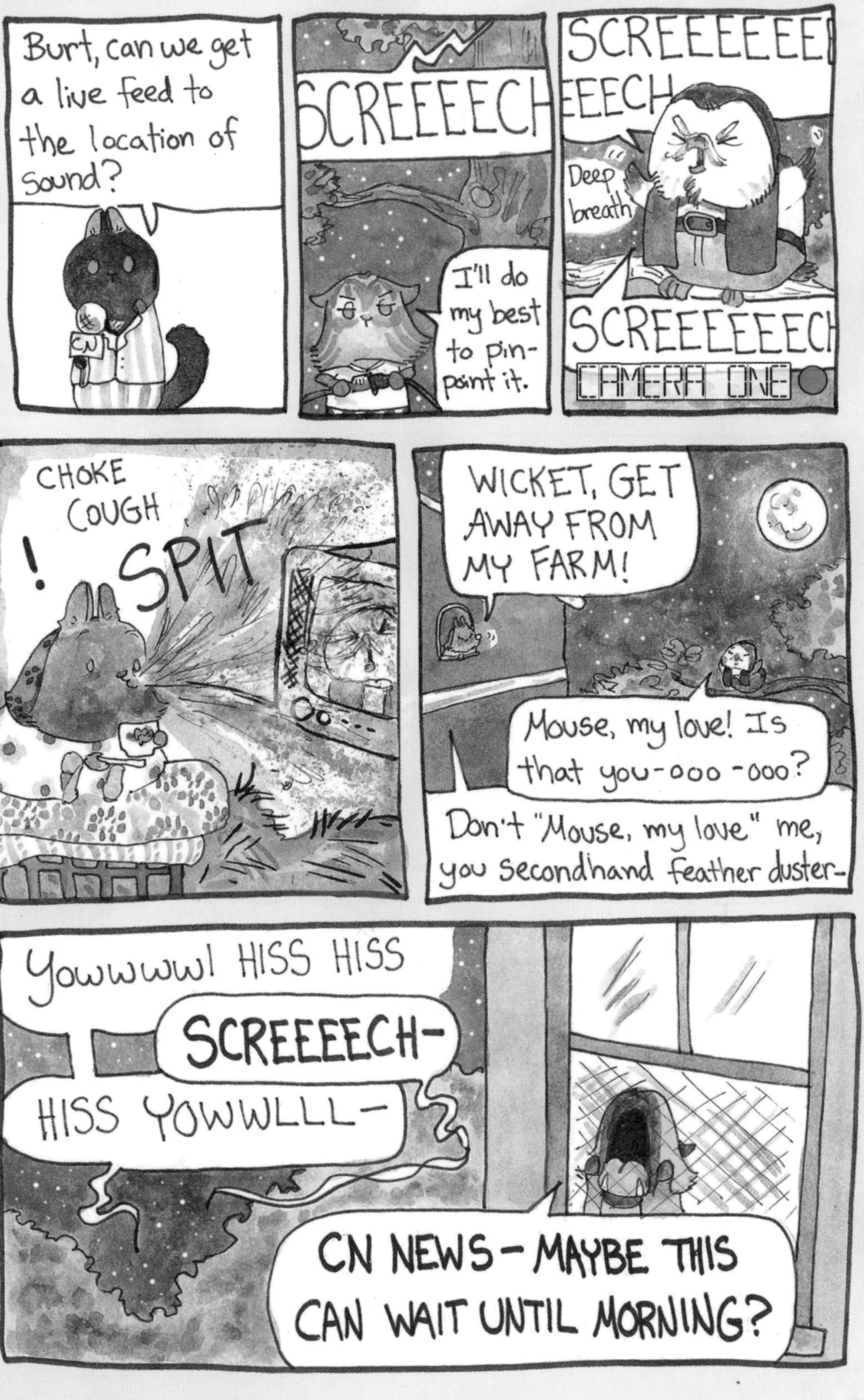
Burt, can we get a live feed to the location of sound?
CN
SCREEEEECH
I'll do my best to pin-point it.
SCREEEEEEE EEECH
Deep breath
SCREEEEEEECH
CAMERA ONE
CHOKE COUGH
!
SPIT
WICKET, GET AWAY FROM MY FARM!
Mouse, my love! Is that you-ooo-ooo?
Don't "Mouse, my love" me, you secondhand feather duster-
Yowwwwl HISS HISS
SCREEEECH-
HISS YOWWLLL-
CN NEWS - MAYBE THIS CAN WAIT UNTIL MORNING?

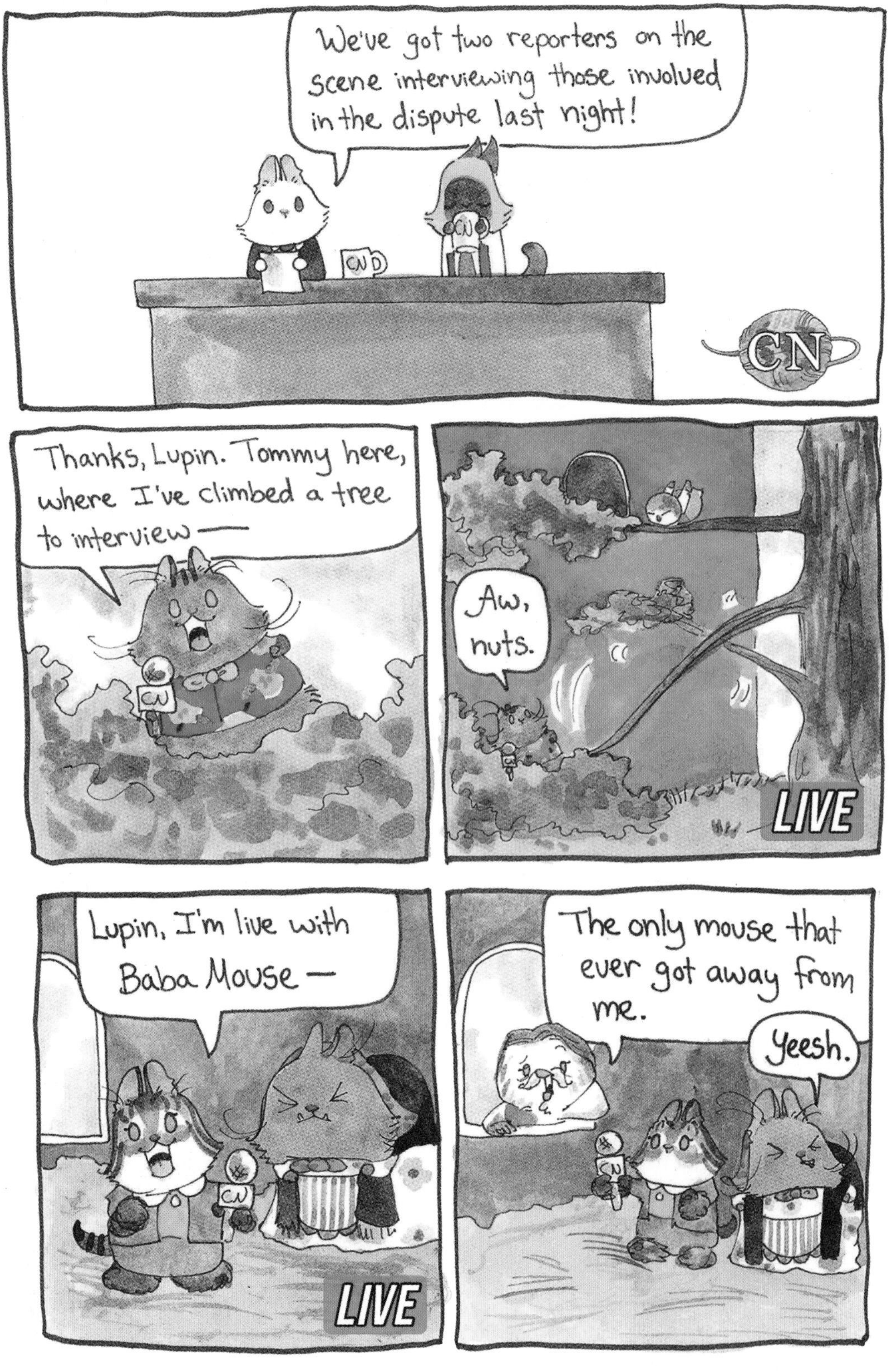
We've got two reporters on the scene interviewing those involved in the dispute last night!
CN
CN
CN
Thanks, Lupin. Tommy here, where I've climbed a tree to interview—
CN
Aw, nuts.
LIVE
Lupin, I'm live with Baba Mouse—
CN
LIVE
The only mouse that ever got away from me.
Yeesh.
CN

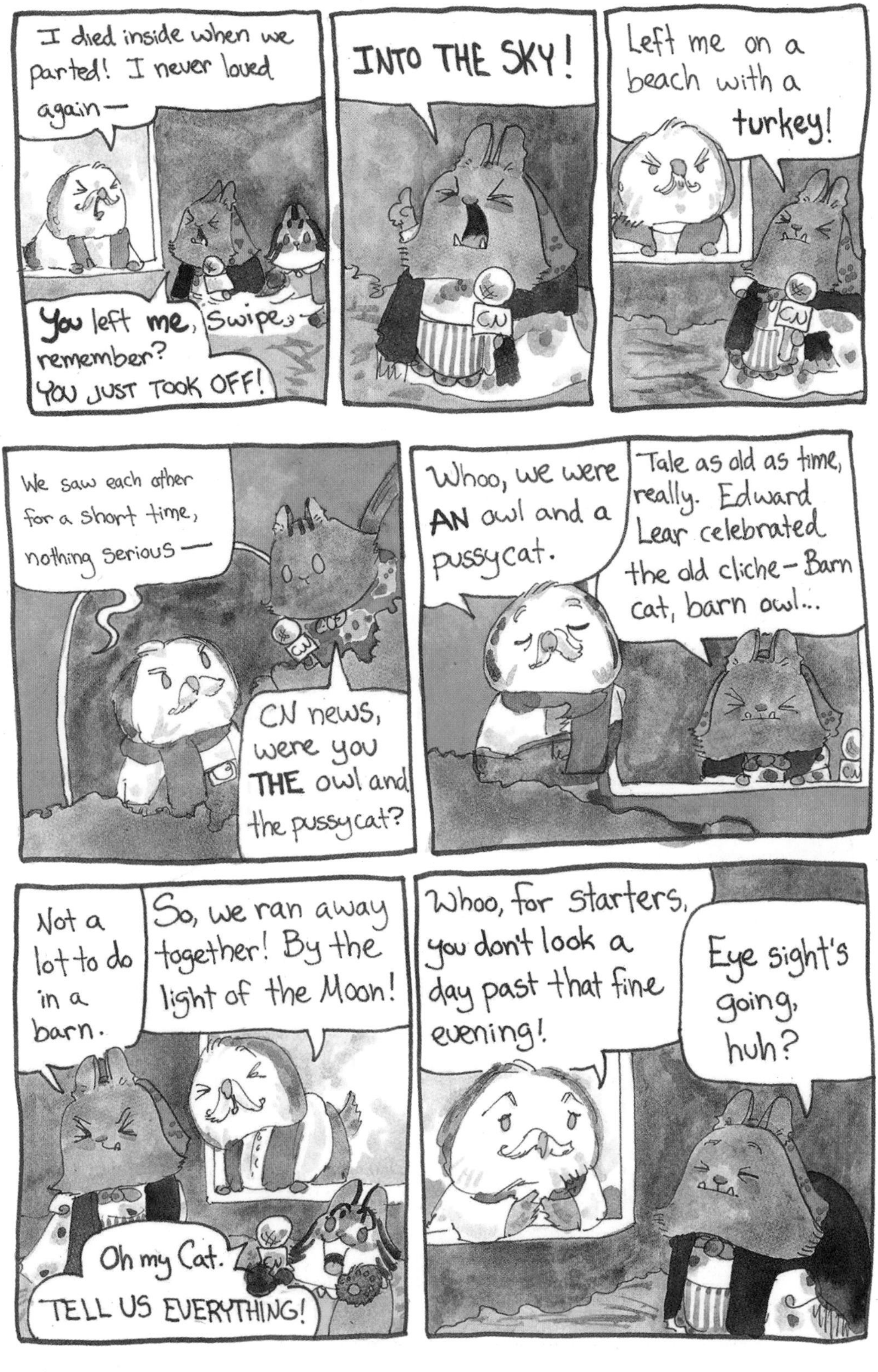
I died inside when we parted! I never loved again—
You left me, Swipe, remember? YOU JUST TOOK OFF!
INTO THE SKY!
Left me on a beach with a turkey!
We saw each other for a short time, nothing serious—
CN news, were you THE owl and the pussycat?
Whoo, we were AN owl and a pussycat.
Tale as old as time, really. Edward Lear celebrated the old cliche- Barn cat, barn owl...
Not a lot to do in a barn.
So, we ran away together! By the light of the Moon!
Oh my Cat.
TELL US EVERYTHING!
Whoo, for starters, you don't look a day past that fine evening!
Eye sight's going, huh?

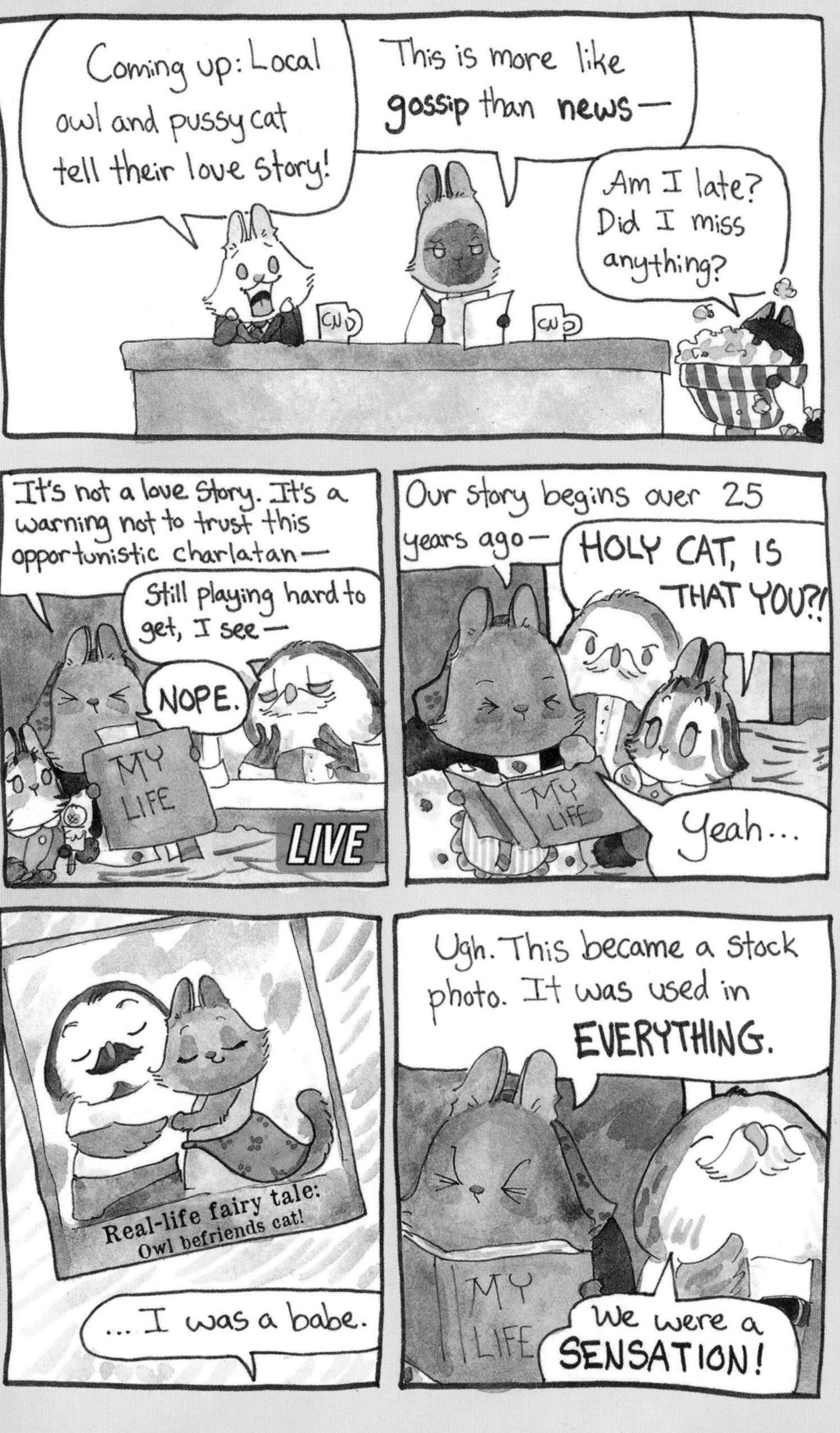
Coming up: Local owl and pussy cat tell their love story!
This is more like gossip than news—
Am I late? Did I miss anything?
It's not a love story. It's a warning not to trust this opportunistic charlatan—
Still playing hard to get, I see—
NOPE.
MY LIFE
LIVE
Our story begins over 25 years ago—
HOLY CAT, IS THAT YOU?!
MY LIFE
Yeah...
Real-life fairy tale: Owl befriends cat!
...I was a babe.
Ugh. This became a stock photo. It was used in EVERYTHING.
MY LIFE
We were a SENSATION!

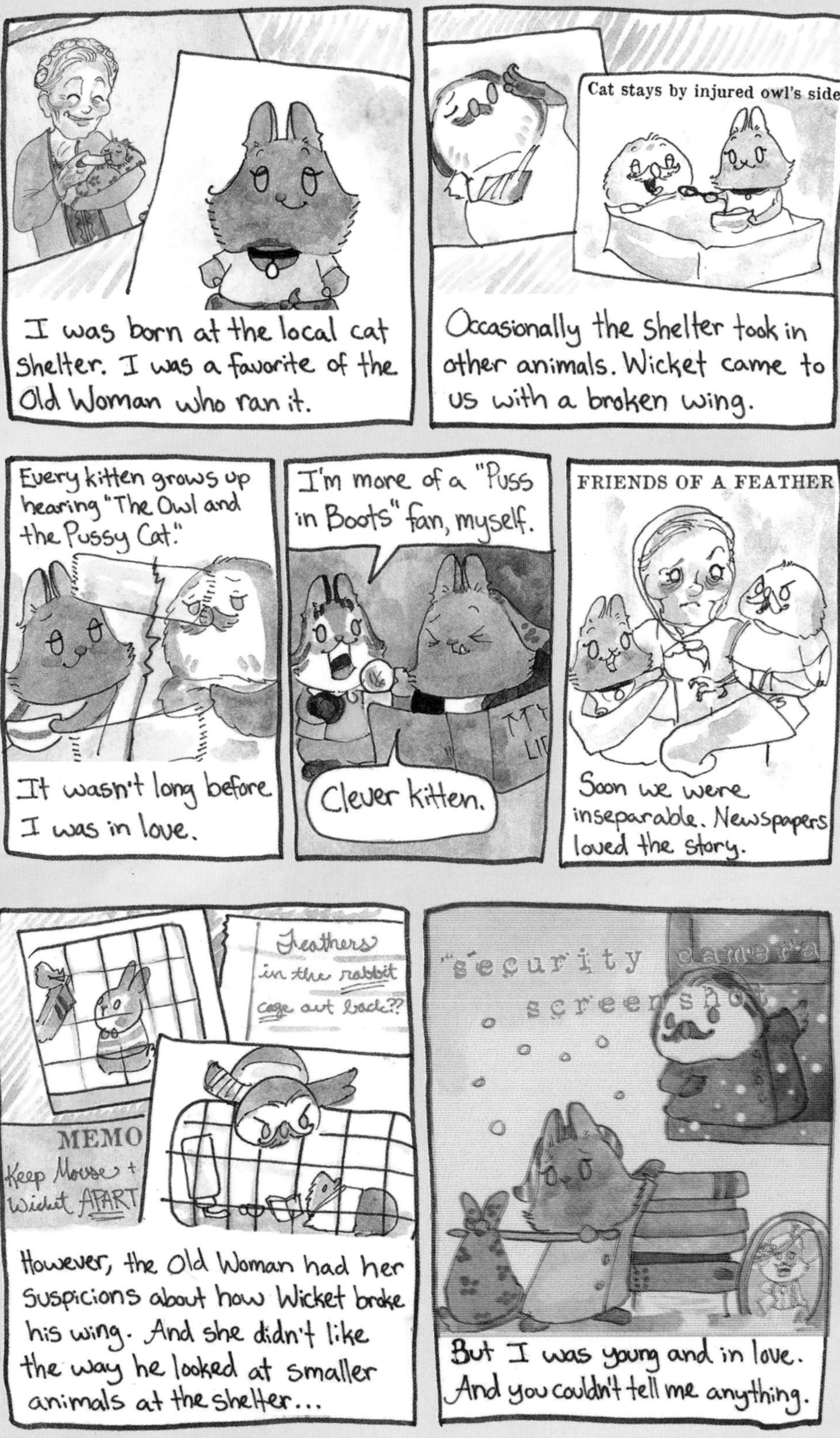
Cat stays by injured owl's side.
I was born at the local cat shelter. I was a favorite of the Old Woman who ran it.
Occasionally the shelter took in other animals. Wicket came to us with a broken wing.
Every kitten grows up hearing "The Owl and the Pussy Cat."
It wasn't long before I was in love.
I'm more of a "Puss in Boots" fan, myself.
Clever kitten.
FRIENDS OF A FEATHER
Soon we were inseparable. Newspapers loved the story.
Feathers in the rabbit cage out back??
MEMO
Keep Mouse + Wicket APART
However, the Old Woman had her suspicions about how Wicket broke his wing. And she didn't like the way he looked at smaller animals at the shelter...
"security camera screenshot"
But I was young and in love. And you couldn't tell me anything.

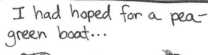

I had hoped for a pea-green boat...

...But all I got was a shopping cart.

That shopping cart was our **CHARIOT!**

Each wheel was determined to squeak the loudest.

So... Does this mean you're single, or...?

Unreal.

It was exciting for a time, but it wasn't long before he bailed.

I had to look for a place for us to live.

For 25 years.

You stranded her?!

Eh, it was for the best. I wanted kittens, he was an owl...

It never would have worked.

My only regret is the Old Woman passed away before I could return to apologize.

Freddie Quinn 85

I always felt bad about that.

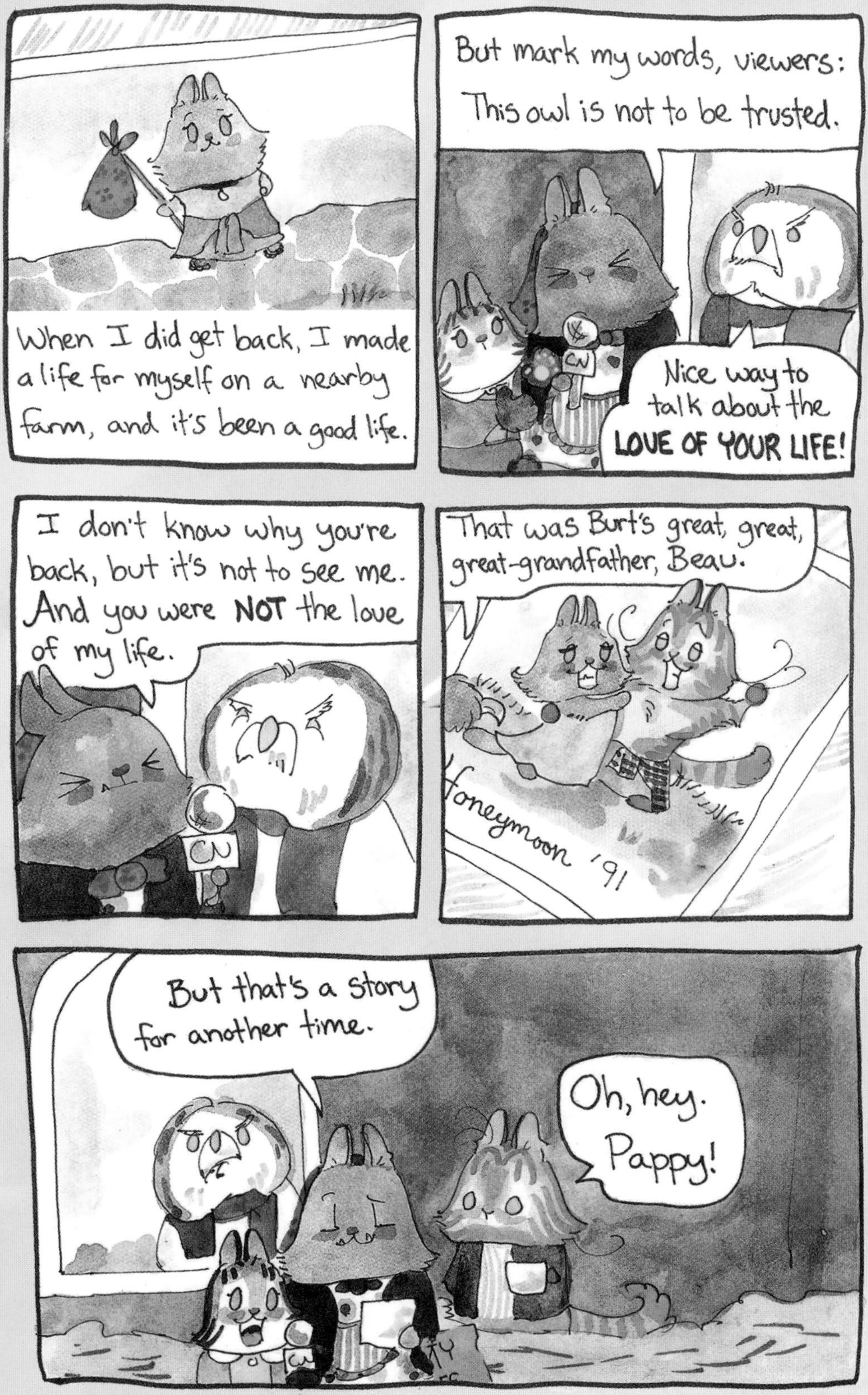

When I did get back, I made a life for myself on a nearby farm, and it's been a good life.
But mark my words, viewers: This owl is not to be trusted.
Nice way to talk about the LOVE OF YOUR LIFE!
I don't know why you're back, but it's not to see me. And you were NOT the love of my life.
That was Burt's great, great, great-grandfather, Beau.
Honeymoon '91
But that's a story for another time.
Oh, hey. Pappy!

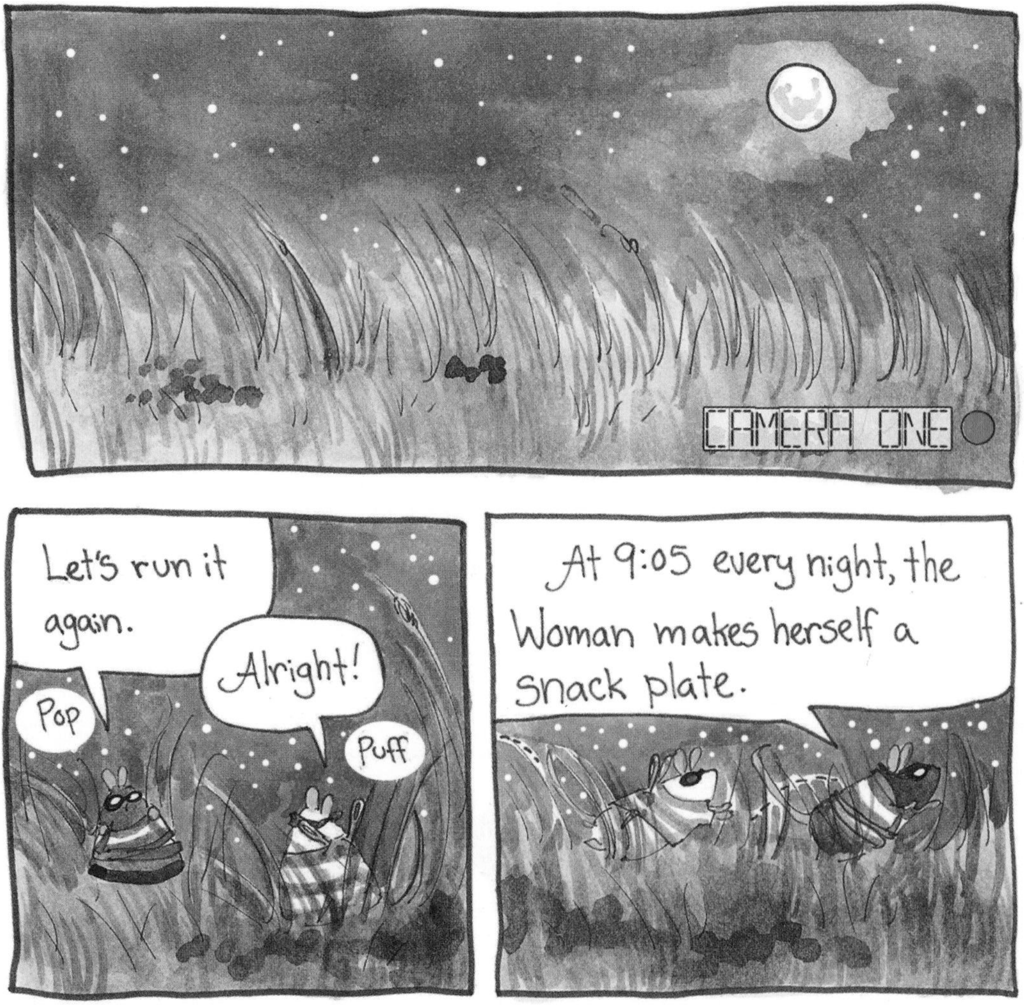
CAMERA ONE
Let's run it again.
Pop
Alright!
Puff
At 9:05 every night, the Woman makes herself a snack plate.

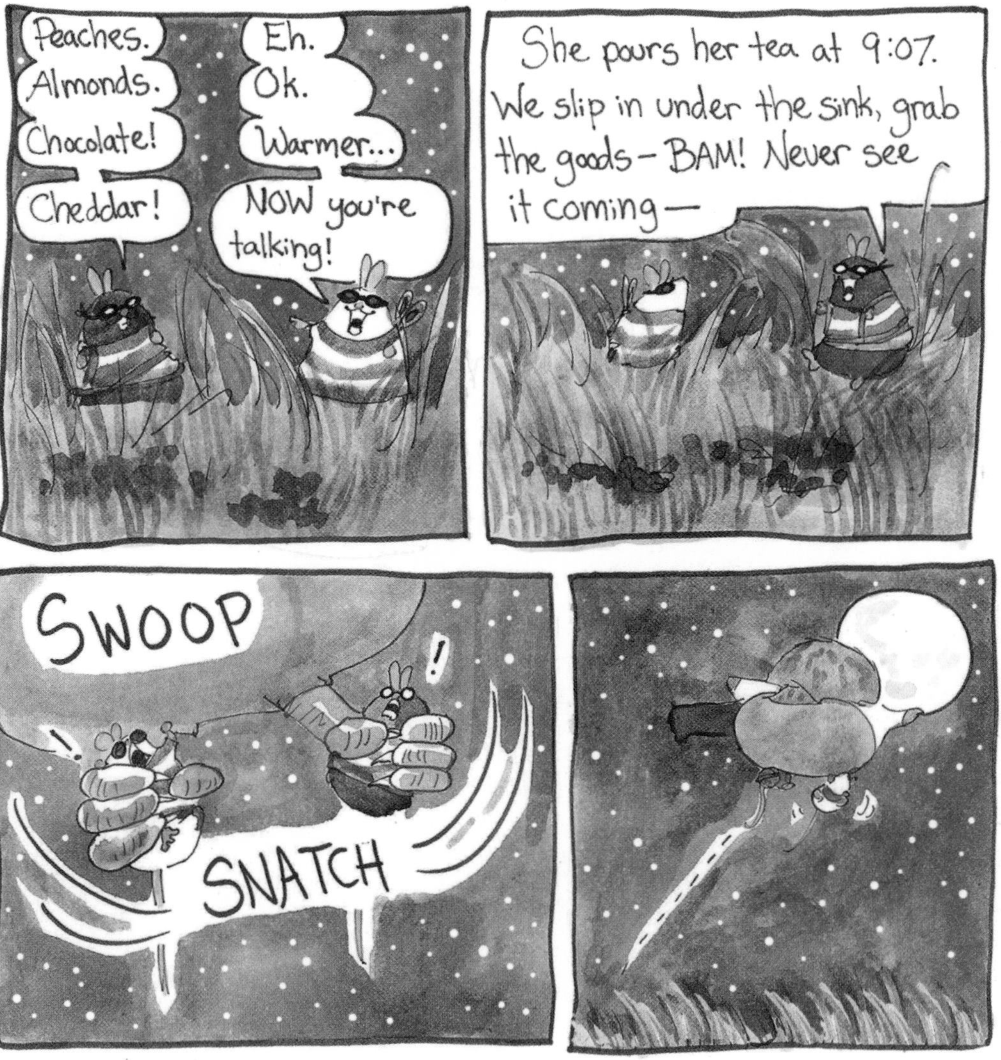
Peaches.
Almonds.
Chocolate!
Cheddar!
Eh.
Ok.
Warmer...
NOW you're talking!
She pours her tea at 9:07. We slip in under the sink, grab the goods—BAM! Never see it coming—
SWOOP
!
!
SNATCH

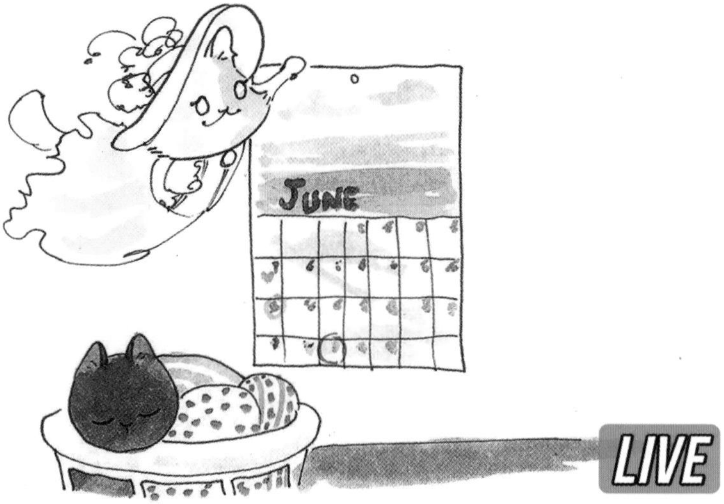
JUNE
LIVE

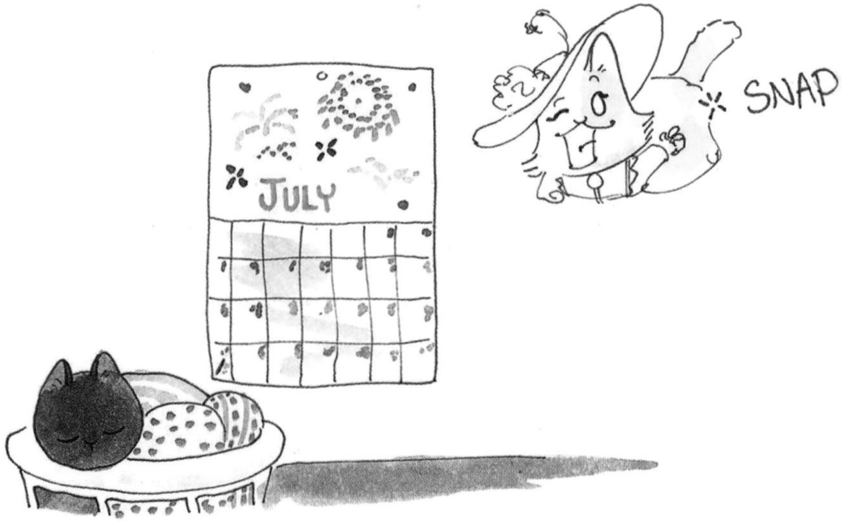
JULY
SNAP

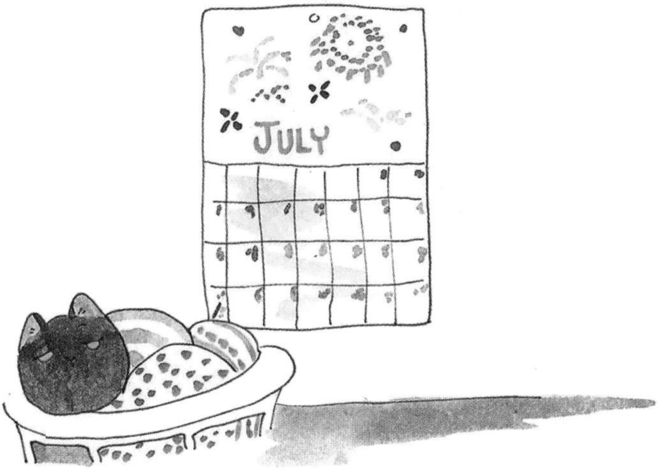
JULY

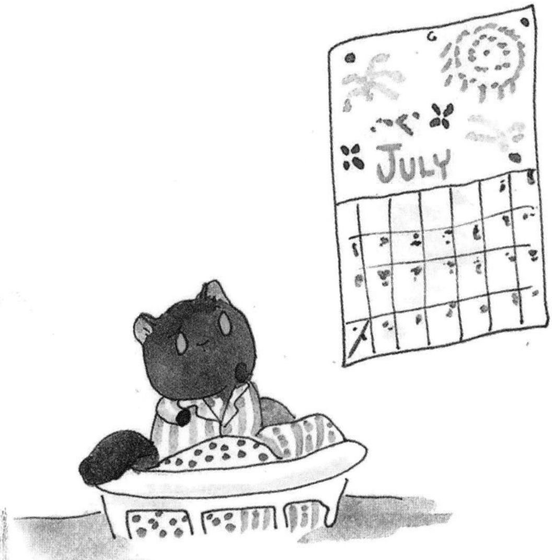
JULY

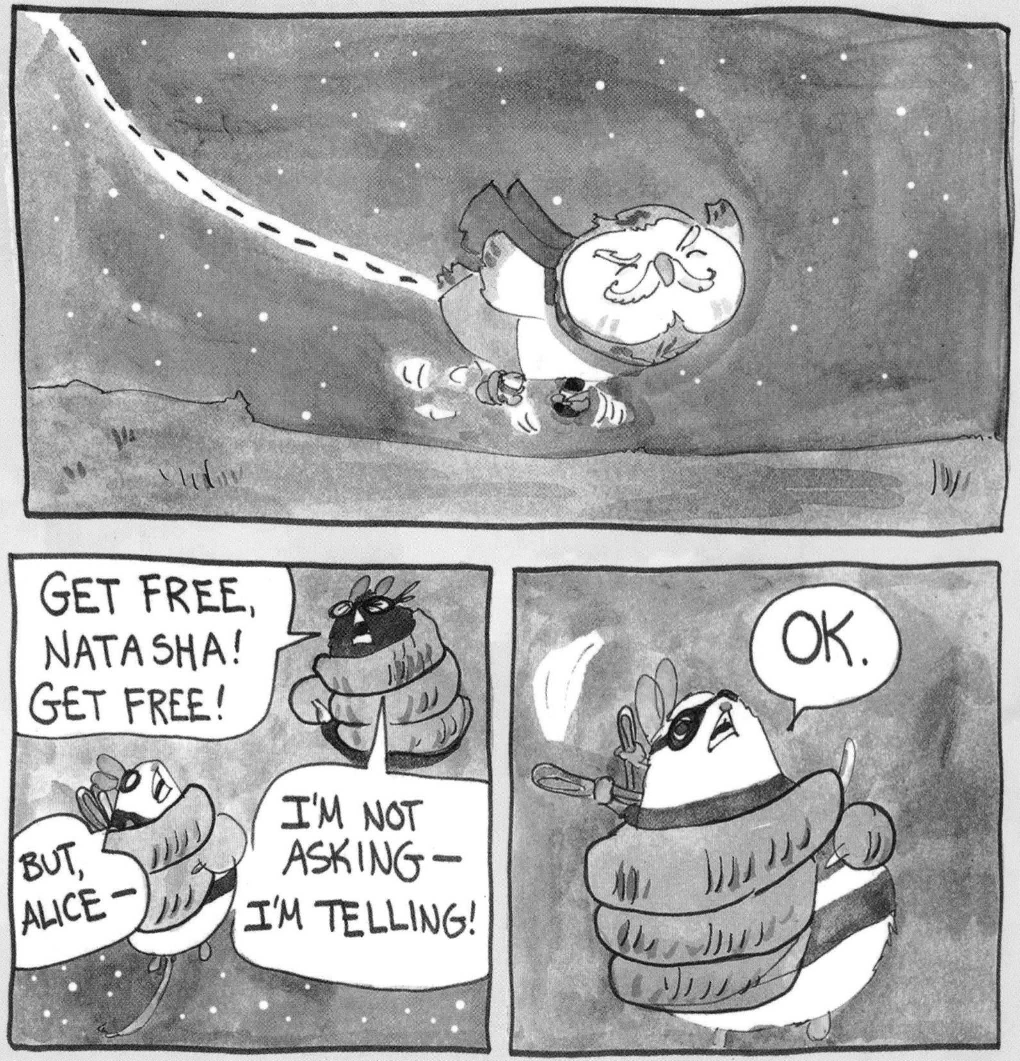
GET FREE, NATASHA! GET FREE!
BUT, ALICE—
I'M NOT ASKING— I'M TELLING!
OK.

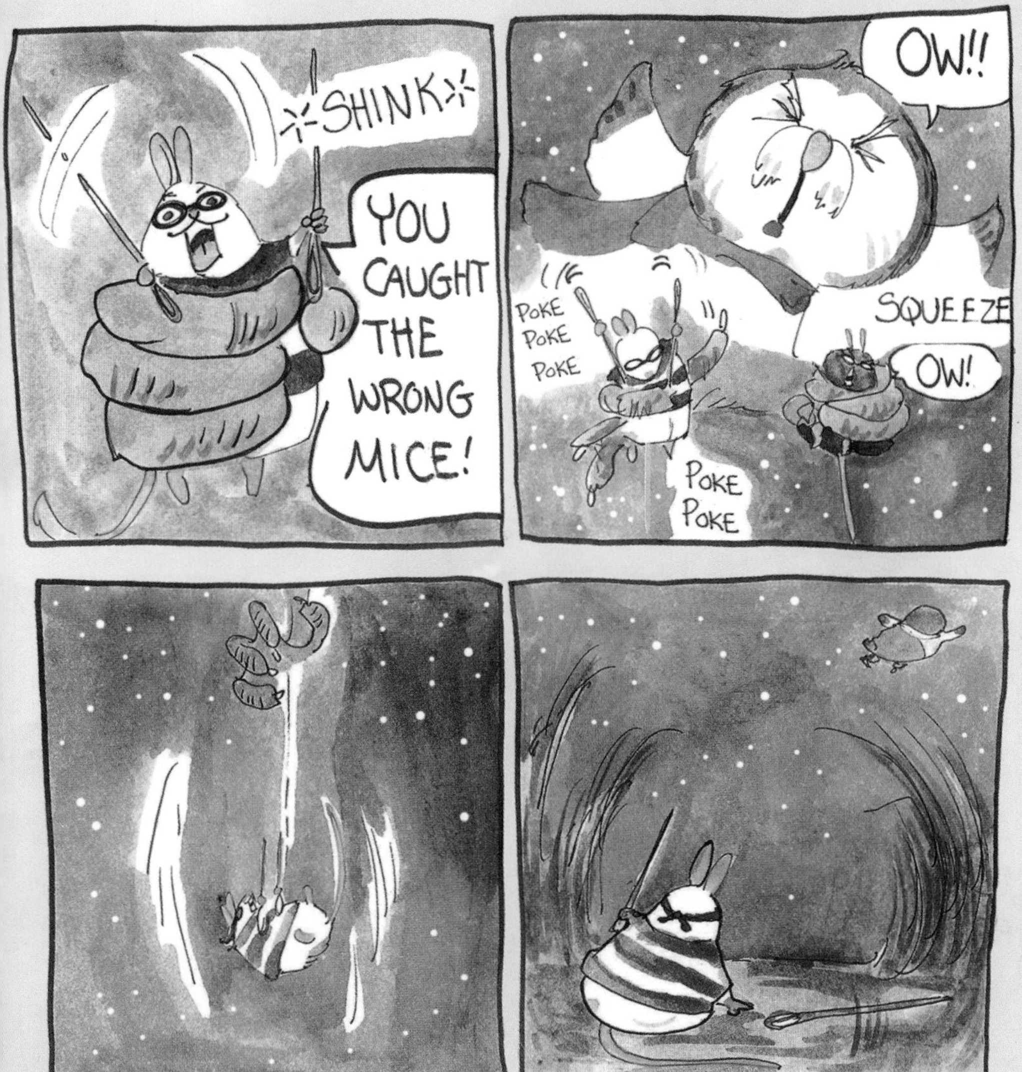
SHINK
YOU CAUGHT THE WRONG MICE!
OW!!
POKE POKE POKE
SQUEEZE
OW!
POKE POKE

Being a mouse is a hard business.
We have one day. The clock starts now!

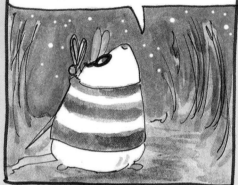

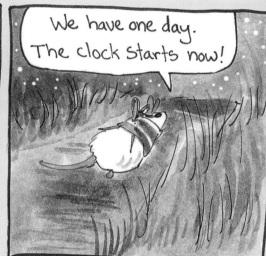

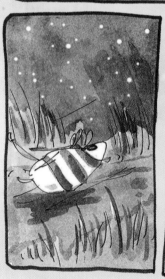

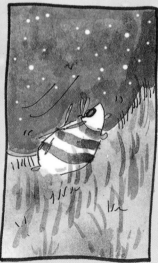

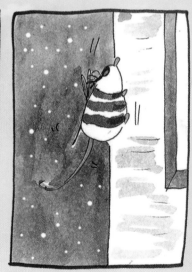

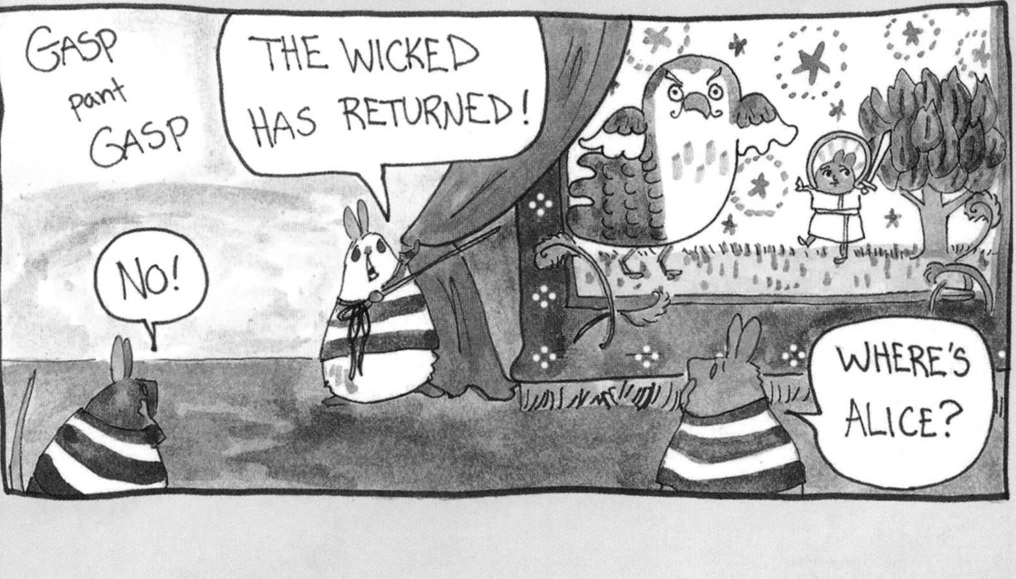
GASP
pant
GASP
THE WICKED
HAS RETURNED!
NO!
WHERE'S
ALICE?

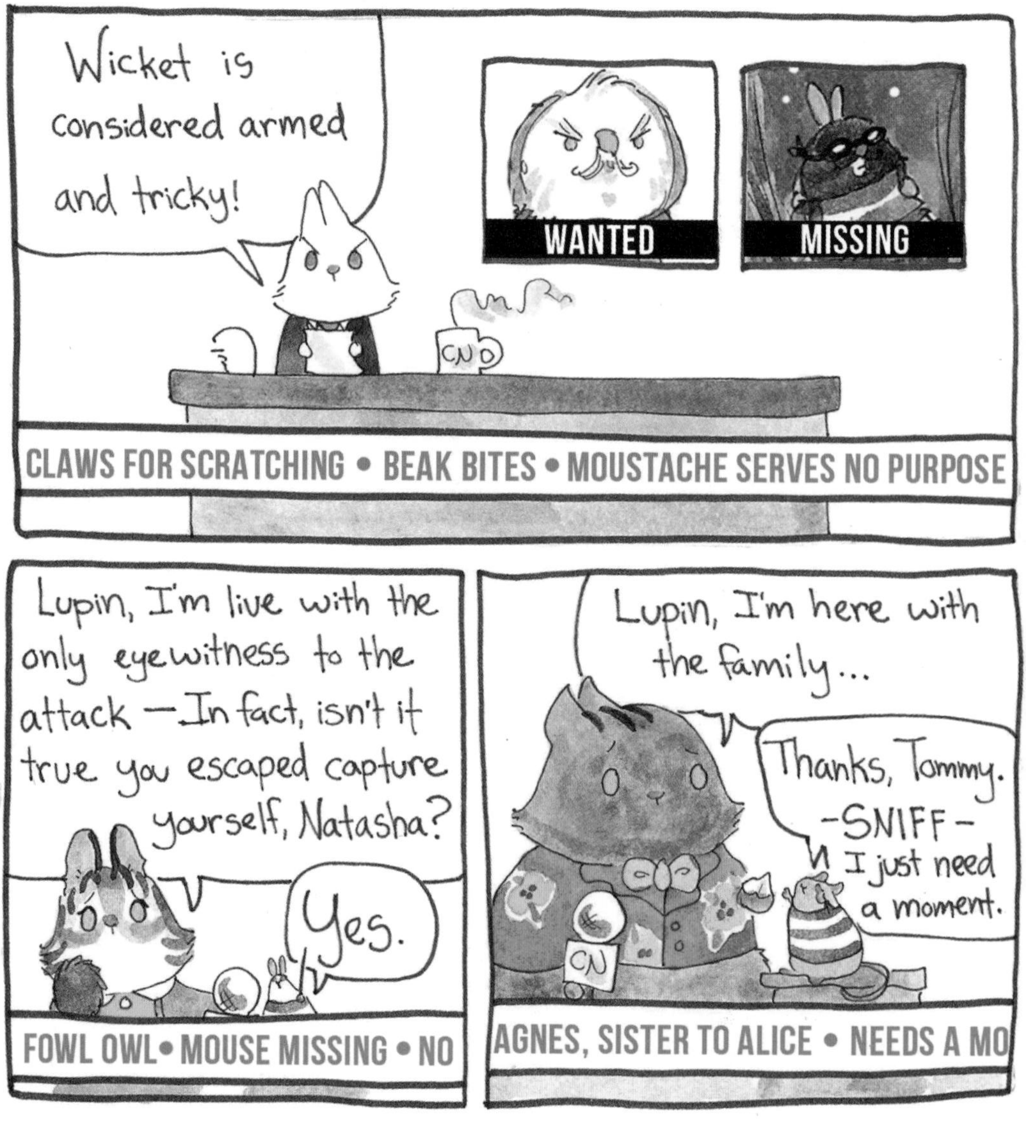
Wicket is considered armed and tricky!
WANTED
MISSING
CN
CLAWS FOR SCRATCHING • BEAK BITES • MOUSTACHE SERVES NO PURPOSE
Lupin, I'm live with the only eyewitness to the attack —In fact, isn't it true you escaped capture yourself, Natasha?
Yes.
FOWL OWL• MOUSE MISSING • NO
Lupin, I'm here with the family...
Thanks, Tommy. -SNIFF- I just need a moment.
CN
AGNES, SISTER TO ALICE • NEEDS A MO

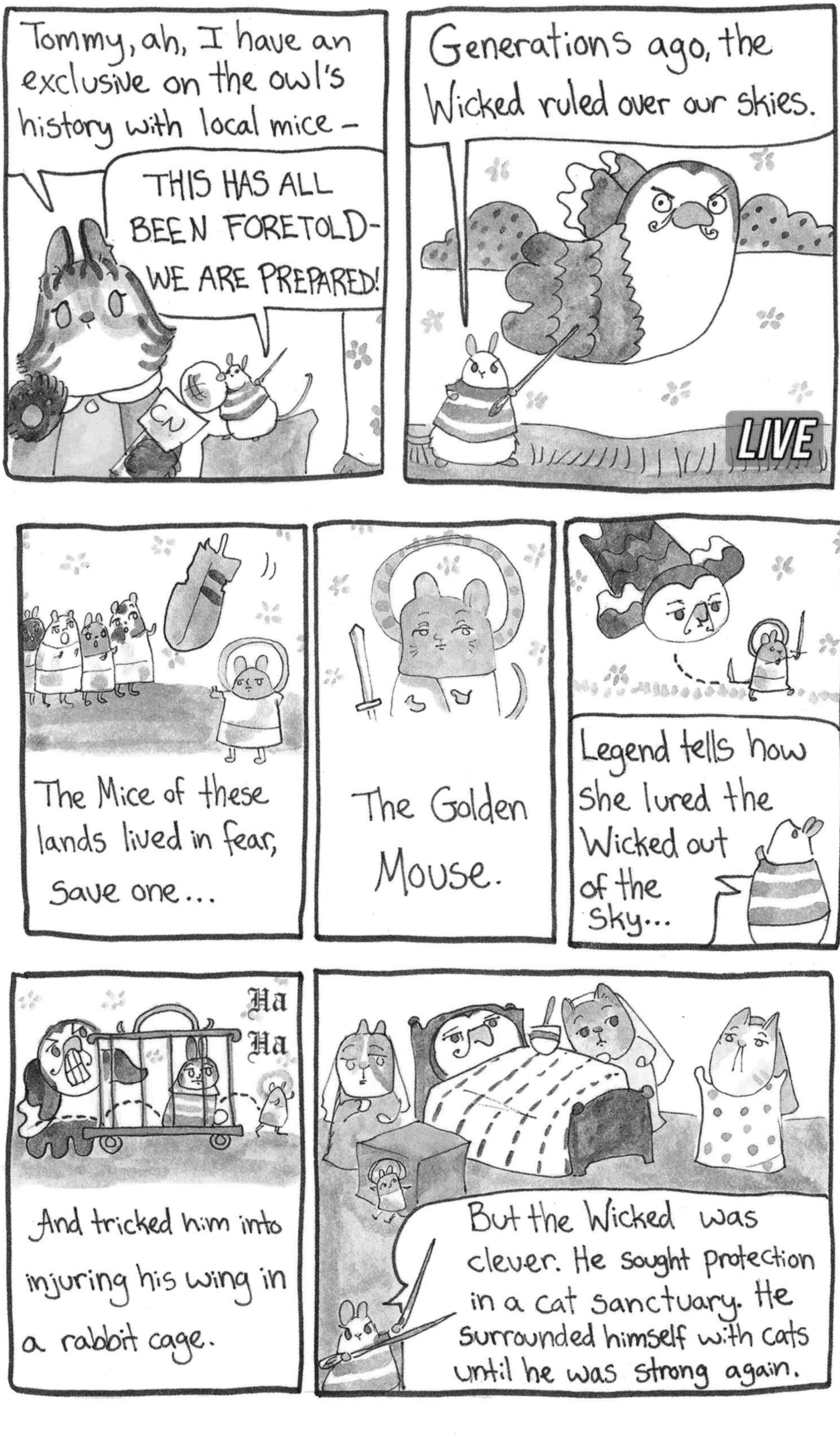
Tommy, ah, I have an exclusive on the owl's history with local mice -
THIS HAS ALL BEEN FORETOLD- WE ARE PREPARED!
CN
Generations ago, the Wicked ruled over our skies.
LIVE
The Mice of these lands lived in fear, save one...
The Golden Mouse.
Legend tells how she lured the Wicked out of the sky...
Ha Ha
And tricked him into injuring his wing in a rabbit cage.
But the Wicked was clever. He sought protection in a cat sanctuary. He surrounded himself with cats until he was strong again.

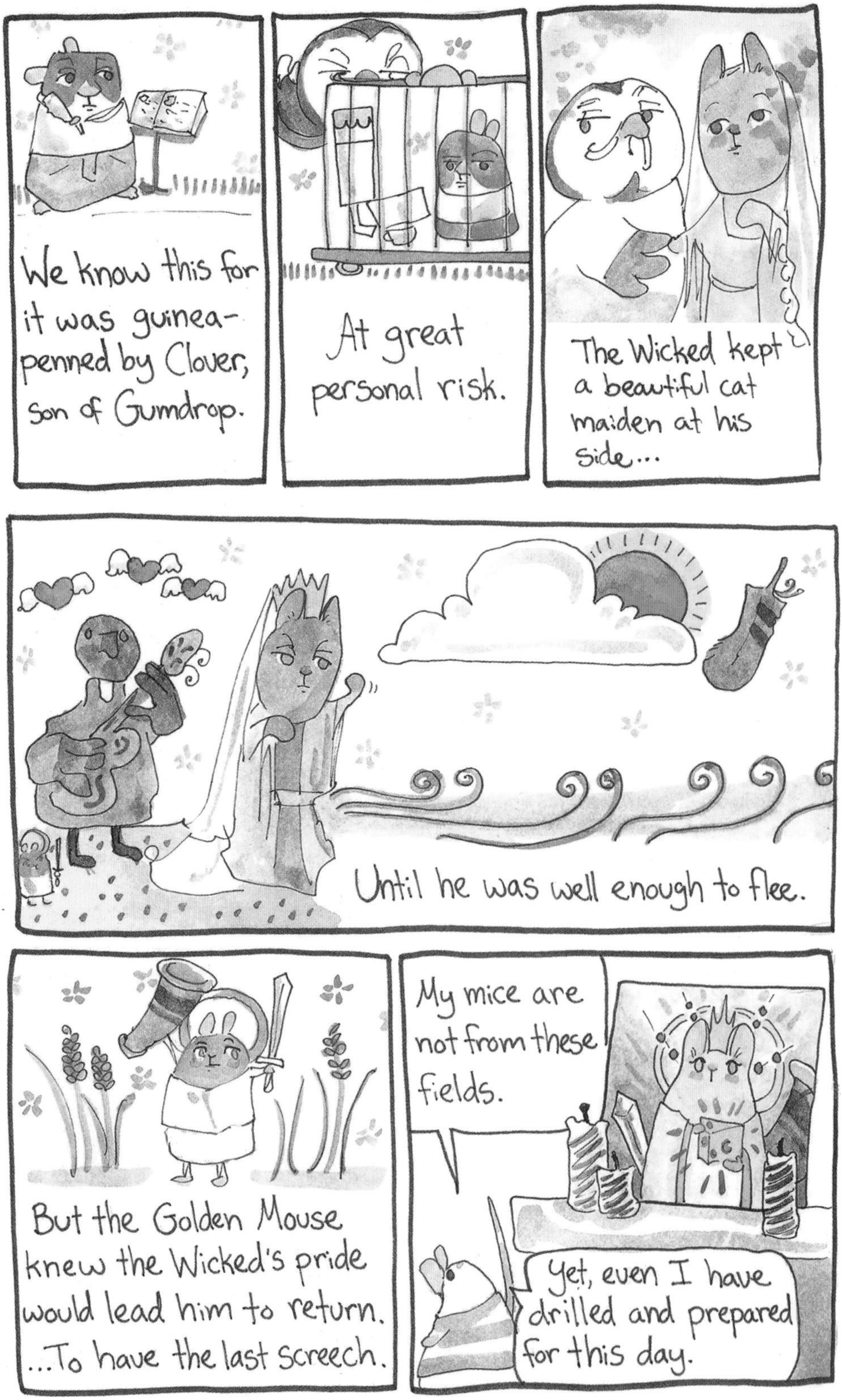
We know this for it was guinea-penned by Clover, son of Gumdrop.
At great personal risk.
The Wicked kept a beautiful cat maiden at his side...
Until he was well enough to flee.
But the Golden Mouse knew the Wicked's pride would lead him to return. ...To have the last screech.
My mice are not from these fields.
Yet, even I have drilled and prepared for this day.

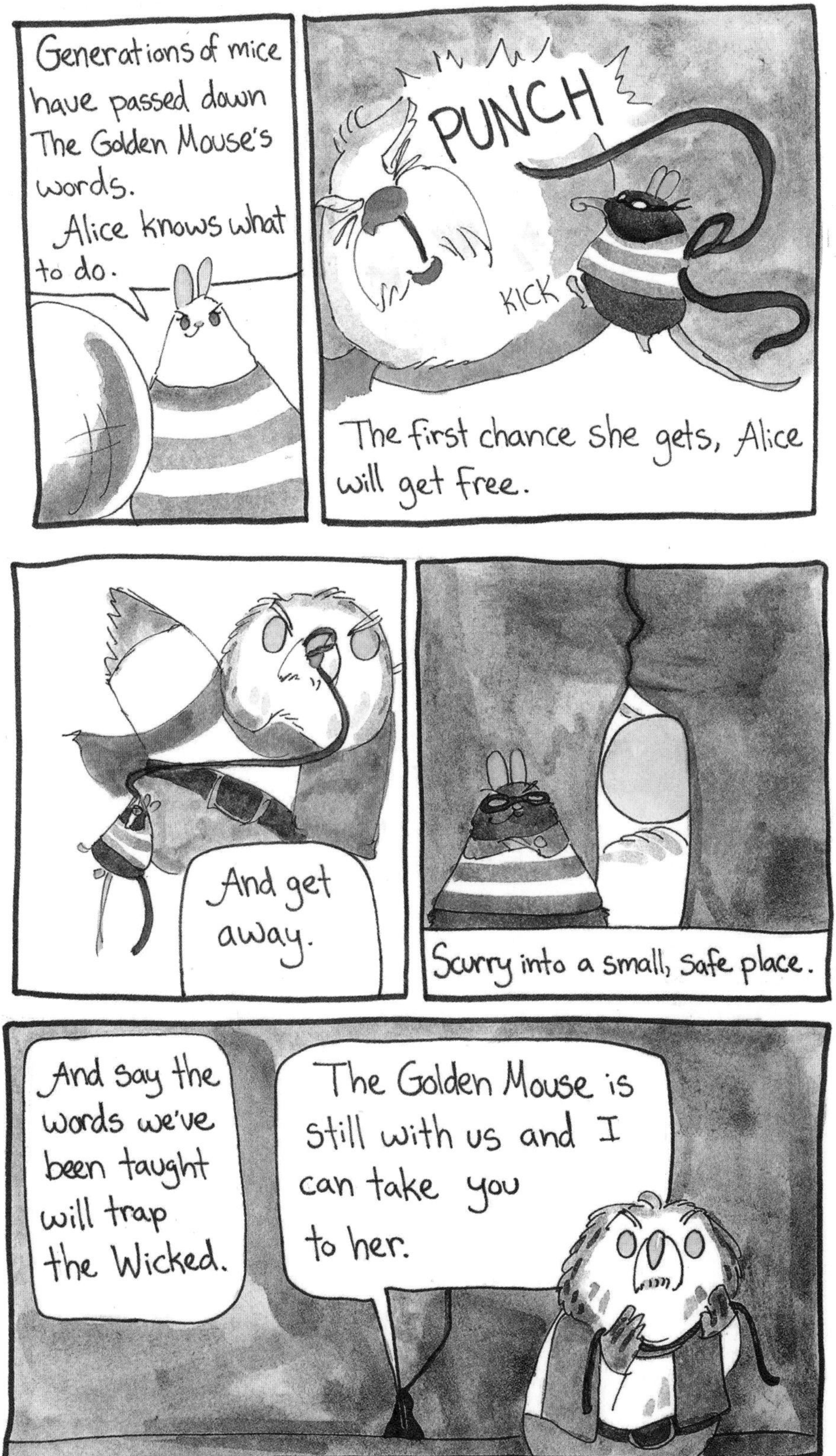

Generations of mice have passed down The Golden Mouse's words.
Alice knows what to do.
PUNCH
KICK
The first chance she gets, Alice will get free.
And get away.
Scurry into a small, safe place.
And say the words we've been taught will trap the Wicked.
The Golden Mouse is still with us and I can take you to her.

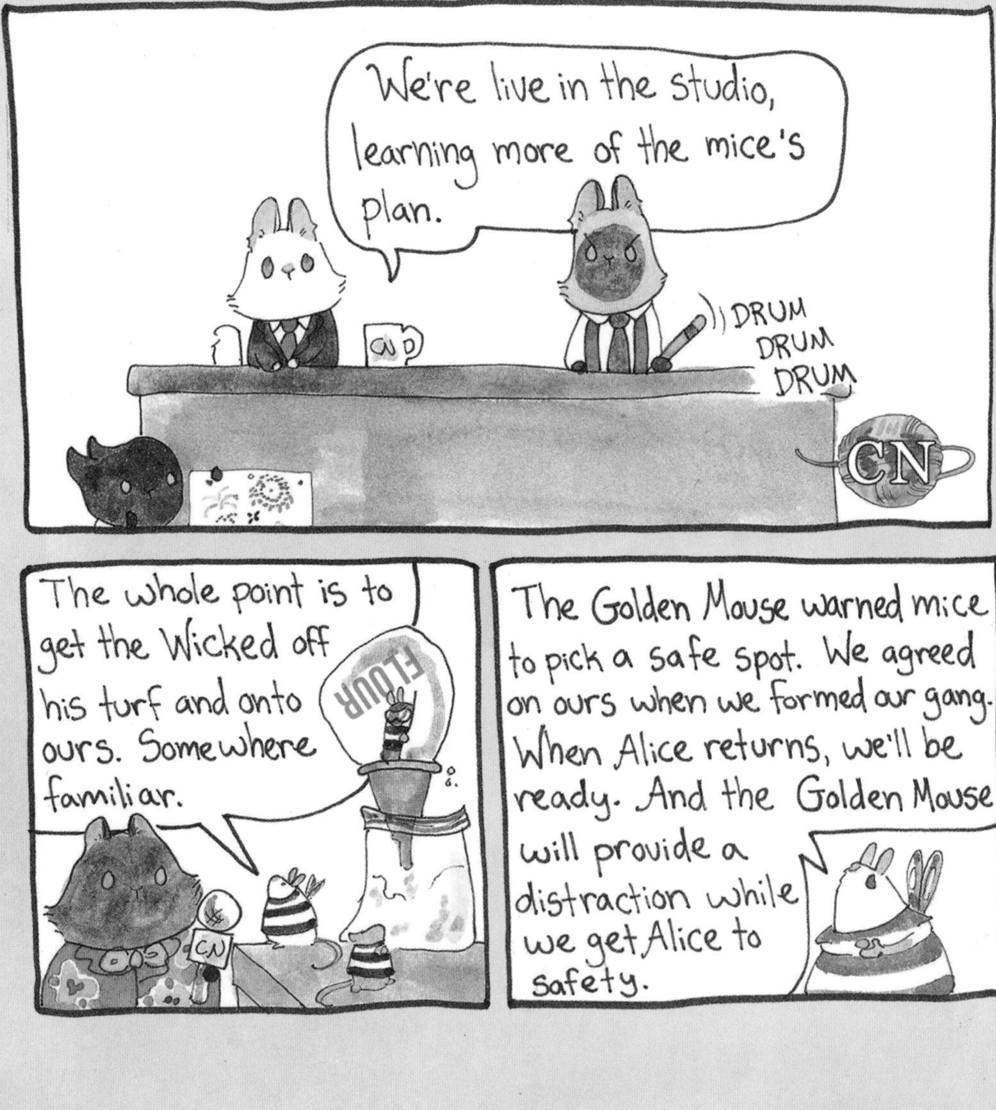
We're live in the studio, learning more of the mice's plan.
DRUM DRUM DRUM
CN
The whole point is to get the Wicked off his turf and onto ours. Somewhere familiar.
FLOUR
CN
The Golden Mouse warned mice to pick a safe spot. We agreed on ours when we formed our gang. When Alice returns, we'll be ready. And the Golden Mouse will provide a distraction while we get Alice to safety.

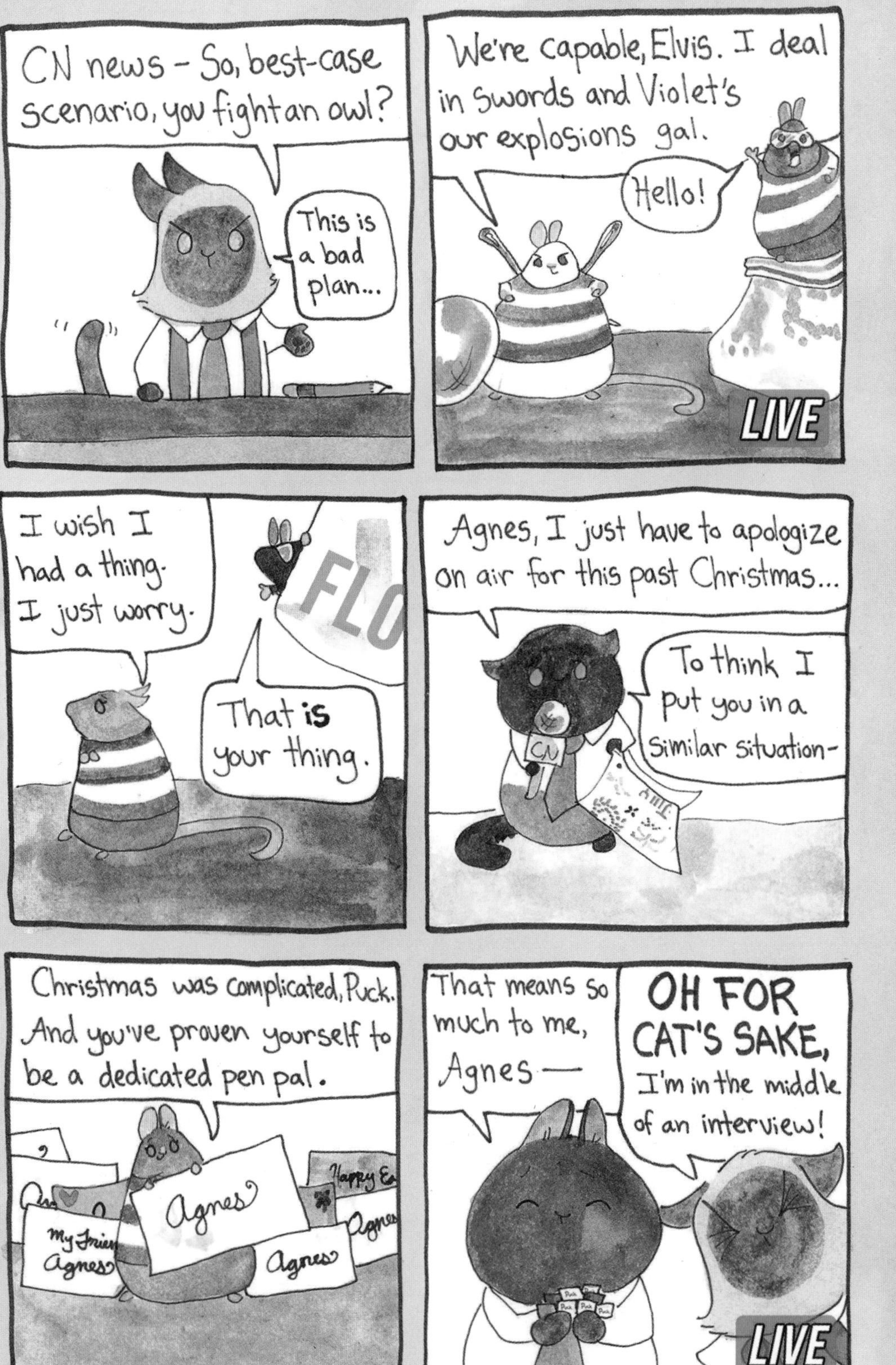
CN news - So, best-case scenario, you fight an owl?
This is a bad plan...
We're capable, Elvis. I deal in swords and Violet's our explosions gal.
Hello!
LIVE
I wish I had a thing. I just worry.
FLO
That is your thing.
Agnes, I just have to apologize on air for this past Christmas...
To think I put you in a similar situation-
CN
Christmas was complicated, Puck. And you've proven yourself to be a dedicated pen pal.
Agnes
My Friend Agnes
Agnes
Happy
That means so much to me, Agnes—
OH FOR CAT'S SAKE, I'm in the middle of an interview!
LIVE

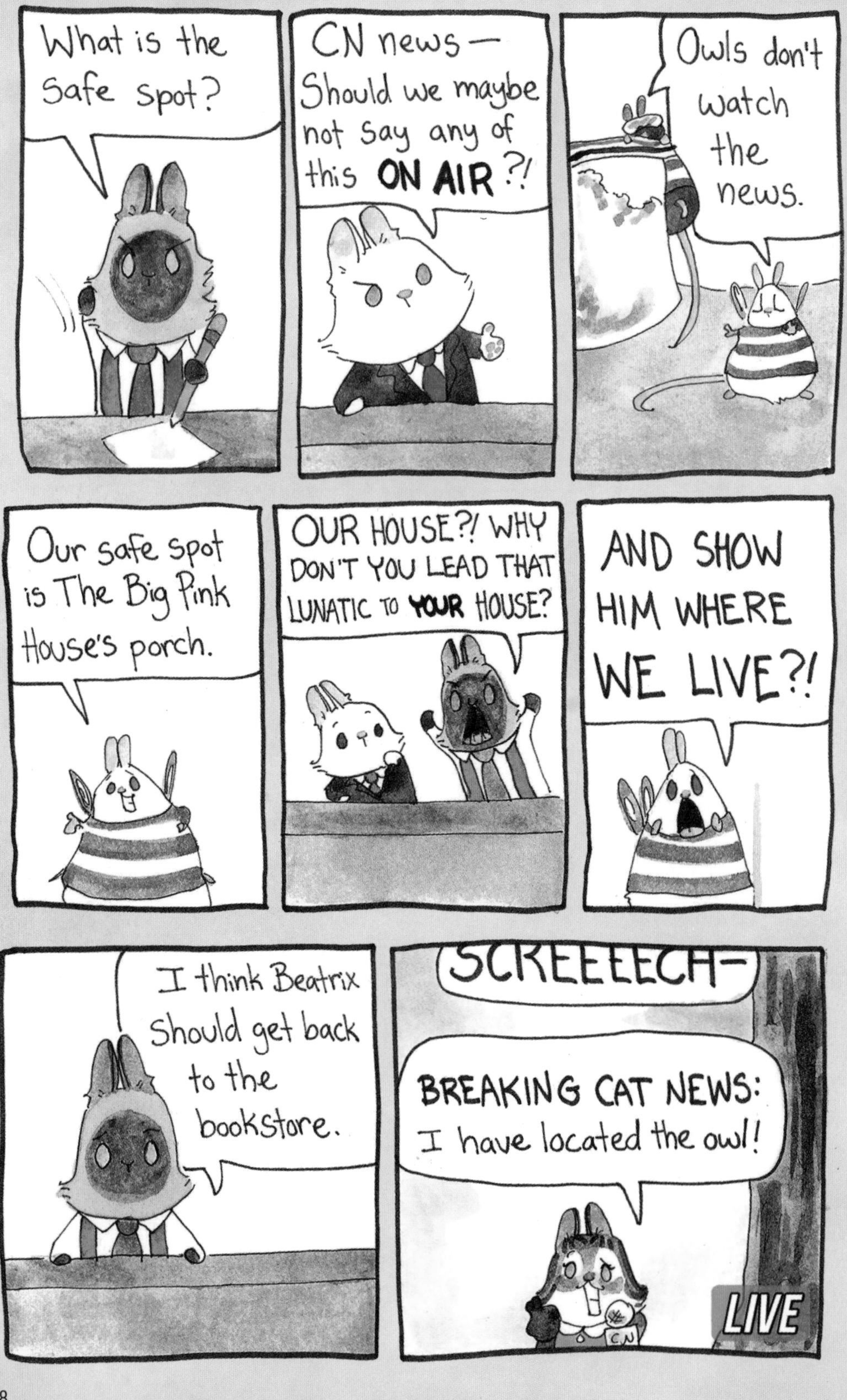
What is the Safe spot?
CN news— Should we maybe not say any of this **ON AIR**?!
Owls don't watch the news.
Our safe spot is The Big Pink House's porch.
OUR HOUSE?! WHY DON'T YOU LEAD THAT LUNATIC TO **YOUR** HOUSE?
AND SHOW HIM WHERE WE LIVE?!
I think Beatrix Should get back to the bookstore.
SCREEEECH—
BREAKING CAT NEWS: I have located the owl!
LIVE
CN

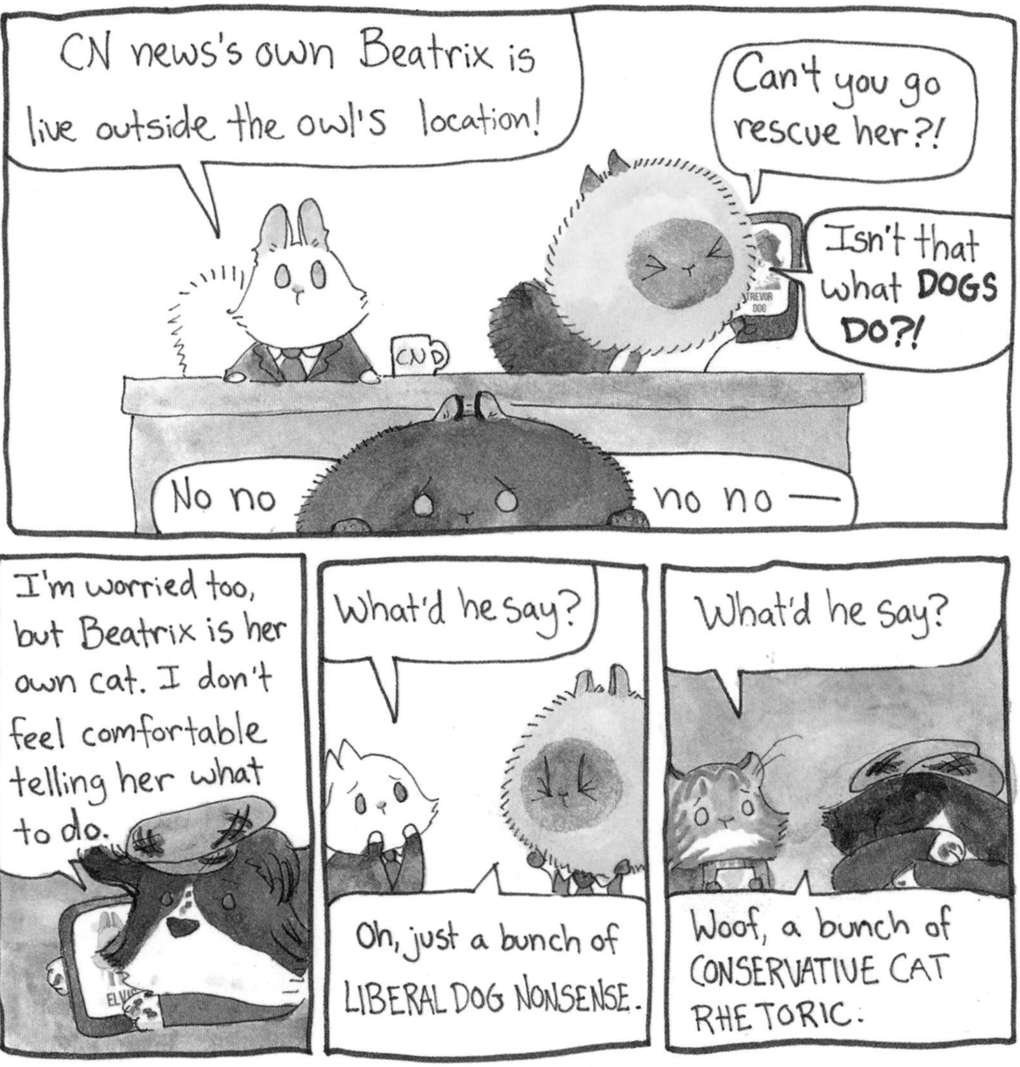
CN news's own Beatrix is live outside the owl's location!
Can't you go rescue her?!
Isn't that what **DOGS DO?!**
TREVOR DOG
CND
No no
no no —
I'm worried too, but Beatrix is her own cat. I don't feel comfortable telling her what to do.
What'd he say?
Oh, just a bunch of LIBERAL DOG NONSENSE.
What'd he say?
Woof, a bunch of CONSERVATIVE CAT RHETORIC.

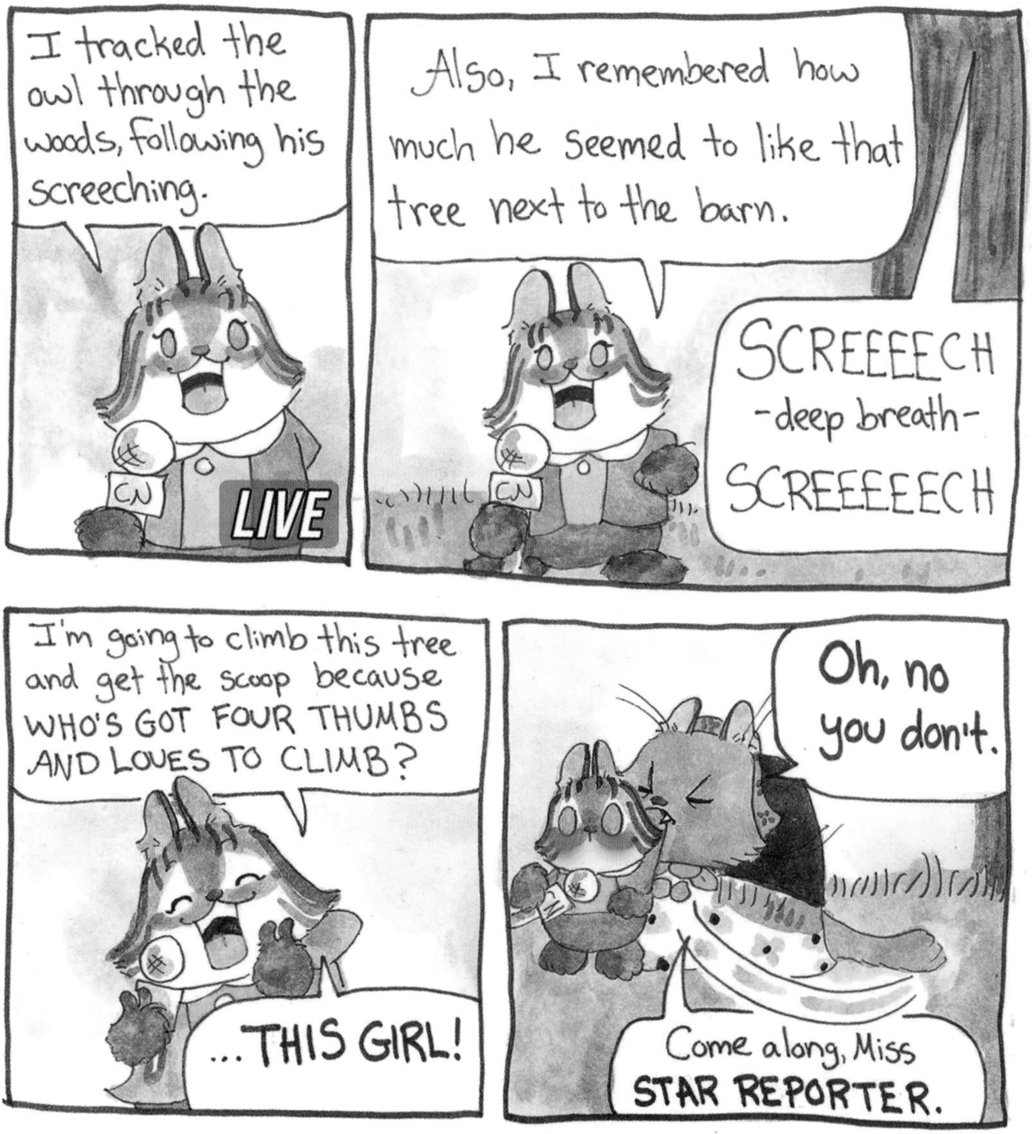
I tracked the owl through the woods, following his screeching.
CN
LIVE
Also, I remembered how much he seemed to like that tree next to the barn.
CN
SCREEEECH
-deep breath-
SCREEEEECH
I'm going to climb this tree and get the scoop because WHO'S GOT FOUR THUMBS AND LOVES TO CLIMB?
...THIS GIRL!
Oh, no you don't.
Come along, Miss STAR REPORTER.

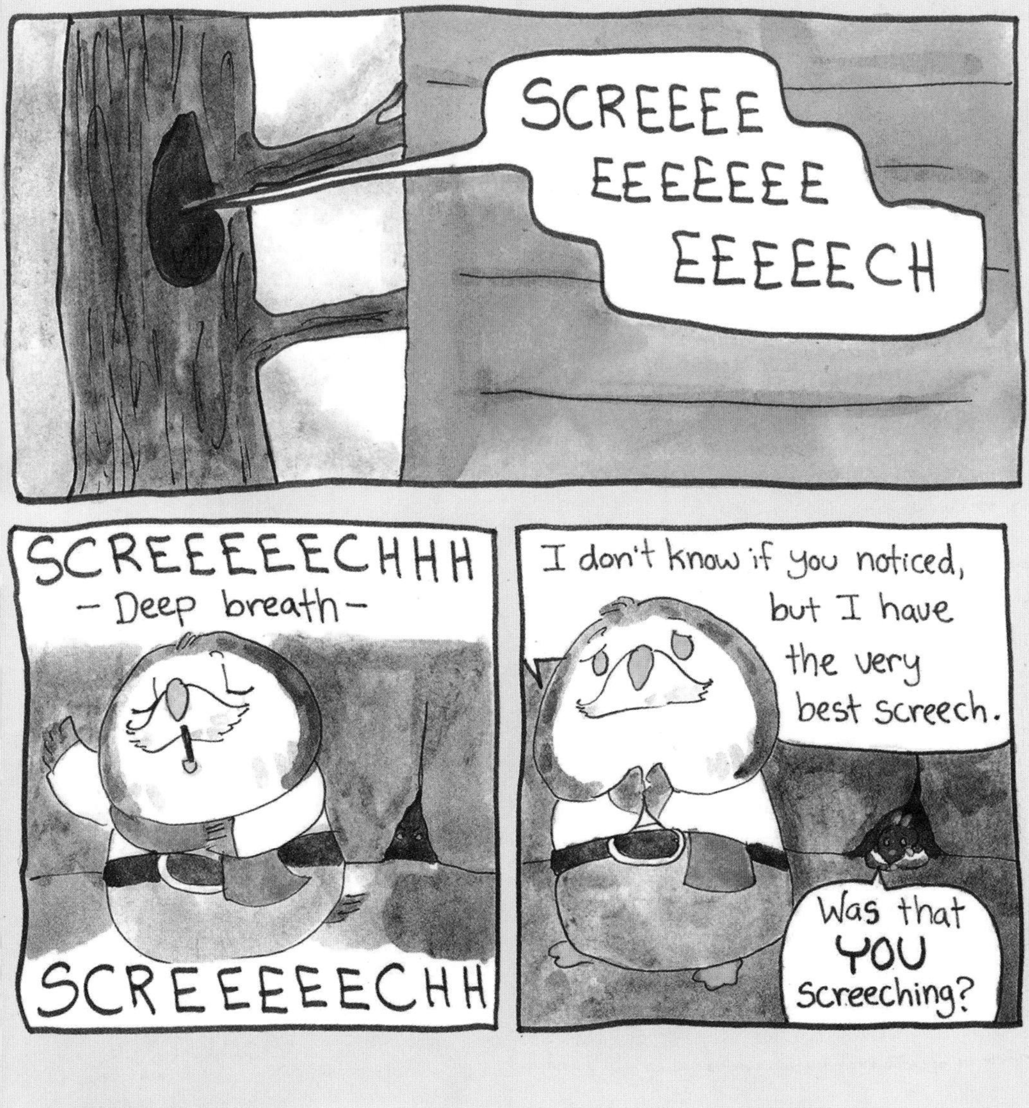
SCREEEE EEEEEEE EEEEECH
SCREEEEEECHHH
- Deep breath -
SCREEEEEECHH
I don't know if you noticed, but I have the very best screech.
Was that YOU screeching?

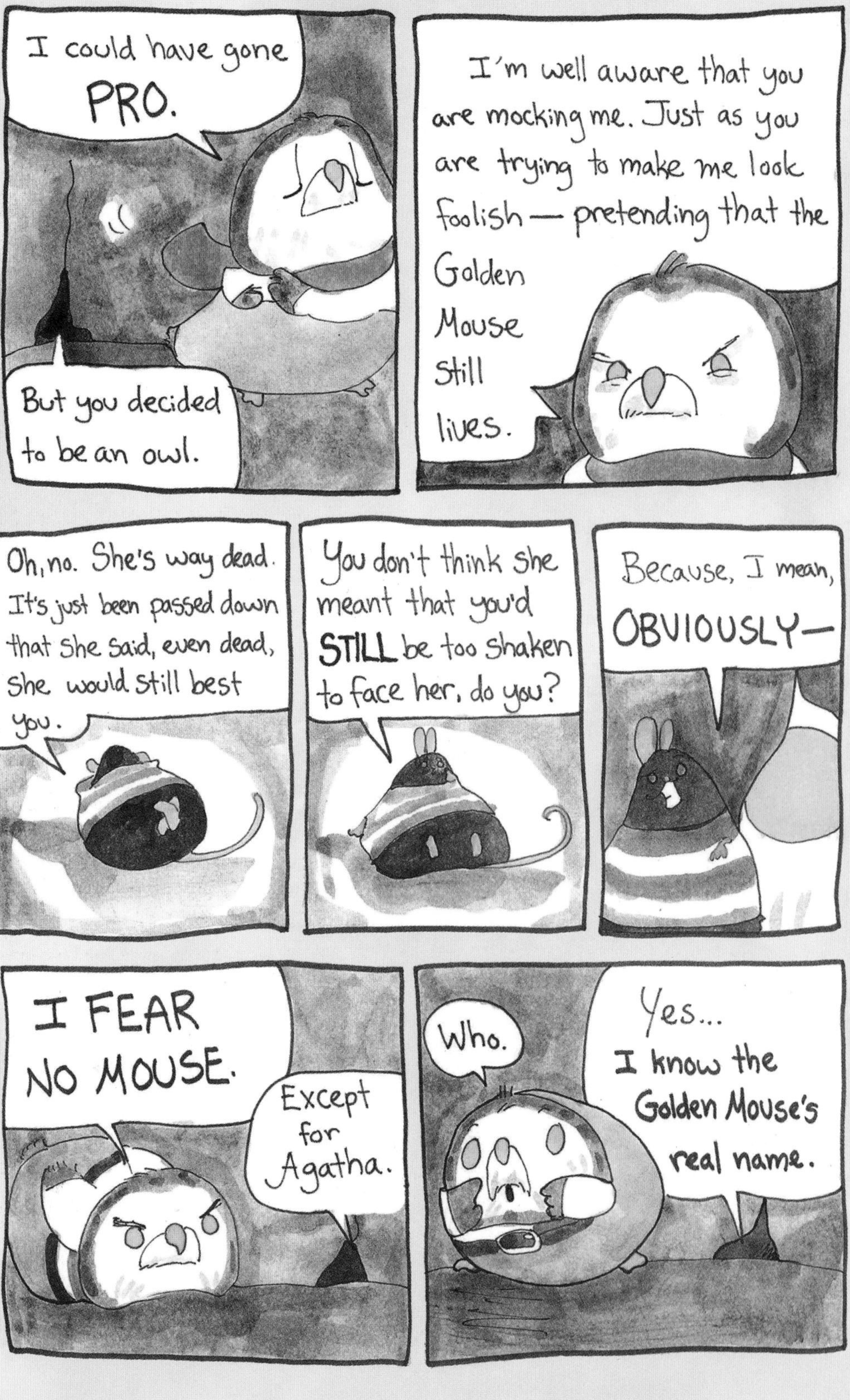
I could have gone PRO.
But you decided to be an owl.
I'm well aware that you are mocking me. Just as you are trying to make me look foolish — pretending that the Golden Mouse still lives.
Oh, no. She's way dead. It's just been passed down that she said, even dead, she would still best you.
You don't think she meant that you'd STILL be too shaken to face her, do you?
Because, I mean, OBVIOUSLY—
I FEAR NO MOUSE.
Except for Agatha.
Who.
Yes... I know the Golden Mouse's real name.

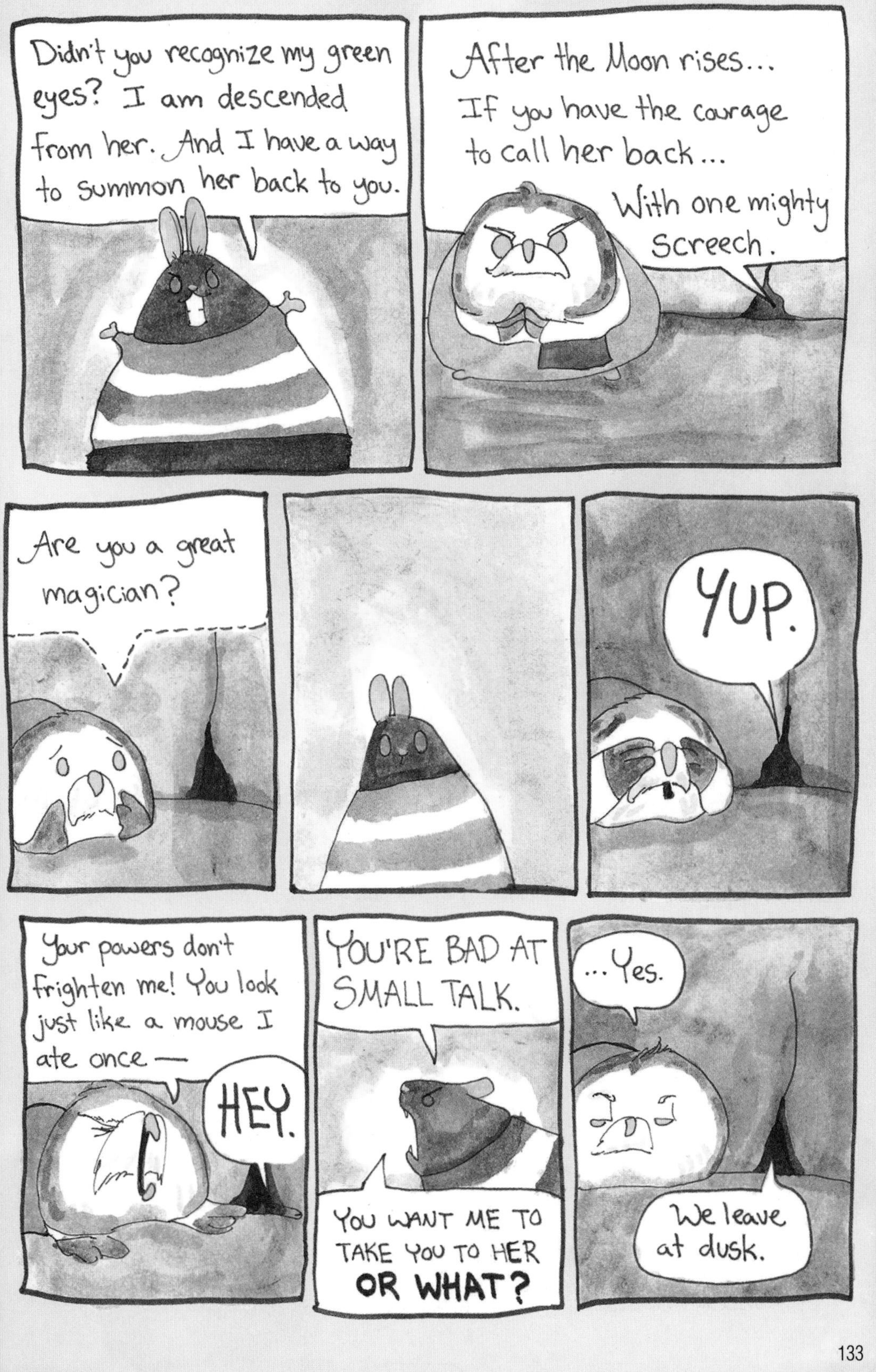
Didn't you recognize my green eyes? I am descended from her. And I have a way to summon her back to you.
After the Moon rises... If you have the courage to call her back...
With one mighty Screech.
Are you a great magician?
YUP.
Your powers don't frighten me! You look just like a mouse I ate once —
HEY.
YOU'RE BAD AT SMALL TALK.
YOU WANT ME TO TAKE YOU TO HER OR WHAT?
...Yes.
We leave at dusk.

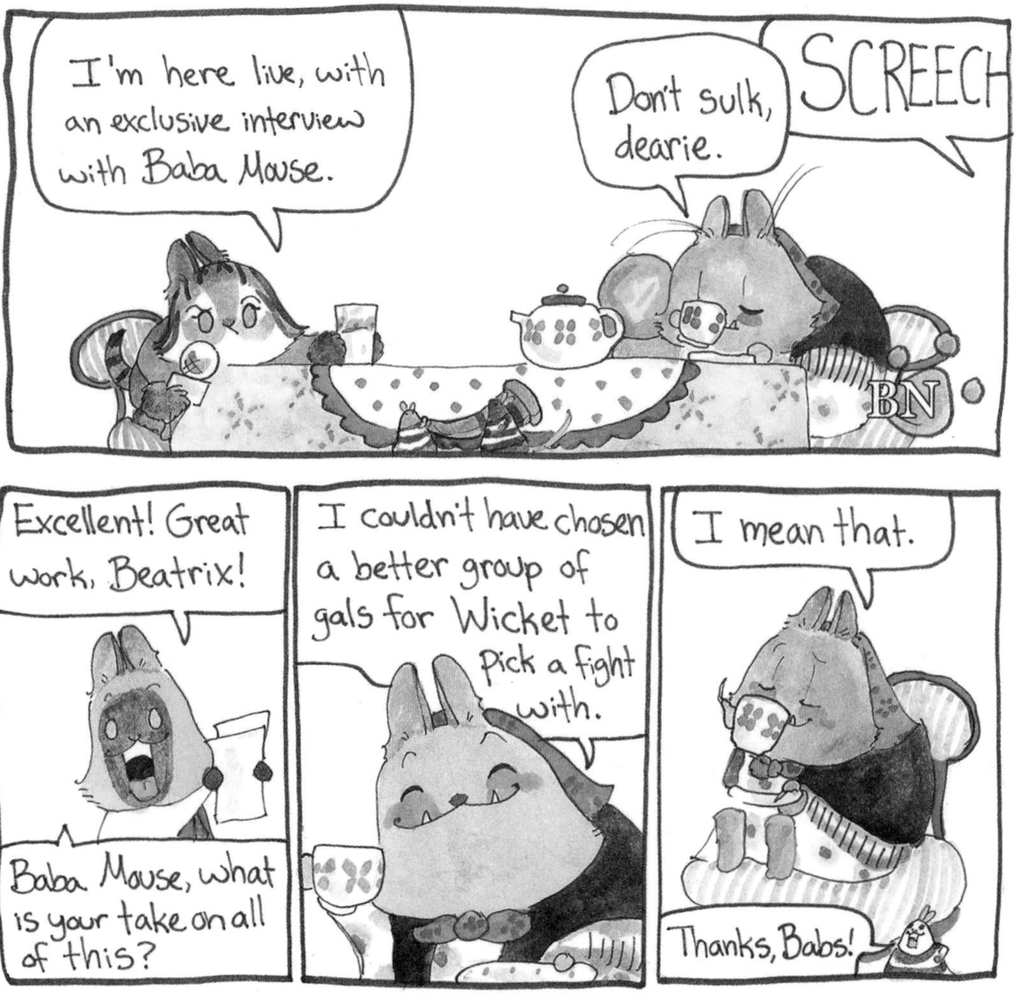
I'm here live, with an exclusive interview with Baba Mouse.
Don't sulk, dearie.
SCREECH
BN
Excellent! Great work, Beatrix!
Baba Mouse, what is your take on all of this?
I couldn't have chosen a better group of gals for Wicket to pick a fight with.
I mean that.
Thanks, Babs!

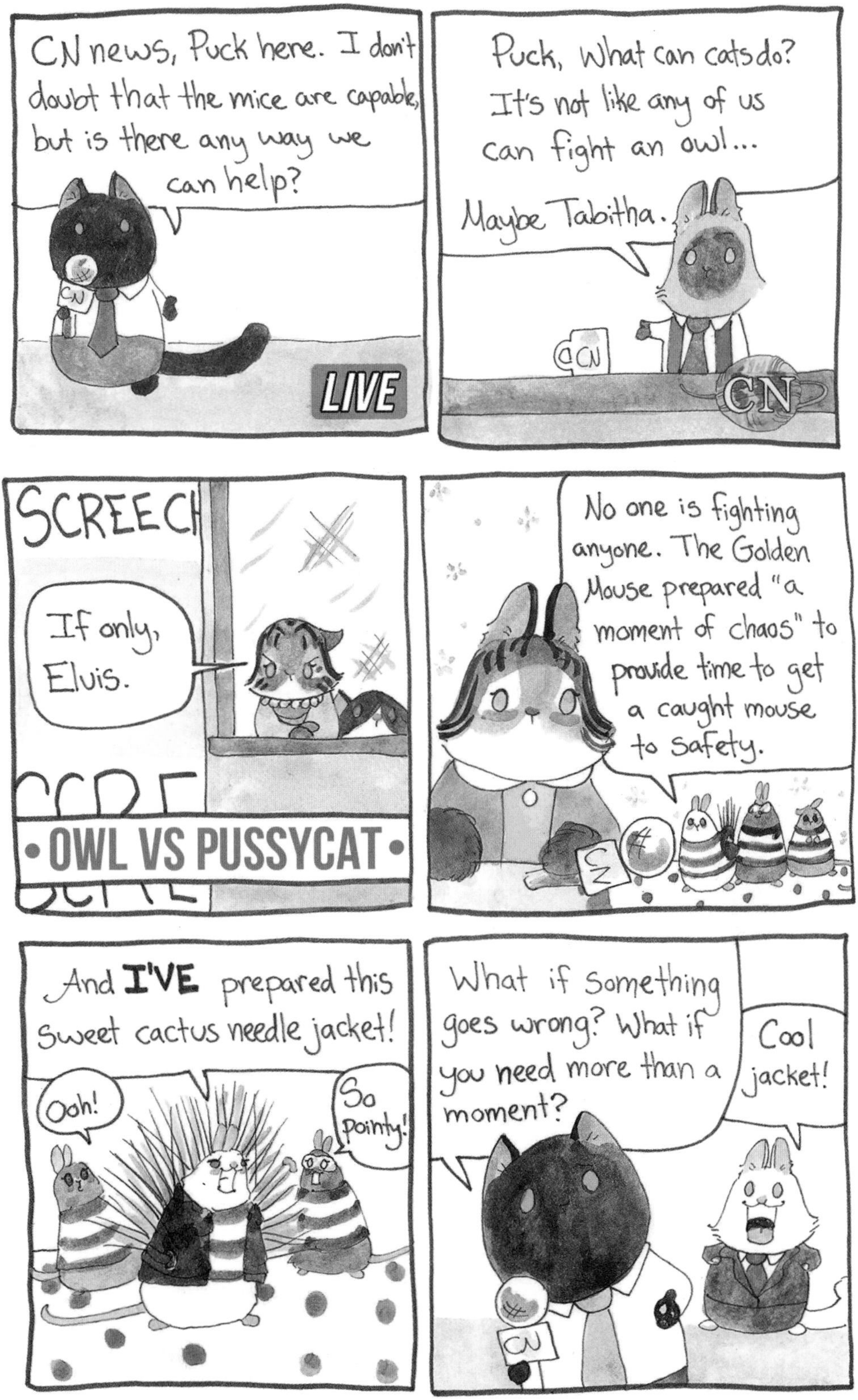
CN news, Puck here. I don't doubt that the mice are capable, but is there any way we can help?
LIVE
Puck, What can cats do? It's not like any of us can fight an owl...
Maybe Tabitha.
CN
SCREECH
If only, Elvis.
• OWL VS PUSSYCAT •
No one is fighting anyone. The Golden Mouse prepared "a moment of chaos" to provide time to get a caught mouse to safety.
And I'VE prepared this sweet cactus needle jacket!
Ooh!
So pointy!
What if something goes wrong? What if you need more than a moment?
Cool jacket!

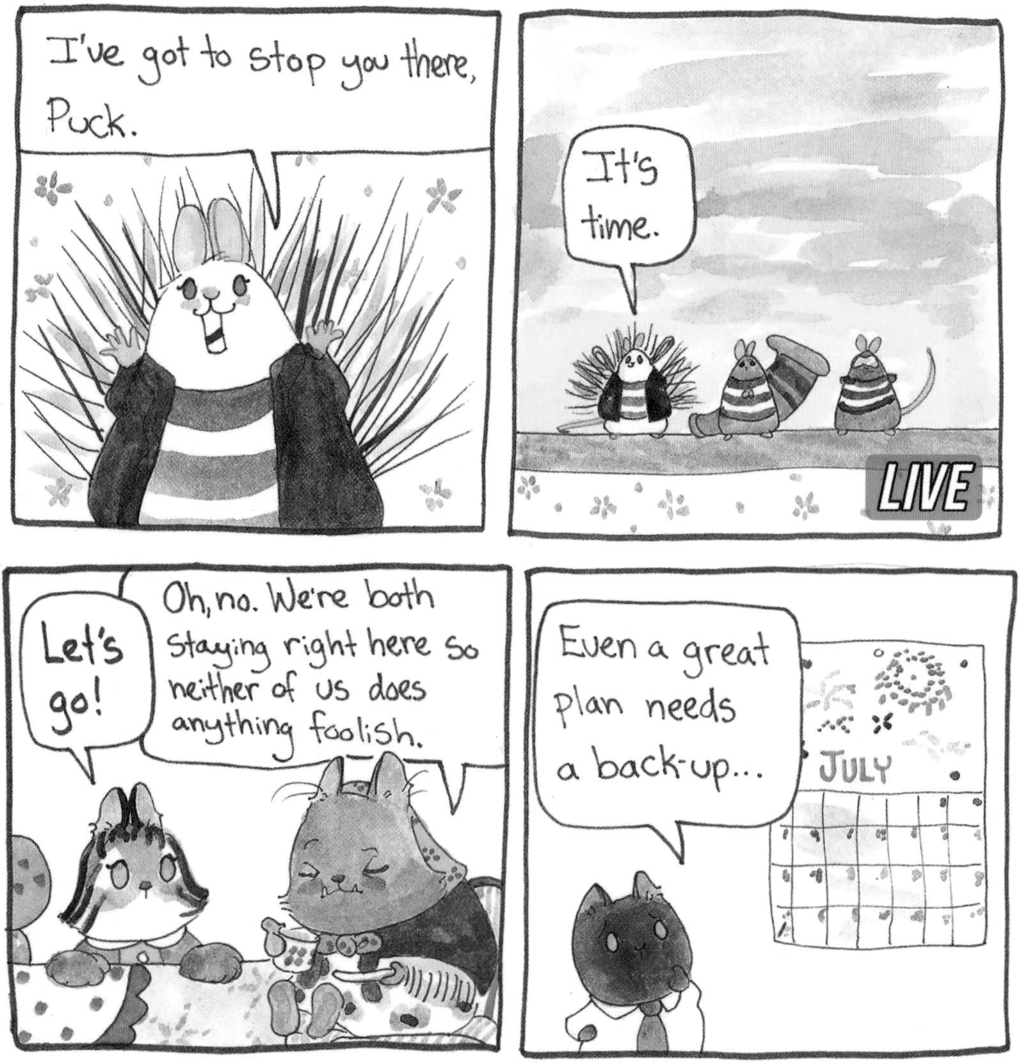
I've got to stop you there, Puck.
It's time.
LIVE
Let's go!
Oh, no. We're both staying right here so neither of us does anything foolish.
Even a great plan needs a back-up...
JULY

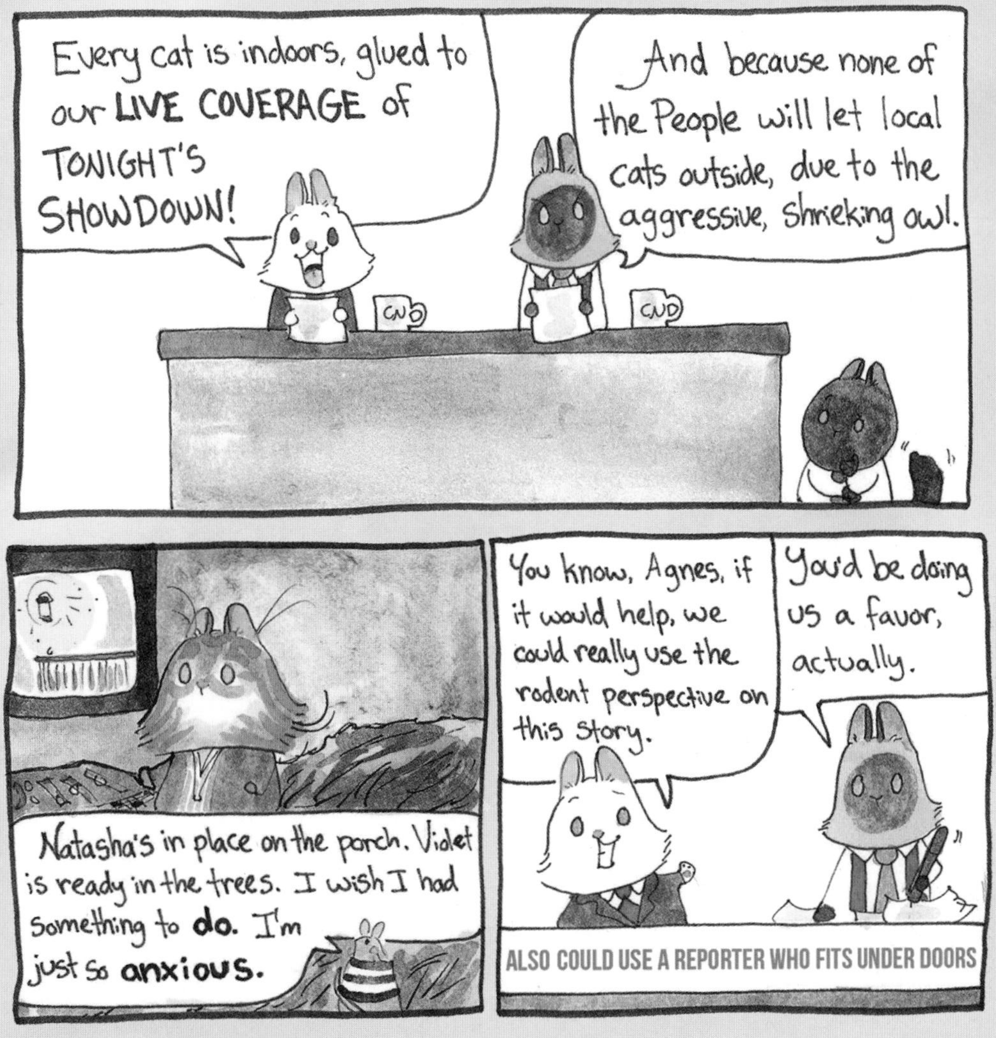
Every cat is indoors, glued to our **LIVE COVERAGE** of TONIGHT'S SHOWDOWN!
And because none of the People will let local cats outside, due to the aggressive, shrieking owl.
Natasha's in place on the porch. Violet is ready in the trees. I wish I had something to **do.** I'm just so **anxious.**
You know, Agnes, if it would help, we could really use the rodent perspective on this story.
You'd be doing us a favor, actually.
ALSO COULD USE A REPORTER WHO FITS UNDER DOORS

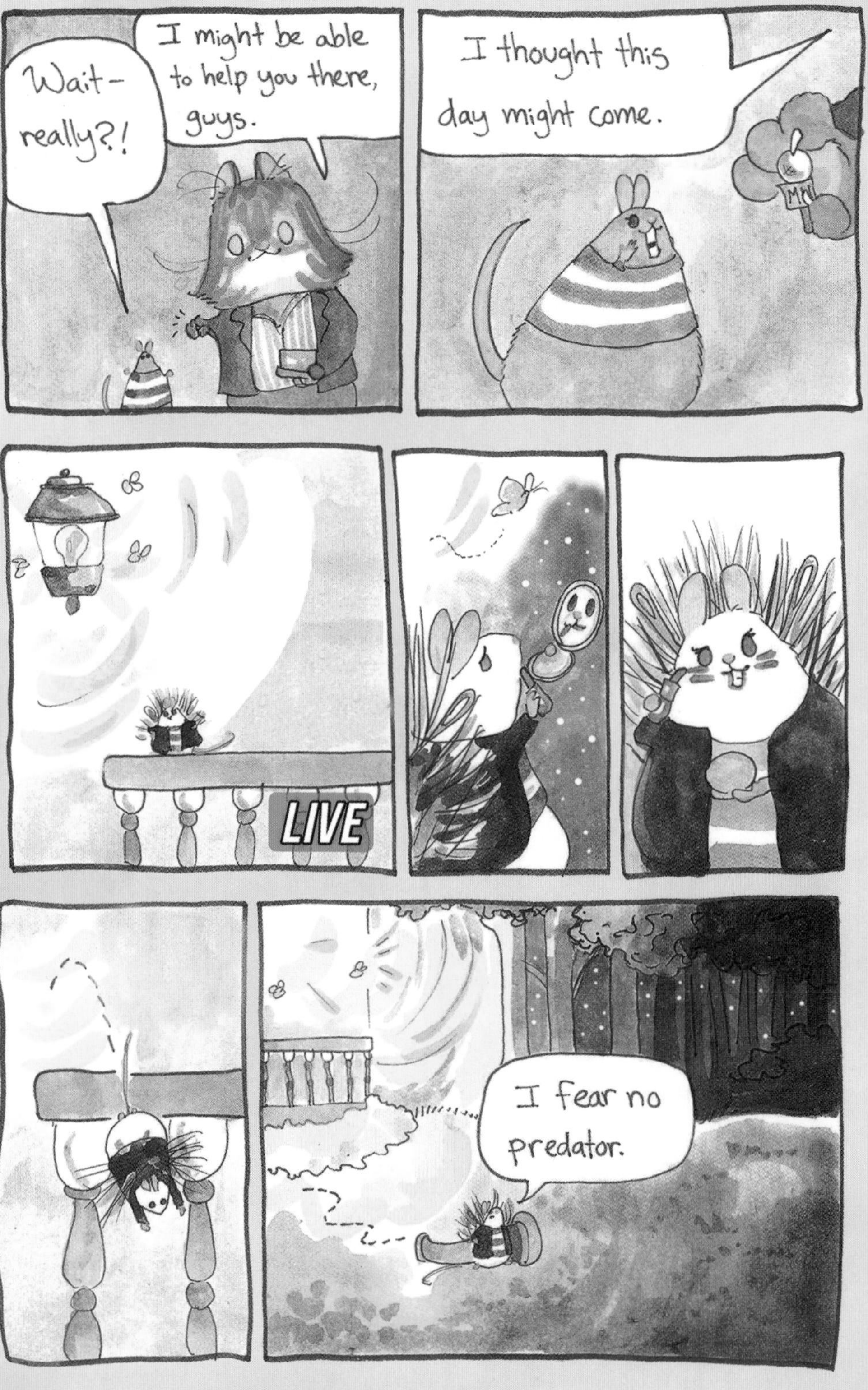
Wait- really?!
I might be able to help you there, guys.
I thought this day might come.
LIVE
I fear no predator.

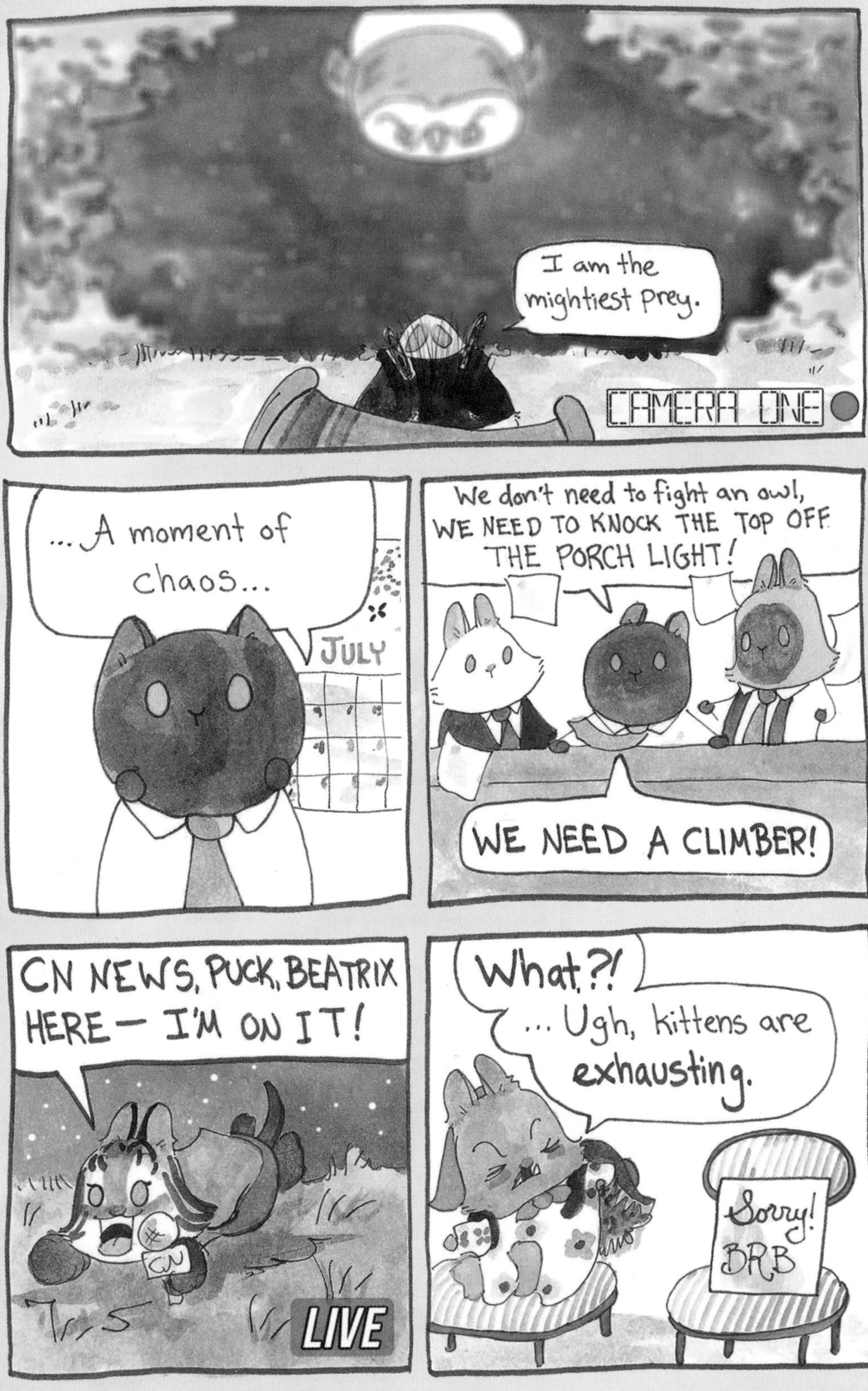
I am the mightiest prey.
CAMERA ONE
...A moment of chaos...
JULY
We don't need to fight an owl, WE NEED TO KNOCK THE TOP OFF THE PORCH LIGHT!
WE NEED A CLIMBER!
CN NEWS, PUCK, BEATRIX HERE— I'M ON IT!
CN
LIVE
What?! ...Ugh, kittens are **exhausting**.
Sorry! BRB

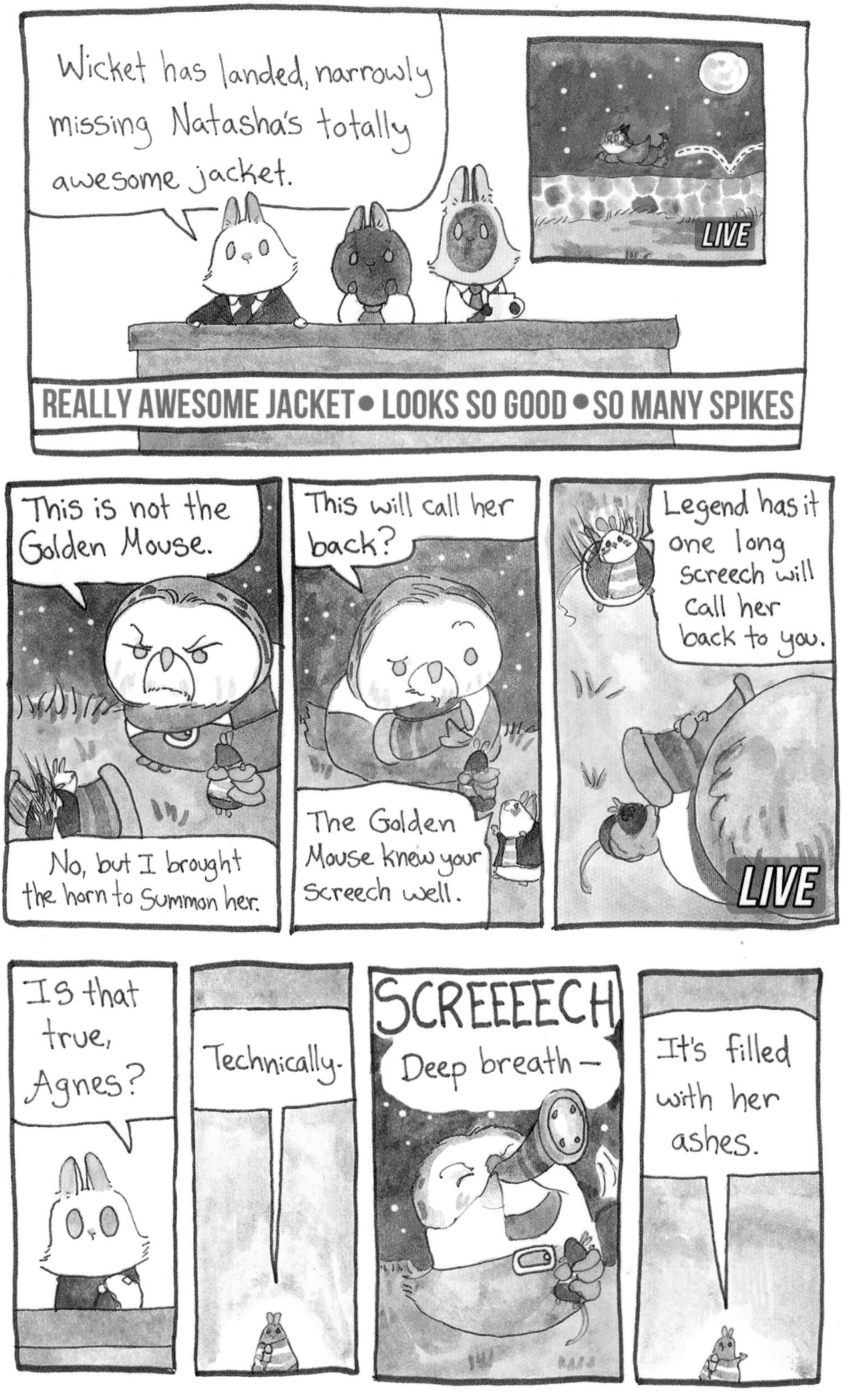
Wicket has landed, narrowly missing Natasha's totally awesome jacket.
LIVE
REALLY AWESOME JACKET • LOOKS SO GOOD • SO MANY SPIKES
This is not the Golden Mouse.
No, but I brought the horn to Summon her.
This will call her back?
The Golden Mouse knew your Screech well.
Legend has it one long screech will call her back to you.
LIVE
Is that true, Agnes?
Technically.
SCREEEECH
Deep breath –
It's filled with her ashes.

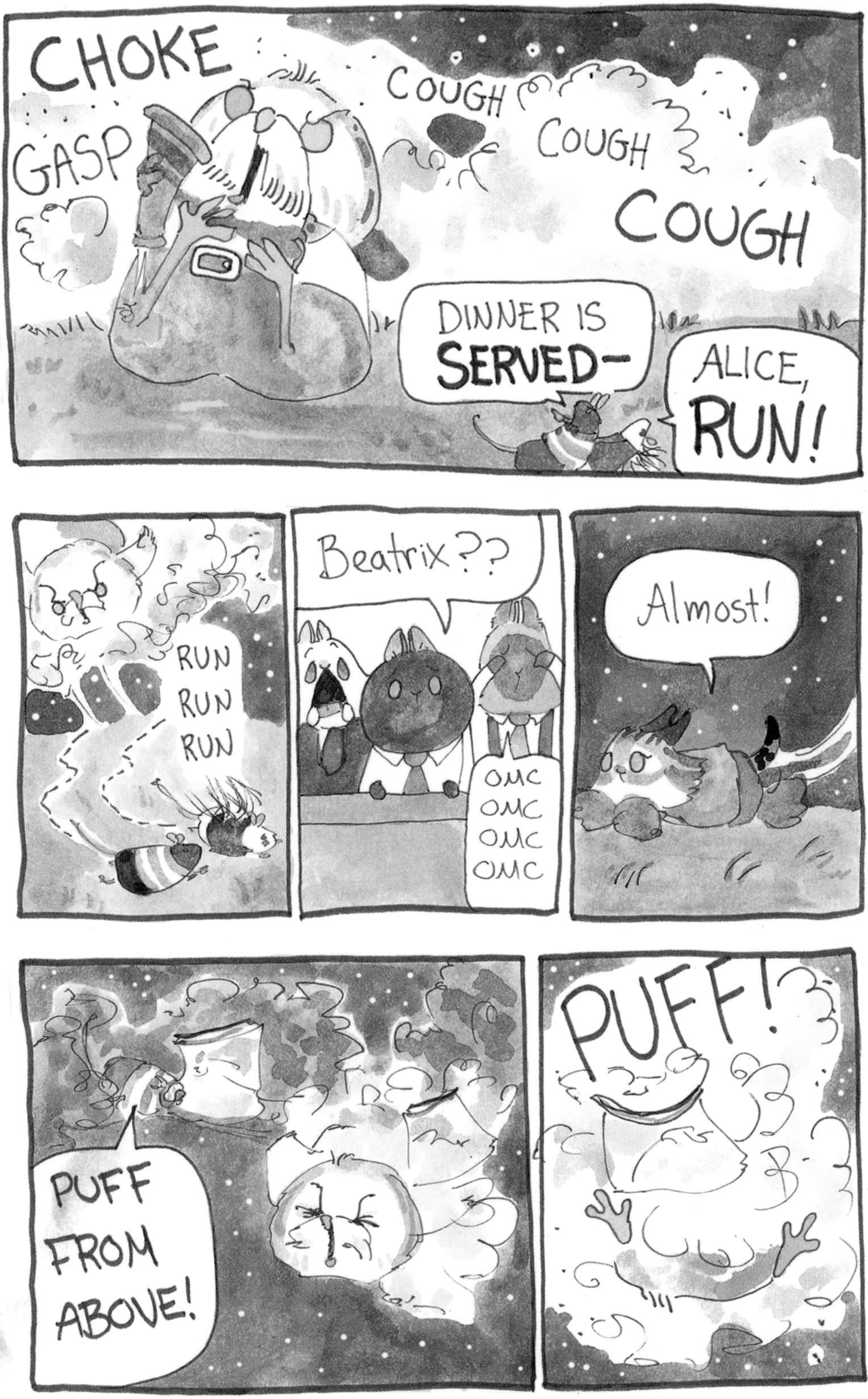

CHOKE
GASP
COUGH
COUGH
COUGH
DINNER IS SERVED—
ALICE, RUN!
RUN RUN RUN
Beatrix??
OMG OMG OMG OMG
Almost!
PUFF FROM ABOVE!
PUFF!

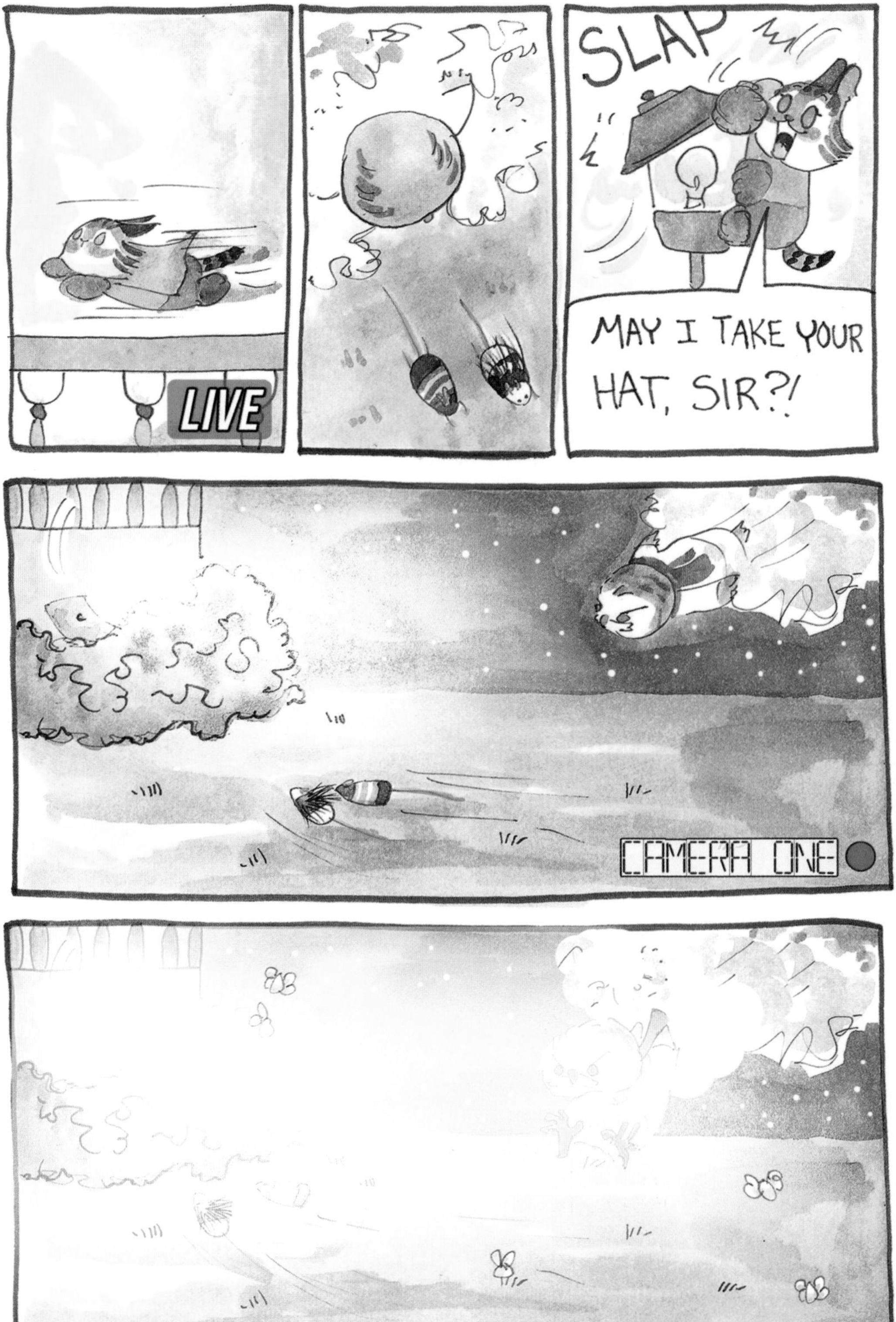
LIVE
SLAP
MAY I TAKE YOUR HAT, SIR?!
CAMERA ONE

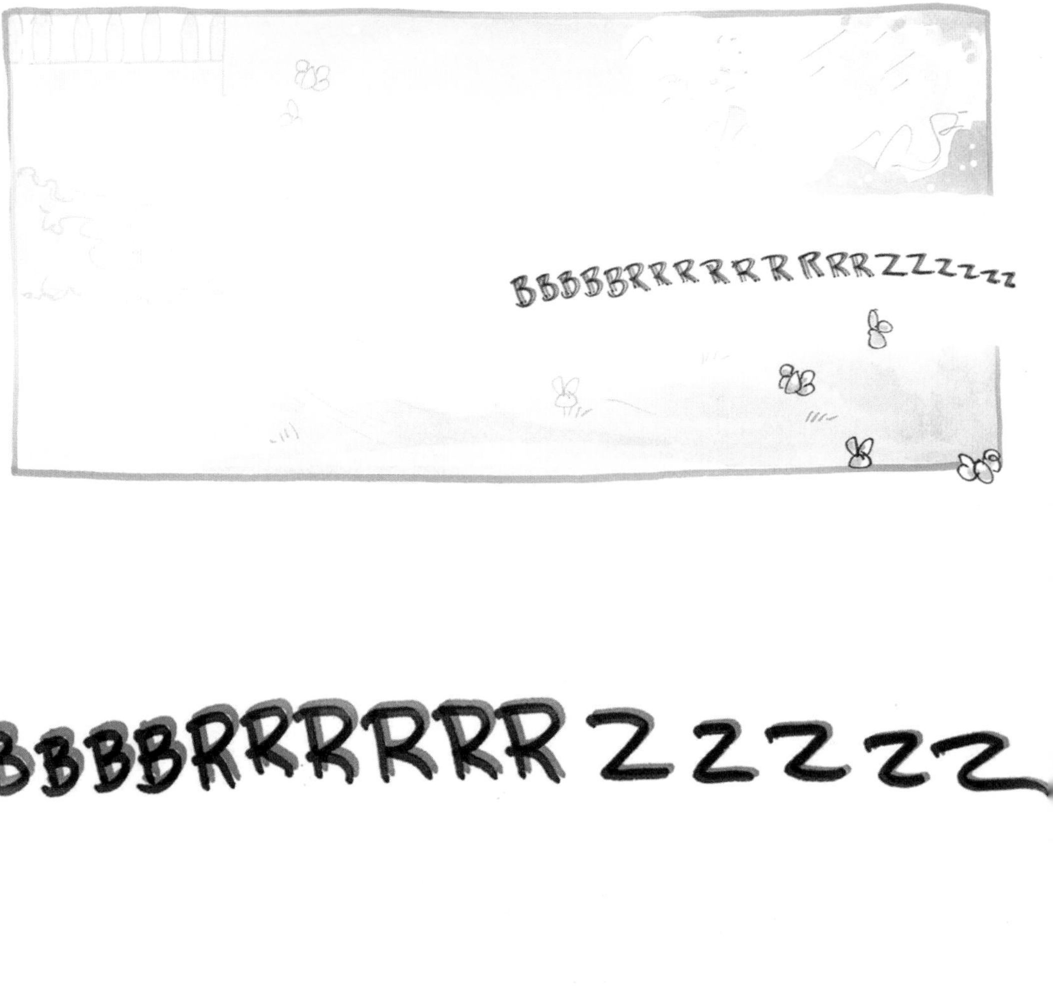

BBBBBRRRRRRRRRZZZzzz
BBBBRRRRRRRZZZZZ
BONK
BBBBBRRRRRRRRRZZzz
LIVE

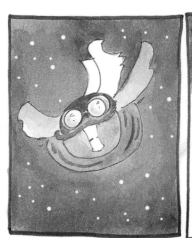

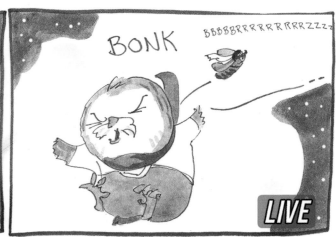

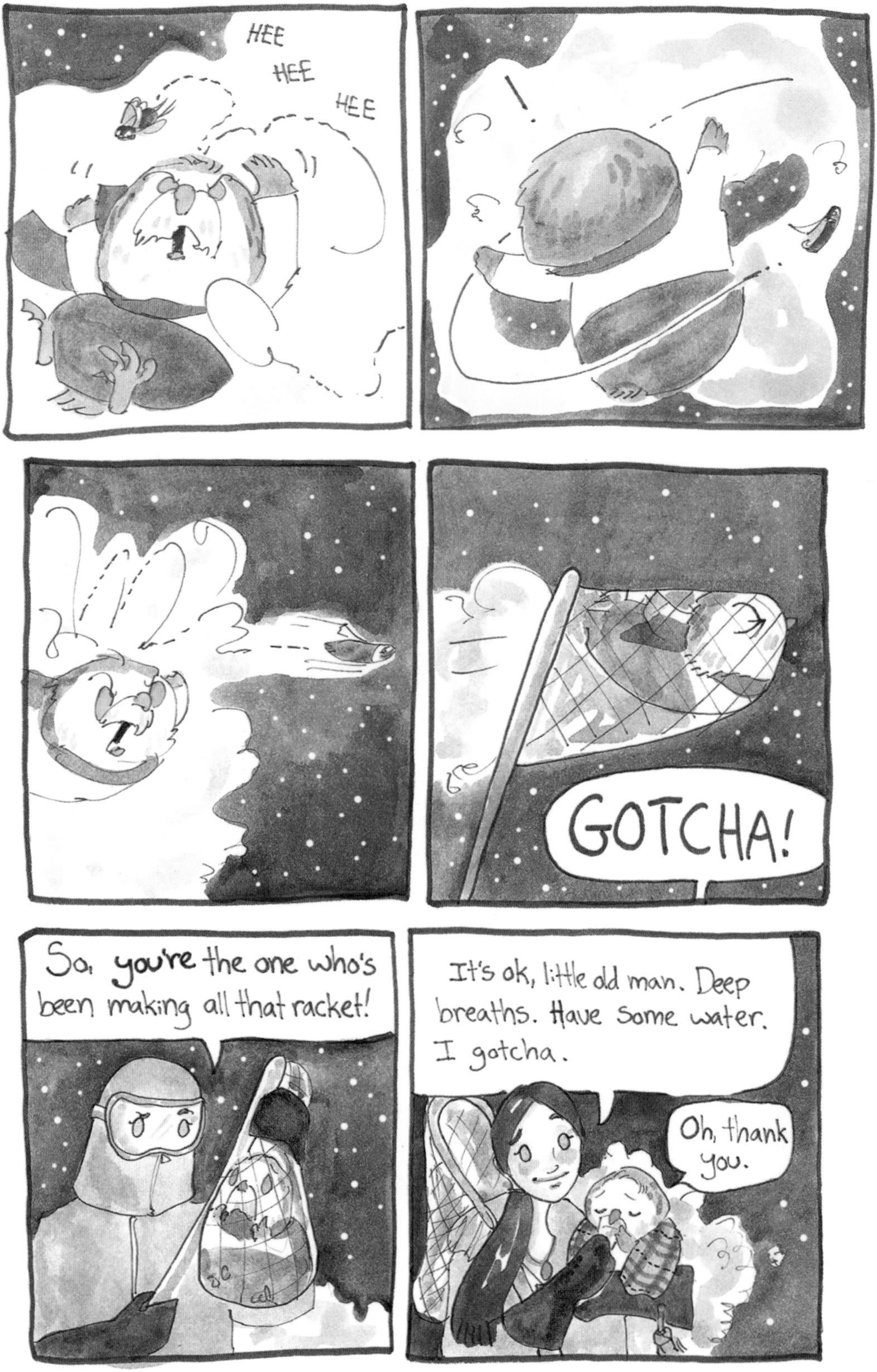
HEE
HEE
HEE
!
GOTCHA!
So, you're the one who's been making all that racket!
It's ok, little old man. Deep breaths. Have some water. I gotcha.
Oh, thank you.

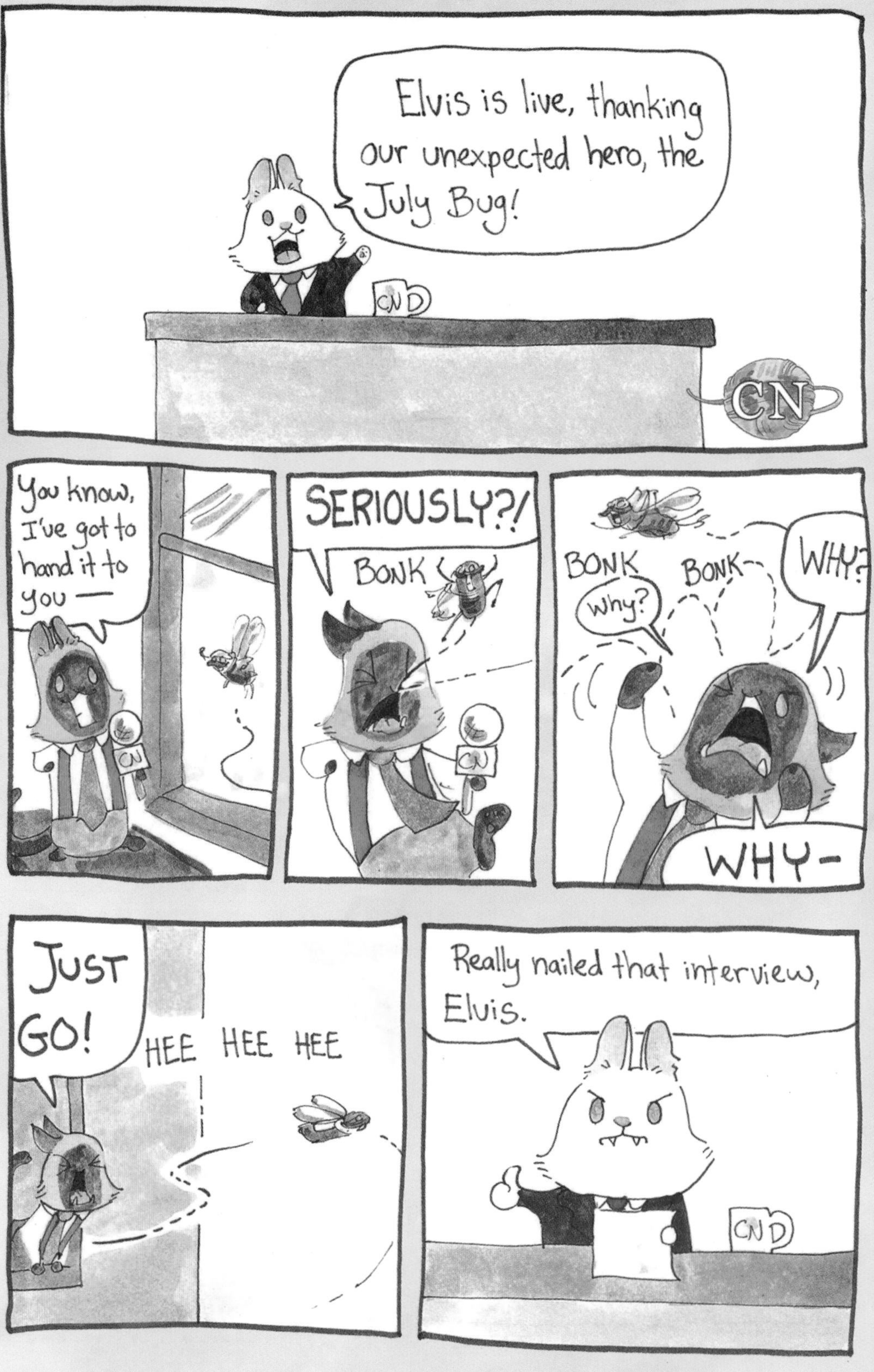
Elvis is live, thanking our unexpected hero, the July Bug!
CND
CN
You know, I've got to hand it to you —
CN
SERIOUSLY?!
BONK
CN
BONK
why?
BONK
WHY?
WHY-
JUST GO!
HEE HEE HEE
Really nailed that interview, Elvis.
CND

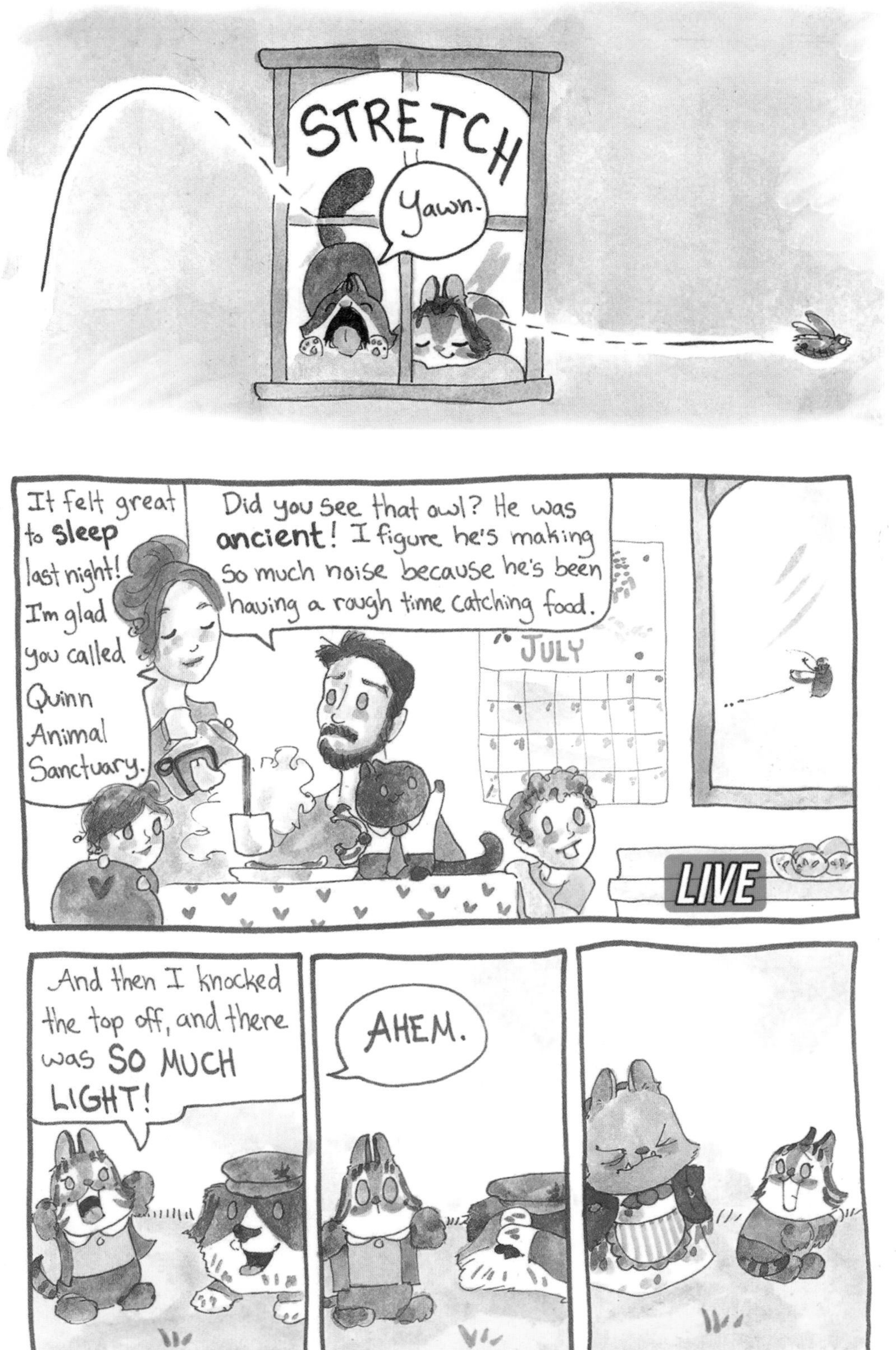
STRETCH
Yawn.
It felt great to **sleep** last night! I'm glad you called Quinn Animal Sanctuary.
Did you see that owl? He was **ancient**! I figure he's making so much noise because he's been having a rough time catching food.
JULY
LIVE
And then I knocked the top off, and there was SO MUCH LIGHT!
AHEM.

Eh... I didn't always listen when I was young, I guess.

You're helping me with some of my gardening and weeding, though.

That sounds fair!

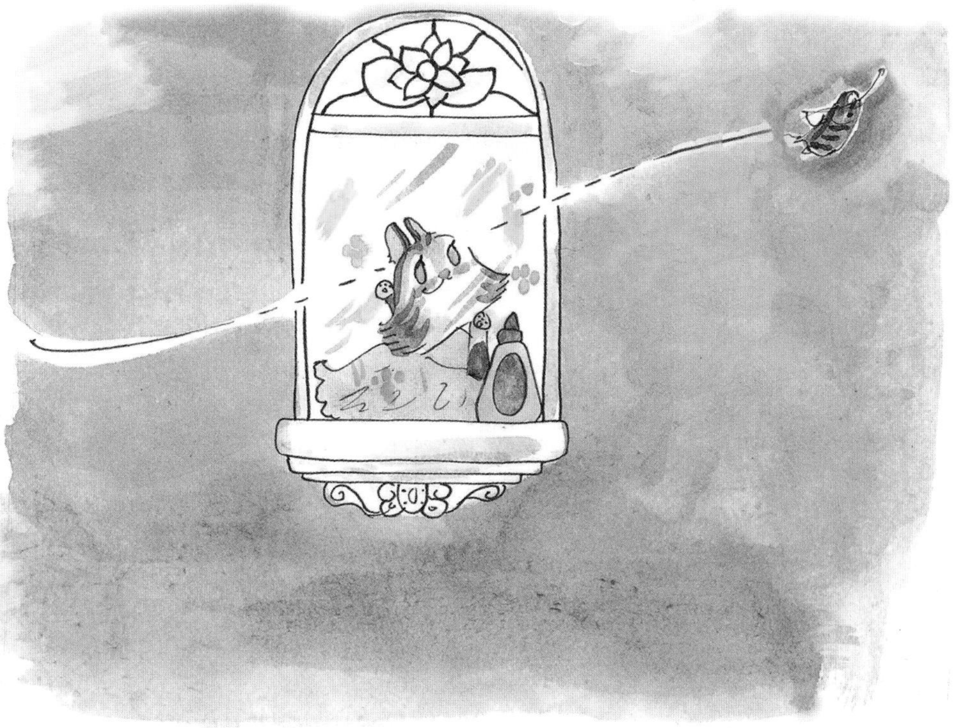

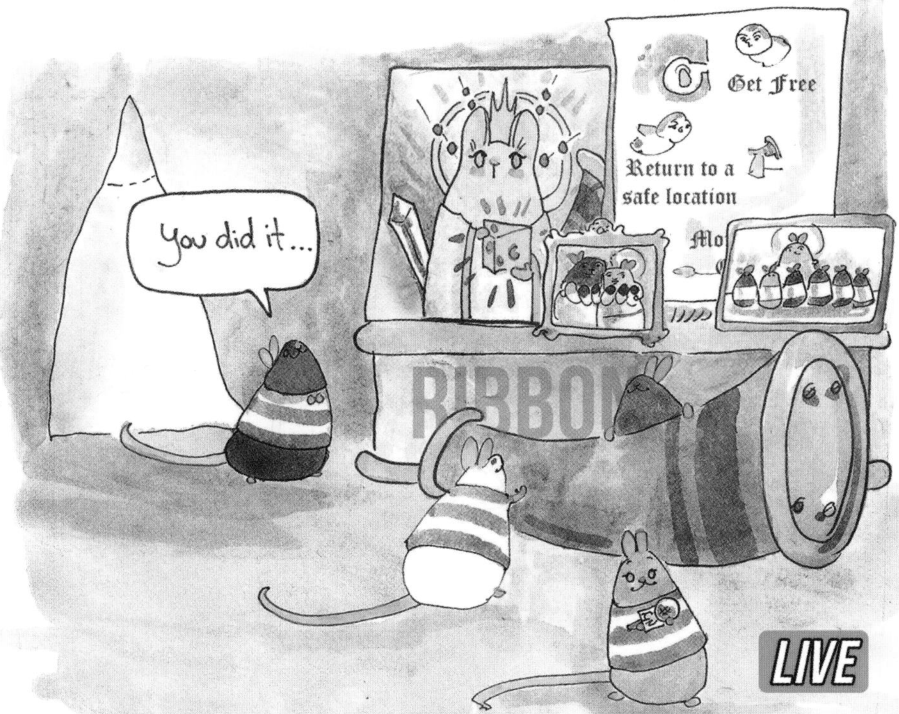
Get Free
Return to a
safe location
You did it...
LIVE

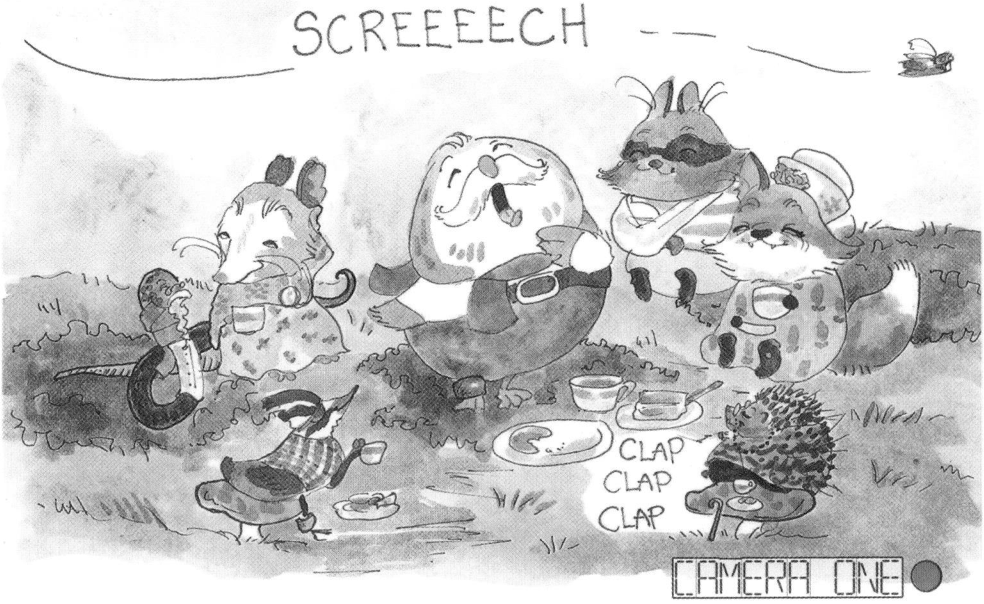
SCREEEECH
CLAP
CLAP
CLAP
CAMERA ONE

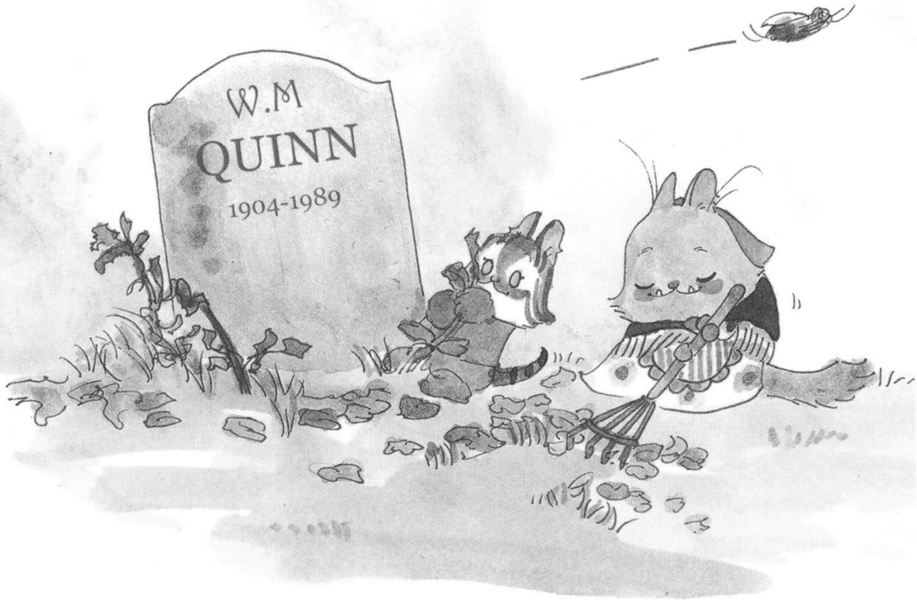
W.M
QUINN
1904-1989

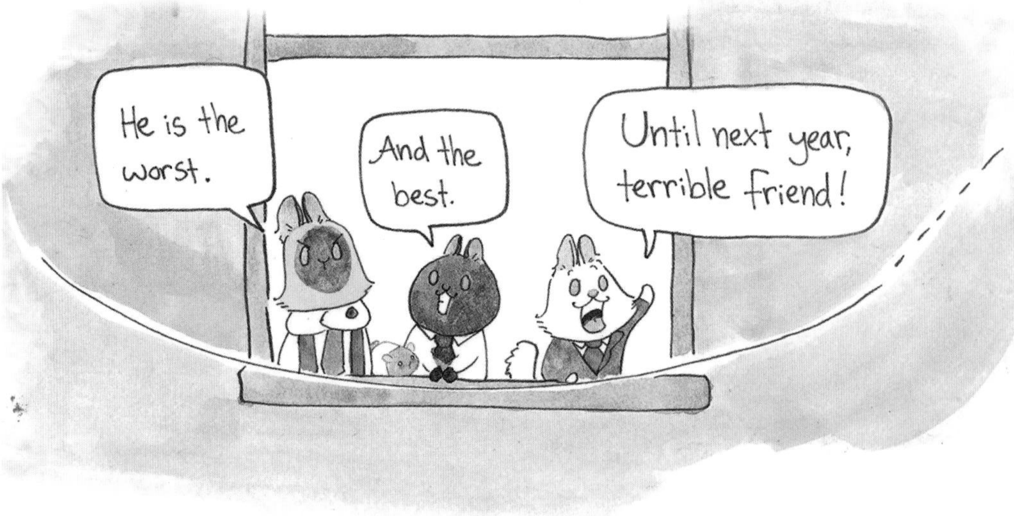
He is the worst.
And the best.
Until next year, terrible friend!

MORE TO EXPLORE! | Featuring cool activities and fun facts!

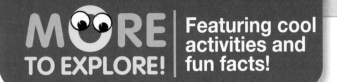

BREAKING CAT NEWS

MORE TO EXPLORE

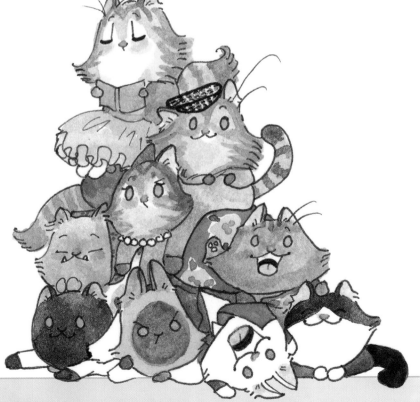

WOODEN SPOON DOLLS

In second grade, I made about 8-9 cat spoon dolls and put on a puppet show for my class with some of my friends. This was one of the first ways I found to tell stories! They're super fun to make (just be sure to ask first before painting the wooden spoons in your house. ...Sorry, Mom!)

YOU WILL NEED:

Wooden spoons
(You can usually get them very cheap secondhand!)

Paint, paintbrushes, markers

Googly eyes, buttons, pipe cleaners, ribbons, felt, etc.

Something to secure felt, ribbon, etc. Glue, needle and thread, glue gun

(Have an adult help you, if you're too young to use these!)

PAINT YOUR SPOONS!

Paint your spoon one light color

Paint the fur/skin/ solid clothing colors

Add fur markings or patterns

Paint the details! Eyes, noses, ties, scarves etc.

These are the kind of spoon dolls I made as a child. I'd use the scoop for the head and paint clothes along the handle.

Felt ears, added with glue

Fun little egg bodies

One of the best things about wooden spoon dolls is making them "walk" around by holding their handles.

After you paint your spoon dolls you can use felt, pipe cleaners, googly eyes, buttons, and such to give your dolls 3-D accessories!

MAKE A THEATER AND YOU'VE GOT PUPPETS!

Cut a window into a cardboard box, decorate the outside, and you've got a puppet theater!

REPORTING NEWS AROUND YOUR HOUSE

There are news stories happening all around you, every day. Maybe you have a new lamp, your cat fell asleep on an open book, or you found a lost pen.

It can be fun to report these stories as news for your friends and family. It is also good practice if you'd like to be a reporter yourself one day!

WHO, WHAT, WHEN, WHERE, WHY?

When you're investigating a story, this is a great place to start. Whether you're reporting on an event or trying to solve a mystery (or both!), these five questions can help you gather your thoughts and guide you to the truth!

WHO: Who was there? Who is involved? Who will this affect?

WHAT: What did they see? What happened?

WHEN: When did this happen?

WHERE: Where did this happen?

WHY: Why did this happen? What led up to this?

GATHER YOUR RESEARCH

Write down your five questions and answer them.
Interview as many of the folks involved as you can.
Be accurate. Be honest. Take careful notes, preferably
in a small notebook. It's old-school, but notebooks
can fit in your pocket and be pulled out, opened,
and ready for facts at a moment's notice.
You need to be quick if you're going to get
the scoop!

IT'S TIME TO REPORT!

Your five questions and their answers are all you need. In a pinch,
they will read as their own broadcast or can be quickly typed up into
a news report. Keep it simple and clear!

WHO: The Woman
WHAT: Made a cup of tea
WHEN: Tonight
WHERE: In the kitchen
WHY: She had a long day.

"The Woman made a cup of tea tonight
in the kitchen, after a long day.
No word yet on whether it was earl gray
or lemon ginger. Elvis, back to you."

WHY REPORT THE NEWS IN YOUR HOME?

When life gets stressful or current events feel overwhelming, it can help to
report—even to just yourself, for fun or comfort—the simple, sweet things
around you. If you can find one or two moments in the day to mark in good
humor and feel grateful for, it can help you
recharge to face the rest of the world
and its challenges tomorrow.

"This just in: Boxes are
never empty because
they are always filled
with adventure."

TIPS FOR PAPER DOLLS!

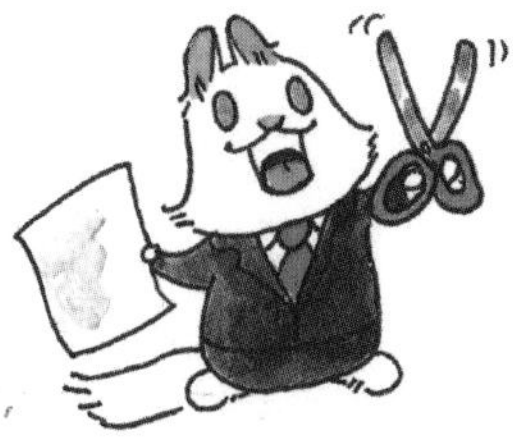

Scissors:
Safety first!
Be careful,
take your time.

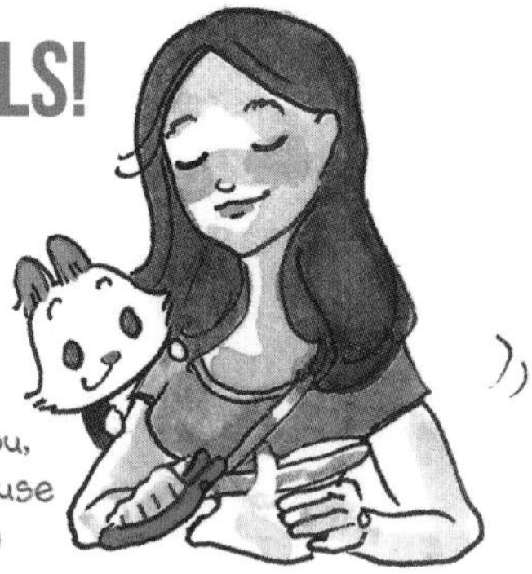

Ask someone to help you, if you're not allowed to use scissors. (...Like Lupin)

Make your own clothes:
Flip a patterned piece of paper over and trace an outfit face down. Cut it out and you've got pajamas or a fancy new suit! (Or draw and color an outfit on the tracing!)

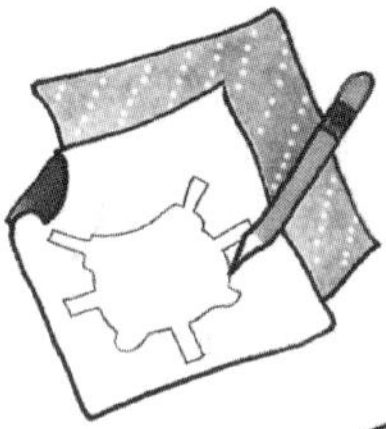

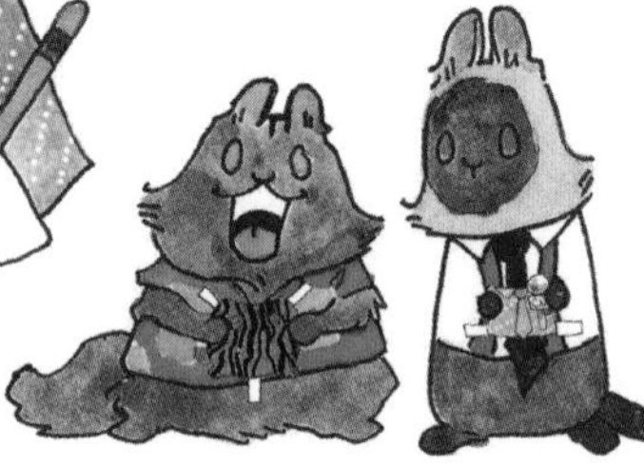

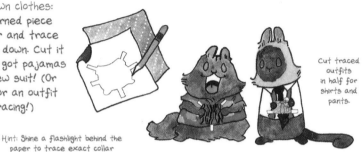

Cut traced outfits in half for shirts and pants.

Hint: Shine a flashlight behind the paper to trace exact collar lines, ties, and shirt hems!

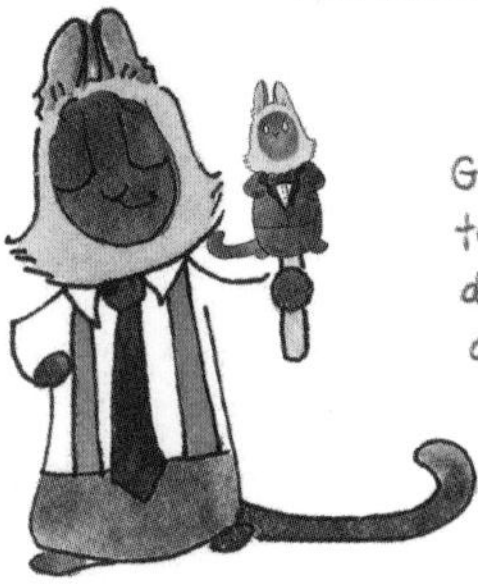

Puppets:
Glue a popsicle stick to the back of each doll, and you've got a little puppet to move around and voice!

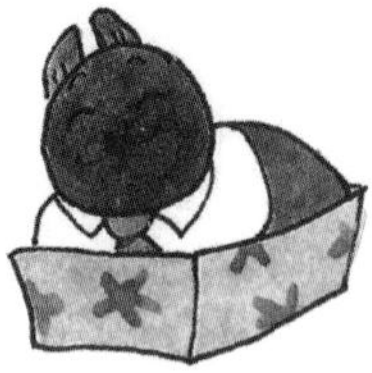

Boxes:
They're not just for naps anymore!
Turn any box into a puppet theater.

Puppet Theaters: By cutting a window into a box, you can create a puppet theater! You can even make your own cardboard television and act out broadcasts inside! Delivery boxes, shoe boxes, and oatmeal containers all make great little theaters.

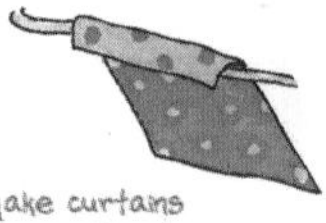

Make curtains for your theater by looping fabric over string and fastening it with glue, thread, or safety pins.

Decorate your theater with paint, crayons, craft paper, scraps of fabric, stickers—anything you have!

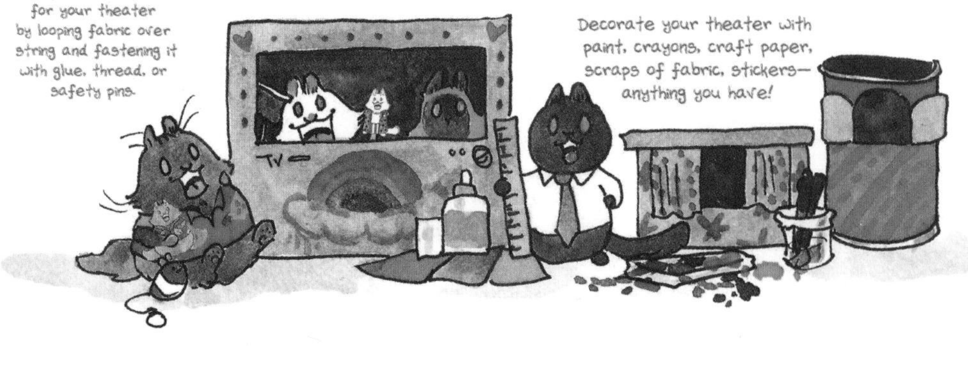
TV

BREAKING CAT NEWS PAPER DOLLS

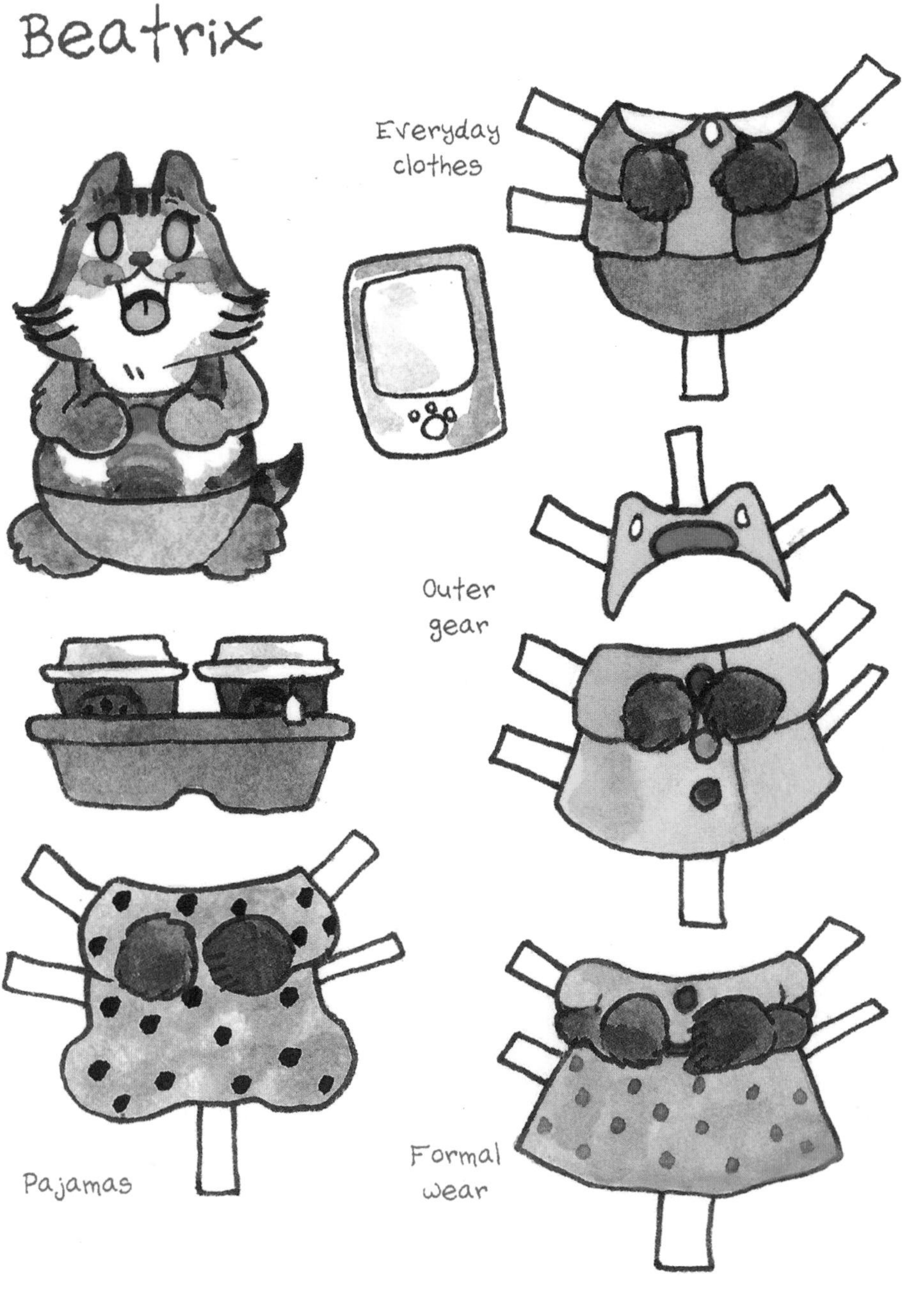
Beatrix
Everyday clothes
Outer gear
Pajamas
Formal wear

Cut page out along dotted line.

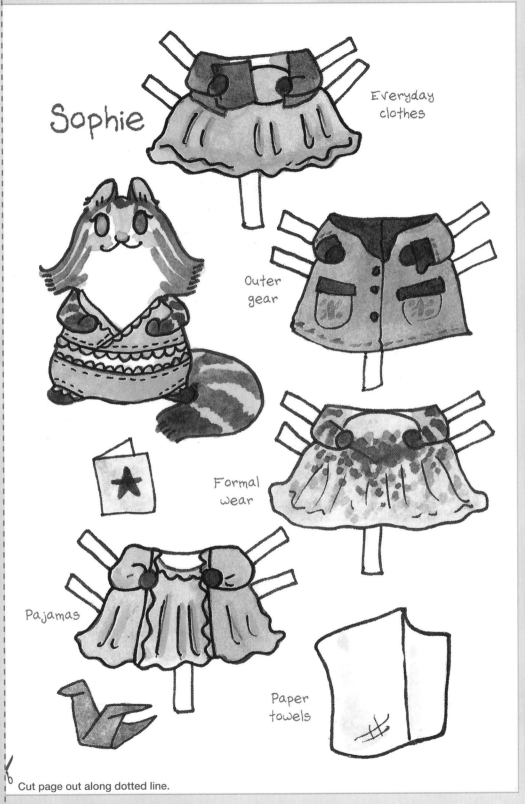

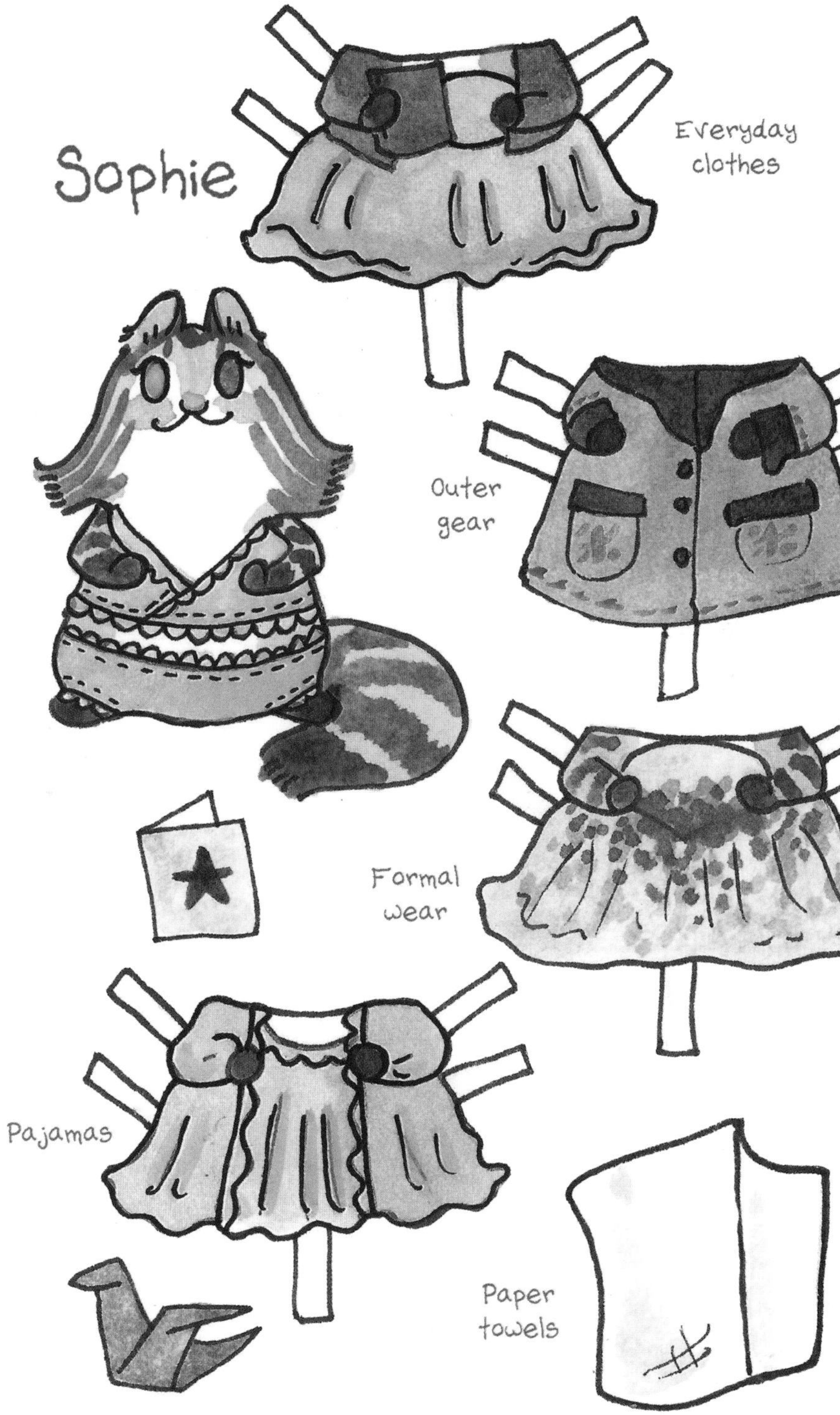
Sophie
Everyday clothes
Outer gear
Formal wear
Pajamas
Paper towels

Cut page out along dotted line.

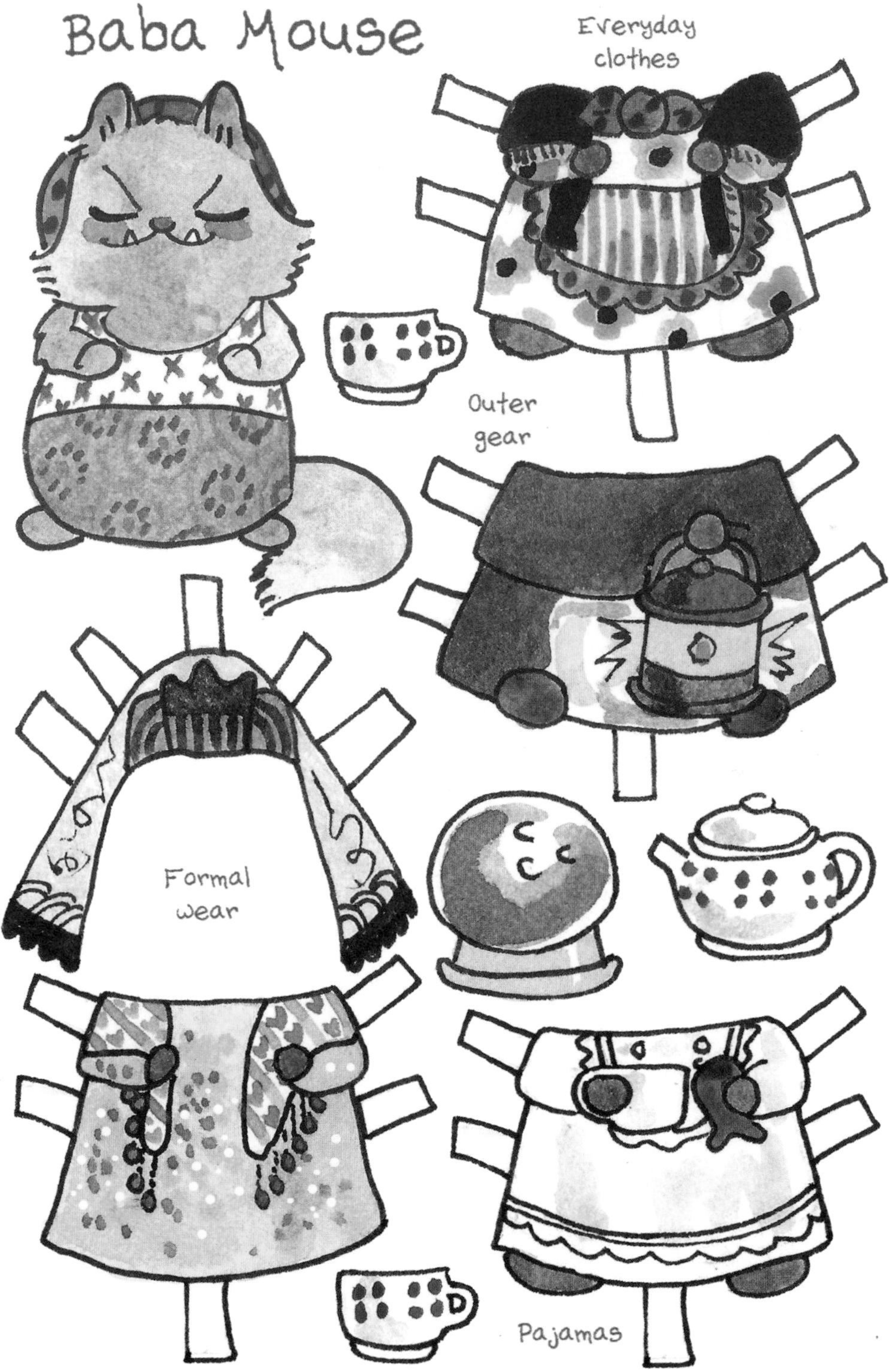
Baba Mouse
Everyday clothes
Outer gear
Formal wear
Pajamas

Cut page out along dotted line.

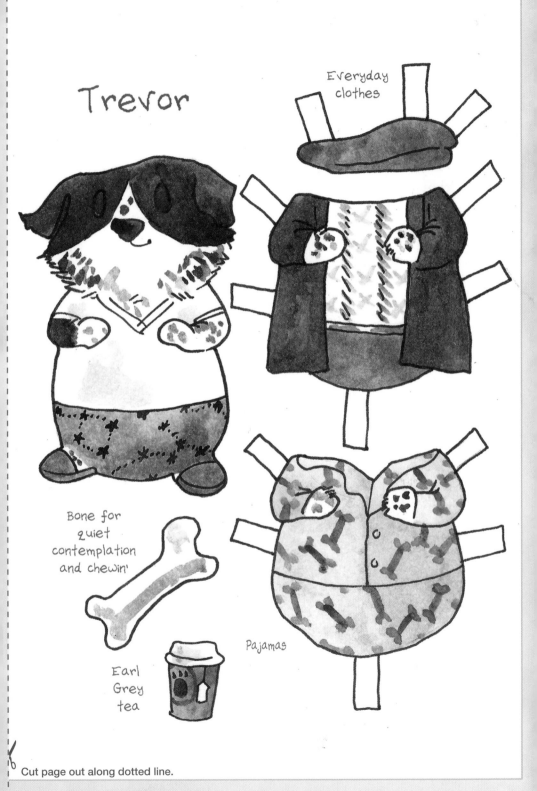

Trevor

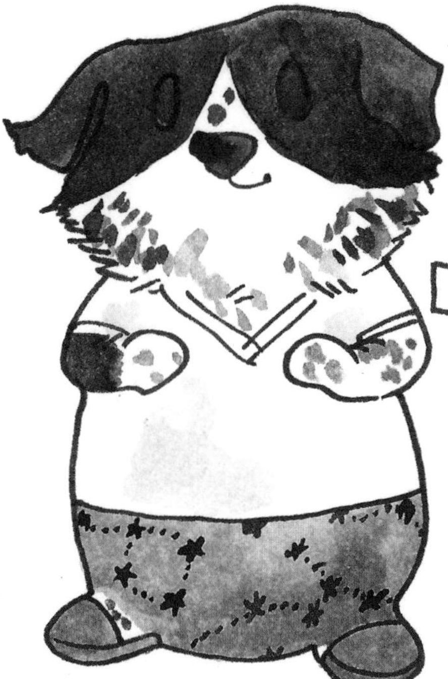

Everyday clothes

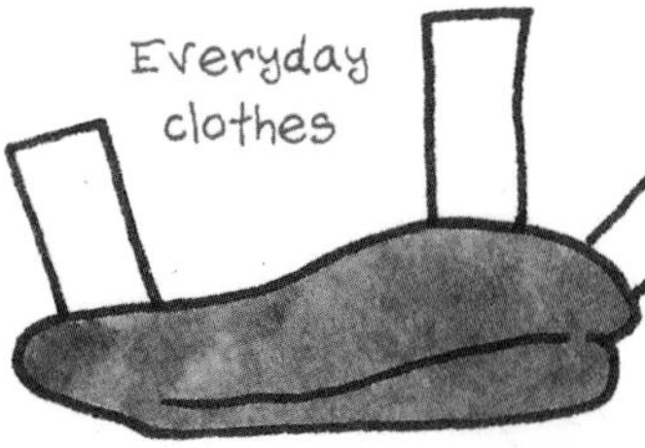

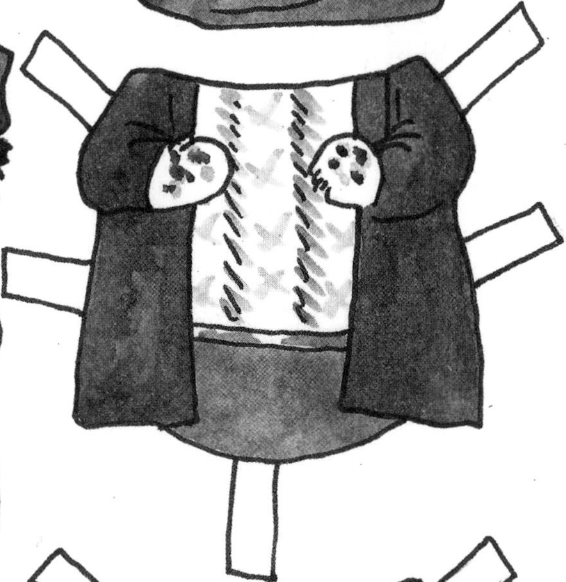

Bone for quiet contemplation and chewin'

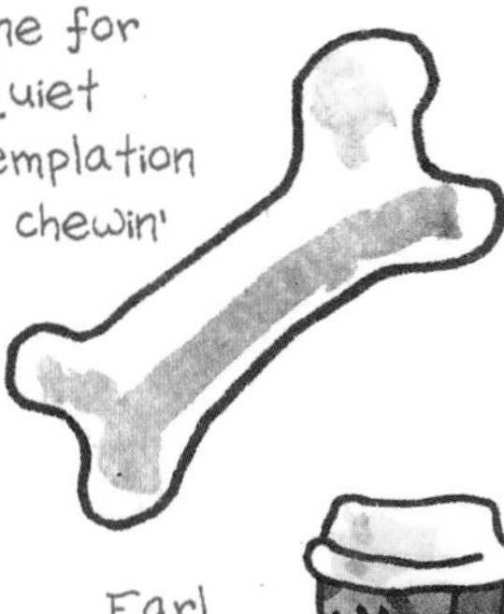

Pajamas

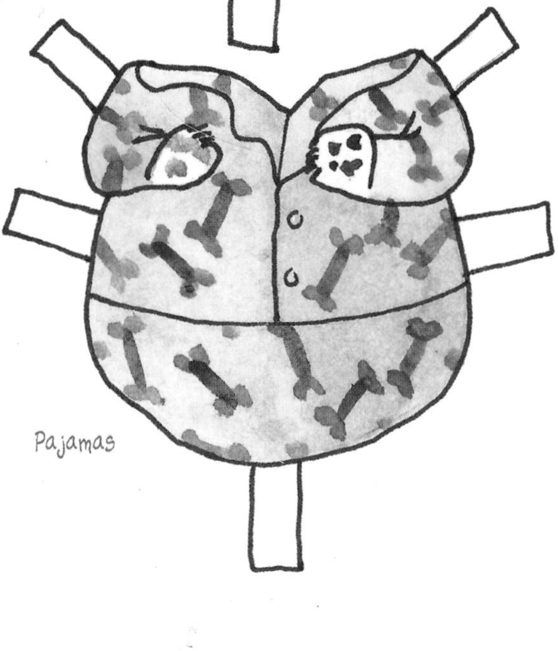

Earl Grey tea

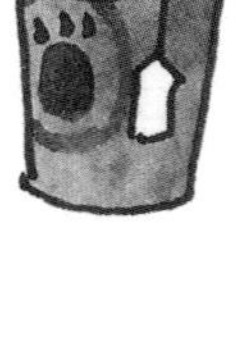

Cut page out along dotted line.

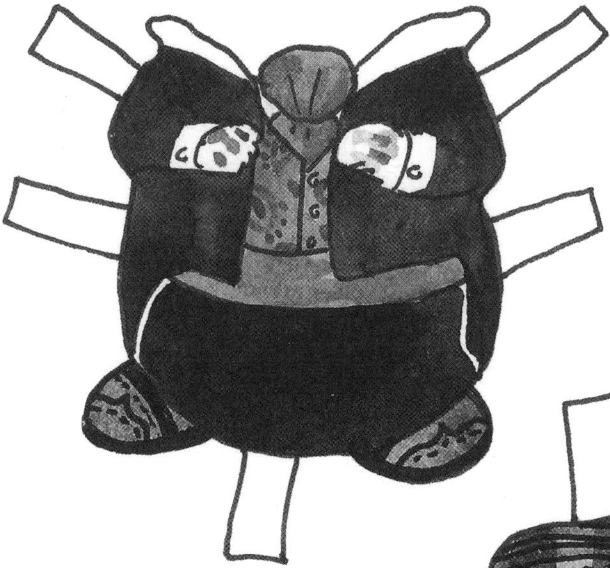

Formal wear

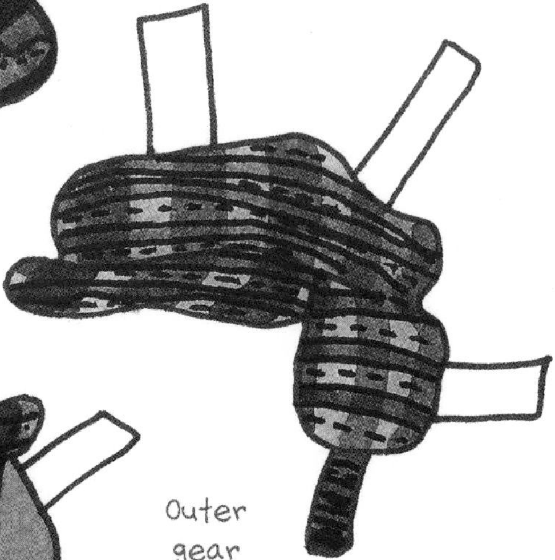

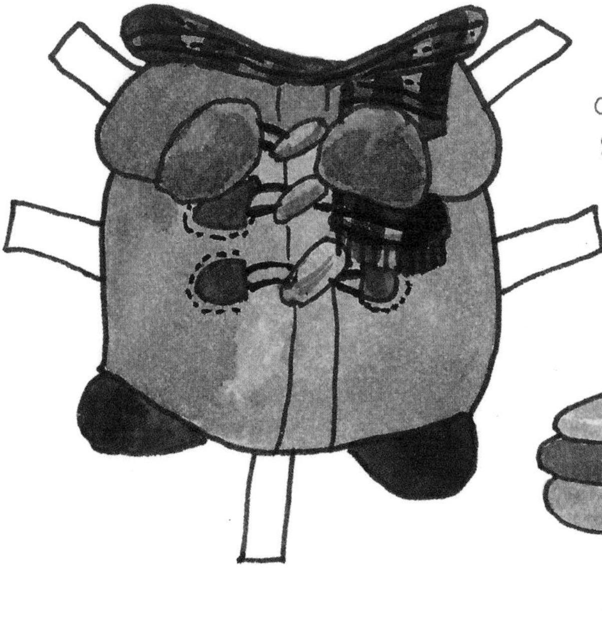

Outer gear

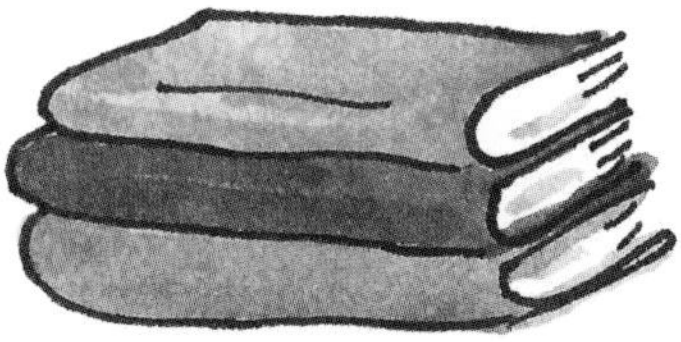

Favorite books

Cut page out along dotted line.

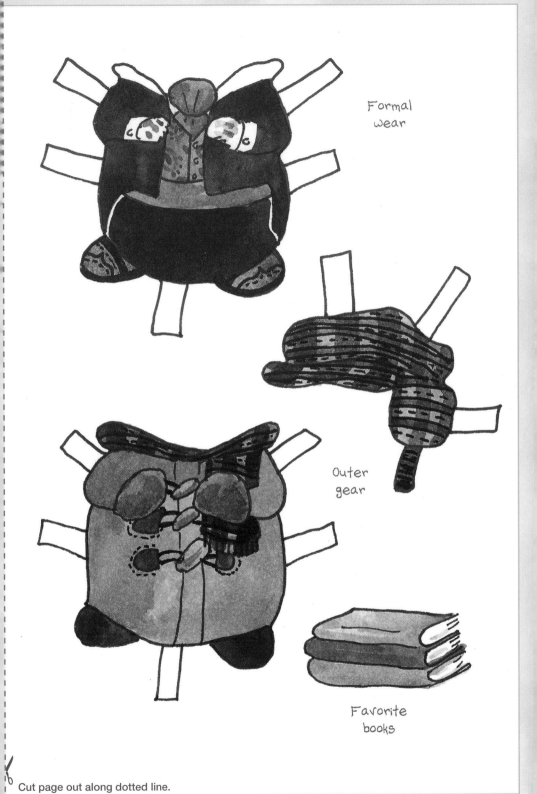

Robber Mice and the July Bug

Alice

Violet

Natasha

Agnes

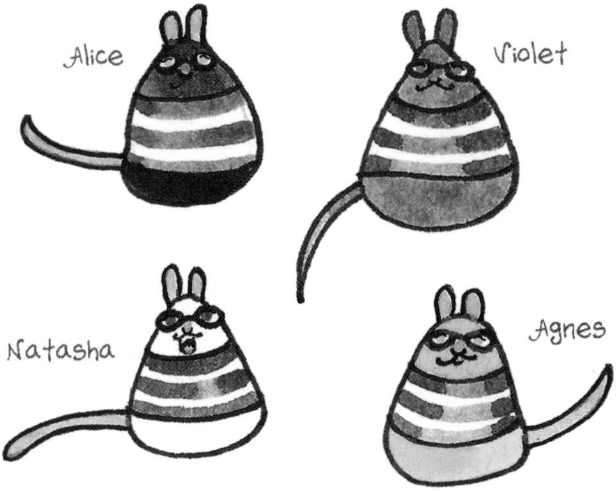

Tommy's Christmas tree

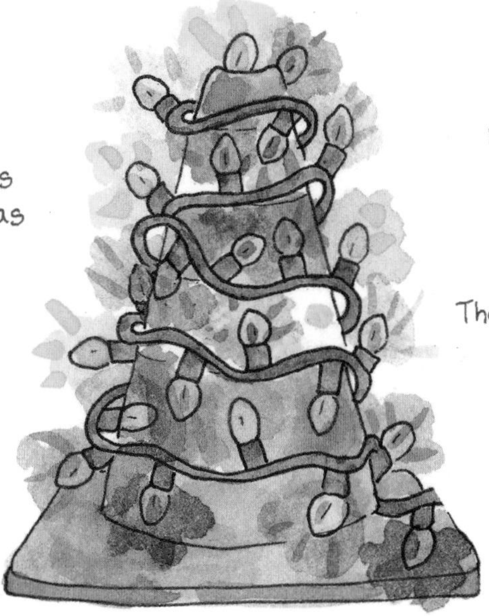

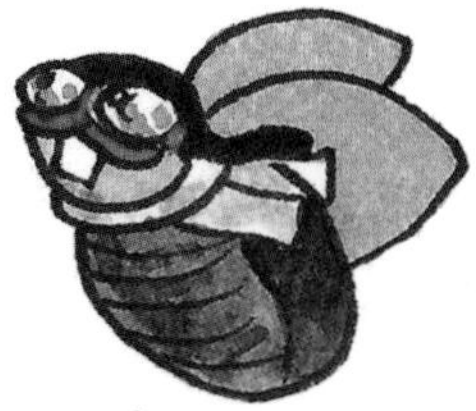

The July Bug

Andrews McMeel Publishing
a division of Andrews McMeel Universal
1130 Walnut Street, Kansas City, Missouri 64106

www.andrewsmcmeel.com
www.breakingcatnews.com

20 21 22 23 24 SDB 10 9 8 7 6 5 4 3 2 1

ISBN: 978-1-5248-5819-3

Library of Congress Control Number: 2020937785

Published under license from Andrews McMeel Syndication
www.gocomics.com

Made by:
King Yip (Dongguan) Printing & Packaging Factory Ltd.
Address and location of production:
Daning Administrative District, Humen Town
Dongguan Guangdong, China 523930
1st Printing — 6/29/20

ATTENTION: SCHOOLS AND BUSINESSES

Andrews McMeel books are available at quantity discounts with bulk purchase
for educational, business, or sales promotional use. For information, please
e-mail the Andrews McMeel Publishing Special Sales Department:
specialsales@amuniversal.com.

Check out these and other books from Andrews McMeel Publishing

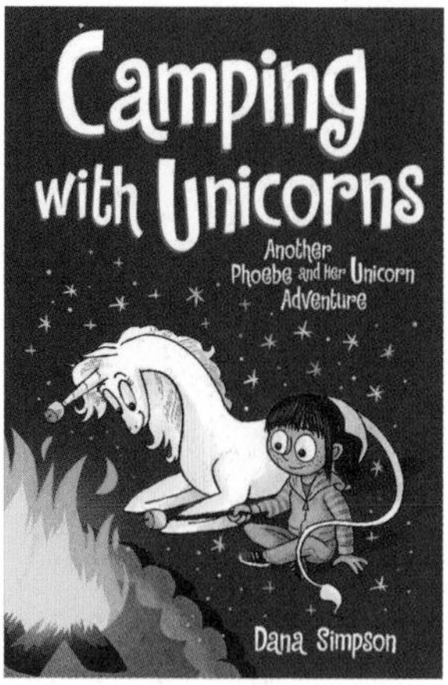
Camping with Unicorns
Another Phoebe and Her Unicorn Adventure
Dana Simpson

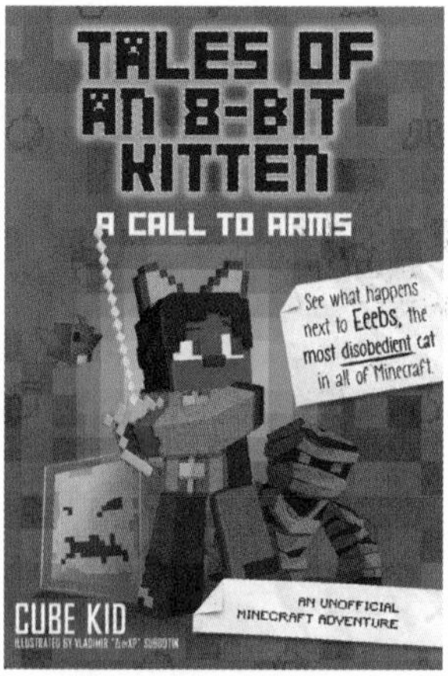
TALES OF AN 8-BIT KITTEN
A CALL TO ARMS
See what happens next to Eeebs, the most disobedient cat in all of Minecraft
CUBE KID
AN UNOFFICIAL MINECRAFT ADVENTURE

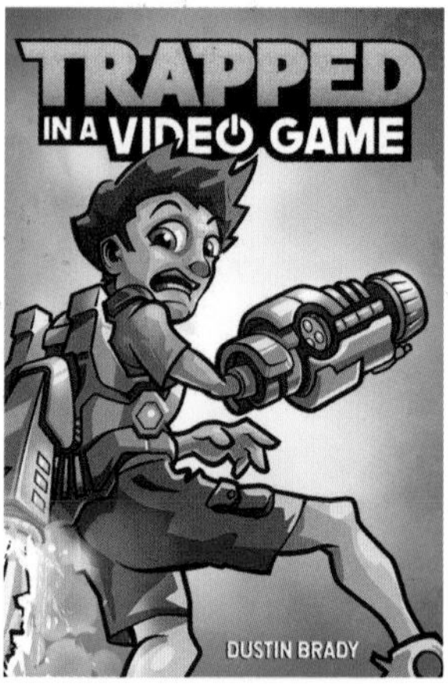
TRAPPED IN A VIDEO GAME
DUSTIN BRADY

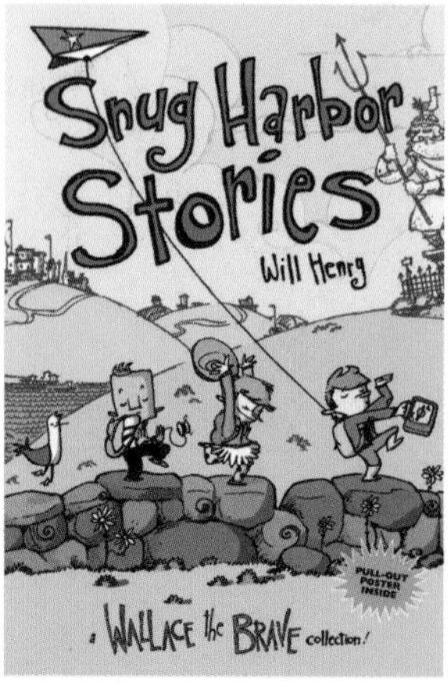
Snug Harbor Stories
Will Henry
PULL-OUT POSTER INSIDE
a WALLACE the BRAVE collection!

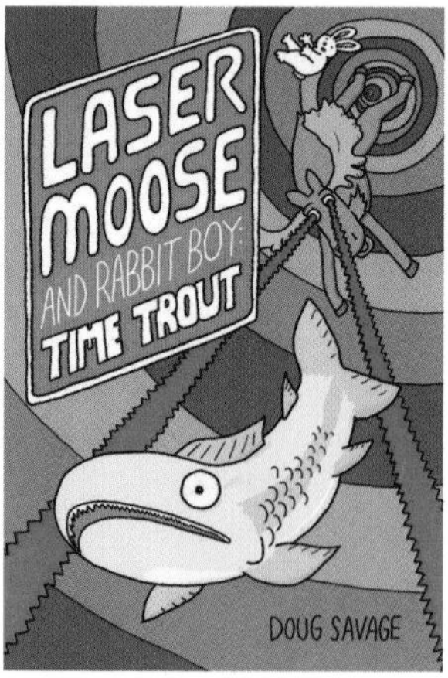
LASER MOOSE AND RABBIT BOY: TIME TROUT
DOUG SAVAGE

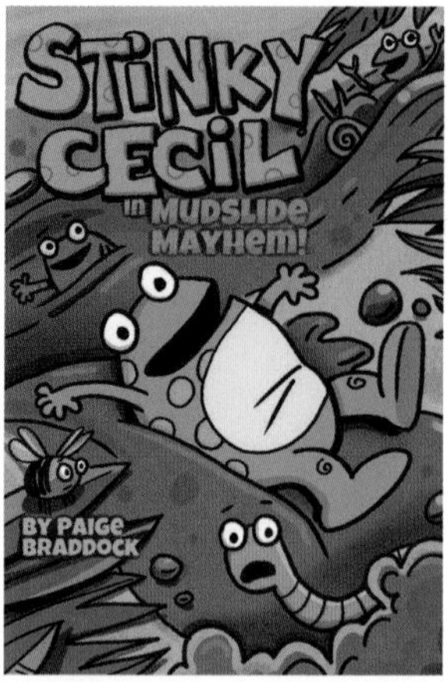
STINKY CECIL in MUDSLIDE MAYHEM!
BY PAIGE BRADDOCK

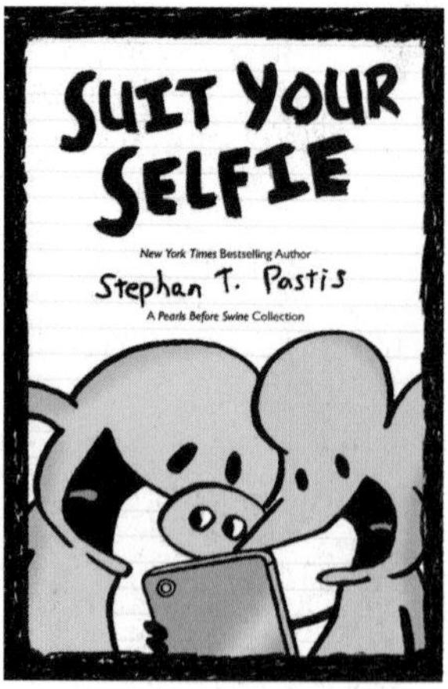
SUIT YOUR SELFIE
New York Times Bestselling Author
Stephan T. Pastis
A Pearls Before Swine Collection

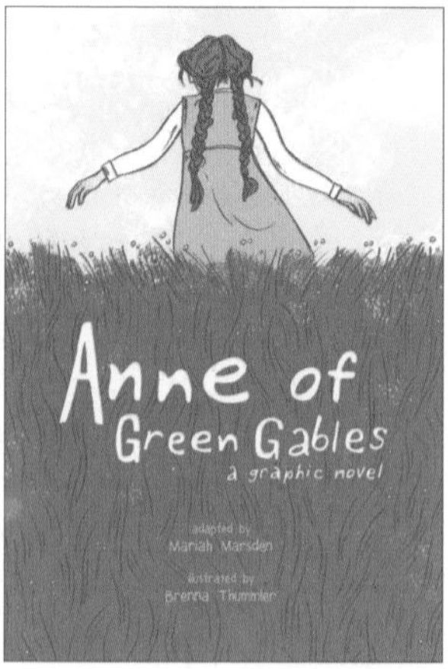
Anne of Green Gables
a graphic novel

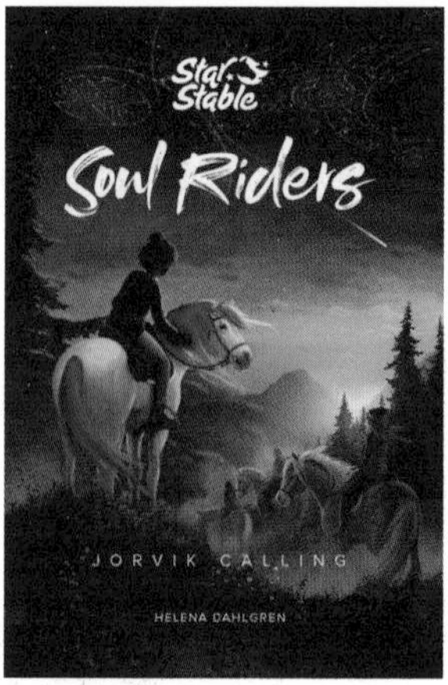
Star Stable
Soul Riders
JORVIK CALLING
HELENA DAHLGREN